"What's the matter? Afraid of a little kiss?"

"Yes. No. Of course not." Penny drew back. "But we came here to work."

"All work and no play is a real drag. Do you ever just relax and have fun, Money?"

"I've never had time for fun."

"That's just not right." Sam's voice lowered. "I see it as my duty to show you how to play."

"Oh, I'm sure that's something you're an expert on. Drinking, gambling, playing."

"And kissing a pretty girl. Don't forget that. It's the most important game of all."

"Oh, you."

His smile grew and he drew her close.

Against her ear he whispered, "All right. I'll let you get back to your work. For now. But before the day is over, you're going to ask me if we can play."

"Don't hold your breath."

As she turned away, she could hear his low rumble of laughter.

MATT

"Ryan has created a gripping love story fraught with danger and lust, pain and sweet, sweet triumph."
—*Library Journal*, starred review

"Touching and romantic, Ryan's portrayal of a city slicker falling for a cowboy delves into the depths of each of their personalities to find common ground in their love for the land. Readers will eagerly anticipate future installments."
—*Publishers Weekly*

THE COWBOY NEXT DOOR

R. C. RYAN

FOREVER

NEW YORK BOSTON

Copyright © 2019 Ruth Ryan Langan
Excerpt from *Born to Be a Cowboy* Copyright © 2019 by Ruth Ryan Langan
Bonus novella *Saved by the Cowboy* Copyright © 2018 by A. J. Pine

Cover photography by Rob Lang. Cover copyright © 2019 by Hachette Book Group, Inc.

Forever
Hachette Book Group
1290 Avenue of the Americas, New York, NY 10104
forever-romance.com
twitter.com/foreverromance

First Edition: February 2019

Forever is an imprint of Grand Central Publishing. The Forever name and logo are trademarks of Hachette Book Group, Inc.

The publisher is not responsible for websites (or their content) that are not owned by the publisher.

The Hachette Speakers Bureau provides a wide range of authors for speaking events. To find out more, go to www.hachettespeakersbureau.com or call (866) 376-6591.

ISBNs: 978-1-5387-1117-0 (mass market), 978-1-5387-1116-3 (ebook)

Printed in the United States of America

OPM

10 9 8 7 6 5 4 3 2 1

To every family's wild child,
who breaks rules and hearts.

And to my very own wild child, Tom,
who stole my heart and owns it still.

THE COWBOY NEXT DOOR

PROLOGUE

Monroe Ranch—Spring—Sixteen years ago

The calendar said it was April, but in the hills above the town of Haller Creek, snow still trickled from low-hanging clouds.

"Over here," Mackenzie Monroe shouted as he and his crew of wranglers moved among the cattle milling about, searching out cows in need of help with birthing. It was calving season, and the grass beneath their boots was a sea of mud.

His three newly adopted sons, twelve-year-old Ben, eleven-year-old Sam, and ten-year-old Finn, were spending their first spring on Mac's ranch.

These troubled brothers, after years of separation in the foster care system, were struggling to adjust to this strange new life. Though they'd finally achieved their goal of being reunited, they weren't ready to trust adults, especially Mac, who expected them to handle ranch chores alongside his wranglers and the three old men who also made their home on Monroe Ranch.

Otis Green, a black man born on the south side of Chicago, may have looked like a fish out of water in the hills of Montana, but in truth, he'd found a forever home here.

Roscoe Flute, an itinerant cowboy who'd come to repair some equipment twenty years previous, had made himself at home in the bunkhouse and had never left.

Zachariah York, a retired lawyer, had come to heal a broken hip and had remained as part-time cook and house-keeper while the others saw to the more physically demanding ranch chores.

As old cowboy Roscoe paused to push his arms, elbow deep, up a bawling cow, the three boys gaped in horror.

While Ben and Finn were speechless, Sam yelled, "What the..." He shot a sideways glance at Mac, who had forbidden cuss words in his home. "Why are you hurting that cow?"

"Not hurting her, boy." Roscoe grinned, showing the gap where teeth once were. "She's about to become a new mama, and having a bit of trouble. She needs a little help delivering her first calf."

"Gross." Finn was thoroughly disgusted, even though he couldn't seem to look away.

"Yeah, gross. I thought nature took care of all that stuff." With a sort of horrified fascination, Sam stepped closer.

"Sometimes a new mama needs a little help. That's what a rancher does." The old cowboy grunted, pulled, twisted.

There was a sudden gush of liquid, and then an opaque sac dropped to the ground. Minutes later the newborn calf broke free of the sac and let out a feeble sound. At once the cow, now as docile as she'd been agitated just moments before, began calmly licking her new calf.

"Ewww." Finn turned to his adoptive father. "If you think I'm ever going to do what Roscoe did, you're crazy. I'm never going to be a rancher. That was disgusting."

Sam, ever the tease, pointed a finger at his younger brother. "Oh, no. Now I bet you're going to cry like a girl."

"Am not." Finn's chin came up like a prizefighter. "And don't tell me you'd ever do what Roscoe just did."

Sam gave a negligent shrug of his shoulders, unable to resist a dare. "Before coming here, I had to do lots worse."

Mac went very still, listening not just to the things these boys said but to what they didn't say. He knew their years of abuse had been painful enough to have the boys setting out during a snowstorm to find freedom. That decision had led them to his ranch, where they'd forced their way inside, searching for food and shelter. His first inclination had been to contact the authorities. Instead, he'd followed his better nature. And now, though there were days when he wondered what he'd been thinking, they were legally his. His sons, though they were still the tough, ready-to-stand-and-fight-the-world delinquents he'd first encountered.

Mac knew it would take years, or perhaps a lifetime, to erase all the doubt and pain and mistrust they'd been forced to endure. Each of them carried scars, both physical and emotional. Ben, the oldest, did his best to look out for the other two. Finn, the youngest, took comfort in the presence of two older brothers. But it was Sam who worried Mac the most. Sam, the tough guy, the free spirit, who always managed to spit in the eye of rules. Sam, who could actually laugh in the face of danger. The boy was fearless, facing every challenge like a superhero, hands fisted, eyes steady, never holding back. And always, when life tossed him to the ground, the boy got back up, laughing.

Always laughing.

Was that healthy? Mac wondered. Did it mean Sam was leaving his past behind? Or was he merely masking his pain with false humor?

While Mac fretted, Sam followed Roscoe to the next cow. Before the old cowboy could pull on his rubber gloves, Sam stopped him.

"Okay. I saw what you did. Now it's my turn."

The old man shot him an astonished look. "You said it was gross."

"Yeah. It is. But like you said, this is what a rancher does."

"Listen, boy. It takes a lot of muscle to birth a calf. I don't think you're ready."

"Maybe. Maybe not. You watch me. If you think I'm getting in the way, push me aside and take over. But at least let me try."

The cowboy did just that, watching as the boy grunted, and sweated, and pulled until his arms had to be nearly falling off. But to Sam's credit, he kept at it until, without warning, the earlier scene was repeated, and a contented new mama stood licking her bawling calf clean.

"I did it." Sam turned to Roscoe and high-fived him.

The old man grinned. "Yes, you did. I think we're going to make a rancher out of you, boy."

While the other wranglers moved on, helping in other births, Sam stayed where he was, watching the cow and calf, and grinning like a proud papa. Mac walked over and dropped an arm around the boy's shoulders. "You did good, Sam."

"Thanks. That was so fuc—" He stopped, started again. "That was cool."

Mac's voice lowered. "And for that cuss word, you'll do Finn's chores tomorrow."

"I could have said a lot worse."

"I know."

When the man walked away, the boy remained, his goofy

grin intact. Hell, yes, he'd do Finn's chores. Right now, he'd do Ben's chores, too. He'd just helped deliver a calf. A year ago, living a life of misery, such a thing wasn't even imaginable. Now here he was, free as a bird, living on a ranch in the middle of nowhere. Living a life he'd never dreamed possible.

Look at him. He was a damned cowboy like those actors in movies. Except this was even better. He was the real thing.

His laughter, unbridled, joyful, drifted on the breeze.

CHAPTER ONE

Monroe Ranch—Present Day

Hoo boy." Ben, dressed in his crisp sheriff's uniform, his badge winking in the late-summer sunlight, held his nose as Sam led his roan gelding past him into the barn. "My brother, the trail bum. How long have you been up in the hills?"

Sam began unsaddling his mount. "Three weeks. I know I smell. I've been in these clothes for days, and eating dust for miles."

"It's not just the smell. You look like one of those wild mountain men. If your beard gets any thicker, it'll completely cover your ugly face. Not that that's a bad thing."

Sam gave one of his rogue grins. "That's not what the girls at the Hitching Post say."

His brother laughed. Sam's prowess with both a pool cue and the ladies was well known at the saloon in the little town of Haller Creek. Men and women alike were drawn to his zany sense of humor and his love of a good joke. "If they could see you now, they'd have a change of heart."

"It's nothing that a shower and shave won't fix."

Ben leaned his arms on the stall's door. "What kept you in the hills so long?"

"I offered to handle the herd while Dad and the others caught up on ranch chores"—Sam shot a pointed look at his older brother—"now that one of us has left ranching behind in favor of being a sheriff. You going to lend a hand, or just stand there trying to look important?"

Ben stood a little taller. "You think the uniform makes me look important?"

"Only in your own mind, bro." Sam flung his saddle over the rail of the stall before filling troughs with oats and water. "I'm still trying to wrap my mind around the fact that my big brother is on the right side of the law for a change."

Ben laughed and Sam joined in.

Sam started toward the house, and then turned. "You coming?"

Ben shook his head. "I just got a call from Becca. She's coming home early, so I'm heading back to town to pick her up. We'll be back in time for dinner."

Sam shot him a sideways glance. "You'd think after almost a year of wedded bliss, things would change. You still rushing home to your blushing bride?"

"You bet." The mere mention of Ben's pretty young wife, Becca, had his grin spreading from ear to ear. "Since we're still in that honeymoon stage, I thought I'd..."

Sam covered his ears. "Stop. Too much information. Remember I'm your brother, not your confessor. Take all that gooey love stuff home, bro."

"Yeah. I'm going. But before I leave I think you should know—"

Sam was shaking his head as he started walking faster. "Not now. I've got the longest shower in history waiting for me. I intend to grab all the hot water before Dad and the others beat me to it. Plan on heading to the Hitching Post after supper. I'm hoping I can lure a couple of suckers from the Murphy Ranch to challenge me to a game of nine ball tonight."

"Okay. But before you go inside, you ought to know. Dad hired a housekeeper."

"What?" Sam stopped dead in his tracks. "What's wrong with Zachariah's cooking and cleaning?"

"Nothing. But I guess Mary Pat told Dad about this woman who needed a job. And Dad—"

Sam held up a hand. Mary Pat Healy, social worker, visiting nurse, and homeschool advisor for the county, was the proverbial bleeding heart, eager to help every needy person in the entire state of Montana. "And Mary Pat asked Dad to work his magic and hire this poor old woman until she can get on her feet."

"Something like that. But…"

Sam eyed a battered car that had seen better days parked outside the barn. "I guess a couple of old men weren't enough for Dad. Now we've added an old woman to keep an eye on." Sam climbed the steps to the porch and pushed open the back door without a pause, leaving his older brother to stare after him with a wide smile splitting his lips.

Once inside the mudroom Sam paused to pry off his filthy, dung-caked boots before strolling through the empty kitchen to the parlor, unbuttoning his shirt as he walked.

That's when he spotted a small figure headed toward him carrying a huge box.

"What the hell?" His reaction was automatic. No sweet old lady should be handling something as heavy as this. "Here. That looks like it weighs more than you. Give me that."

He forcibly took the box from her hands and had to blink twice. He found himself looking into amber eyes so wide, they seemed too big for the pretty face that framed them. To his astonishment, it was a pretty *young* face.

The woman's features went from relaxed to fearful in the blink of an eye. "I don't know what gives you the right to come barging in here, but if you aren't out of here by the count of three, I'll shout down the rooftop. I happen to know the sheriff is right outside."

"I was." Ben's voice came from behind Sam. "Good thing I followed Sam inside."

They both turned to see Ben standing in the doorway. He didn't bother to hide his amusement. "I see I'm too late. You two have already met."

Sam's eyes narrowed. "Okay. What's the joke? I thought you said Dad had hired an old lady."

"That's *not* what I said." Ben turned to the woman. "This smelly cowboy fresh from the hills is my brother Sam." To Sam he added, "Our new housekeeper, Penny Cash."

At the mention of her name Sam's lips curved into a teasing grin. "Really? Penny Cash? You're making that up, right, Miss...Money?"

"What a tired joke. Believe me, I've heard them all." She looked from Ben to Sam before taking the box from Sam's hands. "Now if you'll excuse me, I'll store these things in the mudroom and finish cleaning out the spare bedroom, which is now my bedroom."

She started to brush past Sam, but he stopped her with a hand on her arm. "Okay. What are you doing out here in the middle of nowhere, cleaning up after a houseful of men? Are you on the run from the law?"

She glowered at the offending hand until he removed it. "Mackenzie Monroe knows everything he needs to know about me. If you have any questions, ask him. Or better yet, ask your brother, the sheriff."

Ben slapped a hand on his brother's back. "Better watch out, bro. Looks like she's already made up her mind about you."

She looked Sam up and down and wrinkled her nose at the offending odor before turning to Ben. "I find it hard to believe this trail bum is the brother you and Finn bragged about. The one who charms all the ladies from six to sixty."

Sam puffed up enough to say, "Yeah. They got that right."

She couldn't hold back her laughter. "Poor things. They must be desperate. I pity them all."

Without a backward glance she headed toward the kitchen, shaking her head.

When she was gone, Ben was grinning. "Way to go. I could see she was really impressed." He paused a beat before adding, "Looks like you're losing your touch with the ladies."

A grin spread across Sam's face. "You think I care what one sassy female thinks?"

"Hell, yes. I know you too well. You never could resist a challenge. You're going to brood until you find a way to charm her."

"You got that right." Sam turned away, eager for that shower.

"Welcome back to civilization, Samuel." Zachariah, his lion's mane of white hair framing a handsome, weathered face, looked up from his gin and tonic as Sam stepped into the kitchen.

"It's good to be home." Sam reached into the refrigerator, helped himself to a longneck, and took a long, cool drink.

Mac clapped a hand on his son's shoulder. "Thanks for stepping in with the herd."

"You know I don't mind, Dad. I can't think of anywhere I'd rather be than up in those hills."

Zachariah shared a knowing smile with Roscoe and Otis, who were grinning from ear to ear. "Unless it's in town running the table at the Hitching Post."

Sam chuckled. "Well, yeah. That's a given."

Mac indicated the young woman across the room. "Have you met Penny?"

"We met." Sam couldn't help but study her backside as she bent to remove a roasting pan from the oven. She was wearing slim denims and a faded T-shirt, her dark hair pulled back in a ponytail, making her look even younger.

She barely gave him a glance before setting the pan on top of the stove and lifting the lid.

Sam inhaled the amazing aroma that drifted toward him, making his mouth water.

Zachariah turned as Finn walked in carrying his ever-present briefcase stuffed with legal documents. "Ah. Finnian. Just in time for supper."

Seeing Sam, Finn's face creased into a wide smile and he crossed to his brother. "Hey. How're things in the hills?"

"Quiet. How's the lawyer biz going?"

"I picked up another client today." He tossed aside his briefcase to accept a longneck from Mac. "You know a rancher named Edgar Hanover?"

His father thought a moment before nodding. "Does he have a ranch up on Stony Mountain?"

"That's him." Finn turned to Zachariah. "He wants to take on the county for creating a dam that dried up the branch of the Stony Mountain Creek that feeds into his land."

Zachariah arched a bushy white brow. "I'll remind you. The county has deep pockets, Finnian. They'll spare no expense. You'll be up against an experienced legal team that is kept on retainer for only one purpose—to shoot down the locals who complain about the way things have always been done."

Finn turned to Sam, and the two wore matching dangerous smiles.

Finn took a sip of beer before saying, "I figured as much. That's why I told Edgar Hanover I'd be happy to represent him." In an aside, he said to Zachariah, "And I'm hoping you'll give me the benefit of your expertise."

"Going up against the big guns, are you, lad?" The old man rubbed his hands together. There was nothing he liked better than a chance to step back into the ring and use his years of experience as one of the top trial lawyers in the state. "You have as much of my time and expertise as you want, Finnian, my boy."

They looked toward the door when Ben and Becca walked in holding hands. In Becca's other hand was a leash attached to a big brown dog with floppy ears.

"Hey. What've you got there?" Sam was down on his knees, ruffling the dog's fur and accepting sloppy dog kisses in return.

"This is Archie." Becca's voice was warm with love. "We just got him from the rescue in town. We thought about a puppy, but then we decided to give a second chance to an older dog that needed a home."

"What breed of dog is he?"

"A pure mutt." Ben drew an arm around his wife. "Becca always wanted a dog. I think he'll be good company when I have to work nights."

"And a great watchdog," Sam said with a grin. "He'll lick any intruder to death."

The family was laughing as they gathered around to pet

the dog. If a wildly wagging tail was any indication, Archie was lapping up all the attention.

Ben accepted a longneck from his father. "We were just taking a look at how our house is shaping up. Conway is doing a fine job."

Mac gave a nod of approval. "Conway Miller is a good, honest building contractor. You two hired the best. When does he think you'll be able to move in?"

"Not for another six or seven months. But that's okay. Becca and I are comfortable in the little house in town." Ben looked around. "I'm glad to see we're not too late for supper."

Sam gave a snort of laughter. "Some things never change." He put an arm around his sister-in-law's shoulders. "I thought Mary Pat was giving you cooking lessons."

Becca nodded. "She is. But only when she's in town, which isn't nearly often enough to suit me."

"Or to suit Dad," Sam said in an aside, causing Mac to blush. "Have you met Penny?"

"We met in town before she came to work here." Becca hurried over to give the young woman a hug. "Hi, Penny. I hope it's all right that we've barged in on you without warning."

"You know I'm used to cooking for a crowd. The more the merrier." Penny bent to pet Archie.

It was obvious that Penny and Becca had already become comfortable with one another.

Becca reached for a platter. "The least I can do is help pass things around."

As the others took their places around the table, Zachariah joined the two young women in passing platters of tender roast beef with garden potatoes and green beans, along with rolls warm from the oven.

To keep Archie busy, Becca took a plastic bag of dog food from her pocket and set it in a bowl in a corner of the room.

When they were all gathered around the table, Mac suggested they join hands in honor of their missing member, Mary Pat, who always insisted on a blessing whenever she managed to join them.

He smiled as he intoned, "We're thankful for this food, this family, and those who aren't able to be here with us this day."

With murmured words of approval, they dug in.

"That was a fine meal, Penny." Mac glanced at the young woman seated across the table.

For the most part she'd eaten dinner in silence, content to let the others carry the conversation.

"Thanks, Mr...." She paused and corrected herself. When Mackenzie Monroe had hired her, he'd asked her to call him Mac. "Thanks, Mac."

"Where'd you learn to cook like that, Miss Penny?"

She smiled at Otis, easy in his company. "I have three brothers. I learned early that growing young men like to eat."

"I bet your ma was a good cook, too."

She stared hard at the table. "My mom died when I was ten."

Otis stared helplessly at Mac, who strove to lighten the mood. "I'm sorry to hear that, Penny...Mary Pat said you earned your teaching certificate at the university in Bozeman."

She nodded. "I started studying online, and finished at Bozeman."

Becca put a hand over Penny's. "I went to college there, too. I bet we were there at the same time. Wouldn't it be something if we had mutual friends?"

Penny gave a shake of her head. "I didn't have much time

to socialize. I carried two jobs while I was there. I worked in a little café in the mornings, and right after class I worked in a coffee shop off campus."

"And I thought my schedule was tough. When did you sleep?" Becca asked.

Penny gave a short laugh. "Good question. Mostly I went without it. But I didn't mind. Getting my teacher's certification was worth it."

Sam winked. "I always thought it would be fun to be teacher's pet."

Seeing the heat that stained Penny's cheeks, he added quickly, "But if you're a teacher, why aren't you teaching?"

Mac turned to explain. "Penny was brought to Haller Creek by the school board to replace Nancy Carter."

Sam nodded in understanding. "Pryor Carter was telling everybody that he and Nancy were finally having a baby after six years of trying."

"Unfortunately, Nancy lost the baby." Mac sipped his coffee. "She and Pryor have been really shaken by the loss. Her doctor said work would be the best way for her to move on with her life, so she asked Chet Butler and the board to keep her job available. The board agreed that they were legally bound to honor their commitment to her, since technically she was still under contract."

Sam glanced at Penny. "But what about your job?"

She shook her head. "Mr. Butler explained that since I never got a chance to sign a contract, I had no legal rights."

"Couldn't you teach somewhere else?"

She sighed. "With school already in session, all the positions are filled. Mr. Butler offered to let me sub whenever one of the teachers needs a day, and I'm happy to do that, but I have a lot of college debt to clear. I need a full-time job, and Mary Pat suggested I come here."

Sam arched a brow. "Not surprising. Mary Pat seems to have a logical solution for every problem under the sun."

Sam's words had Mac nodding. "That's our Mary Pat, all right."

"Do I smell pumpkin pie?" Roscoe's question had Penny pushing away from the table, glad for the change in conversation.

Over her shoulder she called, "I think it's cool enough to cut now. I made whipped cream, too."

"I'll help." Sam walked to the refrigerator and removed a bowl mounded with whipped cream. Even before he reached for a spoon he'd dug his finger in to taste. "I'll be darned. Not out of a can or carton, but the real thing." He dipped a big serving spoon into it and ate it in one gulp.

Finn chuckled. "That's the fastest I've ever seen you offer to help. Now I know why."

"So do I." Penny fished a second spoon from the drawer and took the bowl from Sam's hands. "After you've licked that one clean, you can put it in the sink. I don't want you passing your germs around to the rest of us."

"Hey." Sam tried to reach over her shoulder with the spoon, but she was quicker and snatched the bowl away.

She shot him a withering look. "If you want a piece of pie, you'd better not try that again in my kitchen, cowboy."

While Sam stepped back, the rest of the family hooted with laughter.

"Guess the lady told you who's in charge, bro."

At Finn's taunt, Sam was forced to drop the spoon in the sink and take his place at the table. But one bite of pumpkin pie smothered in whipped cream had his smile returning.

Penny Cash may appear shy, but she certainly knew how to take charge. And she could cook. He was willing to overlook her obvious character flaw as long as he could indulge his sweet tooth on something as good as this.

"So," Finn said around a mouthful of pie. "I guess you must have missed your nights in town while you were stuck up in the hills with nothing but cows for company. Planning on heading to the Hitching Post tonight?"

Penny's head came up sharply, and she regarded Sam with a look of disdain, the way she might study a big, hairy spider.

Seeing the look of disapproval on her face, Sam gave a slow, reluctant shake of his head. "That was the plan. But after three weeks in the hills, and a full stomach, I've decided I need to sleep in a real bed."

He saw the rigid line of Penny's back as she walked to the stove and couldn't resist adding, "There's time enough for teaching the yokels the game of nine ball some other time."

CHAPTER TWO

After second slices of pie, and many cups of coffee, the family began drifting from the kitchen to the old-fashioned parlor, where they gathered around the fireplace.

Before Penny could tackle the dishes, Ben and Becca shooed her away.

"We barged in uninvited," Becca explained. "So we'll tackle the cleanup."

"But it's my job…"

Ben gave a firm shake of his head. "You cooked. We'll clean. It's a rule of the house. I'm sure there are plenty of other chores you need to see to."

She shot him a look of surprise, followed by a slow smile. "As a matter of fact, I have baskets of laundry to sort."

"There you go." Ben added with a smile, "Besides, this is the perfect excuse for some alone time with my bride. We've both been putting in too many hours at work lately."

Penny gave them plenty of privacy, heading to the mudroom to pick up a basket of clean laundry. Walking to the parlor, she chose a side table in the corner to sort and fold.

Archie, panting from a run around the room to sniff every corner, settled down underneath the table and curled himself into a ball before falling asleep.

As Penny worked, she couldn't help hearing snatches of conversation.

Mac's voice. Low. Tentative. "With fall closing in, we never know when the weather will turn."

Sam took a pull on his beer. "All I know is, up in those hills I was in a sauna, it was so hot."

"All the same, we need to start getting the herds ready to bring down to the winter range." Mac looked at Sam. "How many wranglers should I hire?"

"That depends. How tight is money right now?"

His father shrugged. "It's always tight. But I remember plenty of years we got caught with an early snowstorm, and the cattle were trapped in the hills."

Ben's voice interrupted. "What's this about trapped cattle?"

They looked up as Ben and Becca, holding hands and wearing matching secret smiles, stepped into the parlor to say good night.

At once, Archie was awake and running up to them. Becca snapped on his leash before straightening.

"You're looking awfully happy about doing kitchen duty, bro."

At Sam's words, Ben merely wiggled his brows like a movie villain. "Wicked happy. We actually managed a little alone time. Now we need to head back home so I can work the night shift. What's this about the cattle?"

"Nothing we can't handle," Mac assured him. "You've got enough on your plate, son."

"You know I'm always available when you need me, Dad."

Mac nodded. "I know that, and I appreciate it."

They called good night to everyone, and Becca paused to hug Penny before taking her leave, with Archie tugging on his leash.

The others returned their attention to the cattle drive.

"We've got some time." Sam glanced at Otis and Roscoe. "If we bring the herds down in smaller bites, instead of one big drive, the three of us can handle it."

Mac sipped his beer. "I can help, too."

Sam held up a hand. "Not this year. With Ben and Finn working in town, somebody needs to keep up with all the chores around the barns. The three of us can handle it, Dad."

Mac clapped a hand on Sam's shoulder. "You've been doing double duty for a while now. Just so you know, we can afford to hire some help."

Penny picked up an armload of towels and headed toward the stairs. As she walked past, Sam's gaze narrowed slightly as he tracked her progress up the steps until she was out of sight.

"Now that's an expense we could do without."

At his muttered comment, Mac shook his head. "I couldn't say no to Mary Pat. The poor girl is stranded here with no family and no job."

Sam turned to Zachariah. "And you've been replaced as chief cook and bottle washer."

"Perfect timing," the old man said. "I'm thinking Finnian here is going to need a good many hours of my help as he muddles his way through his first high-profile trial against the big guns in government."

Finn chuckled before tipping up a longneck. "You got

that right, Zachariah. Looks like you and I will be burning a lot of midnight oil."

After storing the clean towels in a linen closet, Penny closed herself in the guest room she'd been given when she'd been hired. It was on the far end of a long upper hallway. It was a big room, bigger even than the tiny living room at her family home. The scarred wooden floor was cushioned by a rug in soft hues of pale coral, yellow, and spring green. The big bed had a plain white down comforter brightened by a handmade throw in pale coral, folded at the foot. A high, wide window boasted a window seat, with a grand view of the hills rising up in the distance. Best of all, it had its own bathroom, all done in gleaming white tile. Well, she thought, it hadn't been so white or gleaming when she'd first arrived. But after removing years of dirt and neglect, it looked brand new, as did the old hardwood floor.

Every time she stepped into this room she felt a little thrill. All hers. Her very own private sanctuary. No noisy brothers barging in. No demands being made on her.

Not that she'd ever minded caring for her brothers, or her elderly great-aunt, who had moved from a retirement home after the death of Penny's father to be with her family. Without Aunt Lucy, the authorities would have stepped in to place the children in foster care. But having an adult in the home, even one who used a wheelchair, meant that they could stay together. And for that, Penny would always be grateful. It meant more work for Penny, but it was a labor of love. As for Danny, Cooper, and Curtis, they'd been good boys. But boys required a lot of discipline to keep them from going wild. She'd done all she could to give them everything she knew her parents had wanted for them. Now they were men, and in charge of their own lives.

In charge.

It's what she'd studied for, sacrificed for, dreamed of. Being in charge of her own future.

She'd been so deliriously happy when she'd been hired to teach in Haller Creek. It would mean freedom. Independence. But best of all, molding young minds. Helping sweet children be all they could be.

By the time she'd learned that the job offer had been rescinded, she'd already severed all ties with life in Dennison, a little town nearly two hundred miles from here. She'd spent the last of her savings to move to Haller Creek. When she'd met with the board president to consider her options, she'd been in a deep well of fear and despair.

All those years of hard work and studying late into the night to pursue her dream. And the dream had been hers for one brief, shining moment, before it had been cruelly snatched away.

Now, instead of walking into a classroom, she was living among strangers, doing the same things she'd been doing for a lifetime. Cooking. Cleaning. Except, instead of being in her own comfort zone, she was far from home, without a friend.

She shook her head.

That wasn't true. She would be forever grateful to Mary Pat for listening, for caring, and for steering her toward this job. At the moment she may be nothing more than an interim cook and housekeeper, but without the need to pay for room and board, she would be able to save every dollar she earned here, so that by next summer she could accept a teaching position somewhere else and once more pursue her dream.

At least she'd grown up in a houseful of men, so she wasn't completely intimidated by this situation. But her father and brothers had been family. This strange assortment of men seemed completely different from any family she'd ever known. Otis, who spent hours tilling the soil behind the barn and growing the most amazing vegetables. Roscoe, a throwback to the Old West, always smiling, despite the loss of several front teeth, and always courtly in her presence. Zachariah, a lion of a man, with a mane of white hair and a voice that rang with a lifetime of courtroom authority. And Mackenzie, quiet, thoughtful, with the kindest eyes she'd ever seen.

And his sons, Ben, Sam, and Finn. Rough, tough, and, according to rumors that circulated around the little town of Haller Creek, ready to stand together and fight anyone who threatened them.

As Penny undressed, she could hear the low drone of masculine voices drifting from below.

One voice stood out from the others.

Sam Monroe.

Even though their introduction had been prickly, she sensed the affection his family had for him. Even the fact that he seemed to pour a great deal of energy into his pursuit of pool and pretty women, he appeared to hold up his end of responsibilities around this ranch. Mackenzie seemed to trust Sam's judgment.

Still, there was something reckless and a little dangerous about Sam. He made her extremely uncomfortable.

She crossed her arms over her chest and stared at the outline of the darkened hills in the distance.

Despite this huge tract of land, the many buildings, and the vast herds of cattle, she knew, from the bits of conversation she'd overheard, that money was tight. She also knew, from Sam's softly spoken words, that she had added to their debt. She was certain he hadn't wanted her to overhear, but now that she had, it wasn't something she could soon forget.

She'd always been a worker. Now, she decided, she would work even harder to overcome that little twinge of guilt for being the cause of yet another drain on the Monroe finances.

As she turned away and settled into bed, she came to a decision. Mackenzie Monroe would have no reason to regret having opened his doors to her. She would double her work-load until this old house sparkled. And when Mac and his family came in from the fields, she would serve them meals that would make them weep with gratitude.

Take that, Sam Monroe.

As that thought intruded, she felt another twinge of guilt. Why was she letting him get to her? He was just another cowboy, in a part of the country littered with them.

All right, she thought grudgingly. Not just another cow-boy. A really great-looking one with a killer smile. The change in him, after a shower and shave, had been a shock to her system. Not that she'd let him see it. She didn't quite know how to handle him. He'd proven to be as quick with his humor as he'd been with anger when he'd thought some little old lady was carrying too heavy a load.

Still, he'd been silly and charming at dinner.

Without even trying, he was sexy, and just a little bit dangerous.

The thought had her gritting her teeth. That's probably the way he saw himself.

She had no use for cocky, good-looking cowboys with an attitude.

Still, she couldn't afford to forget for even one minute that he was the son of the generous man who was giving her another chance.

If there was one thing she'd learned early in life, it was that she could do anything she put her mind to.

Right now, she needed to put all her energy into making herself indispensable around here.

As for Sam Monroe, she would have to put him in the same category as her brothers. Maybe that would help her forget how appealing he could be.

Right. Good luck with that.

The thought had her sighing in the darkness.

CHAPTER THREE

Sam woke to the tantalizing aroma of freshly ground coffee. He sat up, struggling to get his bearings.

After three weeks in the hills, sleeping in rough range shacks or, more often, under the stars, using his saddle for a pillow, it took him a moment to realize he was home. Last night he'd fallen asleep as soon as he hit the sack, and had slept for ten solid hours.

By the time he made his way downstairs to the kitchen, the rest of the family was just finishing breakfast. He paused in the doorway, listening to the familiar voices, watching his brother Finn going over a document with Zachariah, while Roscoe and Otis were planning their chores for the day. Penny was topping off Mac's coffee. A glance at his father's face showed him looking relaxed and content.

"Oh. You're up." Penny turned to the stove. "I'll have fresh pancakes for you in just a minute."

"Thanks. No rush." Sam picked up a mug and crossed the room.

Before he could pour the coffee, Penny picked up the coffeepot and filled his cup.

He breathed in the wonderful fragrance before taking a long drink. Satisfied, he grinned at her. "Now, this is coffee."

Roscoe nudged Otis. "Are you saying this is better than the stuff made in a blackened coffeepot over a campfire?"

Otis chimed in. "Or better than the odor of stale coffee grounds on the frosty air?"

They gave a grunt of laughter.

Sam held up his mug of steaming brew. "All I know is, this is worth all those long, cold nights up in the hills." He turned to Penny. "What did you do to make this so fine?"

She flushed with unexpected pleasure. "I found an old coffee grinder up in the cupboard and thought I'd give it a try."

"Pure magic," he muttered as he took a seat at the table.

Minutes later, Penny set down a plate of scrambled eggs, thick slices of ham, and half a dozen pancakes laced with maple syrup. Without a word he began to eat, and he didn't stop until he'd polished off everything.

Watching him, Zachariah deadpanned, "Careful, Samuel. You're allowed to lick the plate clean, but don't try eating it. You'll break a tooth."

While the others laughed, Sam sat back with a contented sigh. "After weeks of beef jerky in the saddle, I'd wake up dreaming of food like this. Thanks, Miss Money."

To hide her pleasure she merely gave a nod of her head.

"Yeah, that can make a man yearn for the comforts of home." Mac shoved away from the table. "I'm heading into town for supplies. Everybody got their lists ready?"

Roscoe handed over a page of scribbles.

Otis did the same.

Mac turned to Penny. "Got your list?"

She shrugged and could feel her cheeks grow hot as Sam looked over at her. Thinking of what she'd overheard about their finances, she said softly, "I don't want to be a bother. I can make do with whatever's here."

Mac gave her an indulgent smile. "It's no bother. I'm going to town now, and I may not make the drive into Haller Creek until next week. So, if you're running low on anything, you'd better write it down now."

She shook her head. "I've gone over your supplies. I'm fine."

"Okay." He strolled into the mudroom, where he plucked a Stetson from a hook. "See you later."

The others filed out behind him, with Finn off to his law practice, and Otis and Roscoe heading toward the barn. Zachariah made his way to his room, where floor-to-ceiling shelves housed his legal library.

Sam smiled as the door closed. "Zachariah will spend a very satisfying day looking up legal precedents for Finn to cite in his case."

Penny topped off his coffee before crossing to the sink. "Your brother told me Zachariah was once a famous lawyer."

"One of the best. He's the reason Finn went into law."

"Really?" She glanced over. "Is he a relative?"

Sam chuckled. "Not by blood. But, in case you haven't noticed, we're all family here."

"I've noticed." She filled the sink with hot, soapy water and began to wash the dishes, setting them on a tray to drain. "But I didn't want to pry about the relationship."

"You're living here now. You have a right to know." Sam finished his coffee and sauntered across the room to pick up a clean towel before starting to dry the dishes.

Penny lifted a hand from the soapy water to still his movements. "You don't need to do that. It's my job."

He enjoyed the little thread of pleasurable heat that shot along his arm at her touch. "Running this place and keeping up with a million and one chores means we all work together."

As he reached over her head to move the platter to a high shelf, his hand brushed her hair, sending another curl of heat up his spine.

This morning she wore her hair long and loose, and it spilled over her shoulders and down her back in a tangle of mahogany curls. Curls that were as soft and downy as a new-born calf's coat.

What in hell was wrong with him? It was obvious he'd been in the hills way too long.

"Mac's wife and son are buried up there on that hillside." Sam nodded toward the window, where the gently curving meadows climbed higher and higher, each one folding into the next.

She blinked. "His wife?"

"Rachel. And their son, Robbie."

"They weren't your mother and brother?"

He shook his head. "My brothers and I were adopted by Mac when we were kids. His wife and son were killed in an accident on the interstate before we ever showed up. According to Roscoe and Otis, it was Rachel who opened her doors to each of them years ago when she learned of their troubles."

"What kind of troubles?"

At her look of concern, Sam shook his head before picking up another plate. "That's not my story. Maybe one day Otis and Roscoe will tell you about their lives before coming here. Zachariah, who lived on a neighboring ranch, fell and broke his hip, and Rachel and Mac brought him here to recover. And he was so happy to be here, in the company of good people, he never left. Then my brothers and I arrived on the scene, angry, determined to start a life together, and willing to do whatever it took to do that. So, we decided to break into what we thought was a deserted ranch and steal whatever we could eat or carry."

"You broke in? To steal?" The rumors she'd heard were all true. These three had been dangerous.

"We were scared and mad and desperate. That can make a kid do some wrongheaded things. But instead of calling the authorities, Mac not only allowed us to stay, but, with the help of Zachariah and Mary Pat, he also adopted us legally. And now we're all family."

Penny drained the water and used the towel to dry the counters as Sam stored the last of the clean dishes in a cupboard. And all the while she digested what he'd told her.

"To think Mac adopted three thieves. And opened his door to so many strangers. What an amazing, generous man."

"Yeah. That's Dad. He's a good man. One of the best."

"Now I know why he hired me, even though money is tight. I bet he sees me as just another stray needing a place to land."

"What do you mean...?"

She shook her head and turned away to avoid his eyes. "I heard what you said last night. I'm another expense you don't need, at a time when money is tight."

"Hey." He caught her by the shoulders and turned her around to face him. "Ignore what I said. Dad always used to tell me my mouth runs ahead of my brain. I thought I'd outgrown it." His lips curved into a sexy smile. "I'd really like you to stay and keep on making that fine coffee and those amazing pancakes."

"You're just saying that because you've been on the trail so long. But now that I know your father can't afford to pay me..."

He gave a hiss of frustration at having been overheard the previous night. He must have been a lot more trail-weary than he'd realized. "Please try to ignore what I said. We're not broke."

"But you said..."

"We're just like every other rancher in Montana. Always having to decide if we'll call a vet or save the money to invest in a prize bull to increase our herds, or..."

"Now you're just trying to make me feel less guilty about being here and taking a paycheck."

"No guilt. None." His hands tightened at her shoulders, and he drew her closer before he realized what he'd done.

He turned away, a growl in his voice. "I can imagine how stunned you must have been when the job you were promised was taken away. Life happens. My dad understands that. Now you're here. And I'm telling you straight. You keep on feeding us like last night's supper and this morning's breakfast, we'll fight anybody who tries to coax you away."

Though she still wasn't smiling, two bright spots of color appeared on her cheeks, the only sign that he'd touched a nerve. "I was feeling really guilty for being a burden. I guess..." Seeing him turn to look at her with that fierce expression, she stepped back a pace before stiffening her spine. "I guess I'd better get busy earning my keep."

As she walked away, Sam stayed where he was.

She was an odd little thing. All stiff and stern, and obviously desperate to hold on to her job.

He hoped she'd stay. For his dad's sake. For Zachariah, who had taken on the majority of cooking and cleaning, while neglecting his first love—the law. For the others, who deserved to come home to a fine meal and clean clothes after a day of hard ranch chores.

He thought about the coffee and hearty breakfast he'd practically inhaled. If he was honest, he had to admit he selfishly wanted more of that for himself, as well.

But he'd have to learn to keep his mouth shut and think before he blurted out any more smartass remarks. Penny Cash was too smart for her own good.

Those big, sad eyes and that stiff backbone had gotten under his skin.

She reminded him of a bird he'd once rescued up in the hills, half frozen in a raging blizzard. The minute it spotted him, it flopped around, silently pecking his hand with that sharp beak, all to hide the fact that it couldn't fly.

Was Penny covering a deep well of pain?

He'd know a thing or two about hiding pain.

Sam had learned early in life not to put too much hope in expectations. He was a realist. Most wishes don't come true. Still, he'd already had his one and only miracle. He was here with a good, honest man and a strange assortment of characters who had become family. He was living free and easy on a ranch he loved, living life most men only dream of. He already had more than he could have ever hoped for. He wouldn't ask for more.

He gave an annoyed shake of his head.

Penny was no wounded bird. No storm-tossed, helpless female. She was just another woman, who probably carried a lot of baggage.

So why this flare of heat at the mere touch of her?

Hell, he'd held enough females in his arms to know pure and simple lust when he experienced it.

What he needed, he told himself, was a night at the Hitching Post in Haller Creek. A night with the guys, a couple of cold longnecks, and some satisfying games of nine ball.

And then he'd come home feeling like the old Sam Monroe, who had vowed that no female would ever get to him.

He'd learned early in life not to expect a happily-ever-after. There was no guarantee that tomorrow would be better. There was only today. And a smart man grabbed the day with both hands and enjoyed the hell out of it, expecting nothing more.

CHAPTER FOUR

Weeks later, Sam walked into the kitchen, sleeves rolled to his elbows, hair glistening with drops of water. He studied the familiar scene of his family gathered around one end of the room talking business and drinking longnecks, while the most amazing scents of meat roasting, bread baking, and desserts cooling on a sideboard had his mouth watering. But not nearly as much as the way his mouth watered every time he looked at the woman responsible for all this.

They had all noted the subtle changes since Penny had been here. Sunshine poured in through windows that didn't have a speck of dirt or dust. The rooms of the house were not only clean but also organized. Parkas hung on hooks in the mudroom in an orderly fashion, with hats above and boots below. A thick mat had been added to trap mud and snow beneath the long wooden bench they all sat on to pry off their boots. In the parlor, a copper tub, once discarded in one of the barns, now sat on the hearth, polished to a high shine and filled with logs and kindling. Upstairs, towels that had once been draped over the tub and shower were now collected daily, washed, and rolled into a big basket. Shaving gear that had once cluttered every inch of bathroom space was now arranged in a caddy placed atop the counter for easy access. Every room smelled of soap and disinfectant.

Though the house was still the domain of half a dozen rugged men, Penny's touch could be seen everywhere.

Spying his older brother and wife and their now-familiar pet, Archie, Sam's face creased into a wide smile.

"Hey, Ben. You and Becca just happen to be in the neighborhood?" Sam dropped to his knees to ruffle Archie's fur and accept a few wet kisses.

Ben gave a laugh and dropped an arm around his wife's shoulders. "I doubt I could get away with that lie. But since both Becca and I got off early today, we thought we'd take advantage of Penny's excellent cooking."

Becca nodded.

Finn, who had discarded his ever-present attaché case on a sideboard, arched a brow at Sam. "You planning on hanging around for supper?"

Sam gave a nonchalant shrug of his shoulders, hoping to look disinterested. "Why wouldn't I?"

"I figured as soon as you finished the ranch chores, you'd be on your way to town to wolf down some of Horton's chili and fries at the Hitching Post before fleecing the local wranglers out of their paychecks."

Sam gave a snort of disdain. "Why should I bother with that mud Horton calls chili when I can have whatever Penny's cooking that smells so good?"

Finn nudged Ben. "So it's her good cooking that has you sticking around."

The two shared knowing grins.

Penny lifted a roasting pan from the oven and glanced over to say, "It's pretty simple tonight. I just roasted a couple of chickens."

Becca crossed the room to lend a hand. "My mouth has been watering since Ben and I walked in. What's in all these pots?" She lifted lids, then gave a sigh. "Oh, my. Mashed potatoes. Green beans." She watched as Penny lifted a pan of biscuits from the oven. "I think I'm ready to change loyalties. I've been getting the occasional kitchen help from Mary Pat. But she rarely has time to spare. I'd like to take cooking lessons from you. Would you teach me how to do all this, Penny?"

Penny dimpled. "Of course. It's really simple, once you do it a time or two."

"Easy for you to say." Becca shared a smile with her new husband. "I know it would make Ben really happy if you could teach me to do all this."

Ben crossed the room to press a kiss to his wife's cheek. "I didn't marry you for your cooking, babe."

Becca blushed as the others chuckled. "Of course you didn't. But I'd love to surprise you one night with a meal like this."

They looked up at the sound of another car pulling up behind the string of trucks parked outside.

"Oh, look," Becca announced. "It's Mary Pat."

The minute the words were out of her mouth, Mac set aside his longneck and hurried out the door.

Minutes later Mary Pat, arms laden with mysterious packages, stepped into the mudroom, trailed by Mac, whose smile was as bright as the sun.

Mary Pat turned to Penny. "I can't tell you how lovely it is to walk into this house and smell dinner cooking."

She set aside her burden before circling the room to hug

everyone, her red hair threaded with gray brushing the collar of her faded plaid shirt.

It was obvious, from the warmth of their greetings, that the entire family was delighted to see her.

"You've been gone a long time, Mary Patricia." Zachariah took her hand. He nodded toward the door. "Car trouble again?"

She gave a quick laugh. "No, thank heavens. Roscoe and Otis continue to work miracles on my old van. There's no reason, really, for being away so long, except that I wanted to get in as many visits to the outlying ranchers as I could before the weather turns."

They all knew that her role as social worker, visiting nurse, and homeschool advisor made her welcome everywhere she traveled.

She dropped to her knees to exclaim over Archie. "Oh, look at you. Aren't you just the cutest thing." While petting him she looked up. "Whose doggie is this?"

Becca and Ben said together, "He's ours. His name is Archie. We got him at the shelter in town." Then they both broke out in laughter as they realized they'd spoken in unison.

"A good choice. He suits the two of you." Mary Pat gave him a final pat before getting to her feet.

"Dinner is ready," Penny announced.

While Penny arranged the roast chicken on a platter, the others passed around a bowl of mashed potatoes and another bowl of green beans.

Mary Pat eyed the beans. "These look fresh. I'm betting you didn't get these out of the freezer."

"Otis picked the last of his garden vegetables. We can thank him for the bounty."

The old man was flushed with pride. "I'm afraid those are

the last of them. I had to hunt for every one. But they're so much better than the ones in the store."

"Everything's better when it's fresh." Mac helped himself before passing it along to Roscoe.

As soon as their plates were filled, they joined hands and waited for Mary Pat to offer a blessing.

She smiled as she looked around the table. "Bless this food, these good friends, and the many roads we all travel."

As they dug into their meal, Mac turned to Mary Pat, seated beside him. "Want to fill us in on your latest adventures?"

"I'd be happy to." She took a bite of moist chicken and paused to sigh in pleasure. "Penny, this is pure perfection."

The young woman's cheeks colored at the compliment.

Becca blurted, "Before you tell us about your last few weeks, I have a confession to make. I'm afraid I've traded loyalties, Mary Pat. I know I asked you to give me some cooking lessons, but lately you're gone so much I just asked Penny if she'd teach me instead. I hope you don't mind..."

Mary Pat put up a hand to stop her. "You're not being disloyal, Becca. You're being smart. Besides, now that I've had a taste of Penny's roast chicken, I may ask for some of her cooking tips, too."

"I'll admit," Mac said quietly, "that we've been eating like royalty since Penny came along."

The young woman lowered her gaze, aware that her cheeks were burning. It was obvious that she wasn't accustomed to compliments.

Seeing her reaction, Mac quickly deflected attention. "I believe you were going to tell us where you've been lately, Mary Pat."

"Well, the Gardner ranch is falling into serious disrepair now that young Butch left for the Marines. Olga confided to me that her husband is too proud to hire someone to handle all the chores Butch once did. But doing it all by himself is taking a toll, not only on Cecil's health, but also on their marriage. Olga said Cecil is finding fault with everything. She doesn't know how much longer they can go on like this."

Mac thought a minute before saying, "I may know someone." He glanced at the others. "Foster Egan's boy, Mitch, graduated high school last spring and needs a job. He and Foster have been fighting like two bulls in a pasture. Mitch might be willing to work for Cecil Gardner in return for room and board and a little money. That would get him out of Foster's hair for a while, and ease Cecil's workload without draining their finances too much. Maybe, if Cecil thought he was doing the boy a favor, he could be persuaded to take him in."

Mary Pat put a hand over Mac's. "Oh, Mac. If you can make it happen, it could be heaven-sent for all of them."

He shrugged. "I can't promise, but I'll see what I can do."

By the time they were all enjoying Penny's freshly baked pound cake drizzled with strawberry preserves and vanilla ice cream, Mary Pat had brought them up to date on half the population of ranchers in the county. She regaled them with an account of an elderly widow who, after burying her husband, mucked stalls, helped her wranglers with calving in the spring, and rode with them on the annual drive to bring her cattle down from the hills every autumn.

"She'll be ninety-two this year, and hasn't slowed down at all."

While they were remarking on this, Mary Pat added, "Oh, and, Becca, a classmate of yours, Dakota Meyers, delivered twins while her husband was caught in a storm up in the high country."

Becca's eyes widened. "Did she have help?"

"Their ranch is too isolated. She was all alone. She told me it all happened too quickly to be afraid. She just did what she had to, called the clinic afterward to report the births and to ask what else she should do. They told her I was on the road and would make her a priority. So I did. After checking both baby girls, I told her they were perfect. She's an amazing mother."

Becca caught Ben's hand. "I'm so glad we have lots of family around us. If I'm ever forced to give birth at home, I want as many women with me as possible."

Sam leaned close to say, "Don't you worry, Becca. If there are no women nearby, I'll dash over to lend a hand."

She gave him a playful slap on the arm. "No offense, brother-in-law, but you'd be the last person I'd want attending to me during childbirth."

"Hey. I've delivered enough calves to know what to do."

While the others laughed, Becca rolled her eyes in mock horror. "That's what I'm afraid of."

"That was another fine meal, Penny. Let's take our coffee in the other room." Mac pushed away from the table and led the way to the parlor, where a cheery fire was already blazing.

Mary Pat and the men followed him, while Sam, Finn, Ben, and Becca remained in the kitchen to help with the cleanup. By now, Penny had learned that it did no good to protest. The three brothers had accepted kitchen duty as a necessary part of their routine. After marriage, Becca had happily joined them, mainly because it was too much fun to miss.

Penny was content to let the others play their foolish pranks, while she remained aloof. Although she tried to distance herself, she was soon caught up in the constant laughing and teasing that was as much a part of the cleanup as dishwater and towels.

Ben looked over as Sam picked up a towel and shoved his way closer to Penny, whose hands were deep in soapy water. "You still here, bro? I figured by now you'd be halfway to Haller Creek."

"Not tonight." Sam rubbed his flat, muscled stomach. "All that good food has left me too mellow to hustle pool."

Penny frowned. "You actually shoot pool for money?"

"Well, yeah." He shot her a lazy grin. "What other incentive would there be for me to perform?"

"Perform?"

Ben and Finn shared a laugh before Finn explained. "Sam's the best actor around these parts. If he spots a sucker, you'd swear he can't even figure out how to hold a cue stick, let alone shoot nine ball. But once some poor dumb wrangler falls for his act and ups the bet high enough, Sam suddenly turns into Super Sam."

"Super Sam." She gave a sniff of disdain.

"It's a beautiful thing to watch." Finn used his best courtroom voice to embellish his tale. "I've seen my brother look like a falling-down drunk, slurring his words, using the wrong end of a pool stick, and completely missing the ball when he tries for a shot. When the poor wrangler thinks he's got a sure thing and asks if they can play for a hundred dollars or more, Sam mysteriously sobers up and runs every ball in succession."

She looked horrified. "Isn't that cheating?"

Sam finished the last dish and stored it in the cupboard above her head.

He leaned close. "That's called hustling, little lady. And you're looking at one of the best in the business."

While the others shared his laughter, Penny drained the water and dried her hands on a towel. "Careful, cowboy. Pride goeth before a fall."

"Oh. So prim and proper." He tugged on a lock of her hair. "And don't you forget. Fall goeth before winter."

Despite her good intentions, she couldn't hold back the burst of laughter, and the others quickly joined in.

They were all still laughing as they trooped into the parlor to join Mary Pat and the men, who were listening intently as she shared more news from the trail and began opening the packages she'd brought. A handmade afghan from a grateful rancher's wife. A series of childish drawings made by a family of six young children whose parents lived miles from their nearest neighbor. A stone, cut in two and polished to a high shine by a teenaged rock collector, in gratitude for having been contacted by a college professor recommended by Mary Pat.

Her tales were endlessly entertaining and brought home to all of them how much impact she made on the lives of all those she touched.

CHAPTER FIVE

As the fire burned low, Ben put a hand on his father's shoulder. "Time for us to get back to town. I have an early morning tomorrow."

"I'm glad you two were able to make the drive." Mac hugged his daughter-in-law.

After they took their leave, with Archie between them, Penny couldn't stifle a yawn.

She turned to Mary Pat. "I've been sleeping in the bigger guest room, but since you've been on the trail for weeks, I'd like you to have it. I'll take the other room."

Mary Pat shook her head firmly. "Penny, after sleeping in my old van, any room with a bed will feel like heaven. You have all your things in the big room, and that's where you'll stay."

"But…"

Mary Pat gathered her close for a hug. "No argument, honey. Now go to bed. And thank you for that lovely dinner."

Penny turned away, calling good night to the others.

Sam set aside his empty cup. "I think I'll turn in, too. I'm beat."

He trailed slowly behind Penny.

The others watched until they disappeared up the stairs.

Finn turned to Zachariah. "If you're not too tired, I'd like to ask your opinion on some issues I have with my latest case."

The old man looked pleased. There was nothing he loved more than the chance to discuss any aspect of the law. "Let's go to my room. If I can't help, maybe we can find something in my library that will do the trick."

They called good night to the others and made their way to Zachariah's rooms off the kitchen.

Otis and Roscoe had already hurried off to the bunkhouse to continue their nightly gin rummy game.

Mac put a fresh log on the fire before fetching fresh coffee from the kitchen. He and Mary Pat settled into two rockers side by side in front of the fire.

Mary Pat took a sip. "I've never seen this place looking so organized."

Mac nodded. "It's certainly showing Penny's touch."

"So." Mary Pat took another sip. "Penny's a good fit?"

"As if you didn't know that before bringing her here." He looked over with a grin. "You have a gift for reading people, Mary Pat."

"Some people." Relaxed, she leaned back, letting the warmth of the fire soothe her. "It's so good to be back here, Mac."

"You were gone so long, I was starting to worry."

She put a hand over his. "I'd tell you not to worry about me, but it's kind of nice having someone do that. It's been a lifetime since I had someone care about my comings and goings."

"I care." His gruff voice softly growled his words almost grudgingly.

She kept her gaze fastened on the fire. "I was a little worried about bringing a young woman into this all-male household. I know how your boys love to tease, especially Sam. I'm sure a lot of women wouldn't be able to hold their own against them. But Penny is different. She helped raised three brothers, and I thought that would level the field a bit."

"My boys do like to tease. But they don't take it far enough to be hurtful. If I ever saw something like that, you know I'd put a stop to it."

"I know." She turned to look at him. "But you do know Sam has a crush on Penny."

He arched a brow, and she could see the look of surprise in his eyes. "A crush? That sounds like high school talk. Aren't they both a little too old for that kind of thing?"

"What does age have to do with attraction?"

When he said nothing, she softened her words with a smile. "A fascination, then. I doubt he's even aware of it yet. I suspect it might have something to do with the fact that Penny isn't like other young women he knows."

"What does that mean?"

"From what I've seen, women young and old are attracted to Sam, not only because he's so good-looking, but also because of that zany sense of humor. It's a real bonus. But I'm guessing those are the very things that are off-putting to Penny."

"Off-putting? Isn't that a strong statement?"

Mary Pat shrugged. "From what I know of her, Penny hasn't had much time for fun and games. She's strict, not only with others, but also with herself. I'm sure a laid-back, handsome charmer might seem intimidating to a serious-minded woman like her."

"I know Sam can appear to be…careless. As for any attention he pays to her, I think it's just his way of trying to make her feel comfortable." Mac tapped a finger on the arm of the chair, his mind working overtime. "Penny does seem to enjoy bossing around my boys like they were her brothers."

Mary Pat chuckled. "I've noticed. But they aren't her brothers."

He paused, clearly uncomfortable with the direction this was taking. After a moment of silence, he swallowed before saying, "I guess I'll start paying closer attention. And if I see any issues between Sam and Penny, I'll speak to Sam."

"I don't think that would be wise."

He arched a brow.

"Sam's a man. And a good one. He'll figure out how far he can tease Penny without crossing a line."

Mac sat quietly, mulling over her words.

Upstairs, Penny made her way to her room. When she paused at the door, she was surprised to find Sam directly behind her.

"What are you…?"

"Just walking you to your door."

"Why?"

He gave her one of those rogue smiles that did funny things to her heart. "Hey. Just trying to be nice."

She lifted her chin, determined to ignore the strange tingle of awareness his presence always caused. "When one of my brothers tried to be nice, they always wanted something. Usually money or the chance to borrow my car."

"Penny, I don't want your money or your car. I have my own, thank you." He leaned close, inhaling the soap-and-water smell of her. "You smell so clean. Like the house.

Everything's cleaner, brighter since you took charge of the place."

"I'm glad you noticed."

"You'd be surprised at the things I notice." He pressed his face to her hair. "Like the way you smell. Like sunshine."

As he breathed her in, she was caught by surprise by the rush of emotions that flared like a torch. The nearness of him had heat racing through her veins.

Seeing the way she held herself stiffly, he lifted both hands in a signal of surrender. "Sorry. I didn't mean to . . . I just wanted to . . ." He paused, gathering his thoughts. "I want you to know, even though I tease you a lot, I'm really glad you're here."

"Thanks. But I can't help thinking you've got some ulterior motive for all those kind words. Next you'll be asking me to pack you extra goodies in the lunches I make when you and the others head up to the hills, just the way my brothers always asked."

"That's not a bad idea." Instead of taking another step back, he stood his ground. His smile was that sexy, teasing curve of mouth that always sent her heart into overdrive. "But there's something you need to know. I'm not your brother."

The deep timbre of his voice, the way he was looking at her, had her tingling with warmth. A warmth that spread all the way down her body to her toes.

To cover her reaction, her defensive mode kicked in. Her head snapped up. Her spine stiffened.

In her best teacher's voice she commanded, "You need to step back."

"Yes, Miss Money, ma'am."

There was that rogue's smile again. But he took a step back, hands out, in a sign of surrender. "I get it. You don't like your space invaded."

"Thank you."

"I apologize for catching you by surprise. I just can't help it. Maybe you're not even aware, but you're like a magnet. Whenever I get close to you, I'm caught by an invisible force."

His admission had her going very still.

He turned and sauntered along the hallway until he paused in front of his bedroom door.

When he looked over, Penny was standing, her hand on the doorknob, her eyes, big as saucers, watching him.

"Good night, Money. Sleep tight."

Sam sat on the edge of his bed and nudged off his boots. He stood, stepped over them, and shrugged out of his shirt before tossing it aside. He unsnapped his jeans as he walked to the window. Leaning a hip against the windowsill, he stared at the distant hills, cloaked in shadows.

His mind wasn't on the landscape. He was reliving that scene in the hall.

He hadn't planned it. Hadn't planned any of that. As with most of his life, it had just happened. But the minute he got close, something changed. He didn't know the how or why of it, but that woman had him tied up in knots.

He didn't want this. Didn't want to feel these kinds of things for her. But in that brief moment when he'd leaned close, inhaling the clean, fresh scent of her, he'd felt a strange, rare yearning. A feeling he didn't want to probe too deeply.

She'd felt, in that one tiny second, like the missing piece of his life. As though something unique and wonderful had just materialized and then, just as quickly, had disappeared like mist over the mountain streams.

He crossed his arms over his chest and let his gaze move

over the hills, trying to concentrate on anything except Penny.

He loved the look of the countryside this time of year. With summer faded, and autumn taking over, it signaled a coming lull in ranch activities. Oh, there were still plenty of chores to see to. Enough to keep the family hopping. But once the herds were brought down from the hills, things would begin to slow down. There would be time to mend fences, as well as equipment. Time to linger over late-night coffee in front of a roaring fire. Time to listen to Otis, Roscoe, and Zachariah talk about the old days.

Years ago, as a boy new to all this, he'd been content to wrap himself in an afghan and listen to the old men's voices recounting their often-misspent youth. Did they know, when they were spinning their tales, that they were helping an angry boy find common ground with them?

During his years in foster care, he'd begun to think adults were nothing more than harsh taskmasters, and he a mere servant who would never know freedom, unless he fought his way free. From those good men downstairs, he learned that they'd all been foolish boys once upon a time. Boys who grew up in very different circumstances, yet came together to form a family.

He was smiling as he studied the clouds scudding across a full moon.

Despite his determination to put Penny out of his mind, his thoughts drifted to her. Penny Cash. Money. The very name had his smile growing. She was his complete opposite. So serious. So driven. He, on the other hand, had learned early on to grab all the fun he could manage, in case it would one day be snatched away.

He wasn't careless. He could work circles around his two brothers. When it came to ranch chores, he was the best there was. But when it was time to play, he played even harder.

He was proud of that fact. He'd worked long and hard to carve out a reputation as a pool hustler. When he was holding a pool cue, he wasn't just some hick off the farm. He was a pro. The best.

He'd seen the look of disapproval on Penny's face when Finn had mentioned it. Even though her knee-jerk reaction bothered him, he was quick to dismiss it. He didn't need her approval.

Still, it rankled.

He turned away from the window and shucked his jeans, kicking them aside.

As he slid naked into bed, he breathed in the smell of clean sheets and pillowcases.

In his mind he could see Penny in his room tomorrow, stripping the bed linens. Picking up his discarded clothes.

The thought prickled along his scalp.

He climbed out of bed and stuffed his things in the hamper before setting his boots in the closet.

Satisfied that the room was organized, he climbed between the fresh-scented sheets and waited for sleep. And smiled in the darkness, thinking about Penny's pouty lips, and how they might taste.

She had tried to look all mad and out of sorts. But he'd seen the way she'd looked when he'd leaned in close. Maybe it wasn't the nearness of him that bothered her. Maybe it was her own reaction to him that kicked in, causing her to throw a fit.

He tossed and turned, trying to settle. But thoughts of Penny kept intruding.

He felt itchy. Twitchy. And he didn't know why. He could have his pick of women. Fun, laid-back, pretty women out for a good time. But none of them had ever made him feel like this.

Why now, with this woman? They were absolutely wrong for one another. Complete opposites.

Time to back off and walk away while he could. Because if her reaction to his invasion of her space was any indication of what they'd be like together, it would be an explosion.

Fire and ice.

Prim discipline and reckless abandon.

Saint and sinner.

He chuckled in the darkness.

Yeah. That was it. Saint and sinner. And he knew one thing. He had no intention of being converted. He was very happy being what he was—the biggest sinner of them all.

CHAPTER SIX

'Morning, son."

At Mac's voice, Sam looked over from the stall he was mucking. "'Morning. You're up early."

"I could say the same for you."

"I was awake, and figured I'd get an early start on the chores."

Mac nodded and plucked a pitchfork from a hook on the wall of the barn. "Me, too."

The two men worked in separate stalls, forking dung and wet straw into the honey wagon. When it was full, Sam took the handles and hauled it out the door and around back, returning minutes later with the empty wagon.

Mac had already moved to another stall.

Sam took up his pitchfork and began to work.

"I like what Penny's doing with the house." Mac dug, lifted, dropped a load into the wagon.

Sam did the same.

"She's proving to be a good worker."

"Uh-huh." Sam moved to the next stall.

"She's a pretty little thing, don't you think?"

"Uh-huh." Sam continued working.

"I know it has to be a letdown for her to be working as a cook and housekeeper instead of being a teacher."

Sam made no response.

"I mean, she spent years training to teach, and here she is doing what she always did, cleaning up after a houseful of guys."

Sam took the handles and leaned into the chore, rolling the filled wagon out the door and around back, returning minutes later to start again.

Mac cleared his throat. "I think Penny is special. Don't you?"

"I guess so."

"You guess? Do you like her?"

"Of course I like Penny. Who wouldn't like a woman who cooks like one of those TV chefs? Who turns a man cave into a showplace? And manages to make it all look so easy?" Sam paused. Leaned on the handle of his pitchfork and turned to Mac. "You're circling around something. Just spit it out. You going somewhere with this?"

His father shrugged. Blushed. "I need you to understand that Penny isn't just another pretty woman. Now that she works for us, she has the right to demand respect."

Sam's brow shot up. "Have I done something disrespectful? Something you don't like?"

"Not at all." Mac stepped around the stall to put his hand on Sam's shoulder to soften his words. "Look, son. If you're…feeling an attraction to Penny, I understand. I just want you to treat her with care."

"Attracted? Why would you think that?"

"I…" Mac could feel his face getting all hot. Of all the conversations he'd had with his sons through the years, this was proving to be the most ill-conceived one yet. Why hadn't he listened to Mary Pat when she'd told him this was a bad idea? "I guess I misread the signals the two of you were giving out."

"Yeah. I guess so. You got any more brilliant nuggets you want to toss out?"

"I think I'm done. See you inside for breakfast."

As Mac strolled from the barn, Sam worked up a sweat, straining under the load of dung and heavy straw.

The female he was supposed to treat with care had robbed him of sleep and had him as antsy as a heifer being stalked by a bobcat. And for the life of him, he didn't understand why.

"So you heat the cream before you add it to the other ingredients?" Becca stood beside Penny in the kitchen, watching intently as, together, they prepared her biscuit dough.

Archie had sniffed his way around the room and was now curled contentedly under the table.

"Just enough so it doesn't curdle." Penny stirred, before handing the wooden spoon to Becca.

At the stove, Mary Pat tossed a handful of diced onions, celery, and carrots into the chicken stock heating in a big pot.

She glanced over. "Until you suggested using frozen chicken breasts, it never occurred to me that I didn't have to thaw them first."

Penny smiled. "I discovered it out of necessity. One day time just got past me, my brothers were due home from school, and I hadn't given a thought to supper. By the time I got around to it, all I had were frozen chicken parts. So I tossed them into the pot, along with whatever vegetables I found in the garden. An hour later the chicken was cooked and easy to cut. And the skin and bones made the chicken stock richer. So, from then on, that's the only way I ever made my chicken soup."

Mary Pat chuckled. "You know what they say. Necessity is the mother of invention. From now on, I'm using your quick and easy recipe." She shook her head. "Think of all the time I wasted over the years thawing chicken first."

The three women had spent the better part of a week cooking together every chance they got. While the men boasted that they were the beneficiaries of all that woman power, the three had formed a special bond as they cooked and exchanged stories of their lives.

While the soup simmered and the biscuits baked in the oven, Penny poured three cups of tea, and she and Becca and Mary Pat relaxed around the table.

"Oh." Mary Pat gave a sigh of pure pleasure. "It does my heart good to spend time in the kitchen with the two of you. This time in a real home restores my soul."

Penny glanced over. "Why don't you do it more often?"

The older woman gave a shrug of her shoulders. "A part of me is afraid if I let myself relax too long in one place, I'll lose the discipline I need to do my job. And another part of me really loves the people I serve."

"No more than they love you," Becca turned to explain to Penny. "To a lot of the ranchers who live far from civilization, Mary Pat is their only connection with the outside world."

Mary Pat put a hand over Becca's. "That may have been true years ago, but now they all have computers and are connected to one another through the internet."

"Of course." Becca gave her a gentle smile. "But the internet isn't the same as having a real live person stopping by not only to talk, but also to listen to their troubles, and to give them a hug when they need it."

Penny nodded. "I agree. When I was feeling so alone, raising my brothers, caring for Aunt Lucy, one of my former teachers used to stop by every month to see how I was doing. It meant the world to me to know that I could tell her anything, and she wouldn't judge me for it. She was so kind and compassionate, and often she would bring me some little thing. A jar of homemade strawberry preserves. A plate of cookies. And I was always so touched by her thoughtfulness."

Mary Pat thought about her words. "I guess you've just explained why I do what I do. As much as I dream of staying in one place and putting down roots, I'm reluctant to put my own needs ahead of all those who need that personal touch. That's why I've never given up my little room over the bakery in town, even though I almost never get time to stay there."

Mac paused in the doorway, his sleeves rolled to the elbows, his hair damp from the mudroom sink. Having overheard, he gave her a long, steady look before saying, "Something smells wonderful."

"Penny's chicken soup and biscuits." As Mary Pat started to shove away from the table, Mac put a big hand on her shoulder to still her movements. "You stay right there and drink your tea. The others won't be here for half an hour or more. I was just heading into the parlor to do some paperwork."

"I'll bring you tea."

He shook his head. "You do enough. Just sit and enjoy time with your friends."

With a courtly smile he walked away.

Penny was grateful for the company of these two women.

It helped her take her mind off the fact that Sam had barely acknowledged her since the night he'd walked her to her bedroom door and leaned so close that she'd thought he was going to kiss her.

The almost-kiss.

That was how she thought of it. An imaginary kiss that had rocked her world.

Afterward, in the privacy of her room, she'd lost sleep thinking about Sam and the fact that, though she'd acted angry at his boldness, she'd secretly hoped he would kiss her.

She should have known he was nothing more than a tease. He hadn't wanted to actually kiss her. What he'd wanted was exactly what he'd accomplished—getting her to rise to the bait and lose her temper.

Ever since, Sam had begun spending his nights anywhere but here. She supposed, now that he had satisfied his curiosity about her, he'd moved on to other, more willing women he could find in town. And of course, drinking and gambling.

A man like Sam Monroe wasn't worth thinking about.

She had better things to do.

In the parlor, as Mac worked at his desk, he heard the muffled voices of women and the trills of laughter, clear as a bell, so different from those of the men of the house. The sounds had him smiling to himself as he went over the monthly bills and wrote out checks.

There was something warm and settling about having women around. He'd grown accustomed to a houseful of men. Everyone was free and easy in each other's company. But women softened the edges. Heated the cold breezes that blew across the hills and snuck into the walls of the old house.

It wasn't just the smell of bread baking and meat roasting. It was something more. It was the way the family of men responded to their presence. Having women around seemed to bring out the best in all of them.

Except for Sam. Since their little talk, Sam had reverted to his old ways of heading into town as soon as supper ended. Some nights he didn't even eat a meal with the others, heading to the Hitching Post as soon as he'd showered and dressed after a day of chores.

As always, Mackenzie found himself questioning his good intentions.

Maybe sometimes it would be better to step away and just let life take its course.

"What's this?" Ben eyed the plate holding a brownie with two scoops of vanilla ice cream and smothered with hot fudge, before glancing up at his wife. "Are you telling me you baked this, babe?"

Becca was all smiles. "It's Penny's recipe, but I made it all by myself."

While the others watched, he took a taste and gave a long, deep sigh. "Now that's even better 'n the dessert at Dolly's Diner. And Dolly boasts that nobody makes a better brownie than she does."

While Becca beamed, Sam looked over at Penny. Against his better judgment, he'd decided to forgo a night in town to stay home with the family. "What about the rest of us? Or are we chopped liver?"

While Mary Pat circled the table filling coffee cups, Penny passed around desserts to everyone except Sam.

She put a hand to her ear. "What's that? You'd rather have chopped liver than dessert? I think that can be arranged."

Seeing the wicked gleam in her eye, he jumped up and reached around her, making a grab for the entire plate of brownies. "Aren't you funny? I'll just have to help myself."

She picked up a wooden spoon and rapped his knuckles. "Don't you even think about it."

Before she could stop him, he shoved a brownie in his mouth and reached for a second one.

While the others laughed at their antics, she finally relented, fixing him a plate of dessert.

"Not fair," Finn shouted. "Now he got an extra helping."

"Because he's grabby," Penny announced. "Tomorrow, to make up for it, he'll get the smallest slice of my coconut cake."

Sam put a hand over his heart. "Really? Coconut cake? It's my favorite."

"You said that last week about my cherry pie."

"And it was my favorite. Until you reminded me how much I love coconut cake."

"Oh." She gave him a mock slap to his arm. "You're impossible."

"Am not. Just a guy who loves sweets." He took his place at the table and gave a sigh of pleasure as he ate every bite.

Finn was shaking his head. "You keep on feeding us like this, Penny, and we'll soon be going on diets."

Mary Pat joined in the laughter. "Not likely, the way all of you work."

"Speaking of work." Ben finished the last bite of brownie. "You've been here for a whole week. You thinking of retiring, Mary Pat?"

She sat back with a smile. "Wishful thinking. After a week of so much fun, I have to admit it crossed my mind a time or two, but duty calls."

While the others around the table continued enjoying their dessert, Mac fell silent, draining his cup.

When Penny began clearing the table, Sam caught her hand, stilling her movements.

She looked up. "What are you doing?"

"You and Becca and Mary Pat have been cooking and cleaning like crazy all week. Tonight, the three of you are going to relax while Ben and Finn and I take over the kitchen."

"We can at least help."

"Nope." He nodded toward the door. "You can go in the parlor and sit by the fire, or head on out to the back porch and watch the daylight fade. Your call."

Penny turned to the other two women.

Mary Pat led the way to the mudroom, where she picked up a shawl from a hook on the wall. Penny and Becca did the same, and the three women settled on the swing. Minutes later Mac, Zachariah, Otis, and Roscoe joined them.

They sat in companionable silence, listening to the voices and laughter coming from the three brothers in the kitchen, as always, teasing, joking, and occasionally cussing as they tidied up.

When Ben, Sam, and Finn finally joined the others on the porch, they talked about the day, the weather, and the crops as the shadows lengthened and the glorious red sun began to set behind the peaks of the hills in the distance.

One by one, they all drifted away. Ben and Becca said their good nights and leashed Archie before heading back to town. Otis and Roscoe resumed their nightly gin rummy game in the bunkhouse. Finn and Zachariah locked themselves away in the old lawyer's library, discussing Finn's latest case. Penny called good night before making her way upstairs, trailed within minutes by Sam.

Mac and Mary Pat remained on the porch, seated side by side on the swing.

Mac kept his voice low. "Against your advice, I had that talk with Sam."

"How did it go?"

"Hard to say. Since then, he's mostly been absent, as I'm sure you've noticed."

She nodded.

"I think he got the message to respect certain boundaries."

"That's good, Mac."

"I'm not so sure. I really bungled things. I have a feeling I spoke out of turn. If there are any feelings between those two, they're not aware of them."

"I realize Sam has been spending more time in town these nights. That may because of your talk with him. But when he's here, I see him watching Penny when he thinks nobody's looking."

Mac shrugged. "He teases her a lot, but then Sam has always loved teasing everybody." He took his time, choosing his words carefully. "Penny has shouldered a lot of responsibilities from a really young age. I think that would make a woman unwilling to take on a man who wasn't solid and steady."

"And Sam? You don't think he's solid?"

Mac gave a slow shake of his head. "Sam is my son, and I love him. But he's always been my wild child. He took to ranching like a natural, and that touches my heart. But there's also that side of him that worries me. He loves taking risks. I've seen him at the Hitching Post, swaggering around like an actor in a play he wrote for himself. He's a natural con. He can spot a sucker a mile away. And when he's out to sweet-talk a woman, he turns into a real charmer. Sometimes, watching from the sidelines, I wonder who he is."

"You know who he is, Mac. You said so yourself."

He turned to stare at her.

"He's your son. And you love him."

"Yeah."

They sat in silence, listening to the sounds of the night. Cattle lowing in the hills. Night birds crying in the darkened sky. Crickets chirping. The occasional sound of laughter coming from the bunkhouse drifting on the breeze.

Mac's next words were hesitant. "Were you serious earlier, when you said you may be thinking of retiring?"

She kept her gaze averted, studying the stars winking like diamonds in the black velvet sky. "I have to admit, this week has been special. Becca and Penny are such lovely young women. I can't recall the last time I had so much fun doing nothing more than cooking and cleaning, and just listening to the two of them."

"It's been special for me, too."

"Why?" She looked over at him.

He shrugged. "It's nice to know you're here, and safe, and sleeping just down the hall"—he cleared his throat—"instead of in the back of your old van in the middle of nowhere."

She put a hand over his. "You know I'm only here for a little while."

He closed his other hand over hers. Patted it. "I know that you love what you do, and love even more the people you help."

They sat for the longest time, just watching the clouds and listening as the night grew soft and silent.

And when at last they climbed the stairs, Mary Pat made

her way to the end of the hall, letting herself into the guest room, while Mac stood just outside his door, waiting until he saw her door close.

Only then did he step into his room.

Alone.

The thought mocked him.

CHAPTER SEVEN

T urning downright chilly out there today." Otis picked up a mug of coffee as the others stomped in from morning chores and gathered in the kitchen.

"Yeah." Roscoe nudged him. "That's Mother Nature reminding us what's coming. I can already smell autumn leaves."

"Speaking of which, something smells great." Finn set aside his attaché case and chose a glass of orange juice from an assortment of drinks on a tray.

After the first swallow he looked over at Penny, busy removing a pan from the oven. "What did you do to this? It tastes different."

Penny turned. "Good different or bad different?"

"Really good."

She looked relieved. "It's freshly squeezed." She pointed to a glass bowl with a pointed end in the middle. "I found that fancy little orange juice squeezer in the pantry and decided to try it."

"Fancy?" Mac gave a shake of his head. "That's ancient. The new modern ones are electric. When we used that old thing we had to use plenty of elbow grease."

"I have plenty of elbow grease to spare." Penny began passing around a platter of eggs, sausage, and pancakes. "I can't even count all the boxes of old stuff I've been finding while cleaning out these cupboards." She nodded toward a set of doors beside the mudroom. "And how many treasures I've found in that old pantry. Fancy cookie cutters. Old-fashioned lace doilies. Hand-stitched hot pads."

Mac gave a startled look. "They're still there?" He glanced around at the others. "They belonged to my mother. She lived with us before she passed on. She used to sit up nights knitting, crocheting, and doing all kinds of handwork. She said it kept her old fingers nimble."

Penny held up one of the pretty hot pads. "I was thinking of using this, but if you'd like to save it as a keepsake..."

Mac shook his head. "Use it. Use all the things you find, Penny. I think that's what my ma had in mind when she stored them all away, hoping one day we'd find them and use them for our own enjoyment."

Mary Pat, who had helped herself to a steaming cup of coffee, took a seat at the table before announcing, "I'm glad you made all my favorite things for breakfast, Penny. This should hold me until the next time I come back."

Caught by surprise, the others looked over.

It was Mac who asked quietly, "You're leaving?"

She nodded. "I know I said I was hoping to relax a while longer, but I've heard from several families looking for some assistance. I think it's time I head out for one more long trek into the hills before the weather turns."

"When?" Mac's single word sounded strained.

"I'm planning on packing up my van and leaving later today."

While the others dug into their meal, Mac set aside his coffee before saying, "Would you be willing to hold off leaving until tomorrow?"

She glanced over. "I suppose so. Any particular reason?"

He shrugged. "Just a thought. We haven't gone to town as a family for months. We've been too busy with ranch chores." He turned to Penny. "Don't bother cooking dinner this evening. After our chores, we'll head into Haller Creek. I'll phone Ben and see if he and Becca want to join us at Dolly's Diner."

Roscoe put a hand over his heart. "I hope Dolly has some of her famous meat loaf."

Otis was grinning from ear to ear. "I don't care about anything else, as long as she has collard greens. Although..." His grin widened. "I wouldn't refuse her fried chicken, either."

"Well then." Penny circled the table, topping off their cups. "I guess I'll take some time reading one of my books up in my room tonight."

Mac put a hand on her arm to still her movements. "You're included in the invitation, Penny."

"Oh." She caught Sam staring at her across the table and nearly bobbled the pot of coffee. "I don't want to intrude on a family dinner."

Mac's voice lowered. Softened. "When I say family, I mean all of us here. You're as much family as the rest."

"Thank you." Without another word she took her place at the table and bowed her head as Mary Pat led them in a blessing.

"Bless this food, this... family"—she shot a smile at the shy young woman seated across the table—"and the roads we travel."

*   *   *

Penny brushed her hair long and loose, and fastened one side behind her ear with a pretty butterfly clip that had been a gift from her mother on her sixth birthday. Even though it was childish, she loved it because it had been bought by her mother and was one of the few treasures from her childhood.

She was wearing a simple pink shirt with clean denims. She snagged a denim jacket from the closet for later, when the night would turn cool.

Two ranch trucks were parked beside the back door. As the family stepped outside, Mac held the door for Mary Pat before walking around to the driver's side. The others streamed out the door.

Zachariah slid in beside Mary Pat, while Roscoe and Otis climbed into the backseat.

Finn climbed behind the wheel of the second truck, while Sam held the passenger door open for Penny before sliding in beside her.

As they started along the gravel driveway, he gave her a long, steady look. "You look pretty. And I like that thing in your hair."

She smiled. "A gift from my mother when I was little."

He leaned close. "Mmm. And you smell good."

Her face flamed, and she felt the quick jittery rush of heat that always caught her by surprise whenever he got too close. And, she thought, he seemed to do it more often lately. Or was it just magnified in her mind? Lately she'd had to force herself to concentrate on good, hard work in order to keep from thinking about Sam.

"My brother, Cooper, sent me a bottle of perfume all the way from Paris. He's stationed in Germany, and said his goal is to see as many countries in Europe as possible before he's reassigned."

"Remind me to thank Cooper if I ever get the chance to meet him."

She gave Sam an elbow in the ribs. "I know you're just teasing."

"Is that what you think?" He looked past her to Finn. "I'll just ask an impartial observer. What do you think, bro?"

"I think your brother has good taste, Penny. You do smell good. And you look good, too."

"You see?" Sam draped an arm over the back of the seat, allowing his fingers to play with the ends of her hair.

She sat with her hands gripped firmly in her lap, wondering if he knew what his touch was doing to her. Each brush of his hand sent fresh tingles along her spine. His muscled thigh was pressed to hers in the close quarters of the front seat. His breath, when he leaned past her to talk to his brother, was warm and oh so tempting.

And then he looked directly at her and winked, and her heart took a hard, heavy bounce.

Oh, he was a sly one. Too handsome for his own good. A lean, casual cowboy, completely comfortable in his own skin. That was part of his charm. And if she wasn't careful, she'd start believing all those words that flowed like warm honey from his tongue. But she figured a man like Sam would never settle for one woman, when he could have them all. Besides, he'd admitted to being a gambler. And that was something she would never tolerate.

And so, to keep from thinking about the man beside her, she watched as the pretty countryside flew past her line of vision on their way to town.

Ben and Becca were standing outside the diner as their convoy of trucks pulled up.

Ben hurried over to announce, "We told Dolly how many would be here, and she said she'll have a table ready."

"What did you do with Archie?" Ben asked.

"We had to leave him home." Ben laughed. "You should have seen his reaction. Tail down. Ears down. I swear he was frowning."

They were all laughing as they stepped into the diner.

The little place was packed with hungry ranchers and their families. As Dolly led their party to a big, round table, they were forced to stop and greet half a dozen or more friends. Finally, as they took their seats, Dolly asked if anyone wanted a menu.

"None for me," Mac said.

The others shook their heads, signifying they knew what they wanted.

While most of their party ordered Dolly's famous meat loaf and garlic potatoes, Otis asked for her fried chicken and collard greens, and Zachariah ordered a rare prime rib and a baked potato smothered with sour cream.

"Mmm," Penny said as she dug into her meat loaf. "You think if I asked, Dolly would share this recipe?"

"Not likely," Mary Pat said with a laugh. "Through the years, whenever Dolly is pressured to share her recipe for any of her specials, she always manages to 'forget' one or two key ingredients. It's happened so often, nobody even bothers to ask her anymore. They know she'll sabotage their intentions to duplicate her famous menu."

That brought a round of laughter from the others.

"You can't blame her." Otis used a slice of Dolly's sourdough bread to mop up the bacon drippings used to wilt the greens in a heavy, cast-iron skillet, just the way he remembered his mama doing. "If every female in Haller Creek could cook like this, Dolly would be out of business."

"Oh, I don't know." Sam leaned back, sipping strong, hot coffee. "I don't think Dolly's cooking can hold a candle to our own cook."

Penny's head came up sharply.

Seeing everyone looking from Sam to her, she felt her cheeks flaming. Hoping to deflect attention she said, "You're just saying that so you'll get the biggest piece of cake tomorrow night."

He gave a nonchalant shrug. "If you feel the need to reward me, I certainly won't refuse. But I'm saying it 'cause it's true. I'd rather have your cooking than Dolly's any time."

Beside him, Finn nodded. "I hate to admit that Sam and I agree on something, but this time, he's right. Since you started feeding us, Penny, we've become spoiled."

Seeing the look of disbelief on her face, Mary Pat put a hand over hers. "They're not teasing you this time, Penny. I agree with them. In fact, one of the things I'll miss when I leave tomorrow is all the fine meals you've been serving."

"Then why not stay?" Penny blurted the words before she could stop herself.

Mac nodded. "I agree with Penny. Why not stay?"

Mary Pat let out a long, deep sigh. "You'll never know how much I want to. If only I could ignore my conscience and shut out the voices of all those families who need my help."

Penny happened to glance at Mac and saw, for a fleeting moment, a look in his eyes she couldn't quite fathom. One part sadness. One part resignation. And then it was gone, and he was laughing and talking with the others, and she was caught up in the conversation until she forgot what she'd seen.

After paying the bill, Mac turned to the family. "As long as we're here, we can't head home until we've had a longneck at the Hitching Post." He winked at Sam. "And maybe watch my son indulge in a game of nine ball."

Sam gave his father one of his famous rogue smiles. "A lot of the ranchers around here are taking on extra wranglers for roundup. I'll just have to wait and see how many have *sucker* written on their foreheads."

"Come on, then." With a laugh Mac herded them toward the door.

Finn leaned close to Penny to whisper, "Maybe, if we're lucky, we'll get to watch my brother perform. You won't believe his moves. He's like a magician with a pool cue in his hands."

Penny gave a sniff of disdain. "Drinking beer and shooting pool. I guess I shouldn't be surprised. What does surprise me is that someone like you is bragging about someone like Sam."

Finn gave her a long, steady look. "Someone like me?"

"You're a lawyer, for heaven's sake. And you're acting like Sam's talent on a pool table is something to be proud of."

Finn merely smiled. "I guess you just have to see for yourself." Trailing behind her, he added, "Prepare to be entertained and amazed."

Up ahead, Sam held the door until everyone had exited Dolly's. Then, falling into step beside Penny, he was humming a little tune.

Probably, she thought, in anticipation of a chance to show off to his family.

But she had already dismissed him and his so-called talent. He could give it any name he wanted. It was still drinking and gambling.

Vices she'd sternly warned her brothers about.

CHAPTER EIGHT

It was impossible to miss the Hitching Post Saloon. The sign above the long, wooden building screamed the name in bright neon red and yellow.

Inside, a long bar, every stool taken, ran the length of the room. Behind it was a grill tended by the owner, Horton Duke, a bewhiskered man who looked as if he hadn't shaved in weeks, flipping burgers and onions and peppers, sending up puffs of greasy smoke. Two bartenders were in a state of perpetual motion while a chorus of mostly male voices talked, laughed, cursed. Young women in Daisy Duke cutoff jean shorts and midriff-baring shirts maneuvered between packed tables to deliver trays of longnecks and shots of whiskey. On the jukebox, Dolly was wailing a promise to always love you.

While Penny's eyes adjusted to the murky interior, Sam sauntered across the room, comfortable in this old familiar place, waving to Horton and the bartenders before leading the way to a booth in the rear of the packed room.

When they were seated, Penny found herself squeezed between Becca on her left and Sam on her right side. Once again, it seemed she would be forced to endure the press of his body to hers. Though she fought to ignore the tingle of awareness, the same couldn't be said for Sam. The look on his face was one of pure male indulgence.

One of the waitresses hurried over, smiling at the entire family but saving her brightest smile for Sam.

"Hey, stranger." She leaned down to set the empty tray on the table, aware that she was revealing a good deal of cleavage. "The regulars missed you last night, Sam. Where were you?"

"Sticking close to home. Thanks for asking, Char. It's good to be missed." He returned her smile. "Say hello to my family. Everybody, this is Charlotte."

After quick greetings, Sam glanced at the others. "Longnecks all around?"

They nodded their agreement.

"Anything to nibble? The special tonight is Horton's chili fries, guaranteed to make you sizzle from your head to your toes." To the round of chuckles she replied, "Horton insists we tell everyone that."

"That's not just a slogan." Sam shook his head. "You know I love Horton's chili fries. But we just had supper at Dolly's."

"Okay. I'll tell Horton you've been cheating on him, Sam." With a laugh Char picked up her tray. "Ten longnecks coming up." She turned and wiggled her way toward the bar.

Mary Pat watched her leave before arching a brow at Sam. "I didn't expect to see Charlotte Jenkins working here. The last I heard, she was attending beauty school in Eton. She once told me her dream was to open her own shop right here in town."

Sam nodded. "She was this close to getting certified"—he

held two fingers slightly apart—"when her dad took that fall up in the hills. He's using a wheelchair now, as you know, and Char helps her mother and little brother with the ranch during the day, and works here at night."

"What a shame." Mary Pat gave the young woman a warm smile when she returned with their order. "How is your father doing?"

Some of the light went out of Char's forced smile. "He's in a lot of pain, Miss Healy. But my mom's taking him to a clinic in Bozeman next month, and we're all hoping they'll find him some relief."

"When I get back in town in a few weeks, I'll go by and have a visit with your folks."

"Thanks. I know they'd like that." Char moved quickly, depositing their drinks before hurrying off to another table.

Seeing the way Penny was swiveling her head this way and that, Becca nudged her. "Your first time in the Hitching Post?"

"Yes. Is it always so loud?"

Sam chuckled. "You should hear it on a Friday night. Or maybe you shouldn't. Sometimes it's a deafening roar."

Penny smiled. "Maybe they should lower the volume on the jukebox."

"Why bother? Nobody'd hear it."

"I guess you're right." She sipped her beer.

Finn nodded toward the pool table in the far corner of the room. "Looks like a hot game in progress."

"Yeah." Sam tipped his bottle and drank, all the while keeping an eye on the action.

A circle of cowboys ringed the area, watching the players with interest. Their voices and faces were animated. Suddenly a murmur ran through the crowd. Money was soon changing hands.

Several of the spectators walked away, while a few new-comers took their places.

As two cowboys passed their table, Sam heard one mutter to the other, "The kid's good, but he's too much of a show-boat. He keeps playing for that kind of money, somebody's going to be happy to relieve him of it before the night's over."

The other cowboy added, "And he's had way too much to drink. He keeps telegraphing every move."

Intrigued, Sam stood and turned to Penny. "Want to watch up close and personal?"

She hesitated.

Before she had the chance to decline, he caught her hand and helped her to her feet, and then led her to the edge of the crowd. As two of the onlookers moved aside to give them some room, she could see a bearded cowboy setting up the balls for a break.

The second player, hidden from her view, announced from the other end of the table, "Let's make the game inter-esting. How about two hundred this time?"

She nearly dropped the bottle in her hand as her fingers reflexively dug into Sam's arm as the second player came into view.

"Well now." He looked down at her with a big grin. "I see you're starting to enjoy this."

"Oh, Sam…"

Her words were lost as the bearded player rammed the cue ball into the others, sending up a roar from those watch-ing as several balls sank into a pocket.

Sam's arm came around her shoulders while he kept his attention glued to the game.

He leaned close to say into her ear, "The scruffy cow-boy's name is Luther. He's good. I've played him before.

Right now he's holding back, but I saw the way his eyes lit up when his opponent offered to up the ante to two hundred. I'm betting old Luther will lose this game, then set his opponent up for the big bonus next game."

"Bigger than two hundred dollars?" Her voice was suddenly shaky and breathless.

"I figure Luther will con this kid into thinking he's the greatest player in the world, just so he can get him up to four or five hundred next game. Then suddenly old Luther will run the table." He chuckled. "That's what I'd do."

The game moved quickly, with Luther missing his second shot and his opponent winning.

Just as Sam predicted, Luther made a great show of anger before he demanded a chance to play again to win back what he'd lost over the past hour.

His opponent, drunk with success and happy to oblige, suggested they play for five hundred. As the game started, the kid looked supremely confident as he broke the balls and began running them one by one in succession.

Sam looked down at Penny, her hand clutched firmly in his, her eyes fixed on the game with an intensity he couldn't have imagined mere minutes ago.

"Hey. You're really getting into this, aren't you?"

She didn't say a word as the kid swayed slightly and missed an easy shot. A roar went up from those surrounding the table.

"Sam," she whispered, her eyes suddenly filled as Luther stepped up and methodically ran the rest of the balls into the pockets.

When he'd finished, he lifted his wide-brimmed hat as a salute to his audience before saying to his opponent, "That's five hundred dollars, kid."

The young cowboy dug the money out of his jeans and

counted out five hundred dollars before slinking dejectedly toward the bar.

"Thanks, kid. Nice doing business with you. I appreciate your donation, son. I'm here any time you'd like to ask for a rematch," Luther called to his retreating back.

As the crowd drifted away, Sam looked down at Penny.

"Don't go feeling sorry for that young cowboy. It may be a tough lesson, but anybody who wants to be a player has to learn it. The first rule of gambling is never bet more than you can afford to lose. And there will always be a time when you lose. Next time, he'll be more cautious. The second rule is you can't get drunk when you're running a hustle. Once your brain gets muddled, it's all over. You need to stay sharp and maybe spend some time watching your opponent before jumping into a money game against him."

Seeing tears welling up in her eyes, he put his hands on her upper arms. "Hey now. That's just the way the game is played. Not just the game of pool, but the game of hustling."

One big fat tear rolled down her cheek, and he swiped at it with his thumb.

His voice lowered. "I'm missing something here. The toughest female I know, the woman who orders us all around like a drill sergeant is shedding tears over a pool game? What's wrong, Penny?"

Her lips were quivering, and she was very close to crying like a baby.

"I don't care about your stupid game, or hustling. It's what I saw. Or rather *who* I saw. That wasn't just another cowboy, Sam."

"Are you talking about Luther?"

"No. The other one. The loser. That beer-drinking, pool-hustling stupid drunk cowboy is my little brother, Curtis.

After all the lectures I've given him about doing the right thing, he pulls a stunt like this just to show off to those others."

Despite the tears, her eyes narrowed in anger. "And whether he likes it or not, I'm about to go over there right now and rip a great big patch off his ornery hide."

CHAPTER NINE

Before Penny could do what she'd threatened, Sam caught her by the arm and hauled her up against him. "Hold on, now. You may be his big sister, but right now he's drunk as a skunk, and you're mad as a nest of hornets. You mix those two, you're sure to cause an explosion."

"I don't care. I'm going to..."

"You're going to wipe those tears."

Knowing his family was watching, Sam drew Penny aside, handing her a handkerchief and making certain they were in the shadows while she struggled to compose herself.

When she'd finally wiped away the last of her tears, he leaned close. "Now, if you want to go talk to your brother, I'm going with you. Understand?"

"I don't need a bodyguard to give Curtis a piece of my mind."

"You may want to remember that he's sitting with a

crowd of wranglers from the Lazy K. He's already made a fool of himself in front of them. He won't take kindly to having his big sister chewing him out in public."

"I don't give one hoot what Curtis likes or doesn't like."

As she started away, Sam gave a hiss of annoyance before laying a hand on her arm. "Before you charge in there, take a breath."

Though she shot him a killing look, she dragged in a deep breath before starting toward the bar.

Her brother was surrounded by a group of rowdy men.

"Nice job, kid." A grizzled old cowboy tipped up his beer. "Now that you've given away your paycheck, you'll have to work overtime just to make enough to eat."

A bearded cowboy defended Curtis, slapping him on the back. "Okay, so you lost. But you lost to one of the best hustlers around. So stop beating yourself up and just enjoy the fact that you're still standing."

"Barely," another cowboy hooted. "I think you've had enough beer for tonight, Curtis."

"I don't think I've had nearly enough." Curtis signaled the bartender for another.

Penny pushed her way through the group of men to stand in front of the young cowboy seated on the barstool.

"Curtis."

At the sound of her voice he swiveled. He stared at her in stunned silence.

When he finally found his voice, he said, "What're you doing here, Penny? Last I heard, you were teaching school somewhere."

"Last I heard, you'd found a job on a ranch."

"The Lazy K. In Milton. It's about fifty miles from here."

"You should have stayed at the Lazy K tonight. You would be five hundred dollars richer."

He looked away. "Sorry you had to see that. I'll do better next time."

"Next time? Oh, Curtis, haven't you learned anything from this?"

"Still my teacher, aren't you? It seems you just can't help yourself." He gave her a long, level look. "So? What're you doing in a place like this?"

"I'm here with..."

Sam stepped up beside her. "Sam Monroe."

He stuck out his hand, forcing the young cowboy to accept his handshake.

"Curtis Cash."

The young cowboy looked from Sam to Penny. "Is this where teachers hang out to pick up lonesome cowboys?"

"Don't be rude, Curtis. The teaching job didn't work out. I'm working for Sam and his family."

"Sorry. I know how much you wanted to teach school."

"I don't want to talk about me. I want to know what you think you're doing, Curtis. I begged you to go into the military like Danny and Cooper. You promised me you'd make something of your life."

"And I am. I have a good job at the Lazy K." He looked around at the grinning cowboys, who were watching in silence. "And these are my buddies."

"Some buddies. Egging you on." Penny's agitation made her careless with her words. "How long will the owners of the Lazy K keep you on when they learn you've been out drinking and gambling away your paycheck?"

"It's none of their business what I do when I'm not working."

"You're right. It's not their business until what you do after hours keeps you from doing what they pay you to do every day. How many nights can you gamble and drink too much before you start cheating your boss out of a day's work?" Penny put a hand on his arm and lowered her voice, struggling for patience. "Curtis, I hope you've learned from this, and find some other way to spend your off hours. If you keep doing this, the word will get around that you're unreliable."

He yanked his arm away. His eyes darkened with anger. "Okay, big sis. As usual, you've had your say."

"Curtis, please. I'm trying to help. I raised you better than this."

"And there it is." His words were hissed from between clenched teeth. "It's not bad enough you bossed me around like you were my father and mother when I was just a kid. But now I'm supposed to be grateful to you for the rest of my life?" He slammed down his empty bottle and slid from the barstool. "In case you haven't noticed, I'm twenty-one and in charge of my own life now, big sis."

"Curtis..."

To his friends he called, "I'm outta here. Who's with me?"

Without a backward glance at his sister, he stormed out of the Hitching Post.

While Penny watched in stunned silence, the rest of the wranglers drained their drinks and trailed slowly across to the door. Minutes later a convoy of ranch trucks moved out at a fast pace.

Sam snagged their waitress and pressed money into her hand. "Here, Char. Let my family know the bill is paid and Penny and I will be waiting at the door."

"Thanks, Sam." She counted the money and started to protest. "Wait, this is too much."

"Keep the change."

He steered Penny away from the bar and the two of them

stood at the door watching as his family drained their beers and made their way toward them.

"I'm sorry." Penny greeted them and tried to be heard above the noise. "I'd like to explain…"

"There's no need." Sam held the door as the others stepped outside.

"It's all right. We've already heard." Seeing the look on Penny's face, Mac managed a smile. "I'm sorry about your brother, but I can't say I'm sorry we're leaving. The noise level in there was getting to me."

When everyone had filed past, Sam led the way toward their trucks.

While Finn climbed up to the driver's side, Sam helped Penny before sliding in beside her.

In the darkness he reached for her hand. The fact that she offered no resistance was proof that she was somewhere else in her mind.

"So." Finn turned onto the interstate. "What'd you think about the Hitching Post?"

"It was…loud."

Finn gave a short laugh. "You forgot to mention smelly and noisy and raunchy. But hey, it's home to some of us."

"He means me." Sam squeezed her hand and her head came up sharply, as though coming out of a dark place.

"How can anyone feel comfortable in such a place?"

He shrugged. "It takes all kinds."

"Drunks and hustlers." Suddenly aware that Sam was holding her hand, she pulled it away and held it firmly in her lap. "What sort of man is Horton Duke that he could own such a place?"

"What sort of man? Let's see." Sam lifted his arm to the back of the seat. "When Dolly Pruitt had a grease fire at the diner and had to close up shop for two weeks, he offered to let her cook at his place. That was enough to keep her afloat while the repairs were being made to the diner. And then there's Loretta Everhardt, who lost her husband in a ranch accident. When she went to the bank to ask for a loan, they told her the mortgage had been paid, and she was debt-free. It took her weeks to find out it was Horton who was her angel of mercy."

"And don't forget Charlotte Jenkins," Finn said.

"Yeah. The minute Horton heard about her father's accident, he told her she could have a job with him for as long as she needed it."

"I get the message. Horton Duke is a good man who has helped a lot of people." Penny sniffed. "But does Charlotte Jenkins have to dress in that awful outfit?"

Sam's voice warmed with humor. "That outfit earns her more tips than a pair of bib overalls ever could."

"Somehow," Finn said with a chuckle, "I can't picture Char in overalls."

"You got that right, bro."

The two men shared a laugh while Penny fell silent, trying to digest all she'd just heard.

When they reached the ranch, they parked the trucks and climbed the steps to the house.

Mary Pat gathered Penny close to hug her. "The word filtered to us that the young cowboy losing all that money is your brother."

Penny nodded. "Curtis. My youngest brother."

"I'm sure he's learned a painful lesson."

"Oh, I hope so."

"Me too. Good night, honey. I'll see you in the morning."

Penny nodded and called good night to the others as they stepped into the mudroom.

When everyone had gone inside, she remained on the porch, needing some quiet time to clear her mind.

As she sat on the log swing, she was surprised to see Sam take a seat beside her.

"You don't need to stay, Sam."

"Yeah. I do. Especially tonight. I feel responsible. I was the one who took you there."

"This isn't your fault. I'd rather be alone. I'm not very good company."

He set the swing into motion, and for long minutes they remained silent, content to let the night breeze offer comfort.

Penny's voice, when she finally spoke, was filled with pain. "I always knew my brothers resented the fact that I was constantly telling them what to do. They called me bossy when I lectured them, and stingy when they wanted money. And mean when I refused to let them drink with their buddies when they were too young. I guess they thought it was easy for me to be the enforcer. But I hated having that responsibility. I felt so alone. With Mom and Dad gone, and Aunt Lucy failing more every day, I was all my brothers had. And I was terrified it wouldn't be enough."

"They were lucky to have you, Penny."

"Lucky." She spoke the word on a huff of breath. "Sometimes, after they fell asleep, I'd sit at the table and cry, and wonder if I'd said one nice thing to them the whole day. I was so tired of constantly nagging and pushing and fighting. But they were just kids who wanted the moon, and all I had to give them were rules. And now, look at what Curtis did with the rules. He's thrown them all away, and has turned into a drinker and a gambler."

"Curtis is young, Penny. He's having his first taste of freedom. And like a kid in a candy store, he looks around and wants it all."

"That's just it. He can't have it all, Sam. And what he's apt to find at the end of the day is nothing. Or worse, so much debt, he can't ever climb out of it. Just like my ..." She paused, swallowing back the rest of the words she'd almost blurted.

Sam took her hand in his. When she didn't resist, he closed it between both of his. His tone lowered. Softened. "I know you're worried. You have a right to be. But as someone who's broken most of the rules, I can tell you that each rule broken becomes a lesson learned."

She looked at their joined hands, and then up into his eyes. "You aren't just saying that to make me feel better?"

"I'm saying it because it's true. You did the best you could for Curtis. Now it's up to him to do the rest. Give him a chance to make some wise choices."

"Oh, Sam."

She got to her feet, and he stood up beside her.

She looked so wounded. So vulnerable.

Without thinking it through he gathered her against him and brushed his mouth over her temple.

The flash of fire was instantaneous. One moment he was intent on comforting her. The next his hands were in her hair, though he couldn't recall how they got there. His mouth was moving on hers with an urgency that had all his blood rushing to a single part of his anatomy.

Her arms twined around his neck, and she returned his kiss with a passion that had him backing her across the porch until she was pressed to the door.

The kiss spun on and on, with both of them practically crawling inside each other's skin. And still it wasn't enough to satisfy the sudden hunger that swamped them.

Their mouths were greedy. Their breathing labored.

It was Sam who finally managed to lift his head, though

he couldn't bring himself to break contact. With his hands on her shoulders he stood, taking in deep breaths while his heartbeat pumped furiously.

"I want you to know I didn't plan for this to happen."

She nodded, unable to find her voice.

His tone was gruff with passion. "Go inside. I'll stay out here awhile."

"You don't have to..."

"I do." He stepped back, his eyes dark and dangerous. "You need to go. Now."

Without a word she turned away and stepped inside.

Sam remained on the porch, listening to the receding footsteps as she made her way through the mudroom, the kitchen, the parlor, and up the stairs.

He watched the light go on in her bedroom. Saw the shadows move and sway as she prepared for bed.

Finally he saw the light go out, and darkness stole over the household.

Knowing he wouldn't be able to sleep, he made his way to the barn and saddled his horse.

A midnight ride across the hills might be enough to erase the wanting. But he knew in his heart that nothing would erase the taste of her from his lips. Or the need that was growing stronger, deeper, with every day she stayed here.

CHAPTER TEN

Penny woke to a chill wind rattling the windows. Her sleep had been disturbed by images of her brother talking tough and losing his entire paycheck to a shadowy figure. He took off across the vast hills without a job, without a future. What was worse, in her dream Curtis had morphed into Sam, who was sweet-talking her one minute, and then hustling a group of wranglers in a game of pool the next. She sat up feeling dazed and vaguely disoriented. Even though it had only been a dream, she felt a sense of doom. Her sweet, restless baby brother was now a drinker and pool hustler. And she was feeling things for a man who was the exact opposite of everything she'd ever stood for. Hard work. Discipline. Playing by the rules. None of those words could describe Sam Monroe. He was, by his own admission, much like Curtis. A man who enjoyed spending more time in a saloon than in his own home.

None of this made any sense to her. Her world as she'd

known it was upside down, not just in her dreams, but in real life as well.

After years of hard work and study in preparation for the future she'd planned for herself, she was right back where she'd started—cooking and cleaning up for a bunch of men.

Wasn't life strange? Strange and . . . confusing.

When she opened the shade, her windowpane was covered in frost. She could see the outline of snow in the distant hills. Hadn't school just begun? Yet here it was, looking like winter outside her window.

The sounds of doors opening and closing, and booted feet moving along the hallway, told her the household was already awake and ready for the day.

She dressed quickly and hurried down the stairs to begin breakfast.

Mary Pat stepped into the mudroom, her cheeks pink from the cold. "'Morning. My car's all loaded."

"'Morning." Penny looked up. "There's coffee. I'll have eggs and sausage in a few minutes."

"That'll give me time to make one more sweep of the bedroom to see if I've forgotten anything." Mary Pat left the room, her footsteps sounding on the stairs.

One by one the others came in from the barns, pausing to wash at the big sink in the mudroom before stepping into the steamy kitchen. Minutes later Mary Pat joined them.

As Penny passed around platters of toast and eggs and sausage, the conversation centered on the sudden change in the weather.

Roscoe gave a shiver. "Barely September, and these old bones are aching like it's January."

"Soon enough it will be." Mac closed both hands around a mug of steaming coffee before turning to Mary Pat. "You might want to think about holding off your latest trek to the wilderness. There's a lot of snow up in those hills, and it could be just the beginning of a really big storm sweeping though."

"I know." She managed a smile. "But there are too many ranchers and their families counting on me. If I postpone this, the winter is bound to get even worse, and then I won't get a chance to visit them until the spring thaw."

"Would that be so bad?"

She smiled. "It would for some lonely rancher's wife who is desperate for medical or emotional support. Or a scared and confused parent or child counting the days until I can help out."

Mac put a hand over hers. "When you say things like that, I understand."

He glanced at Sam. "You'll need to take on a few extra hands so we can bring down the herds early."

"Otis and Roscoe and I can handle it."

"Of course you can. But only if you want to separate the herds and do it in dribs and drabs. If the snow increases, we'll need to bring them down to the lower pasture as soon as possible, in case this is just a taste of what's coming."

"You're right. What was I thinking?" Sam nodded. "I'll put in a call to Horton. He always knows which ranchers around here are in need of some extra money and willing to help out. And Ben will have a few leads of his own in town. I'll go there this afternoon and finalize things."

"Good." Mac set aside his coffee and began to eat. "I'll want to get started as soon as we have enough hands. I've already asked Clive if he can stop over and handle the barn chores." He turned to Penny. "Clive Hughes is our closest neighbor. He owns the ranch to our north. You probably won't even see him. He'll just muck the stalls and head back home. Once we have a crew, we'll be up in the hills for the next week or so, rounding up strays before bringing down the herd. Think you can cook and haul enough food in a truck to feed an army of wranglers?"

She circled the table, topping off their mugs of coffee. "You tell me how many you hire, and I'll make it happen."

He squeezed her hand. "Good girl. Sam will have a number for you by the end of the day. If you need to take on extra supplies, give your list to Sam after breakfast. He can fill it while he's in Haller Creek."

Penny nodded, her mind already racing ahead to all the things she would have to cook and bake and pack. A daunting task. But at least, she thought, it would keep her mind off Curtis and the mess he was making of his life. And with Sam in the hills, she would have one less temptation to deal with while she struggled to set her own life back on course.

Sam walked into a kitchen and gave a smile of pleasure. "Something smells amazing." He glanced around. "You're baking bread?"

Penny straightened from the oven. She wore a stained apron over her jeans, her hair tied back in a knot, her face dusted with flour. "I will be, when all that dough finishes rising."

A dozen loaves of bread were swelling under linen towels on a sideboard, giving off their yeasty scent. A giant pot of chili was simmering on the stove, sending up a rich cloud of steam. A huge tenderloin was roasting in the oven, adding to the mouthwatering fragrances that filled the house.

"It looks like you took Dad at his word. You really are cooking for an army."

"Maybe a small army. How many wranglers were you able to hire?"

"A dozen. A couple of cowboys migrate from ranch to ranch each season. The rest are ranchers who live around these parts and need an extra income. All of them are good workers, so we'll get the job done."

"I've no doubt of it." She smiled. "From what I've seen, you and your family know how to work together."

"On a ranch of this size, we have no choice. If we don't pull together, it could all fall apart." He glanced around. "I thought Zachariah would be helping out in the kitchen."

"He'd planned on it. But Finn called and asked him to drive into town and lend a hand with his latest court case. Because of the fickle weather, the two of them plan on staying in town until the case is resolved."

Sam frowned. "Finn's timing couldn't be worse."

She gave a shake of her head. "That's what Zachariah said, but I assured him I could handle things here without him. I don't think a lawyer ought to be spending his valuable time in the kitchen when he's needed in court."

"So he left a teacher in charge?"

At Sam's grin she couldn't help laughing. "I never thought of it like that. But yeah, it looks like I'm the last recruit."

"And the best."

Penny turned away so Sam wouldn't see the heat that rose to her cheeks. All he had to do was pay her a single compliment and her silly heart betrayed her. She needed to remember that compliments were easy for a charmer like Sam Monroe. All those sweet words just rolled off his tongue like honey.

His cell phone rang, and he answered with a curt word before saying, "I'll be right there, Dad."

When he was gone, Penny removed the roasting pans from the oven, placed the first half-dozen loaves inside, and set the timer. She was grateful for all the hard work ahead of her. It would leave her no time to think. After last night her brain felt scrambled, and she kept replaying that scene in her mind. One minute she was being consoled by Sam, and the next they were practically tearing off each other's clothes.

She couldn't help wondering if those kisses had meant nothing more to Sam than the peck on the cheek he'd given Mary Pat when she'd taken her leave this morning.

Penny paused to touch a finger to her lips.

Maybe it was no big deal to Sam, but it shamed her to admit that his kiss last night had rocked her world.

Penny loaded the back of the ranch truck with supplies. A huge pot of chili. Several prime cuts of beef, roasted to perfection and sliced so that they were ready to eat with the mashed potatoes that filled two foil pans, as well as a green bean casserole. The leftovers would be made into sandwiches, easy to carry on the trail. There were a dozen loaves of sourdough bread, eggs to go with their breakfast, gallons of coffee, and cases of bottled water in coolers.

The past few days had been filled with dawn-to-dusk work, keeping her so busy she had no time to think about Curtis and his problems or to dwell on her feelings for Sam.

When she wasn't cooking and baking, often starting at dawn, she was loading up the truck and driving into the hills with a hot supper.

There were two range shacks spread across the hills. One offered emergency dried food and shelter, with a wood-burning fireplace and outhouse. The second, larger one had bunks for two dozen wranglers, as well as a small bathroom and a galley kitchen stocked with dried and canned foods for emergencies. Several groups of wranglers had been assigned a specific area to hunt strays, which were rounded up and driven to a holding corral until it was time to drive the entire herd to the lower elevations for the winter.

Penny planned to set up a hot meal for the cold, hungry wranglers, with enough left over for breakfast and a cold meal along the trail the next day. Then she would drive back to the ranch and fall into bed before starting over the next morning.

At night she was asleep as soon as her head hit the pillow. She'd never worked as hard or as long, and yet she found the entire process exhilarating.

Each morning, as she began the day, she felt a thrill of anticipation, knowing she was playing a small part in the success of the Monroe ranch.

Today, on her drive into the hills, the snow began falling. At first it was a gentle sifting of white through the clouds. Within an hour, just as she reached her destination, the snow had become a curtain of white, nearly obliterating the trees on either side of the trail.

Zipping up her heavy parka, she strained to see, off in the distance, the wranglers scouring the brush, chasing up strays and herding them toward the corral.

The sound of horses and all-terrain vehicles approaching alerted Penny to the arrival of the wranglers after another day of chasing after strays.

There was no time to think about the snow as she began carrying the prepared food from the truck.

Otis had arrived in time to help her set up a long table on the covered porch of the little cabin. The men, fresh from the trail, didn't bother with formalities as they filled their plates and sat wherever they could find a dry spot. Some sat with their backs to the cabin wall. Others settled under a towering evergreen that offered shelter from the wind and snow. A few went inside to eat in front of the fireplace.

Mac loaded his plate with slabs of roast beef and potatoes before sitting on the porch next to Otis and Roscoe.

Sam walked from the corral, slapping his wide-brimmed hat against his leg, sending up a cloud of snow. Despite the cold, he looked hot and sweaty from his hours chasing strays.

He shot her a grin. "I don't know what looks better—you, all cool and composed, or this amazing meal."

Her heart did a quick somersault, and she itched to brush the damp hair from his forehead. Instead, she dug her fingers into the pocket of her jeans. "I'd go with the food if I were you, cowboy."

He chuckled. "Yes, ma'am." His smile deepened. "Looks like you've been working overtime."

"No harder than you and the others."

"Yeah, but I don't look as fresh as a daisy."

"You don't smell like one, either."

That had him throwing back his head and giving a roar of laughter. "Just stay upwind of me, ma'am, so you're not offended."

"Don't you worry. I'll keep my distance, cowboy."

He shot her a long, level look that had her blush deepening before he filled his plate and strolled over to sit beside his father and the others.

Penny finished loading the empty pans into the back of the truck. She'd used the leftovers to prepare dozens of roast beef sandwiches, which she stored in a cooler. The men who rode the perimeter of the herd during the night hours knew they could always stop by the range shack and help themselves.

The others were heading inside, where bunks lined the walls. They were grateful for the warmth of the log fire blazing on the hearth.

Penny dug the keys out of her pocket and opened the

driver's-side door. Before she could climb inside, Sam stopped her with a hand on her arm.

She turned with an arched look. "Did I forget something?"

He motioned over his shoulder to where Mac was standing in the shelter of the porch. "Dad and I were talking. We don't like the look of this storm."

"I'm sure, once I get down from the hills, it won't be so bad."

"You're right. It won't. But it's getting there that worries us. It's already too dark to see the trail. One slip, and you could find yourself buried in a ravine."

"I'll be fine, Sam." She made a move to climb in, and his hand tightened on her arm.

"There's nobody at the ranch to help if you're in trouble. Finn and Zachariah are in town, more than an hour away."

"I have my phone."

"Service is bad enough in good weather. With a storm like this, you'd never be able to reach anyone."

She gave a sigh of exasperation. "What do you want me to do? Snap my fingers and stop the snow?"

"We think you should stay here tonight."

She blinked. "Stay here? You want me to sleep in there, with all the wranglers?"

"I know it isn't the most comfortable place to spend the night. But at least you'll be safe, not to mention warm and dry."

"And forced to listen to men snoring."

He bit back a smile. "But you'll be safe, Penny, and that's what matters. You can leave first thing in the morning, if the trail is passable. But for tonight, we just can't let you go."

"Let me...?" She sucked in a breath. "I've been taking care of myself for years, Sam."

"But now you work for us. We're responsible for your safety."

She looked beyond him, to where Mac stood waiting and watching with a worried frown. With a sigh of resignation, she slammed the truck door and moved along beside Sam.

When they reached the porch, Mac put a hand on her shoulder. "I'm sorry, Penny. I know this isn't the most comfortable situation, but it's just for tonight." He handed her a steaming mug of coffee. "If you'd like, you can sit out here for a while and relax. I know a lot of the wranglers are wandering around in long johns while their clothes dry by the fire. Sam can let you know when the men are all asleep. Then you and he can fight over who gets the top bunk and who gets the lower one." He studied her face. "Think you can handle it?"

She nodded. "I'll be fine, Mac. Remember, I raised three brothers."

"Good." Mac turned away and walked inside.

Sam couldn't help teasing. "I call the bottom bunk."

She shot him a withering look. "Why?"

He gave a negligent shrug. "I think it'll be fun watching you climb the ladder to the top, and knowing you're sleeping just above me."

She gave a huff of annoyance and turned away to stare morosely into the falling snow.

He tugged on a lock of her hair. "Hey, Money. Look at it this way. Spending the night up in the hills with a bunch of smelly wranglers ought to prove to be a real experience."

"So is getting sprayed by a skunk. But it isn't something you'd ever want to repeat."

He gave a shake of his head, all the while laughing. "I'm betting this will be a step above running into a skunk."

She joined in his laughter. "Okay. Maybe. But just barely."

Relieved that she'd found her sense of humor, he touched a big rough palm to her cheek. "Finish your coffee and I'll let you know when it's safe to come inside."

When the door closed behind him, Penny turned to watch the curtain of snow drifting past her line of vision. A snowfall so thick, it now completely obliterated the corral just a hundred yards away.

Though she wouldn't admit it to Sam, now that she'd had time to assess the situation, she was grateful that she didn't have to drive through this storm tonight. Without proper roads or familiar landmarks, she could have easily ended up in trouble.

And now, knowing she was here for the night, her work ended until morning, she was free to enjoy the beauty of the season's first real snowfall.

She settled herself on the porch, her hands closed around the coffee mug, drinking in the sight of a countryside softened by mounds of glittering, pristine snow.

CHAPTER ELEVEN

Sam stepped out the cabin door and settled himself beside Penny.

"Sorry it took so long. I thought old Ed Whittier would never hit the sack."

She looked over with a smile. "I don't mind. Actually, I'm grateful for the time to just enjoy all this."

He followed her gaze. "I know what you mean. I always feel like a kid at Christmas each time we have a first snowfall."

"You do?" She turned to him with a look of surprise. "I guess I figured this storm would mean more work."

"It does. But it's work I love."

"I can see why." She paused. "Look at all this."

"Yeah. Like a postcard."

"It is. And listen."

He gave her a puzzled look. "I don't hear anything."

"I know. It's as if the snow has blotted out everything. As

though I've landed in an alternate universe where nothing familiar exists."

As the muted sound of cattle lowing reached their ears, Sam smiled. "Now that's a familiar sound. And one I love to hear."

She nodded. "But the hills all covered in snow make it seem like something otherworldly. Like something out of the old West. Cowboys bundled in dusters tending their herds. Coyotes howling at the moon. No sign of civilization. Just the snow and the hills and the cattle." She turned to him. "How does it feel knowing all this is yours?"

He paused and seemed to gather his thoughts before answering. "It took me some time to accept that fact. Even after Mac adopted my brothers and me, I didn't trust him. Hell, I didn't trust any adult. I figured they were all alike, just willing to use me as hired help, without having to pay me."

"Why would you think that?"

"My life before coming here wasn't anything like this. Looking back, I think of it as hell on earth. The worst part about it was being separated from Ben and Finn. My brothers and I vowed we were going to band together and run as far and as fast as we could, and do whatever necessary to stay free."

"But you were all so young."

"Old enough to make a pact. We were desperate. We knew one thing. We were never going to let any law separate us again."

Her voice was hushed. "I'm trying to imagine having my brothers taken away from me when we were young. I would have been so afraid for them. And so lonely without them." She turned. "It must have been really painful for the three of you."

He shrugged, unwilling to let his mind go there. "I'd rather talk about the here and now."

She understood his reluctance and quickly changed the subject. "Are the men asleep?"

He grinned. "If you listen, you'll hear the snore roar coming from inside. They're all sleeping like babies. Or maybe I should say baby bullfrogs."

She was laughing as she got to her feet.

Sam stood beside her, and stared into her eyes before his gaze lowered, centering on her mouth.

In that instant she knew he was going to kiss her. And though she'd warned herself about the consequences of falling under his spell, she felt a flutter of anticipation. After all, what could be the harm? It was only a kiss.

He lowered his head and brushed her lips with his. Just the merest brush of mouth to mouth, but the effect was electric.

Her arms came around his neck and she returned his kiss with a hunger that invited more.

He took what she offered with a wild, almost desperate need that caught them both by surprise.

With a moan he moved his hands inside her parka and drew her closer. "You taste so damned good." His hands moved along her sides, his thumbs encountering her breasts.

"Sam." She felt the sexual tug that left her gasping.

"Don't tell me to stop. Not yet." He murmured the words against her throat.

"You can't...we can't..." Her words were swallowed by his mouth on hers, as he backed her across the porch until she scraped the wall of the cabin.

Without a thought to the consequences, she slid her hands inside his parka, and she felt the ripple of corded muscles with each touch. "Sam." Her voice was breathy. "We have to stop."

"I know. We will." But he didn't. Instead, he kissed her again, long and slow and deep, until a little moan escaped her lips.

"I wish we were really in that alternate universe you talked about, Money." His words, whispered against her neck, had her shivering. "This scene would have a..." He nibbled his way to the little dip between her collarbone and shoulder. "Very different ending."

Penny was so lost in the kiss, all she could do was hold on while his lips whispered over her face, from her forehead to her cheek to the corner of her mouth.

When at last he lifted his head, she sucked air into her starving lungs and wondered why she felt suddenly chilled. The heat of the moment dissolved.

Resting his forehead on hers, he closed his eyes and dragged in a labored breath. Then he took a step back and lowered his hands to his sides.

"You go ahead inside and get ready for bed."

"What about you?"

He shook his head. "I need a long walk in the snow. I'll check on the cattle in the corral before I come in. By then I should be cooled down enough to sleep. And you'll be safely in your bunk."

"Good night, Sam." She touched a hand to his cheek.

He closed his fingers around her wrist and she felt her pulse leap.

With a dangerous gleam in his eye he smiled. "Good night, Money. I hope one of us gets some sleep."

Penny lay in the upper bunk, fully dressed except for her boots.

She heard the door open and close. Heard the slight shuffling as Sam nudged off his boots and climbed into the lower bunk.

"You asleep, Money?"

At his whispered words she smiled in the darkness. "No."

"Want to climb down here? I'll warm your feet."

"They're warm enough."

"You can warm mine, then. They're freezing. Come on down."

"Not a chance."

"I could climb up there."

"Don't try it, cowboy."

He sighed. Twisted. Turned. "You're cruel, you know that?"

"Yeah. That's me. You can call me Mean Miss Money."

That had him chuckling. "I'd like to be teacher's pet."

"Good try."

Across the room someone snorted, then began snoring again.

She couldn't resist saying, "This is so romantic."

"You want romance? I could..."

"Good night, Sam."

She rolled to her side and drew the blanket to her chin. She couldn't help wondering what it would be like to lie beside Sam Monroe. He was funny and charming. And oh so sexy, without even trying. And despite the men asleep all around her, the only one she could think of, the only one who mattered, was Sam.

It was the last thought she had before sleep finally overtook her.

Though the cabin was still dark, and the men in the bunks still snoring, Penny was instantly awake. Awake and alert to a shadowy figure standing by the window.

Curious, she climbed from the upper bunk and padded in her stocking feet across the room.

Mac was holding a mug of lukewarm coffee and frowning as he stared intently out the window at the falling snow.

He turned and gave her a forced smile. "Sorry, Penny. I didn't mean to wake you."

"Are you worried about getting the herd through this snow?"

"I'm worried about Mary Pat, and hoping she isn't stranded somewhere out there."

"So that's what has you awake. Tell me, Mac. How many years has she been doing this?"

He shrugged. "Too many. Thirty years or more."

"Thirty years." Penny shook her head in wonder. "I'm betting she's learned a lot about survival."

"Of course. But in a storm like this..." His voice trailed off.

"In all those years of delivering services to lonely ranchers, an awful lot of people have come to love Mary Pat. How could they not?"

Seeing his interest sharpen, she added, "With a big, open, loving heart like Mary Pat's, I bet she has more friends than she can count."

Mac nodded. "That she has."

"There you are. And you have to know any one of them would welcome the chance to have her stay for more than her usual visit. They'd probably fight for the chance to have her stay over so they can pick her brain on a dozen different matters. I can see her sleeping comfortably in one of their ranches right now, after enjoying a fabulous supper and getting caught up in their family lore."

Mac's smile came quickly. "You paint a pretty picture, Penny. And you're right, of course. What was I thinking?

I have to believe she's safe and comfortable." He turned to look out the window at the snow-covered hills. "She had plenty of time to see this storm blowing in and prepare for survival. And plenty of time to reach a nearby ranch before dark."

Penny touched a hand to his arm. "Would you like me to make some fresh coffee?"

He turned toward her, shaking his head. "Thanks, but I think I'll go back to sleep now." He clapped a hand on her shoulder. "You should do the same."

"I will. In a few minutes."

Penny watched as Mac crossed the room and slid between the covers of his bunk.

She turned toward the tiny galley kitchen and nearly bumped into Sam, standing in the shadows.

"Sam." His name came out in a whoosh as he caught her in his arms before she could slam into him.

He pressed his mouth to her ear. "Shh. Let's not wake the entire cabin."

His whispered words sent a cascade of fire and ice trickling along her spine.

For the space of a heartbeat she merely held on. Despite the cold, he was barefoot and naked to the waist, his jeans unsnapped and riding low on his hips.

She looked up into his face. "You scared the daylights out of me."

"Sorry." His mouth was inches from hers. "That was a nice thing you did for my dad."

"It was the truth. I'm sure Mary Pat is staying at someone's ranch, and safely out of this storm."

"From your lips, Money..."

She smiled.

"Now, can you ease your own fears just as easily?"

She arched a brow. "What's that supposed to mean?"

"I mean, you're better at solving other people's problems than your own."

She shot him an arched look.

His fingers tightened on the tops of her arms and he drew her fractionally closer. "I agree that Mary Pat will find a safe shelter from this storm. And so will Curtis. All he needs is some time to grow up."

"Like you grew up?"

Instead of getting angry, he merely smiled, his teeth gleaming in the dim light. "Yeah. I'll remind you again. In case you haven't noticed, I'm not one of your little brothers."

His hands were moving ever so slowly along her arms, across her shoulders, spreading warmth wherever they touched.

With that same gleam of humor he lowered his face and touched his mouth to hers.

If she'd thought he intended a sweet kiss, she was caught completely off guard when his arms came around her, molding her firmly to the length of him. His mouth moved on hers, tasting, coaxing, before taking the kiss deeper, then deeper still.

She was forced to wrap her arms around his waist and hold on to all that warm flesh as the walls began to sway. Beneath her feet the floor dipped and shifted, and she returned his kisses with a need that bordered on desperation.

By the time they came up for air, their chests were heaving, their lungs straining.

He took a deliberate step back, and she was grateful that he kept his hands on her shoulders. She knew if he let go, her trembling legs would betray her and she would slide like a jellyfish to the floor.

When their breathing returned to normal, he framed her face with his hands and stared down into her eyes.

"I'll say good night now. But when this cattle drive is over, we have some unfinished business, Money."

He brushed a quick, hard kiss over her mouth before turning her toward the bunk.

"Now let's hope we can grab an hour or two of sleep before starting the day."

Penny climbed to the top bunk and lay with her eyes open, staring at the shadows cast by the flaming embers on the hearth.

Below her, Sam could be heard turning, sighing, before the bunk below her fell silent.

What was she going to do about him?

What had started out as a simple kiss had turned into something very different. All Sam needed to do was touch her and she became completely caught up in needs she'd never had before. The need to be held. The need to be kissed. The need to be loved fully. Completely.

Now that she had some distance from Sam, she could see just how foolish she must look to him. While he was engaging in mindless play, she was allowing herself to think about romance, and love, and happily-ever-after. She couldn't help herself. She wasn't the type to indulge in a brief relationship. Maybe it was the loss of her parents. Maybe it was the disintegration of her family as her brothers grew up and left. Whatever the reason, she knew in her heart she was falling hard for Sam, and when it ended, as it surely would when a teaching position opened up, she would have her heart broken.

There was only one solution. She would have to strengthen her resolve to keep her distance from him.

The next time Sam Monroe made a move, she would have

to be quick enough to walk away. Even though she didn't really want to. What she wanted, what she *craved*, was the very thing she would have to avoid, if she wanted to survive the winter with her heart intact.

Agitated, she lay very still and waited for sleep to take her away from her troubling thoughts.

CHAPTER TWELVE

Miss Penny." Otis gave a sigh of pure pleasure as he tasted the omelet Penny set in front of him. "I'm sorry you had to spend your night up here on the mountain with all of us, instead of your comfortable room back at the ranch, but I can't help wishing you could stick around so we could start every morning like this."

The rest of the wranglers were too busy eating to speak, but they gave her nods or a thumbs-up as she topped off their mugs of coffee.

"Since I was up early anyway, and I had all those leftovers, I figured you and the other men have earned a special breakfast. I call this my kitchen sink omelet."

That brought a rumble of laughter from the wranglers.

"No matter what you call it, it's tasty," Ed Whittier called. "A breakfast like this will hold me until supper tonight."

"You keep on feeding us like this," another man said,

"and we'll be standing in line to work the Monroe roundup every year."

Across the table Mac grinned and lifted his mug of coffee. "That's music to my ears. I'll drink to that."

When he finished his meal, he put an arm around Penny's shoulder and leaned close to say, "Thanks for your comforting words last night. I guess I was letting my nerves get the best of me." He nodded toward Otis, just polishing off the last of his omelet. "I've asked Otis to drive you back to the ranch. He'll wait until you finish cooking, and drive you back up in time for supper. And he'll repeat that each day until this drive is over."

"I don't like taking him away from his work."

Mac gave her a smile. "He'll be grateful for the break. Otis works as hard as any man on this ranch, but at his age, he can use a rest, and the chance to sleep in his own bed for the next few nights will definitely recharge his batteries. And he can lend a hand with Clive out in the barns."

"All right." She returned Mac's smile. "Thank you. In truth, I was a little worried about navigating these hills by myself."

"Whenever you're not comfortable with something, you need to let me know." He gave her a steady look. "Are you good with that?"

She nodded. "Yes. Thanks, Mac."

When she turned, she saw Sam watching.

As his father walked out the door, he crossed the room and tugged on a lock of her hair. Bending close he whispered, "I'd kiss you, but there are too many eyes." In a loud voice he called, "Stay safe, Money."

She absorbed the quick rush of heat that put fresh color on her cheeks. She hoped her voice wouldn't betray her emotions. "You, too, cowboy."

*   *   *

Within the hour, Otis was at the wheel of the truck, while Penny sat beside him, white-knuckling the ride and trying to remember to breathe.

In the back of the truck were the empty pots and pans and assorted trays that would be cleaned and filled with fresh hot meals in time for supper. That is, if they made it back safely. Here in the hills the snow was several feet deep, and the wheels of the truck often slipped and slid when they couldn't gain traction.

"Have you ever seen a storm like this before, Otis?"

The old man grinned. "Since coming to Montana, I've seen plenty of 'em, Miss Penny."

"When did you come here, Otis?"

"Oh, more'n thirty years now."

"Were you lured to Montana by a dream of becoming a cowboy?"

He chuckled. "Now I have to admit, I never saw myself riding a horse, let alone riding the range. But life has a funny way of happening while we're busy making other plans."

"What were you planning for your life, Otis?"

He kept his hands steady on the wheel. "I was living on the south side of Chicago. And I planned on being the best husband and father in the world."

"You have a wife and children?"

"Had."

Penny heard the pain in that single word. Before she had a chance to react, he said, "I was so proud and happy. I'd just landed a good job that would allow us to move from our cramped upper room of a tenement to an apartment in a better part of town. That night my wife and I celebrated our good fortune and started reading ads in the newspaper for two-bedroom apartments. Sometime just before dawn, while I was sound asleep, someone firebombed the place where we were living. I heard a loud boom, and found myself lying in the street, my clothes on fire, my wife, Ruby, and my two little boys dead."

Penny lifted a hand to stifle the cry she couldn't hold back.

When she found her voice, she asked, "Did the authorities find the person who committed that horrible crime?"

He shook his head. "I never heard. For the next few weeks I was in a dark place in my mind. It shames me to admit that one night I drank myself into a fog and stumbled off toward the railroad tracks."

Penny's eyes went wide. "Oh, Otis. You weren't thinking of...?"

He shrugged. "I wasn't thinking at all. But I fell into an empty boxcar, and when I woke up, sober and hungry, I was hundreds of miles from home. My first thought was to get a job so I could eat and find a place to sleep. And I did, but I couldn't seem to settle. As soon as I'd find work in a town, I'd move on. I knew I didn't want to return to Chicago, so I just kept hopping into empty boxcars, wondering where I'd end up. And finally I found myself in this place, which is as far removed from my hometown as a place can be. To a city boy like me, Montana was the other side of the moon. More cattle than people. No traffic jams. Hills covered with wildflowers. Streams so clean you can drink from them. And when I walked up to the Monroe ranch to ask for a job and a place to spend the night, Miss Rachel, Mac's wife, bless her, fed me and said I could stay in the bunkhouse. Not for a night, or until a job was finished, but for as long as I wanted to stay on and work. And I never looked back. Mac and his boys and Roscoe and Zachariah are my family now. This place is heaven on earth. This is my forever home."

Penny had to blink away the tears that welled up. "I'm so glad you found your home, Otis."

"I didn't find it. It found me. I believe that's the way of life, Miss Penny. Some of the things that feel like they happened by accident are really part of a heavenly plan. We just have to be patient enough to keep riding that train until there it is, right in front of us."

When she was able to compose herself, Penny turned to Otis. "Thank you for sharing your story with me."

He gave her a gentle smile. "We've all got a story, Miss Penny. Anyone who's ever lived has one."

When they pulled up alongside the ranch, Otis took her hand and helped her from the truck. The two of them plowed through the snowdrifts to the back porch.

Otis stopped and looked around. "Looks like Clive shoveled the snow from the porch."

Penny nodded. "Or maybe Finn and Zachariah finished with the trial early."

"Maybe." He returned to the truck to carry in the empty pots and pans, while Penny stepped inside.

"Becca." She hurried over to hug Ben's wife. "How did you make it here from town in all this snow?"

"The same way you made it here from the hills." Becca gave a laugh. "Ben offered to drive me here before he started work so I could spend the day giving you a hand with all the cooking and baking. When I found the house empty, I figured I'd come all this way for nothing."

"Oh, I'm so grateful you stuck around."

When Otis walked into the kitchen, he found the two women hugging and laughing.

"Miss Becca, I'd say you're just what the doctor ordered."

He turned to Penny. "As long as you have an assistant here, I'll give Clive a hand with the barn chores. If you two ladies need anything at all, just holler."

"Thank you, Otis."

When he was gone, Penny located an apron and began assembling ingredients for the day's meal.

While she and Becca worked together, Penny said, "I'm so glad Otis was able to drive me back. Without our time together, I'd have never known what a remarkable man he is."

Becca looked over. "He told you about his past?"

When Penny nodded, Becca said, "He told me about it when we were working in his garden last fall."

Penny paused. "When I heard his story, he had me in tears."

Becca measured and stirred under Penny's direction, while nodding her understanding. "I had the same reaction. It's heartbreaking."

Penny nodded. "When I watch Otis tending his lush garden, or laughing with the others, he gives no hint of the pain he's suffered." She kneaded a lump of dough before setting it aside and picking up a second one. "He said everyone who's ever lived has a story. And he believes that nothing that happens is an accident, but rather part of a heavenly plan." Penny paused to look over at her friend. "Do you ever wonder if your life was planned?"

Becca shrugged, and in reply told her an abbreviated version of her own story.

"My father made up his mind years ago that Ben was nothing but trouble, and he was determined that his only child was never going to be allowed to spend time with that 'hell-raiser,' as he called him." She shook her head, remembering. "When I think how opposed my parents were to Ben, and how hard they worked to keep us apart, I can't help thinking we were fated to be together." Seeing the look of concentration on Penny's face, she gathered her courage. "How about you, Penny? I can sense that something's wrong."

Penny finished kneading the last loaf and covered it with a clean linen towel before filling the kettle. "Let's take a break with some tea."

Minutes later the two women sat across the table from one another, and Penny admitted her horror at seeing her little brother drinking and gambling.

"How old is Curtis?" Becca asked.

"Twenty-one, and in charge of his own life, he reminded me."

"And so he is. But he's young, Penny. If I had to admit to all the mistakes I made at that age, I'd be so embarrassed."

"That's pretty much what Sam said to me. But of course he would defend Curtis, since Sam is doing much the same things."

Becca shook her head. "I'm not going to defend Sam just because he's Ben's brother, but you have the wrong idea about him. He rarely drinks more than a longneck or two, and never when he's shooting pool."

"But you do admit he shoots pool for money."

"Of course. For Sam, it isn't so much a gamble as a hobby. He's just very good at the game, and he loves to challenge himself by playing against the best pool players around."

"No matter what you call it, it's gambling. And in Curtis's case, it cost him an entire paycheck."

"After he loses a couple of times, he'll learn to either stay sober when he's playing or quit altogether."

"Oh, I hope you're right, Becca."

Becca broke open a biscuit and nibbled before deciding

to change the subject. "Now tell me how it felt being caught in a blizzard up in the hills with an army of wranglers."

Penny chuckled. "I thought I'd feel really awkward having to sleep in a range shack with a bunch of men. But Sam made it easy for me. I sat outside drinking coffee and enjoying the beautiful scenery until all the men were asleep. Then Sam came out and said it was safe to come in."

"And that's it?"

Penny stared down at her tea. "I did feel uncomfortable knowing Sam was sleeping in the bunk right below me."

"Yeah. That would be awkward." Becca sipped her tea. "I'm sure you've noticed that whenever you're around, Sam can't take his eyes off you."

Penny felt the heat rise to her cheeks. "That's his reaction to any female."

"If you think that, you're kidding yourself."

"Becca, when I first came here, Finn bragged about his brother's appeal to women. *All* women."

"Oh, they're attracted. No doubt about it." Becca smiled. "But he seems immune to all of them. Except you. He acts different when you're around."

"Different how?"

Becca shrugged. "He loves to joke and tease, but with you, there's a sweetness to his teasing. Like that nickname he gave you. Money. There's a tone in his voice..." She shook her head. "I can't describe it, but it's almost like a kiss."

"Now you're being silly." Penny started to push away from the table, but Becca reached across and laid a hand over hers.

"Yes. Exactly. His teasing is like a kiss, only with words instead of lips." She paused, then forged ahead. "Has he... Have the two of you...?"

Penny gave a long, deep sigh. "He's kissed me."

"And...?"

Penny swallowed. "And I've kissed him back."

"All right." Becca was practically rubbing her hands together in glee. "Well? Were there fireworks?"

After a very long pause Penny couldn't contain herself. "Yes. Were there fireworks the first time you kissed Ben?"

"Uh-huh." Laughing, Becca rounded the table and gathered Penny into a warm hug. "And I wanted more. What about you?"

"Oh, Becca." Penny joined in the laughter. "I'm scared to death of what I'm feeling. But it's good to know it's happened to you, too."

As the two women put aside their tea and returned to their chores, Penny's heart felt lighter than it had in days.

She'd missed this. In order to chase her dream, she'd severed all ties and moved far from her childhood home in a small town. She'd left behind all her old friends with whom she could talk openly.

It was so good to have a friend she could confide in here on this ranch, so far from all she'd ever known.

Otis had said there were no accidents in life.

If someone told her Becca Monroe had just been dropped from heaven, she wouldn't argue. Right now, Becca was her angel. Sharing her load in the kitchen, and sharing the secrets of her heart, as well.

Whenever worries about her little brother began to weigh her down, she would cling to these simple facts.

It was so good to have a friend.

It was also good to have a job that, though it wasn't the one she'd planned on, was satisfying and fulfilling.

For the moment, life didn't get much better than this.

CHAPTER THIRTEEN

The next days passed in a blur of hard work from dawn to dark. Each day, after endless hours of cooking, Otis drove Penny into the hills in time to deliver hot suppers to the wranglers before driving her back to the ranch to start all over the next day.

The few times she saw Sam, he was hot and sweaty and working alongside the wranglers at a furious pace. But all he needed to do was wave his hat in the air in a salute, or tease her in front of the others, and her face would go all hot. Sometimes he would lean close to say something more intimate, and she could feel the quick rush of heat through her veins. She could feel him watching her as she set up the meal, and again when she and Otis were loading up the empty trays and pans for the trek down to the ranch. Whenever she looked over, he would be wearing that rogue smile that did such strange things to her heart.

Though there was no time alone, his very presence made her feel special.

Often in the night, alone in the privacy of the big guest room upstairs, she would replay in her mind the things he'd said that day. Each thought, each simple word stirred longings in her.

Oh, the restless longings he stirred in her.

Then she would remind herself that she was nothing more than an interim employee here. After all, teaching had been her goal for a lifetime. It was what had driven her to study so hard. It had been the reason she'd struggled with college and two jobs. It was why, after her brothers were grown and gone, and her great-aunt buried, she'd sold the family house, paid off the last of her father's debts, and took a job far away.

Even though it hadn't yet worked out, she knew that someday a teaching position would finally become available, and she was determined to enjoy the fruits of her labors. She would leave the Monroe ranch and begin the future she'd planned. And no sexy cowboy would change her mind.

She often fell asleep wondering why that thought no longer brought her the sense of anticipation it once had. Instead, it left her with a vague feeling of sadness and loss.

"Well, Miss Penny, the day's finally come." Otis helped Penny load up the hot breakfast she would serve before the wranglers began the final push to bring the herd down.

"I can't believe I'm going to be allowed to watch a real roundup."

"It's something to see." Otis smiled. "I remember my first roundup. To a city dude like me, it seemed like a lot of blood, sweat, and tears trying to wrangle a bunch of ornery cows that seemed to want to go anywhere except where they were supposed to." He gave a shake of his head. "At first it looked like mass confusion. But in no time I sorted things out and just moved along with the rest of the wranglers behind the herd. And when it was over, and the cattle were all safely in their winter pasture, I enjoyed the satisfaction of a job well done." He looked over. "Just remember to stay out of the way. Those cowboys have a lot going on. They can't allow for distractions."

"I'll remember." She climbed into the truck and stared out the window at the spectacular sight of the predawn sky streaked with ribbons of pale pink, mauve, and deep purple.

Her heart beat faster as she thought about the day to come.

Or was it the fact that she would see Sam?

She pushed aside the thought and concentrated on the meal she would serve.

At first light they reached the range shack Mac referred to as the staging area. From here they would begin the long trek to the lower range.

The wranglers were already busy saddling their mounts and checking their equipment when Penny and Otis set up a hot meal on the long porch of the cabin. Within minutes the men gathered around, filling their plates with fried chicken and scrambled eggs and thick slices of sourdough toast. They downed steaming mugs of coffee before picking up bottles of water on their way to climb into the saddle.

Sam paused beside Penny and touched a hand to her shoulder. "I see you brought the warm weather and sunlight with you."

She looked up at him with a bright smile. "And here I thought you did that."

He glanced at the line of cowboys already moving out. "I wish there was time…"

"Let's go, Sam." Mac's shout carried above the din. "Get a move on."

Penny was grateful for the distraction. "You need to go."

He closed a hand over hers. "If you climb that hill over there, you'll have a clear view of the roundup from a safe vantage point."

"I will. Stay safe, Sam."

"Don't I always?" He winked before sprinting to his waiting horse.

Penny's heart leapt to her throat and seemed lodged there for the next hour as she and Otis cleared the table and stored the pans and containers in the small, cramped galley kitchen of the cabin before hurrying to the hill to observe the action.

The wranglers had already moved out, forming a loose circle as they fanned out behind the herd. And then the land was black with cattle and men on horseback as they began their downward trek.

It was an amazing sight, and one Penny knew she would never forget.

"Otis." Breathless, she grabbed the old man's arm.

"I know what you mean, Miss Penny. Isn't it a pretty sight?"

As far as the eye could see was a steady stream of cattle undulating like a great black wave moving over vast hills and valleys, on their way down the mountain.

Sam and the others were astride their horses, whistling, shouting, waving lariats as they kept the herd moving.

The melting snow was soon churned into mud by the thousands of hooves.

Whenever a cow made a break for freedom, a wrangler and his horse became a team, turning on a dime, racing ahead, keeping order. The men, unshaven from their time in the hills, were constantly swinging lariats and whistling or cursing as they drove the errant strays back to the herd. It was a blur of sight and sound and mind-boggling activity.

And in the midst, working harder than any of them, Sam seemed to be everywhere, as though anticipating every need, whether fetching a wandering cow, or helping another wrangler turn back a group of strays.

As he passed the spot where Penny and Otis were watching from the safety of a snow-covered knoll, he lifted his hat in the air and sent them a smile that had Penny's heart swelling with sudden emotion.

Otis grinned at her. "Sam's in his element. He surely does look forward to this drive every year."

"Why does he love it so much?"

"Just look at him. In the thick of everything, where he loves to be." The old man shrugged. "Roundup is a chance to release all the tension of making a ranch a successful operation. After all, ranching isn't just a way of life for these men. It's a business, and one that fails as often as it succeeds. For a man like Sam, who grew up without an anchor, he can see that long line of cattle and know he had a hand in making it all happen. Though he wasn't born to it, he took to ranching like a duck to water. The first time he saw a calf being born, he jumped in without any fear. Now when it comes to assisting in birthing calves, he's one of the best. And then there's the fact that it's just a man and his horse. Here on the Monroe ranch, there are no cattle haulers, or trucks, or all-terrain vehicles used at roundup. Just nature, the way it's been for hundreds of years."

As the long line of men and cattle swooped past, Otis turned toward the truck. "We may as well get started back to the ranch."

"What about all those pots and pans?"

"I need to get down to the ranch and out to the meadow

before the herd gets there. But the pots and pans will be here tomorrow when Mac sends someone up here to get the range shack ready for winter. Once the roundup is over, there's all the time in the world."

Penny climbed into the passenger side before turning for a final glimpse of Sam and the others.

They looked, as Otis had said, like pictures in books depicting cowboys in the Old West. The very sight of them had her heart drumming in her chest.

She didn't want to admit to herself that seeing Sam had anything to do with the crazy way her heart was behaving. But the sight of him in the saddle, doing the thing he most loved, had touched her in a special way.

Doing the thing he most loved.

Now that she'd experienced roundup firsthand, she could understand why ranching meant so much to him.

She found herself wondering why her own goal of being a teacher had become less important to her than being near Sam.

She glanced shyly toward Otis, his concentration fixed on the snowy, muddy trail before them.

"After visiting so many places, how did you know the Monroe ranch was where you wanted to stay?"

He took his time answering. "I guess I've seen just about every big city and small town from Chicago to Bozeman. Folks are pretty much the same, no matter where you stop. Some friendly"—he shrugged—"some not so much. But there was a special feeling here. At first I thought it was because of Miss Rachel." He looked over. "You would have liked her. Mac's wife was a good woman. But after she and her son, Robbie, were killed in that terrible accident, I realized her goodness lived on in all of us. And especially in Mac. He was in shock for a long time, and we all worried about him. Then those three hell-raisers came along."

"Ben, Sam, and Finn. Becca told me they were pretty angry when they broke into Mac's house looking for food and warm clothes."

"Angry doesn't even come close to describing them, Miss Penny. Those three swore like sailors, were ready to beg, steal, or borrow to stay together, and stood shoulder-to-shoulder ready to fight anybody or anything that threatened any one of them."

"How could they possibly help a man locked in grief?"

He chuckled. "Heaven only knows. Maybe their needs were so great, Mac didn't have time to think about his own. He became a man on a mission. He made them do extra chores if he caught them swearing. He taught them to use their brains instead of their fists. And most of all, Mac taught them how to become good men." Otis shook his head. "Don't tell him this, but while Mac was busy saving them, those three juvenile delinquents were saving him."

As they continued along the snowy trail, Penny sat back, trying to picture the three men she knew—a sheriff, a rancher, and a lawyer—as those angry, defiant boys Otis had just described. It simply wasn't possible.

"I guess Mac did a good job."

"That he did." Otis chuckled again, a long rumble of laughter. "But every now and then I get a glimpse of the boys they used to be. Especially Sam. He still has a lot of those rough edges. He and his brothers surely did stir up a whole lot of trouble. Life here was never the same after they joined the family."

Otis swung around the barn and drove through puddles of melted snow streaming from the roof before coming to a halt at the back porch.

Once inside, Penny shed her boots and parka in the mud-room before stepping into the kitchen.

Home.

The feeling washed over her like a giant ocean wave.

As Otis headed toward the barn and the chores awaiting him there, she began moving about the kitchen, setting everything in order before beginning the next round of cooking and baking.

She couldn't wait to prepare a feast for the men who'd been in the hills for a week.

In truth, she couldn't wait to feed Sam. To see a light in his eyes as he bit into tender roast beef and devoured her creamy mashed potatoes. To hear his hum of pleasure as he spooned whipped cream over the chocolate layer cake she was planning.

To have him tug her hair and call her Money.

And maybe, after the house grew quiet, he would kiss her again. A dangerous wish, she knew. But there it was.

"Here you are."

At the sound of Becca's voice, Penny's head came up sharply.

When she turned, Becca gave a little laugh before kneeling to release Archie from his leash. "I don't know where you were just now, but you look like a kid caught with her hand in the cookie jar."

"Sorry." Penny actually blushed and dropped to her knees to pet the dog, grateful for the chance to duck her head. "I was thinking about Sam and the others, and how they looked rounding up the herd."

"Isn't it an amazing sight?" Becca sighed. "Ben took me to the hills last fall to watch. But this year, with his position as sheriff, he couldn't take the time off." She chewed her lower lip. "I think he's feeling a little guilty about leaving all the ranch work to Sam. He's out in the barn right now with Otis. They're saddling up a couple of horses so they can ride out and join the others on the final leg of the roundup."

"That's nice. Does Ben miss the ranch chores?"

Becca nodded. "I know he does. But he's here often enough to get his fill of ranching when he needs a fix. The rest of the time I think he's so busy with his sheriff duties, he doesn't have time to think about it. But he has twinges of guilt about leaving it all for Sam and Mac."

Penny put a hand over Becca's. "Tell Ben not to worry. Otis told me Sam's in his glory up in the hills." She turned toward the cupboard. "Now. Let's get started. Those men are going to be starving by the time they get back here. Let's give them a feast to remember."

CHAPTER FOURTEEN

Okay." Becca followed Penny's lead. "Where do you need me to start?"

"I'm thinking comfort food. Roasted turkey, mashed potatoes, garden vegetables Otis picked and stored."

"All right." Becca pulled an apron from a drawer. "I'll handle the vegetables. Where are they?"

"Before that snowstorm, Otis picked his garden clean and stored them in crates of dirt down in the fruit cellar."

"Why in dirt?"

Seeing Becca's frown, Penny laughed. "It keeps them from getting dried up and puckered. They think they're still in the garden. You should be able to dig up carrots, beets, turnips, onions."

"Okay. I'm on it." Becca walked to the mudroom and pulled open the little trapdoor in the floor that revealed steps leading to a cellar below the house.

A short time later she returned with an armload of vegetables and proceeded to scrub them at the sink.

Archie settled down in his favorite spot beneath the table.

The two women worked in companionable silence until Becca casually remarked, "As hard as it was for Ben to walk away from the day to day life on this ranch, I think it would be impossible for Sam."

Penny paused in her work. "Otis said Sam is the most like Mac. A rancher to his core. He told me the minute Sam witnessed his first calving, he jumped right in and took to ranching like he was born to it." She glanced over. "You said you knew the three brothers when they were young. Were they as tough as Otis said, or was he exaggerating?"

Becca gave a short laugh. "If anything, they were worse than you can imagine. If one was threatened, then all three were threatened. I never saw them back away from a fight. But Ben..." She paused, and her voice took on a softness. "Ben was always my hero." She put a hand to her mouth. "In truth, he still is."

"That's sweet." Penny floured a cutting board before uncovering a dough ball and setting to work kneading it. "I can still remember my mother thinking my father hung the moon."

Becca put a hand to her heart. "Oh, what a wonderful memory to carry in your heart."

"Yeah. Theirs was a real love match. My dad was devastated when my mother died. He...changed. Fell into some bad habits. He lived a few more years, but I've always thought he lost the will to go on the day he buried my mother. After that, he just went through the motions of living."

"It had to be hard on you and your brothers to lose both your parents so young. I can't imagine being a teenager and raising three boys alone."

"My great-aunt Lucy saw to it I wasn't alone. Even when she became so crippled up with pain she couldn't lend a hand, it was a comfort having her with me."

"And a lot of extra work I bet."

Penny shook her head. "I didn't mind. I did what I had to. But now I doubt I did a very good job of it. At least with Curtis."

Becca crossed the room to wrap her arms around her friend. "Don't think like that, Penny. Your little brother will learn from his mistakes and make you proud. You'll see."

"Oh, Becca, I hope you're right." Penny took in a deep breath. "Now let's not dwell on anything unpleasant today. Let's get this feast started."

The two young women shared childhood memories and were soon laughing together as they stirred, chopped, peeled, and baked.

"Cooper was big for his age, and so good-looking." Penny turned from the stove with a smile. "He was only fifteen when a high school senior asked him to be her date for the prom. He was so proud, I didn't have the heart to tell him we couldn't afford it. So there I was, racing to our town's little thrift shop to find a suit and shirt and tie and proper dress shoes that would fit him. Then, just before she arrived to pick him up in her dad's car, I realized I'd forgotten a corsage. I ran to a neighbor's to ask if I could cut a couple of her roses. I taped them together and covered a wide rubber band with some old lace, and when Cooper placed it on her wrist, she nearly swooned and said it was the prettiest corsage she'd ever seen."

Becca put her hands on her hips. "I hope your little brother appreciated all you did for him."

"I don't know." Penny couldn't help giggling. "When he

got home that night, he said for the last hour of the dance he asked if she'd mind just sitting in the corner so he could hold her hand. When I asked why, he said the pants I'd bought him at the thrift shop split down the seat, and the only way he could hide what happened was to sit out the last dances."

"Oh, poor Cooper."

Becca and Penny were convulsed with laughter.

"Yeah. But he figured he got away with it because a week later the girl picked him up again in her father's car and took him to the movies."

"Young love..." Becca managed between giggles.

"Can even overcome the humiliation of ripped pants," Penny finished for her before the two young women nearly fell down they were laughing so hard.

Penny and Becca looked up at a sound that rolled through the house like thunder.

"That's the herd. They're coming." Becca caught Penny's hand. "Come on. If we hurry to the meadow behind the barn, we'll be able to watch them bring the cattle down."

The two young women untied their aprons and raced out the back door, leaving Archie barking frantically at being left behind.

Minutes later they stood watching from a perch on a tractor as Otis and Ben opened the gates of a narrow pathway. Becca explained that each cow had to pass through to be counted before being turned into a meadow divided into two sections with a temporary fence. One side was designated for those that would be sold, and the other for the rest of the herd that would winter in this sheltered area.

A convoy of cattle-hauling trucks was idling alongside the meadow. When the last cow had been tallied, the cowboys herded the cattle that had been sold into the vehicles that would take them away. The fence between the two meadows was removed, and the herd was able to spread out.

Their jobs done, the wranglers headed toward a corral, where they unsaddled their mounts and turned them loose.

Ben strolled up to wrap an arm around Becca's shoulders. "Another successful roundup. Another profitable year." He kissed her cheek. "I'm going over to join Dad and Sam. I'm thinking those tired wranglers are ready for a cold longneck and a hot meal."

"They'll get both," she said, turning to Penny.

The two women raced back to the house.

After washing up in the bunkhouse, the men gathered around the back porch, helping themselves to longnecks or bottles of soda or water in a tub of ice.

Penny and Becca carried out platters of sliced turkey, three kinds of salads and vegetables, bowls of mashed potatoes, and assorted baskets of breads, an apple pie, a cherry pie, and a chocolate layer cake mounded with whipped cream in the middle and rich buttercream frosting on top. Everything was placed on the big log table under a giant oak, and the men were soon piling their plates high with food.

A huge carafe of coffee stood at the end of the table, along with an assortment of mugs, cream, and sugar.

Midway through the meal Ben found Becca and leaned close. "Sorry, babe. I just got a call from town. We have to leave."

"Oh, Ben. I can't leave Penny to deal with all this alone."

Penny put a hand on her shoulder. "I'm so grateful for all your help, Becca. I couldn't have done it without you." She leaned close to press a kiss on her friend's cheek. "But don't worry about cleaning up. I'll be fine."

With handshakes all around, Ben fastened Archie's leash before taking Becca's hand and leading her to their truck.

Becca turned to wave as they left in a swirl of mud and melting snow.

After much talk and laughter, Penny glanced around. There wasn't a thing left on the table except empty plates.

Mac stepped out of the house, where he'd completed his payroll, and walked among the men, many of whom were good friends and neighbors, and handed out envelopes.

In a loud voice he called, "I know these weren't the best working conditions. Unseasonably cold. A ton of snow to navigate. But you did it. On behalf of all of us here at the Monroe ranch, we're beholden to all of you. We couldn't have accomplished this on such short notice without your hard work. We thank you."

The men were smiling as they tucked away their paychecks and shook hands with Mac, Sam, Otis, and Roscoe.

Several of the men took the time to thank Penny for the fine meals she'd provided.

Caught by surprise, she accepted their compliments. "I'm just glad I could do my small part."

"Not so small, ma'am," a bewhiskered wrangler said. "Your supper made the day's work seem a whole lot easier."

"And the nights," another chimed in. "There's nothing better than sleeping on a full stomach after a satisfying supper."

Seeing Sam watching and listening, she blushed clear to her toes before turning away to begin clearing the table.

Otis picked up the tub and tossed ice and water aside before setting it on the picnic table. "Just put all those dishes in here, Miss Penny, and I'll haul them inside."

"Oh, thank you, Otis." With a warm smile she filled the tub to the brim.

The old man lifted it and turned away.

Before he could start up the steps of the porch, Sam was there, taking the heavy burden from his hands. "You've done enough, Otis. I've got this."

Penny, trailing behind, watched as the old man gratefully relinquished his grip on the heavy tub.

She followed Sam up the steps and into the kitchen, where he carried the tub as easily as if it weighed nothing at all.

He set it on the counter beside the sink.

Instead of walking away, he turned on the taps and filled the sink with hot, soapy water.

"Sam, what are you doing?"

He glanced over. "I'll wash. You dry."

She was shaking her head. "You've been in the saddle for hours and..."

He put a finger to her lips. "It's the rule in Mackenzie Monroe's house. All members share the work equally."

"But all I did was cook. You've just spent a week in the hills in snow and cold, chasing after..."

She may as well have been talking to the air. Sam simply ignored her protest and began washing the dishes.

Penny pulled a clean towel from a drawer and began drying.

When the dishes were put away and the kitchen tidied, Sam drained the water and took the towel from Penny's hand, drying his hands before giving it back.

He leaned close and put a finger under her chin, tipping up her face.

For a moment she forgot to breathe as she clutched the towel to her chest. But instead of the expected kiss, he merely gave her one of those heart-stopping smiles. "I almost forgot. I smell like a trail bum."

She wrinkled her nose in mock horror. "It's a good thing there's still plenty of hot water."

He stepped back and headed toward the living room. "That's my cue to head upstairs to take the longest bath of my life." He paused to look back. "Want to scrub my back, Money?"

In reply she tossed the wet towel at him.

It landed with a thud at his feet.

"You're got a lousy aim, Money. Better work on that."

Laughing, he sauntered away.

CHAPTER FIFTEEN

With the wranglers gone, Otis and Roscoe were eager to retire to the bunkhouse to catch up on the gin rummy games they'd missed for the past week.

Finn and Zachariah had rolled up after dark and spent a few minutes bringing Mac up to date on what had transpired so far in the trial, before huddling in Zachariah's rooms to go over strategy for the next few days.

Mac had gone upstairs for a much-needed shower, only to find Sam nearly asleep in the tub. He'd sent Sam off to his room and had claimed the bathroom for himself.

Penny made herself a mug of hot chocolate and turned off the kitchen light. As she passed through the parlor, she was surprised to see Mac, freshly shaved and showered, sitting in the dark, his gaze fixed on the fire, which had burned low.

He looked up. "Is that coffee?"

She shook her head. "Hot chocolate. Would you like some?"

"I'd love some."

She handed him her cup and retreated to the kitchen for another. Minutes later she returned with a second steaming mug.

He indicated the rocking chair beside his. "Care to sit a minute, Penny? Or are you in a hurry to get to bed?"

"I'm too wired to sleep." She sat and sipped her chocolate. "This was my first glimpse of a roundup, and it was really something to see."

"Yeah." He sipped. "I've seen a lifetime of them. But every one is new."

"You have good neighbors."

"I do. I couldn't do all this without them." He looked over. "And without your help, too. If it hadn't been for your fine meals, we'd have been in trouble, Penny."

"I'm sure Otis could have come up with something."

Mac shook his head. "Don't minimize what you did. This roundup wouldn't have been nearly so successful without your outstanding meals."

"I'm glad I could help." She took a swallow of the sweet chocolate. "And I'm so grateful for this job. You don't know what it means to me."

"Then we've helped each other. And that's a good thing."

She saw the way he continued staring into the embers. "Have you heard from Mary Pat?"

"Not a word."

She tried to think of something uplifting to say, but her mind drew a blank. This weather, always so unpredictable, could prove to be a blessing or a curse. A man like Mackenzie Monroe, born here in Montana, would know all too well the pitfalls of driving through the wilderness in a fierce snowstorm.

Mac broke the silence. "Tell me about your home in Dennison."

She smiled. "We lived just outside of town on a little bit of land my mother's father left her. We weren't ranchers and we weren't townies. We were just…" She shrugged. "Getting by in the middle of nowhere. The house was tiny. My dad built it when he and my mom first married. The original house was just a bedroom, a bathroom, and a big kitchen. Then, as babies started coming, Dad added a second bedroom and bathroom for me, and finally a big dorm room upstairs for my three brothers."

"That's a lot of mouths to feed."

She sighed. "Dad did his best. He started out wanting to be a carpenter. But with a family, he had to take whatever work he could get. Mostly he worked for ranchers, doing whatever was needed. Sometimes he was gone for weeks at a time. But it paid the bills. When my mom died, he…" She struggled for words. "He was sad a lot. Some days he just wouldn't get out of bed." She set aside her unfinished chocolate. "At first, after my dad died, I was angry. Angry that he died, leaving us alone. Angry that I had three little brothers who needed me, whether I was up to the job or not. Angry that it all fell on my shoulders."

"That's a lot of responsibility for someone in her teens."

"I couldn't have done it without my great-aunt. She left the comfort of a retirement home to live with us so the state wouldn't break up the family and send us into foster care. She knew we would be separated without an adult present in the home."

"Having a frail woman had to require a lot of extra work for you."

She shrugged. "Some. In no time she was in a wheelchair. But she sacrificed her comfort for us. And that's what I had to come to terms with. Yes, I was sixteen and caring for three brothers and an elderly woman. But my brothers and I were healthy. My dad left us with debt, but the house had no mortgage, so all I had to worry about was staying current with taxes and insurance, and paying off the debt. Eventually I had to let the insurance lapse, and I just concentrated on saving enough to pay the taxes. And while my brothers were in school, and Aunt Lucy was sleeping, I was free to study online. So, despite the challenges, it was all good."

Mac gave her a gentle smile. "Do you always look for the silver lining?"

She chuckled. "How else can I have hope?"

He sat back. "You remind me a lot of Mary Pat. She's the most positive woman I know."

"I'll take that as a compliment." Penny glanced at the photo on the mantel of a teenaged girl and a little boy. "Is that boy you?"

He nodded. "And the girl is my sister, Ellen."

"Where does she live?"

"She's dead." Mac stared down at the cup in his hands. "When Ellen was sixteen, she ran off with Shepherd Strump, a cowboy my father had hired as a wrangler."

"So young. How did your parents react?"

"My mother was shocked and heartbroken. To say my father was furious would be an understatement. He was breathing fire and brimstone when he first heard the news."

"Did they try to find her?"

"Not at first. I think they both believed she'd realize her mistake and come home. When she didn't, it caused a rift between my parents, and my father disowned Ellen. When he died, my mother wrote a new will and decreed that, upon her death, the southern portion of our land would be set aside for Ellen or her heirs."

"Did any come forward?"

He frowned. "Not long after my mother died, an official

document arrived from the county seat, declaring that southern portion adjoining my ranch were now claimed by Shepherd Strump, the surviving husband of the late Ellen."

"He never notified her family of her death before that?"

Mac gave a shake of his head. "That's what hurt the most. That he couldn't even bother to let us know, but was quick to claim what was hers."

"Couldn't you contest it in court?"

He shrugged. "Why would I want to go against my mother's wishes?"

"But that could be part of your legacy. Isn't the land valuable?"

"A lot more valuable than the portion of the land we're on here. That southern parcel is some of the finest grazing land around. It's considered prime cattle country." He turned to stare into the fire. "And there it sits, vacant and unused, and claimed by a ghost nobody has ever seen."

"I'm sorry, Mac. I wish there was something you could do to change things."

"There's nothing to be done about it."

Hearing the note of sadness in his voice, she got to her feet. "Can I get you anything before I go up to bed?"

He seemed distracted. "Nothing, thanks. Good night, Penny."

"Good night."

As she made her way up the stairs, she heard his long, deep sigh of distress. Even after all these years, it seemed, the loss of his sister and the division in his family caused Mac unresolved pain.

In her room upstairs, Penny slipped out of her jeans and shirt and pulled on an oversize T-shirt before making her way to the bathroom to get ready for bed.

Minutes later, face scrubbed, teeth cleaned, her hair brushed, she returned to the bedroom and paused by the window. The pastures were dark with cattle. Snowflakes drifted past her line of vision.

Winter had come early to this part of Montana.

Though she ought to be tired, she felt a strange sense of exhilaration. She crossed her arms over her chest and thought about all she'd seen in the past week. Though the roundup was hard work for the wranglers, in her eyes it had been like a dream. That endless sea of cattle, and the men on horseback herding them across hills white with snow, had made such a pretty picture.

And then there was Sam.

He seemed to be everywhere at once. Chasing errant cows, coming to the aid of a fellow cowboy, racing headlong across a stream to keep the cattle moving. And always with that dangerous gleam in his eye and that endearing grin that did such strange things to her heart.

She looked up at a light tap on her door. When she opened the door, the object of her thoughts was standing there, leaning a hip against the doorway, looking at her with a wolfish smile.

"I saw your light and figured you were still awake."

He was naked to the waist, his jeans unfastened and riding low on his hips, as though hastily thrown on. His hair was mussed, his eyes heavy-lidded from sleep.

"Your dad said he found you asleep in the tub."

He laughed. "Yeah. I must be losing my touch. There was a time when I could stay awake all night and not even give a thought to sleeping."

"You need to go to bed. You should listen to your body."

"My thoughts exactly." He closed the door behind him and started toward her. "I do believe in listening to my body.

It's telling me I shouldn't waste time on any more sleep tonight when there are better things to do."

She started to laugh until she caught sight of the fierce look on his face. "Sam…"

"Shhh." He gathered her close and covered her mouth with his.

The purely sexual jolt that shot through them had them both sighing and taking the kiss deeper.

"Now that's what I'm talking about." He spoke the words against her mouth. "Oh, Money, I've been thinking about this for days."

He backed her up until she was pressed to the wall. Her arms were around his waist, her fingers tingling from contact with his bare, heated flesh.

"Mmm, you taste even better than your cooking." His voice was a growl of pure pleasure as he ran heated kisses over her upturned face. And all the while his hands moved along her back, drawing her ever closer, until she could feel the pounding of his heart inside her chest.

"I like what you wear to bed." His gaze strayed to the thin material covering her breasts.

He dipped his head and ran nibbling kisses down her throat.

Penny absorbed the shock waves all the way down her spine to her toes.

Her breathing labored, her heart racing, she could barely speak. "Sam…"

He was beyond hearing as he continued assaulting all her senses, his hands moving sensuously along her back, up her sides, while his mouth, that hot, clever mouth, drove her half-mad with need.

"Come to bed with me, Penny." The words were torn from his lips.

"Sam, I don't think..."

"Don't think. Just go with your feelings." He took her hand and began leading her toward the bed.

Penny struggled to get her bearings. He had her so hot, her mind so clouded with passion, it was impossible to think. She wanted what he wanted. But a voice in her head was warning her that it was the wrong time, the wrong place. She knew so little about this man. She was an employee, for heaven's sake. And she was here at the invitation of his father.

His father. Probably asleep by now, just down the hall.

"Sam, wait. This isn't right. I—"

Her head came up at the sound of loud knocking on the door downstairs.

Hearing it, Sam glanced toward her bedroom door, while keeping his hands at her shoulders.

He turned back and drew her close, whispering against her mouth, "Let's just ignore that."

She drew slightly away. "But it's late. Everyone's asleep. You need to go, Sam. It could be an emergency. Otis or Roscoe or..."

He took in a long, deep breath and pressed his forehead to hers. "Money, I feel like the entire universe is against me. How else to explain this lousy timing?"

Despite the heat of passion, she found herself laughing. "Whatever the reason, I've just been saved by the bell. Or should I say by the door?"

"Saved? Woman, this little interruption has just robbed us both of paradise. Don't move. I'll be back." He brushed a quick, hard kiss over her mouth before striding toward her door, just as another, louder knock sounded downstairs.

When he was gone, Penny sat down weakly on the edge of her mattress, aware that her legs were trembling.

Another minute and she would have been lost.

She pressed her hands to her hot cheeks.

Or maybe she would have been found. She no longer knew. No longer felt like fighting these feelings.

It was impossible to listen to her brain when she was around Sam. Whenever he touched her, kissed her, she lost all common sense.

She closed her eyes and imagined what it would be like to give in to the feelings he aroused in her.

He'd called it paradise. Her blood heated at the very thought of lying with him.

Hearing voices coming up the stairs, she got to her feet and hurried across the room to peer out her door at their nighttime visitor.

"Mary Pat." The name came out in a rush of joy. "Oh, we've all been worried about you."

Just then Mac's bedroom door was thrown open and he stepped out, barefoot, his jeans unsnapped, slipping his arms into a plaid shirt.

He stopped and stared, before a wide smile touched all his haggard features with light.

Mary Pat paused to give Penny a warm embrace. "Oh, it's so good to be back."

She glanced beyond Penny to the man who was watching in silence. "I heard I caused you all to worry. I'm sorry about that. I'm here now, all safe and sound."

When Mac remained perfectly still, she turned toward the empty guest room. "If I don't get into that bed soon, I'll fall asleep right here on the floor. I've been driving for hours just to make it back."

Mac found his voice and hurried forward. "I'll get you some clean linens."

As the two of them walked past, Penny looked up to see

Sam standing at the head of the stairs, watching her with a smoldering look.

She took in a deep breath before calling softly, "It's late. Good night, Sam. See you in the morning."

"Yeah." He winked. "I guess I'll take comfort in the fact that there's always tomorrow."

Penny watched him make his way to his room at the other end of the hallway.

She closed her door and crossed the room. Instead of slipping into bed, she paused at the window and drew her arms around herself. With her eyes closed, she could still taste him. Dark and dangerous and...and sexy enough to make her forget every rule she'd ever set for herself.

As a novice teacher, she'd promised herself that she would adhere to higher standards than others.

As a woman, she now realized this dangerous bad boy made all her promises seem silly and useless, in light of everything he offered.

CHAPTER SIXTEEN

With morning chores behind them, the family gathered around the kitchen table, eager to hear the details of Mary Pat's latest adventure.

Penny was aware of Sam, sleeves rolled above his elbows, his hair still damp, watching her. When he caught her eye, he winked. There it was again. That quick, unnerving tingle in the pit of her stomach.

"So." Mac tipped up his mug of coffee and drank. "How many ranches were you able to visit this time?"

"Only half a dozen." Mary Pat accepted a plate of eggs scrambled with grilled onions and peppers and topped with melted cheese, and gave a sigh of pleasure. "Penny, I can't tell you how wonderful this is. The thought of your incredible cooking kept me going the last endless, snow-covered miles."

"Then I'm happy to oblige." Penny set a basket of freshly baked cinnamon biscuits in the middle of the table and blushed when Sam winked.

Breakfast had become a festive affair, now that the worries over Mary Pat's safety had been put to rest.

Mac's relief was palpable. He seemed more relaxed than ever as Mary Pat began regaling them with funny stories about her latest venture into the wilderness.

"On the day of the storm I phoned ahead to the Matthews ranch, knowing Bert and Ivy Matthews would probably lose power before the storm ended. I told them I was headed their way, and if I didn't make it by suppertime, they should send one of their boys out on a snowmobile to find me."

"Good thinking," Roscoe muttered. "Send out the troops."

Mac grinned. "She's a smart woman. Always has a plan B."

Penny glanced from the stove to see the look on Mac's face. Now that Mary Pat was back safely, he had already forgotten his earlier fears for her. He looked...She studied him a moment. He looked proud and content.

Or like a man who'd just found a pot of gold at the end of a rainbow.

The thought left her slightly stunned, before she started grinning.

"How are Bert and Ivy holding up?" Mac asked casually.

"As well as two old folks who are about to celebrate sixty-five years of marriage. They're amazing. And still so much in love. Two of their eight sons were staying there during the storm, just to make sure their parents were safe."

"That's so sweet." Penny set down a platter of thick ham slices.

"They all dote on their parents." Mary Pat helped herself to ham before holding out the platter to Mac while he stabbed at a slice. "I stayed there until noon the next day, before driving to the Merriweather ranch. Tim and Cora were so grouchy, I only stayed the night and beat a hasty retreat in the morning."

Sam chuckled. "I guess those two just turned the old saying on its head."

When the others looked at him he added, "They're not getting better. Just older."

That had everyone laughing.

Mary Pat nodded. "You got that right, Sam. Poor things. They've spent a lifetime bickering. And maybe," she added, "that's their only way of communicating."

"Or avoiding communicating," Sam put in.

Mary Pat laughed. "After the Merriweather place I made it as far as the Boone ranch in the foothills. They had their daughter-in-law Grace with them, and her new baby, Madeline. Grace's husband is in Granger for a month, helping out his uncle Ned, who suffered a heart attack. So Tommy suggested I leave my van at their place and visit the higher elevations on one of his extra snowmobiles."

"I'm glad Tommy Boone had the brain," Mac muttered.

"I heard that." Mary Pat playfully smacked his arm, while the others around the table laughed. "Actually, I had intended to ask Tommy for the use of one of his snowmobiles, if he hadn't offered it first."

"Like I said, a smart woman." Looking mellow, Mac sat back with a contented smile.

Mary Pat's voice softened. "I'm glad I made it through the hills and up to old Hinkle Carstairs's ranch. Hinkle suffered a stroke a few months ago, and his daughter moved in to take care of him. She's doing a good job, but it's taking a toll on her. But it's also brought the two of them closer than ever. For fun and therapy, knowing how competitive he is, she has him playing checkers every night after supper, since it improves both his eye-hand coordination and his mental faculties. Hinkle is always so proud when he can beat her."

She sighed. "Do you have any idea how many good people I'm privileged to meet?"

Mac turned to her. "Do those good people have any idea how lucky they are to have you crossing the county on their behalf? In a Montana snowstorm?"

Mary Pat brushed aside the compliment and turned to Finn. "Enough about my adventures. I want to hear about the trial that I'm told has been keeping you and Zachariah in town for the past week."

Mac stepped out the back door and lifted a hand to shade the sun from his eyes. "I'm thinking this might be a good time to head up to the high country and winterize the range shack while this weather holds."

Sam paused beside him. "I'll go. The last thing you need is another day away from the ranch. Besides, I heard Mary Pat asking Penny to let her take over kitchen duties tonight. I think she missed cooking and is planning a special supper to celebrate her return. I'm not going to let you miss that."

"So, if you're running late, you'll miss it instead?"

"Better me than you, Dad."

While they were talking, Otis drove up in one of the ranch trucks and parked it beside the porch.

When he stepped out, he spotted Mac and Sam. "I promised to drive Miss Penny up to the range shack. We need to bring down all the supplies we left behind, and clean up any mess before winter sets in."

Sam shook his head. "No sense both of us driving up there. Since I'm heading up anyway, I'll take Penny with me.

She can do whatever she needs to do while I winterize the cabin and stock it with logs."

Mac nodded his approval. "Good thinking, Sam. Now Otis and I can give Roscoe a hand patching the barn roof."

Otis handed over the keys. "Suits me. I've had enough of snow-covered mountain trails to last me until next year."

As he and Mac started toward the barn, Penny bounded down the porch steps.

Seeing Sam, she paused. "I thought Otis was driving me to the cabin."

"Change of plans. He's giving Dad a hand with the barn roof. So I'm driving you." He took the bucket filled with rags and cleaning supplies from her hands. "I'll stow these for you."

"Thanks. I've got bread and cheese and milk. Otis was hoping for grilled cheese sandwiches for lunch."

"Suits me fine." As Sam opened the passenger door, she stepped past him and tossed her parka and food in the backseat before climbing in.

Sam rounded the hood and placed the bucket in the back before settling into the driver's side.

As the ranch truck moved slowly along a muddy path behind the barn, Otis stared after them and paused to rub his shoulder.

He turned to Mac. "More snow coming."

Mac arched a brow and glanced skyward, seeing the blazing sunlight, melting the snow on the barn roof and turning the pastures to mud. "I figured we were in for a thaw. I didn't hear about any more snow on this morning's weather report."

"Maybe not." The old man chuckled. "But I don't need a

weatherperson to tell me what these old bones already know. Snow's coming."

"Oh, look at those glorious trees." Penny couldn't seem to get enough of the brilliant autumn colors, turning her head from one side to the other as the truck climbed through a heavily forested area. "With all the snow that fell earlier, I never got a chance to really see them. But now that it's melting, they're picture-perfect."

"So are you." He shot her an admiring glance that had her cheeks flaming.

Her smile faded. "Don't do that."

"Do what?"

When he looked over, she crossed her arms over her chest. "Compliments are so easy for you, aren't they?"

"They are when I mean them."

"Sam, I'm trying to stay grounded. How can you say I'm picture-perfect when I'm wearing my oldest pair of jeans and a faded work shirt? I'm dressed for drudge work up in the hills, not for some fancy fashion shoot."

"And you think that somehow makes you less beautiful in my eyes?"

"Beautiful? Are you blind?"

"I've never seen things more clearly. Money, if you could see yourself the way I see you, you'd understand why I can't stop staring at you."

"There you go. You're doing it again."

"You bet I am. And I'm going to keep on telling you how beautiful you are until you believe me."

His words, spoken so seriously, had her falling silent.

"I see I finally got your attention." He chuckled and floored the accelerator, causing Penny to grab the door handle and hold on for dear life, while muttering under her breath about the perils of riding with a smug, reckless cowboy. A cowboy who made her heart sing.

They drove in an upward, circuitous route past miles of trees in every imaginable shade of red, orange, and yellow.

When they reached the high country, the hills were shrouded in dark, ominous clouds.

Sam brought the truck to a halt beside the range shack. As he stepped out, he sank to his ankles in mud.

After a few muttered curses he rounded the front of the vehicle and opened Penny's door. Before she could step out, he lifted her in his arms.

She tried to push away. "What're you doing?"

"Saving you from stepping into what I just stepped into."

She looked down. "Oh." Seeing the way his boots sank deep with each step, she couldn't help chuckling at the frown that marred his usually cheerful face. "Sorry about your bad luck, cowboy."

"Uh-huh." When he saw the mischievous gleam in her eyes, his smile returned. "And if you don't stop wiggling, I may just drop you right here."

"You're too much of a gentleman."

"Now that's one thing I've never been called."

Penny bit back her smile before wrapping her arms around his neck. "Thanks for saving me from the mud."

He turned his head slightly, his mouth skimming hers. She jerked back and shot him a dirty look. "And here I thought you were just being a gentleman."

"I warned you, Money. Nobody's ever accused me of that." He carried her to the long front porch that ran the length of the cabin before setting her on her feet. "But you can't blame a guy for trying to enjoy a little reward for a good deed."

Without waiting for the sharp retort that was on her tongue, he turned away with a wicked grin and returned a minute later with the cleaning bucket.

She took it from his hands without a word.

After unlocking the door and holding it open for her, he circled the cabin and disappeared inside a small storage shed. Within minutes he returned with several sheets of plywood and proceeded to set them down to form a dry pathway from the porch to the truck.

When he was finished, he sat on the step and pried off his muddy boots before stepping inside.

Penny was standing in the small galley kitchen unloading her cleaning supplies.

"How can you hope to clean when it's so cold in here I can see my breath?" Sam crossed the room and set a log and kindling on the grate.

Minutes later he'd coaxed a thin flame that soon grew into a cozy fire. Satisfied that the little shack would soon be warm, he went outside to begin his chores.

Penny filled a huge pot with water and set it on the grate that covered the fire. While she waited for it to heat, she set about scrubbing the scarred wooden table and chairs, the long kitchen counter, and finally the floor, littered with muddy boot prints from the crew of wranglers. Then she attacked the small bathroom with the same vengeance, until it sparkled.

Once the water came to a boil she carried it to the small sink. Using a long-handled scrub brush and gritty cleanser, she soon had the serving dishes and pots and pans looking like new.

Nesting them one inside another, she picked up an armload and nudged the cabin door open. As she began storing them in the back of the truck, she found herself thankful that Sam had thought to cover the mud with plywood, providing a dry path over the mud.

Sam.

Earlier she'd heard him hammering up on the roof, where he'd apparently replaced some of the shingles. Now she heard the sound of an ax biting into wood and looked over to see him chopping firewood.

Despite the fact that snow had begun falling, he'd stripped off his parka and rolled up the sleeves of his plaid shirt before tackling such a daunting chore.

She stood transfixed, watching as he lifted the ax high over his head before bringing it down to bite cleanly through a log.

The wood splintered into several pieces, and he bent to stack them neatly alongside the others at the rear of the cabin, before positioning another log and repeating the process.

Penny didn't know how long she stood there, watching the play of muscles along his arms.

As the ax landed again and again, she shivered at a sudden thought: he was magnificent. His body, sculpted from years of ranch chores, was so perfect, she had a sudden yearning that left her staggered. A yearning she'd been struggling to deny since she'd first met him. A hunger to be held in those arms and kissed until she was breathless.

At that moment he bent to pick up the fallen logs and caught sight of her.

"Hey, Money. Want to give it a try?"

"Not on your life. If I tried to do what you're doing, my arms would fall off."

He drove the ax into a log before walking toward her. "Now that's something I wouldn't like."

"Seeing my arms fall off?"

"Yeah." He gave her a dangerous smile. "Such pretty arms. They're not made for chopping logs. These arms are made for holding." He surprised her by gathering her against him. "Like this."

"Sam…" Caught by surprise, she remained perfectly still.

"Relax, Money. It's just a hug."

"I have work…"

"Me, too. And I'm good at my work. But right now, I feel like playing."

As he lowered his face to her, she turned away and his mouth grazed her ear.

Laughing, he caught her chin. "What's the matter? Afraid of a little kiss?"

"Yes. No. Of course not. But we came here to work."

"All work and no play is a real drag. Do you ever just relax and have fun, Money?"

"I've never had time for fun."

"That's just not right." His voice lowered. "I see it as my duty to show you how to play."

"Oh, I'm sure that's something you're an expert on. Drinking, gambling, playing."

"And kissing a pretty girl. Don't forget that. It's the most important game of all."

"Oh, you."

His smile grew, and he drew her close.

Against her ear he whispered, "All right. I'll let you get back to your work. For now. But before the day is over, you're going to ask me if we can play."

"Don't hold your breath."

As she turned away, she could hear his low rumble of laughter. "I'll bet you a hundred dollars on it."

She stopped and turned her head. "If I were a gambler,

which I'm not, that would be an easy bet for me to win. There's no way I'm ever going to ask you if we can play."

"You're on, Money."

"I told you. I don't believe in—"

"I know. Anything that's fun." His laughter followed her as she stalked to the door of the cabin.

CHAPTER SEVENTEEN

Penny looked up when the cabin door opened and Sam trudged in carrying an armload of firewood. His parka and hair were dusted with snow.

She saw more flakes on his back as he knelt and fed wood to the dying fire.

She gaped at the curtain of snow falling outside the open doorway. As she hurried across the room to close the door against the blast of cold air, she was even more surprised to see that the ground was no longer visible under a thick blanket of white. The plywood he'd set down as a path to the truck was completely obliterated.

"This looks bad. Are we going to be able to make it back down the mountain?"

"I doubt it." Sam looked over. "It's been howling for hours."

"Hours?" She paused. "I guess I lost track of time."

He stood and wiped his hands down his pants. "Easy to

do when you're working." He looked around admiringly. "I don't think I've ever seen this old cabin so clean."

She hauled a bulging laundry bag toward the door. "I found clean bed linens in a storage closet, so I figured I'd strip all the bunks and make them up while I was here. That way they're fresh whenever the next wrangler has need of shelter."

He took the laundry from her hands. "I'll store this in the back of the truck."

As he reached for it, she became acutely aware of the heat from his body and felt a flush all the way to her toes.

From the way he was studying her, she was sure he could see her discomfort. She'd never been any good at hiding her feelings.

He was smiling as he strolled out the door and when he returned. He hung his parka on a hook beside the door. When he turned, he was adjusting the rolled-up sleeves of his flannel shirt.

Penny couldn't seem to look away.

"The snow's coming harder now. I figure the trail will be slick and dangerous. That is, if we can even find it. Are you going to be okay if we have to spend the night here?"

"Do I have a choice?"

"Now that you've asked..." He winked. "We don't have a prayer of getting through this. Looks like you're stuck spending the night with me, Miss Money."

She crossed her arms over her chest, tapping her foot as she considered the implications. She could make a fuss and insist on returning to the ranch. She was pretty certain Sam would try to accommodate her. But if her insistence should cause an accident, she would never be able to forgive herself. Still, the thought of spending the night alone with Sam had her nerves fluttering.

His words broke into her musings. "I don't know about you, but I'm starving."

"Why am I not surprised? A guy and his stomach. The only thing that matters more to him is…" Her face flamed at what she'd almost said.

His smile widened, and she braced herself for the teasing words she knew would follow.

"Why, shame on you, Miss Money. I'm shocked, I tell you. Shocked and appalled that a prim and proper teacher like you should even know about such things."

"I told you. I have—"

"Brothers. And that makes you an expert on men."

His silly grin had her cheeks flaming. She forced herself to walk to the kitchen and open a cupboard door. "I noticed you have these cupboards stocked with boxes and cans of food."

"Emergency supplies. We never know when we could be stranded up here. Even when the lowlands are sunny and bright, a blizzard can happen in these hills in early spring and even in late summer."

"Thank heaven for emergency supplies." At a glance her hopes lifted. At least there was plenty of food, and that was something she could be comfortable discussing. "I guess I could open a can of soup."

Sam nodded. "Whatever you'd like. Just so it's hot, and there's plenty of it."

He stirred the ashes and added another log while Penny rummaged through the cupboards.

She carried a pan to the fireplace and set it on the heating rack. In no time it was steaming hot. She replaced that pan with a flat griddle, and carefully turned sandwiches as they browned and the thick slabs of gooey cheese melted and sizzled.

A short time later she carried a tray to a low table Sam had moved in front of the fireplace with a wooden high-backed bench positioned alongside it, softened with a plaid afghan.

"Life doesn't get much better." Sam eyed the food. "Tomato soup and grilled cheese sandwiches."

"Actually, grilled ham and cheese." She nodded toward the kitchen. "I found a canned ham and thought, after all that wood chopping, you've probably worked up a mean appetite."

"You got that right." He dug in, sighing from time to time as he devoured the meal.

She started to get up. "I'll make more."

"No." He put a hand on her arm. "That was just right." He sat back, staring into the flames. "You're amazing, Money."

"Another compliment? What's it about this time? That my soup and sandwiches could win prizes over any made by top chefs? Or maybe they're simply the best in the entire universe."

"Oh, I wouldn't go that far." He couldn't stop the smile that split his lips. "I was just going to say it can't be easy for you to cook over a fire, but you did it like you were born to it."

She laughed. "Maybe I haven't had to cook over an open fire, but I was definitely born to work."

"Yeah." He reached over and squeezed her hand. "I admire that."

She arched a brow. To hide her pleasure, she adopted a trace of sarcasm. "And yet another compliment from the smooth and oh-so-sexy cowboy."

"Sexy?" He latched on to the single word. "You surprise me. I thought mean Miss Money didn't even think about such things."

"Did I say sexy? I meant stinky. I'm sure you're a little ripe from all that wood you chopped."

"I'll let you be the judge of that." He stood and caught her hand, dragging her to her feet. As he teasingly wrapped his arms around her, he pressed her face to his neck. "Go ahead, little missy. Inhale nice and deep, and let this stinky old cowboy know what you think."

She couldn't help laughing at his silliness.

Hearing it, Sam joined in.

But in the blink of an eye their laughter died.

Penny was aware of the press of his big hand at the back of her head, his fingers tangling in her hair. Aware, too, that she'd already tasted the salt of his skin. A taste that lingered on her lips.

The rush of heat was instantaneous. A pulse of need began deep in her core, and without a thought to what she was doing, her arms were around his waist, and her lips were moving along his throat.

It took her a moment to realize that he'd gone completely still.

She lifted her head to steal a glance at his face.

The look in his eyes was so hot, so fierce, she started to step back.

His arms tightened around her, holding her close.

His voice was little more than a strained whisper. "I hope you aren't going to ask me to pretend this didn't just happen."

"I…" When her voice wavered, she lifted her chin. "No. I won't try to hide from it."

"That's you, Money. Honest, even if it kills you. Right?"

She held her ground.

"A word of warning. I may look strong, but I'm just a man. A man who's been on the brink of something…

something I can't define since you first came into my life, but it feels a lot like madness. You should know that I'm barely holding on. So either you walk away right now, or…" He drew her fractionally closer, until she could feel him in every pore. "We let this happen."

She swallowed before whispering, "And you need to know I'm not what I pretend to be. I'm not frigid, or always in charge. And right now I'm just a woman. A woman, thanks to you, who's on fire. If you try to walk away, I may have to resort to begging."

In the silence that followed, he let out a long, deep sigh and rested his forehead on hers. "Thank heaven for answered prayers."

"I should explain something." She avoided his eyes. "I'm not very good at this. The few times…"

"Shhh." He framed her face with his hands and pressed soft, butterfly kisses over her forehead, her cheeks, the tip of her nose. When she pursed her mouth, a slow smile curved his lips and, unable to resist teasing, he kissed her chin instead.

"Oh you." Laughing, she brushed her mouth over his.

His laughter died as he took the kiss deeper, then deeper still, until they were both struggling for air.

Suddenly he lifted his head and gave her a smoldering look before reaching a hand to the buttons of her shirt. When she tried to help him, he took her hands in his. "No. We've fought this long enough. Let me indulge my fantasies. One of them is to undress you."

Without a word he slid the shirt from her shoulders and let it drop to the floor at their feet. Beneath the rough shirt she wore a simple white cotton bra. With quick movements he unhooked it and tossed it aside.

His eyes narrowed. "You're so beautiful."

She smiled. "I don't care if you've said that a thousand times before. I don't care if you mean it or not. Right now, I feel beautiful."

He lifted her face and forced her to meet his steady gaze. "Money, trust me. Those aren't just words. And I don't toss them around casually. You're the most beautiful, the most amazing woman I've ever known." He ran his hands down the soft column of her neck, across her shoulders, all the while staring into her eyes.

Without warning he scooped her up and carried her across the room to a bunk. He laid her down with a tenderness she'd never known.

Seeing the way she trembled, he surprised her yet again. Instead of hot, passionate kisses, he held his own needs at bay as he pleasured her with long, slow kisses, soft as snowflakes, and featherlight touches.

As she relaxed in his arms, he showed her a side of him she would have never expected. A careful, tender lover.

With great care he finished undressing her, before tossing aside his own clothes.

When they were lying flesh to flesh, he ran a hand down her arm, then up again, his rough fingers caressing the softness of her arms, her face, tracing the curve of her eyebrow, the slope of her cheek.

At first she lay very still, absorbing his gentle touch in every pore of her body. But as he continued running nibbling kisses over her face, her throat, her shoulder, need rose within her and she found herself wanting to do the same with him.

Tentatively she reached her hand to his shoulder, feeling those corded muscles she'd admired.

"You have such an amazing body, Sam. You're so strong."

"And you're so small and slim. So perfect. At first, I

thought you were fragile. But now that I know you, I see such strength in you." He traced the outline of her mouth with his tongue before kissing her. Against her mouth he whispered, "I promise you, I won't hurt you."

She blinked. "Even if they're just words, I love hearing you say them."

"What will it take for you to believe me?"

She shook her head. "It just seems so easy for you to say them. But I don't need to hear the words."

"I need to say them." He leaned up on one elbow and ran soft wet kisses down her throat. "I've watched you work until most women would drop from exhaustion. But not you. What drives you?"

She gave a dreamy smile. "Survival, I suppose."

"I'd know a thing or two about that." He drew her close and covered her mouth in a long, slow, lazy kiss until she wrapped her arms around him, giving herself up to the pleasure.

Aware of the subtle change in her, he traced the slope of her shoulder with his mouth and heard her sigh.

Growing bolder, she ran her hands up his back, down his arms, across his chest.

When he did the same, he felt the sudden jolt that shot through her system, alerting him to the deepening of her arousal. He thrilled to the quick, shuddering change in her heartbeat. He lay a hand over the spot, then followed with his mouth.

Her entire body arched upward as his lips and fingertips teased her, moving over her at will.

"Sam..."

"Trust me, Money."

And she did. As his lips and fingertips continued their ministrations, his name was torn from her. Her body trembled and her breath shuddered when she suddenly reached the first shocking peak.

Though he was half mad with need, he was determined to hold back and treat her with the care she deserved.

With a patience he'd never known before, he gave her no chance to recover as he took her even higher.

Now free of all those self-imposed restraints, he watched her lose herself in the pure pleasure of the moment.

This was how he'd imagined her. Leaving all the cares of her world behind. Wild with need. Joyful. Without a thought except this moment, this place, this passion they were sharing.

When at last he entered her, he fought to be gentle. But as she opened to him, and began to move with him, he forgot everything except the bright, blinding need for her.

The storm raging outside their little cabin was forgotten. All that mattered was the storm raging inside them. A storm that was all fire and need, heating their blood, their very core, until they were consumed by it.

Heartbeats thundering, breathing labored, they moved together, climbed together, until at last they reached a shuddering, shattering, all-consuming climax.

"Money." When Sam could find his voice, he murmured her nickname against the soft, damp flesh of her throat.

"Mmm?"

They lay, wrapped around one another, their bodies slick, their heartbeats slowly beginning to return to normal.

"I thought you said you were no good at this."

She touched a hand to his cheek. "I'm not...I wasn't... It's never been like this before. I guess...I guess you're a good teacher."

He laughed. He couldn't remember the last time his heart

felt this light. As though he'd spent a lifetime crossing a barren desert, only to come upon an oasis paradise, complete with a banquet of delights and a delectable goddess to feed his every need.

"You're incredible."

"You're not bad yourself, cowboy."

"I believe, in the heat of passion, you said I was sexy."

She sighed. "I may have slipped and said something like that."

"Uh-huh." He caught her hand and pressed a kiss to the palm. "I know you don't trust my compliments, but I think you're sexy as hell."

"I've been called a drudge and a bossy tyrant. Never sexy."

"You've been hanging with the wrong crowd. Believe me, I know sexy when I see it." He leaned up on one elbow and pressed kisses down her neck, across her shoulder. "Since we have all the time in the world, there are so many things I want to show you. To share with you."

"I'm sure you'll need a little more time before you can...show me more."

"Want to bet?" He gave her a lazy grin. "You already owe me a hundred dollars. Want to go for two hundred?"

"I owe you?"

"I bet you that you'd be asking to play. And you did."

"I told you I don't hold with gambling."

"So. You're back to being serious and somber." He laughed and dragged her on top of him.

Her hair spilled around him, tickling his chest. With a laugh of pure delight he dug his fingers into the silken strands and drew her face down to rain kisses over her pouting lips.

"Money, stick with me and in no time I'll have you not

only gambling, but doing all kinds of fun things you've never even imagined."

"Fun things?" Despite her best intentions, she found herself giggling. "Aren't you just a little worried about the work we're missing?"

His lips curved in one of those dangerous smiles that had a way of tugging at her heart. "We're trapped in the mountains in a blizzard. The trails are slick and hazardous. We have no choice but to hang out here and find ways to fill the hours."

As she arched her eyebrow, he wiggled his brows in return, like a mock villain. Suddenly, he rolled them both until he was looming over her. "I'm betting we'll find a hundred ways to amuse ourselves."

She put a hand on his chest, holding him at bay. "If I didn't know better, I'd think you ordered this storm just so you could win a bet."

"Maybe I did." He shot her a smug look before running hot butterfly kisses along her throat.

He paused and stared into her eyes, seeing the dazed expression in them. "Admit it. You're starting to believe in me, aren't you?"

"I hope I won't regret this in the morn—"

His hot, hungry kiss stopped her.

And then there were no words as they lost themselves in a storm of their own making.

CHAPTER EIGHTEEN

In the midnight hour Penny lay in the warmth of Sam's arms, feeling thoroughly loved. The only light in the little cabin came from the glowing embers on the grate.

They'd spent the hours alternately loving and talking. Now that they had shared such intimacy, it seemed the most natural thing in the world to talk about things they'd never shared with another.

Penny's voice was barely a whisper in the night. "I remember being so afraid when my mother died."

"You had a right to be scared. You were only a kid."

"Yeah. But if losing my mother wasn't enough, it was my dad's reaction that had me even more scared. He changed after Mom died. Some days he didn't get out of bed. Other times he went into town and didn't come home for days. I didn't know what was happening until the sheriff's deputy brought him home one day and I overheard him telling my dad he had to stop gambling."

Sam went very still. "Your dad gambled?"

She nodded. "Until there was no money left. Then he just seemed to give up on life."

"What did you do?"

Her voice trembled. "I never told anybody. I told my brothers our dad died of a broken heart." She sighed. "And maybe he did. He was never the same after my mom was gone. I'm sure that's what drove him to gamble."

"No wonder you're so worried about Curtis."

"I'm scared to death he'll end up like Dad. So deeply in debt he can never crawl out. And then he'll just give up."

"Then you need to tell him."

"How can I do that after all this time? He'll hate me for keeping the truth of our father's problem from him all these years."

"Penny, you were a kid yourself. And you were only trying to shield your brothers from more pain."

"But keeping it from them is the same as lying. And I told them there was never a good reason to lie." She took in a deep breath. "I can't believe I'm telling you all this. I've never told another soul about my dad's weakness. I've always felt so ashamed."

"It wasn't your weakness, Penny. And don't be too hard on your dad's memory. He was just trying to cope with the loss of the woman he loved."

Sam saw the tears shimmering on her lashes and gathered her close. "Thank you."

"For what?" Her words were whispered against his chest, stirring a fresh flame deep inside him.

"For sharing that with me. I know what a private person you are. I know that wasn't easy."

"You're easy to talk to, Sam. I don't know why. You just are."

"The reason is simple. I care about you, Money."

And then he showed her, in the only way he knew, just how deeply he cared.

Embers sparked in the fireplace, and flames cast shadows on the ceiling.

Penny's fingers played with the hair on Sam's chest. "Becca told me you and Ben and Finn were so wild and tough, half the town thought Mac was crazy to adopt the three of you."

"My brothers and I thought so, too. After all, we'd broken into his house while he was away, and when he confronted us, we were ready to fight rather than face the authorities."

"Why were you running away?"

"After our folks died, the county sent us to live with a distant relative we'd never met. He had no wife or kids, and resented our disruption of his life. But I guess he figured we'd be cheap labor. He worked us like dogs. One night, after he was asleep, I crept downstairs and helped myself to his favorite ice cream. He walked in and caught me and hauled me out to a shed and locked me inside. It was cold and dark, and I was barefoot, with nothing but thin cotton pajamas. I figured I could tough it out until I saw feral eyes looking at me in the darkness."

Penny's hands tightened on Sam's. "Eyes? What were they?"

"Rats. The shed was used to store feed for the stock. I was lying on the sacks of feed to stay warm." He gave a dry laugh. "When I realized what they were, I screamed and hollered, but nobody came. That's when I realized I was on my own. I felt my way around the walls until I found a pitchfork. Then I slipped between the sacks and sat shivering, waiting for one of them to come close. I fell asleep still holding that pitchfork. But it helped me realize I wasn't helpless. I could fight back."

"Oh, Sam." Penny hugged him fiercely. "How old were you?"

He shrugged. "Six. And to this day, I hate rats with a passion."

"That's . . ." She struggled for words. "Simply hateful. To leave a little boy all alone in the dark, for eating ice cream. I hope he got what he deserved."

Sam's voice was low in the darkness. "When a social worker reported him for abusing us and practically starving us, we were removed from his house, and we thought our lives would be better. Instead, we entered the foster system. By then we'd become three angry boys who'd come to expect the worst. Add to that the fact we were separated and sent to live with different families, making us even more hostile and ready to stand and fight. None of the families wanted anything to do with us when they realized what we'd become."

"What do you mean?"

"You beat a boy long enough, he learns to either roll over and die or he learns to fight back. Ben, Finn, and I are fast learners. We became mean, ornery, hostile kids willing to fight at the drop of a hat. It was Ben's idea that we should pick a day to run away, meet up at a designated location, and disappear. We chose the middle of a snowstorm and landed in Mackenzie Monroe's kitchen. When he asked if we would agree to adoption, we didn't believe him. We figured all adults lied. But Mac isn't like others. He meant what he said, and though we fought him every step of the way, he became our father."

"And that's why you're always laughing and joking? Because you're so happy?"

He smiled in the darkness. "The truth? When I was living through my deepest, darkest misery, I decided I'd take in every little bit of happiness I could and enjoy the hell out of it. That's been my mantra ever since. Grab all the good with both hands and enjoy it, because tomorrow it can all be taken away."

"Oh, Sam." Penny was so touched by his admission, she found herself wanting desperately to soothe that broken little boy he had been.

She wrapped her arms around him, burying her face against his chest.

He lifted her up to kiss her and tasted the salt on her lashes. "What's this? Tears?"

"You were so young. You must have been terrified."

"Hey, now." He wiped her tears with his thumbs. "It was a long time ago. That little boy doesn't exist anymore."

"Yes, he does. You hide him under that mask of laughter and teasing. But he's still there, and I can't bear to think of the pain you were forced to endure."

He framed her face and stared down into her eyes, swimming with tears. "Do you know what it means to me to have you care so deeply?"

And then, because the words were too painfully intimate, he kissed her.

Penny felt the mattress sag and looked up as Sam crossed to the fireplace to stir the ashes before tossing a log on the embers. Within minutes the log was in flames and the heat began spreading its warmth through the little cabin.

When he returned to bed, he carried two steaming mugs and handed one to her before crawling in beside her.

She took a sip and sighed. "Hot chocolate. Oh, Sam, this is so good."

"Yeah. It's not bad. Especially with the jar of marshmallow topping I found."

"I could have made this while you took care of the fire."

He closed a hand over hers. "Let me pamper you."

"Pamper." That brought a throaty laugh. "I don't know the meaning of the word."

"Exactly. You've spent a lifetime taking care of others. So now let me turn the tables and take care of you."

She rested her head on his shoulder. "That's so sweet."

He kissed the tip of her nose. "Maybe I have ulterior motives."

"I just bet you do."

He put a hand on his heart. "You wound me deeply."

"Sorry."

"You don't sound sorry."

"You're right." She was already laughing.

He closed a hand over hers. "You know what I like?"

She shook her head. "What?"

"The sound of your laughter. You should do it more often."

"How can I help it? You're so silly. So...irreverent. Sam, just being with you makes me laugh."

"I'm glad. I see that as my mission. I'm here, Miss Money, just to bring a smile to those gorgeous eyes and that kissable mouth. And now..." He took the empty mug from her hands and set it on a wooden stool beside the bed. "If you've had enough sustenance, I think it's time for our next marathon."

"We're runners?"

"Close." He gathered her into his arms and kissed her until they were both breathless. Against her throat he whispered, "Marathon lovers."

*   *   *

The next time Penny woke, the little cabin was filled with the wonderful aroma of coffee perking over a fire. When she sat up, Sam stepped away from the fireplace and settled on the edge of the bunk.

Seeing the sunlight outside the window, she gave a little gasp of surprise. "It's morning already? Why didn't you wake me?"

"Because I didn't let you get much sleep last night."

"I'm not complaining." She tossed aside the covers.

Before she could slide out of bed, Sam put a hand on hers. "Slow down, Money. We're not punching a time clock here."

"But you've already made the coffee."

"And flapjacks, and heated the rest of that canned ham."

"But I…"

He kissed her, cutting off her words.

"Mmm. That's nice." She wrapped her arms around his neck and kissed him back.

"That's even nicer," he muttered against her lips. "And as a reward, you get breakfast without having to do the work." He winked.

"But…"

He kissed her again. "Pamper, remember? I promised, and I'm delivering."

"Oh." Her eyes lit with pleasure. "This is all part of your plan?"

"Exactly. I'm sure you'll find a way to thank me later."

She batted her lashes. "I could thank you now."

A slow smile spread across his face. "Why, Miss Money. I do believe you're starting to get with the program. You're actually flirting."

"Indeed I am." Her smile widened. "How am I doing?"

In answer he slid into bed beside her and began nibbling her neck. "Instead of telling you, I'd rather show you."

"But the flapjacks..."

"Will just have to wait. What I have in mind is more satisfying."

And then, with long, slow kisses and sighs of pleasure, they came together in a languid dance of love.

"Why didn't you ever let me know what a good cook you are?" Penny helped herself to the last bite of ham, before draining a mug of steaming coffee.

"When I'm up in the hills, I have to fix something or starve. But it's mostly reheated chili or packaged food I can carry in my saddlebags. The truth is, sometimes I indulge in a steak grilled over an open fire. That, along with an ice-cold longneck under the stars, feels like a feast."

"It sounds heavenly."

He studied her. "It is. To me, the best part of being a rancher is the freedom to spend time up here in these hills."

"You're not afraid to sleep outside? What about wild animals?"

He smiled. "The truth is, you can find danger anywhere. But I'm not afraid of things that go bump in the night."

She gave a dreamy smile. "I think it would be fun to sleep beside a campfire up here on a summer night."

"If you'll stick around long enough to try it, I promise to do all the cooking." He caught her hand. "Now let's go outside and assess our chances of making it out of here."

They pulled on boots and parkas and headed outside.

The scene was a winter wonderland. The trees were bent double with the weight of the snow. The woodpile was barely visible under a layer of white.

Despite the snow, the sun overhead was brilliant, and the air had lost its bite.

Sam caught her hand. "Come on. There's something I'd like to show you."

Penny heard a new note of excitement in his tone. Puzzled, she kept her questions to herself as they climbed hand in hand to a high meadow.

When they paused, Sam pointed. "This is my land."

"I thought all of this was your ranch."

"It is. It belongs to the family. But after Mac adopted my brothers and me, he told each of us to pick a spot that we wanted to call our own. With Zachariah's help, he drew up legal documents ceding a parcel to each of us. A parcel that nobody could ever take away from us. And this is the spot I chose. This is all mine."

Penny turned this way and that, seeing the land through Sam's eyes. "I can see why you chose this."

"You can?"

She nodded. "It's high enough so you can see the town of Haller Creek way over there." She pointed. "And far enough from the ranch house that you have some privacy, if you want. But close enough so you can get there in a hurry if anyone has need of you."

He was looking at her with sharp interest. "You see all that in one glance?"

"Don't you?"

His smile came then. "Yeah. But it took me more than a year of riding across this land before I realized why I kept coming back here. No matter where else I tried to see myself, it wouldn't work. It was here. Only here. It calls to me. But I never thought anyone else would understand."

She thought of the painful past he'd revealed during the night, of the angry, desperate boy he'd been when he'd arrived on this ranch, and of the unspeakable pain he'd endured, though he'd refused to go into detail about it.

"Everyone deserves a place of their own, Sam. But especially a man who was denied such a thing as a child. I'd say you've found heaven on earth."

"I have. Twice. When Mackenzie Monroe adopted me." He paused and again gave her a fierce look. "And when you came into my life." He drew her close and pressed a kiss to the top of her head. "I never shared so much of myself with another person. Not even my own brothers. And now I know why. You're easy to talk to because you get it. You get me."

Tears welled up and she closed her eyes to keep them from spilling over and spoiling the moment.

Wrapping her arms around his waist, she managed to murmur against his throat, "I love your special place, Sam. Almost as much as I love—"

At that very moment he tucked a hand under her chin, lifting her face for a long, draining kiss, and the words she'd been about to speak faded away.

She had a sudden thought. "So the dream home Ben and Becca are building is on the plot of land Ben chose?"

"Yes. And Becca loves it as much as Ben does."

"Oh, I'm so happy for both of them."

"Me, too. My big brother lucked out and found the perfect woman to share his life." He lifted her hand to his lips and pressed a kiss to the palm. "Maybe it's what everybody dreams of, but it's especially important to someone who never had that kind of love in his life. I guess I never believed it was in the cards for me. Now I'm starting to believe."

As they left the meadow behind to begin the long trek back to the cabin, Penny found herself replaying Sam's words in her mind.

Caring and sharing were universal yearnings. But when

they'd been denied for a lifetime, they often seemed like an unattainable goal.

Hadn't she convinced herself of that? It was one of the reasons why she'd hungered to teach. The classroom would become her home. The students her children.

Why then had the dream begun receding since coming to the Monroe ranch?

She knew the answer. She glanced at Sam's proud, chiseled profile, and felt her heart take a quick, hard bounce.

She'd done the unthinkable.

She'd lost her heart to this cocky, teasing gambler.

When they reached the cabin, Sam made his way toward the woodpile and stopped to pick up several snow-covered logs. When he turned, a snowball hit him squarely on one cheek.

"What the...?"

Caught by surprise, he dropped the armload of wood before catching sight of Penny scooping up more snow. Before she could toss it he had a snowball in his hand and took aim. She managed to duck, avoiding being hit, but when she stood up, a second toss caught her on the ear.

"You'll pay for that, cowboy." She scooped up a handful of snow and lobbed it at his face.

"Oh, lady, now you're in big trouble."

Laughing, he wiped at the snow on his cheek. Seeing her take cover behind a tree, he started toward her on the run, dodging snowballs as he did.

When he came around the tree, she was just about to toss another snowball. Before she could act, he made a dive for her.

Together they fell into a mound of snow that nearly buried them.

She reached out, trying to grab more snow, but Sam was

quicker. Pinning both her hands above her head in one of his, he leaned close. "I claim victory and demand an apology."

"In your dreams."

"Now this is the tough little cookie I know. I'd expect nothing else." He kissed her.

When he lifted his head, he was grinning. "You can refuse all you want. But until you concede"—with his other hand he scooped up snow—"I'm going to hold you down and cover your pretty little face in snow." He arched a brow. "Now what're you going to do, Money?"

"I'm never declaring defeat. And I'll never apologize."

"Fair enough." He tossed aside the snow. "But the least you can do is kiss me back."

When she did, he got to his feet and took her hand, helping her up.

As she stood, she brought her other hand up and smeared a handful of snow over his face.

His grin disappeared. For a second he merely stared at her. "I can't believe it. Miss Money conned the con."

With a roar of laughter, he bent and scooped up enough snow to smother her.

She held up her hands. "Wait. I concede."

He put a hand to his ear. "What was that? Did I hear you admit defeat?"

"Never..." She started to turn away.

He dragged her close and held up a handful of snow menacingly. "Now I'll demand not only your admission of defeat, but also an apology. Or..."

She couldn't hold back the laughter any longer. "All right. You win. I'm sorry."

He paused a moment, dropping the snow before hauling her close and kissing her until they were both breathless.

When they came up for air, Penny caught his hand.

"Come on, cowboy. I'll help you carry some firewood inside."

"You think lending a hand will make me forget how you conned me?"

"No, but I'm freezing. I think even your hottest kisses can't drive away the chill of this weather."

"You wouldn't want me to prove you wrong again, would you?"

They were both laughing as they strolled hand in hand to the pile of firewood and began picking up logs.

Once inside they shed their boots and parkas. While Sam set about starting a cozy fire, Penny made a fresh pot of coffee.

As the day slipped into evening, they sat, wrapped in an afghan, sipping coffee and talking about all the things they'd kept in their hearts for a lifetime.

And as they lay together throughout the long, loving night, they could feel the pain of the past slipping away with every passionate kiss, every whispered word of endearment.

It was another night of not only passion, but also healing.

CHAPTER NINETEEN

Looks like the sunlight is doing its thing." Sam opened the cabin door and stepped onto the porch, with Penny trailing.

He pointed to the roof, where melting snow caused rivers to run down the shingles to form puddles along the porch.

The trail, snow-covered just that morning, was now a muddy path leading down the mountain. Rushing water formed gullies of mud and snow as it cascaded down the rugged terrain.

He turned to Penny. "I guess we'd better pack up and head home."

"Or we could hope for another blizzard."

He touched a rough palm to her cheek. "I know how you feel. I'm feeling it, too. If I thought there was a chance in hell that we could get a few more days to ourselves, Money, I'd lock the door and throw away the key."

"Your family would send out the troops to find us."

"Yeah." He opened the door and led her inside.

They worked in silence. Penny gathered the few empty cans and cartons into a trash bag, to be taken with them back to the ranch. Sam cleaned out the hot ash remaining in the fireplace and buried it in snow behind the cabin.

When he checked the cupboards, he glanced over at her. "This knob was loose. I was planning on getting my screwdriver to fix it and forgot. How did you do this?"

She laughed and produced a small gadget from her back pocket. "This was my dad's. I've carried it ever since his passing."

Sam took it from her hand. "A Swiss army knife. My brother Ben swears by his. Is it as good as he says?"

She began opening the sides, producing a knife, a screwdriver, scissors, a can opener, and half a dozen other tools. "My dad claimed this was all a person needed to survive."

"Sounds good to me, Money. And it saved me a chore." He bent to kiss her. "Maybe you'll lend it to me?"

"Not on your life, cowboy." She tucked it into her back pocket. "Get your own."

With a laugh he hurried away to finish packing.

When they had secured the range shack for the season and climbed into the truck for the drive home, they both turned for a final glimpse of their own private paradise.

Sam reached over and took Penny's hand. "I'm going to miss Shangri-La, Money."

"I was thinking the same thing."

He winked.

She smiled.

When they had descended from the high country far enough to get service, Sam called the family on his cell phone and let them know they were on their way home.

And then, to lighten the mood, he turned on the radio and began singing along with Willie, changing the lyrics to some bawdy words that had Penny laughing so hard, she had to wipe tears from her eyes.

By the time their truck rolled to a stop at the back porch, their mood was considerably lighter.

The family spilled out the back door and hurried down the steps to greet them.

"How bad was the storm?" Otis called from the porch.

"Bad enough," Sam told him. "But we've had worse."

Penny hugged Mary Pat. "I'm sorry we couldn't get word to you."

"No need." Mary Pat stood aside to allow the others to welcome Sam and Penny. "We could see the storm clouds from down here and knew you were in the thick of it."

Mac nodded. "I figured as long as Sam was there to take care of things, you'd be safe."

"What could go wrong? I had my personal chef with me." Sam exchanged a look with Penny. "We were snug and warm."

Needing to say something, Penny started toward the rear of the truck. "I need to get those supplies into the kitchen."

He dropped an arm around her shoulder and, without thinking, drew her close. "I know you're dying for a hot shower. Don't worry your head about this. Otis, Roscoe, and I can handle it."

When she turned toward the porch, she could feel the others watching with sharpened interest.

Her cheeks were burning as she climbed the steps and let herself into the house.

Penny descended the stairs feeling reborn. After a long hot shower, a chance to wash her hair and blow it dry, and putting on a soft denim shirt and jeans, she was ready to cook in a real kitchen again.

As she stepped into the parlor, she saw the family had gathered in front of a roaring fire.

Mac looked over. "Penny, you won't be fixing anything for supper tonight. Finn phoned and said the jury just brought in a verdict. Finn's client won and was awarded damages. I told him and Zachariah to meet us at Dolly's in town to celebrate. We're ready to leave."

Sam waited until everyone was gone before crossing the room.

"You smell good." He leaned close and nuzzled the back of her neck.

"So do you."

"Nothing like a shave and a shower to make me a new man."

"I sort of liked the old one."

He winked. "That hairy old thing?"

She touched a hand to his freshly shaved cheek. He caught it and pressed a kiss to her palm. But when he dragged her into his arms she pushed slightly away. "Sam, your family…"

"It's not my family I'm thinking of. Right now I'm re-membering way too much. I'm just hoping when this day is over, you and I can take up where we left off last night."

"I can't…"

He wrapped his arms around her and pressed his mouth to her ear, stealing all her breath.

Without thinking she turned and brought her hands to the front of his shirt, pulling him close for a quick, hard kiss.

Caught by surprise, he dragged her against him and re-turned her kiss with one that had her breath backing up in her throat.

Hearing footsteps on the stairs, he lifted his head and

gave her one of those killer smiles. "I guess that will have to hold me until later tonight, Money."

He turned away and sauntered out the back door, whistling a little tune.

She stood a moment, struggling to gather her thoughts.

That cowboy did have a way about him. Right now, she wasn't sure of anything except the fact that, with just a quick kiss, she was feeling thoroughly disoriented.

She put a hand to her heart and reminded herself to breathe.

Two ranch trucks pulled onto the interstate. Mac and Mary Pat were in the lead vehicle, with Otis and Roscoe in the backseat. Sam drove a second truck, with Penny beside him.

She turned to him. "Why didn't we ride with the others?"

"Too crowded." He glanced over with a grin. "Not that I'd mind being pinned up against you, but I figured we might want to stay in town after dinner."

"Why?"

"Maybe I'll give you a crash course on playing nine ball at the Hitching Post."

"No, thanks."

Seeing her little frown, he reached across the seat and caught her hand. "Hey. Don't knock it until you've tried it. It doesn't have to be anything more than a game."

"I'm no good at games."

"You've said that before. But up at the cabin, you were all kinds of fun."

"It was fun." She smiled, remembering. "It was like a dream vacation. And you're right. Once I had the time, not to mention the place, I have to admit, it was fun learning to play."

"Now that's a real shame, Money."

"That I learned to play?"

"That it took you so long. Every kid ought to play."

She rolled her eyes. "Says the biggest kid of them all."

He threw back his head and roared. "You got that right."

Ben and Becca were already standing outside the diner, along with Finn and Zachariah, when they arrived. The minute their group walked in, Dolly was there to greet them, menus in hand.

"Another evening in town?" She led the way to a table in the corner. As they settled in, she asked, "What's the occasion this time?"

Mac merely smiled. "Do we need an occasion to eat here?"

"I should hope not." She passed around menus before saying, "The special tonight is stuffed green peppers." She leaned close to add, "Millie Spriggs had to hurry and clean out her garden before the snow flew and brought me a bushel of peppers."

When she walked away, Mac picked up his water glass and turned to Finn. "Here's to you, son. I'm so glad you got the verdict you were hoping for."

Zachariah was positively beaming. "I wish you could have seen your boy, Mackenzie. The minute his closing argument was concluded, I saw the look on the faces of the jury. After such an impassioned speech, if Finnian's client had been found standing over a body with a smoking gun, they would have refused to convict him."

"That good?" Mac clapped a hand on Finn's shoulder. "I'm proud of you, son."

"Thanks, Dad." Finn accepted congratulations from the entire family. After scanning the menu, he turned to Penny. "What're you having?"

"The house special. Stuffed peppers."

He set aside his menu. "Okay. I say, if a great cook like you is ordering it, I'd be a fool to order anything else."

Sam caught the flush on Penny's face. It was plain she wasn't used to getting compliments.

He caught her hand beneath the table and squeezed.

Though she smiled, she kept her gaze averted, content to let the others carry the conversation over the course of a long, lazy meal. A conversation that touched on Mary Pat's restlessness as she considered her next trek to the wilderness, and concluded with Zachariah reenacting Finn's courtroom drama, much to the enjoyment of the entire Monroe family.

Mac sat back, taking it all in with a look of contentment.

Penny glanced at the others, as they listened with rapt attention to the proud old lawyer.

What an amazing family they were. Though not blood related, it was impossible for her to think of any one of them belonging anywhere but here.

She thought of her brothers, now scattered, making lives for themselves far away. Not that she resented the distance between them. They had a right to pursue their own dreams. But ever since seeing Curtis drinking and gambling, she had to fight a nagging fear that she had somehow failed him, and possibly the others, as well.

Heaven knew she'd done her best. But the needs of an aged great-aunt and the desire to protect three teenaged brothers from the truth of their dad's addiction had seemed beyond her ability. There had been plenty of times she'd gone on pure adrenaline, hoping it was enough.

"What do you think?"

At Sam's question, her head came up sharply. "I'm sorry. What . . . ?"

He squeezed her hand. "Ben suggested that we head over to the Hitching Post. The old-timers want to head home."

"Who're you calling old?" Mac asked with a mock frown.

"You and the rest of these spoilsports." Sam nudged Penny, causing her to laugh. He added, "As long as there's room in your truck for Mary Pat, Otis, Roscoe, and Zachariah, Finn can ride home with us."

They walked out of Dolly's and gathered around Mac's truck.

After many good night hugs, the older members of the family climbed inside, while Ben and Becca held hands and led the way down the street to the Hitching Post, with Finn, Sam, and Penny trailing behind.

CHAPTER TWENTY

The din of voices could be heard out on the street even before the doors were opened. Once their group stepped inside, they were hit with a wave of sound. Men and women laughing, cheering, cursing. Above it all, a sound system blasted out Willie's distinct wail, praising the woman always on his mind.

The long scarred wooden bar was three-deep with cowboys reaching over heads to pick up a longneck or slapping a pal on the back after a raucous joke.

At one end of the bar there was a heated discussion about the harsh winter recently predicted and the sudden snowstorm throwing ranchers into a panic, trying to get their herds down from the hills.

Horton Duke, manning the grill behind the bar, saluted their party and pointed through a haze of smoke to a booth across the room.

As they made their way through the crowd, Sam signaled to a waitress by lifting one hand. She was at their table with five longnecks as soon as they took their seats.

"You got some live ones tonight, Char." Sam passed a beer to Penny, and one to Finn, before handing two across the table to Ben and Becca. "What's going on?"

Charlotte Jenkins nodded a head toward the pool table, where a crowd had gathered. "It started out simple enough. Just a couple of cowboys playing for a free beer. Now it's turned into a high-stakes game."

Sam tried to see the players, but the crowd around the table was too thick.

"Who're the players?"

"The big guy is Dex Cantrel. He doesn't stop in Haller Creek often, but when he does, he usually plays until there are no more challengers."

"Yeah." Sam's eyes narrowed. "I've played him a time or two. He's good."

The waitress leaned over the table, keeping her voice just above the din. "Horton said he walked in with a stack of hundred-dollar bills so thick, he wouldn't be surprised if Dex had a couple of thousand in his pocket."

"Yeah?" Sam grinned at his brothers. "Who's the sucker playing against him?"

"Some kid. He's been in here a couple of times. Mostly he wins, but when he loses, he starts chasing his money." She shook her head. "Horton says if Dex smells the kid's fear, it's all over."

Just then a roar went up from the onlookers, and Char turned away. "That's my cue to bring them both a beer before the next game."

As she hurried away, Penny put a hand on Sam's arm. "You don't think Curtis would be playing, do you?"

"I'm sure he's learned his lesson by now." Sam patted her hand. "You just sit here and I'll take a look."

He crossed the room and pushed his way through the crowd. A few minutes later he returned, his smile gone.

Penny clutched his hand even before he was seated. "It's Curtis, isn't it?"

He gave a reluctant nod. "Yeah." He closed his other hand over hers. "I got the scoop from Skeeter Norris, a regular here at the Hitching Post. He works with your brother at the Lazy K ranch. He said so far Curtis is holding his own against that shark."

"Shark?" Penny's voice shook.

"Dex."

"Do you think Curtis can beat him?"

Sam could see both Ben and Finn watching him with matching looks of concern. "I think…" He chose his words carefully. "Curtis may be good at the game, but he may be too wet behind the ears to realize there are other ways to get beaten besides having skill with a pool cue."

"How?" Her fingers tightened on his arm.

"If Dex can't outplay him, he'll try to outmaneuver him."

"What does that mean?"

"You heard our waitress. The players have a standing order for longnecks after every game. Sober, your brother's hard to beat. Drunk, he's probably an easy mark. If I know Dex, he'll set aside his beers and concentrate on his game. He'll wait to drink until he has something to celebrate."

Her eyes widened. "This Dex person will wait until Curtis drinks too much and…"

Sam nodded. "And move in for the kill."

She started to slide out of their booth. "I have to stop Curtis."

"Penny." Sam's fingers closed around her wrist. "That's the worst thing you could do."

She pushed against his chest. "Let me go, Sam."

He stood and put his arms around her, holding her still. "Listen to me. I know you think big sister can still convince her little brother to do the smart thing. But if you make a scene, all you'll do is make things worse. Curtis will not only lose his cool, but he'll also be prodded to drink more and bet more, just to prove to everybody he's his own man and doesn't take orders from his bossy sister."

Her voice caught on a sob. "You heard Charlotte. His opponent walked in here with more money than Curtis could earn in months."

"Which is why he's caught up in this. It's the pot of gold at the end of the rainbow. And right now, Curtis is in no mood to listen to anybody tell him he can't have it all."

She lowered her head, shame washing over her. "I know you're right, Sam. But I can't bear to think about my little brother willingly stepping into such a mess."

"He isn't the first. He won't be the last." Sam ran a hand down her back and could feel her trembling with fear and anger. Against her ear he whispered, "Stay here with the others. I'll see what's happening, and report back soon."

He settled her in the booth, and shot a warning look at both Finn and Ben before walking away and blending into the crowd.

After watching the next game of nine ball, Sam returned to their booth and was greeted by somber silence.

He slid in next to Penny. "I have to give it to Curtis. He's good."

She brightened. "He's winning?"

"They're staying even. He wins one. Dex wins one. But

according to Skeeter, Dex keeps upping the stakes, and Curtis keeps agreeing."

"How much are they playing for now?"

Sam shrugged. "Skeeter thinks it's a couple of thousand. He isn't sure anymore. Too much going on. Plus there are a lot of side bets among the cowboys watching."

"Thousands." The word came out in a whisper from Penny. "Curtis doesn't have that kind of money."

"With every win, Curtis starts to believe he's bulletproof. Right now, a herd of mustangs couldn't haul him away from the chance to win big." Sam tossed some bills on the table. "I say we leave now."

Ben nodded in agreement.

"I can't go, Sam." Penny's voice wavered. "I can't leave without knowing whether Curtis wins or loses."

"This could go on for hours." He glanced around for help from his brothers.

Ben nodded. "My night patrol starts at midnight. I need to get Becca home before I start my shift."

Finn added, "After the day I put in at court, I'm falling asleep in my beer."

Sam took Penny's hand. Squeezed. "I'll call Horton first thing tomorrow, and find out who won and who lost."

As their party got to their feet, a roar went up from the crowd, and Penny shot a stricken look at Sam.

He turned her toward the door. "You go ahead with my brothers. I'll see who won this round."

When she started to follow Sam, Becca wrapped an arm around her waist and began steering her toward the door, with Ben and Finn trailing behind.

Once outside, the cold air slapped at them as they stood huddled inside their parkas until Sam stepped out the door.

Penny looked over expectantly.

He managed a smile. "Your brother took this one."

"Oh." She put a hand to her heart. "Please tell me this is over."

Sam dropped an arm around her shoulders and started along the sidewalk leading to Dolly's Diner, where they'd left the truck.

When he said nothing, Penny dug in her heels and turned to him. "He didn't take his money and leave, did he?"

Sam shook his head. "I don't really know. Dex ordered another round. Curtis didn't look like he was ready to leave. He was in the corner of the room, talking on his cell phone."

"His phone?"

Sam nodded.

"Who in the world would he be calling?"

Sam shrugged.

Seeing the glint of tears in her eyes, he fought a wave of annoyance at the young cowboy whose pride had him heading for a terrible fall. A fall that would add another layer of guilt to Penny's already overburdened heart.

At the diner they bid good night to Ben and Becca before climbing into the ranch truck for the drive home.

While Sam and Finn struggled to keep up a steady stream of banter to keep Penny's mind off her troubles, she fell silent. As the truck ate up the miles, she stared straight ahead, watching snowflakes dancing against the windshield wipers.

There was a time, she thought, that the sight would have had her heart soaring. She'd always loved winter in Montana. But tonight the view seemed as bleak as her thoughts.

Curtis had changed from a fun, fearless little boy to a drunk and a gambler. All the years she'd spent trying to make up for the loss of their parents had now fallen by the wayside.

What was it Aunt Lucy was fond of saying?

I know these are hard times, Penny, but all the good you're doing now will come back to you one day.

Just look at us, Aunt Lucy, Penny thought miserably. *What a mess I've made of things.*

Penny looked up as Sam parked the truck alongside the back porch, and Finn stepped out.

Sam circled the front of the vehicle and took her hand.

"You're cold. You should have said something. I would have kicked up the heat."

"I'm fine, Sam."

He waited until Finn walked inside. "You're not fine. I know you're hurting. And probably blaming yourself for your brother's lack of self-control. But you need to stop, Money."

"I wish I could." She started wringing her hands. "Oh, Sam. How I wish I could."

He dragged her close. Against her temple he said fiercely, "I hate seeing you hurt like this. I'd give anything to put your mind at ease."

"I have no right to burden you with this. It isn't your problem, Sam."

"As long as it affects you, it's my problem too, Money. That's just the way it is, so stop fighting it."

"But I..."

"Shh. Just let me hold you." He dragged her close and wrapped his arms around her, burying his face in her hair.

For long minutes they stood, swaying in the wind and cold, until he scooped her up and carried her up the steps of the porch and into the warmth of the mudroom. Instead of setting her down, he continued carrying her through the kitchen, the parlor, and up the stairs to her bedroom.

At the door he set her on her feet. "Get some sleep. First

thing in the morning I'll call Horton and learn how this whole thing ended."

He drew her close and kissed her, before holding open her bedroom door. When she closed it, he made his way down the hall to his own room.

After tossing aside his clothes, he crawled into bed, wishing he could sleep down the hall with Penny. But he wanted her to get some sleep.

For the longest time he lay there, wondering how it had come to this.

Until Penny, he'd been perfectly content to while away his hours in town, drinking with his buddies, showing off with a game of pool.

Now, all he could think of was Penny. Her comfort. Her fears over her brother.

Hearing footsteps on the stairs, he pulled on his jeans and shirt and padded down the hall. Seeing all the doors closed, he made his way down the stairs, expecting to see his father.

Instead, he was startled to see Penny, still fully dressed, arms crossed over her chest, pacing back and forth in the parlor.

"What are you doing?"

She whirled. "Sam. I didn't want to wake anybody."

"I wasn't asleep. Penny..." He crossed to her and caught her hand to still her movements. "You can't keep this up."

"I can't sleep, Sam. I have to know what's happening with Curtis."

He took in a long breath before starting toward the kitchen. "Come on. We'll head back to town."

She shot him a look of gratitude. "You mean it?"

"Money, I thought by now you'd understand. I'd walk through fire for you."

He picked up the keys to the truck and paused in the mudroom to put on boots and grab a parka.

Taking her hand, he led her outside. Once in the truck he turned to her. "Besides, I probably wouldn't get much sleep anyway. I've discovered I don't like sleeping alone. I'd rather be sleeping with my favorite chef."

His attempt at a joke fell on deaf ears.

Penny was staring out the side window, her hands clenched in her lap, a look of such sorrow etched on her profile that Sam had to fight a rush of desire to take her in his arms and offer her whatever comfort he could.

Instead he had to be content with the unbroken silence between them as the truck ate up the miles back to Haller Creek.

CHAPTER TWENTY-ONE

Sam was surprised to see the parking lot of the Hitching Post still crowded with trucks. He found a parking space a block away, and caught Penny's hand as the two of them stepped inside the bar. At once they were assaulted by a wave of noise.

He glanced around. Usually, by this time of night, a lot of the couples would have been gone. Tonight, the crowd remained. He wondered if that was a good omen or a bad one.

Though there were couples on the dance floor, and many more standing around the bar, the majority of customers had gravitated to the rear of the room. There was an air of expectancy as they watched the pool game that had become a high-stakes contest between a professional and a brash amateur.

Knowing Penny wouldn't be placated by anything less than the truth, Sam led her toward the crowd.

When they'd pushed their way toward the front of the circle, Sam turned to a cowboy beside him. "Who's winning?"

"The kid." The old man shook his head. "Every time I figured he'd lost it all, the kid came back stronger. But Dex is one tough con. He just asked for a chance to win back all he's lost in one final game, and the kid agreed."

Sam tensed. "What's the purse?"

The old man shrugged. "I don't know if it's true or not, but folks are saying ten thousand."

Penny's eyes went wide. "Ten...?"

Sam put an arm around her shoulders and leaned close to whisper, "Just remember. No matter what happens, you need to keep your cool. You do or say anything to disrupt the flow, you could cause Curtis to lose his concentration."

She nodded, her eyes following every move her younger brother was making.

Curtis took a long swig of beer and looked supremely confident as he chalked his cue stick and made the break. The crowd let out a cheer as two balls rolled across the felt and dropped, one after the other, into a pocket. He eyed the remaining balls, then bent over the table and took careful aim at a ball slightly apart from the others.

"An easy shot," Sam whispered to Penny, to ease the tension he could feel in her. She was vibrating like the strings of a violin, holding herself so tightly, he wondered that her bones didn't snap.

Curtis smiled as he took his shot and waited for the ball to drop. When it did, a ripple of approval moved through the crowd.

Sam glanced around. The dancers had stopped to join the rest of the people. The crowd around the bar had thinned, as well, crossing the room to join the throng of onlookers.

With his grill now shut down for the night, even Horton Duke stood in the crowd.

Curtis took a moment to take a sip of beer before he chalked his cue stick.

Sam noted the slight trembling of Curtis's hand. Maybe the others hadn't noticed it, but it was something Sam had always watched for in his opponents. An unsteady hand meant an unsteady shot. A single miss could mean the difference between a win or a loss.

Curtis leaned over the table and took his shot.

The ball wobbled and touched a ball nearby, causing it to veer to one side, missing the pocket.

The murmur grew loud as the spectators realized what had just happened. Instead of running the table, and winning everything, the young amateur had probably lost his best chance.

Unless Dex should miss a shot, as well.

The pool hustler showed no emotion as he stepped forward and claimed the next shot. He made it with ease, and continued dropping ball after ball, until only the nine ball was left.

The old man next to Sam whispered, "If he makes this shot, it's all over. He'll win the ten thousand. I was hoping the kid might do it, but since I've never seen Dex miss, I have to put my money on him."

Penny's hand was gripping Sam's so tightly, her nails were digging into his flesh. She was completely unaware of anything except the outcome of the game.

Dex made a smooth motion with his cue, and the ball started down the green felt.

To those watching, time seemed to stand still. The ball banked off the side of the table and started toward a pocket as if in slow motion. Just as it reached the designated pocket, it paused on the lip.

The crowd went deathly silent, all eyes fixed on the spot.

In the blink of an eye, as though pulled by an invisible thread, the ball tipped closer to the very edge.

There were whispers and murmurs from the crowd.

"It's going in."

"A hundred says it won't."

"He's going to win it."

"The kid's still got a chance."

After hovering for what seemed an eternity, the ball dropped into the pocket.

The spectators let out a roar that could be heard a block away.

Around the table, money exchanged hands as the cowboys collected their side bets.

Dex turned to Curtis. "You're good, kid. So good, I thought for a minute there, you'd beat me. Someday you may get the chance again. But for now, you owe me ten thousand."

As reality began to sink in, Curtis stumbled before catching hold of the edge of the pool table.

He dug his hand into his pocket and held out a pile of crumpled bills.

Dex frowned. "There can't be more than a few hundred there."

"Six..." Curtis cleared his throat and tried again. "I've got six hundred here."

"I said ten thousand big ones, kid. You knew we weren't playing for nickels."

"I don't have that much on me. But I'm happy to sign something saying I owe you the rest."

"An IOU is nothing more than a useless piece of paper if you skip town. It doesn't pay the bills. I played you in good faith. You were the one who agreed to the prize."

"I can get your money. Just not right away…"

Dex's hands fisted in Curtis's shirt front, dragging him close. "Now you listen, kid…"

"Hold on a minute." Curtis's hands came up, breaking his hold. "I'll go to my boss and see what he'll advance me. Then I'll write you a check if you'll agree to hold it until I can cover it."

With each excuse, Dex's face darkened. "Do I look like a freakin' banker, kid? I'll take my money now." He looked around. "All those good buddies of yours, who were cheering you on when they thought you were winning, can just pitch in now and save your hide. Otherwise, we're going to go outside and have a little meeting. Just you and me. And they won't like what they find when I'm through with you…"

Before Sam realized what she was doing, Penny raced to her brother's side and stepped in front of him, putting herself between him and his opponent. "If you'll just be patient, Curtis will have the money."

Dex's eyes narrowed. "Who's this? And don't try to pass her off as your banker, kid."

Someone in the crowd laughed.

"I'm his sister. His only kin in these parts."

"Lady, unless you're holding on to ten thousand dollars, I don't care if you're an angel come down from heaven to help this lost soul. A bet is a bet."

Though Penny's face flamed, her spine stiffened and her chin jutted defiantly. She put a proprietary hand on Curtis's arm. "I want you to know that my brother is an honorable man. If you'll give him the time, as he's asked, he'll have your money."

"Oh, he'll have it. That's a promise." Dex ignored her and spoke directly to Curtis. "Tomorrow before noon. I'll be outside the gates of the Lazy K, waiting. If you don't have my money, be prepared to pay some other way."

"Some other...?" Before Penny could say more, Dex stormed out of the Hitching Post, slamming the door with such force it sent the windows rattling.

Curtis shook off Penny's touch and turned on her with a look so filled with anger, she blanched. "What in hell are you doing here?"

Before she could say a word he backed away. "You have no right stalking me, Penny."

"I'm not stalking..."

"You don't know what you're getting yourself into, Penny. Now get out of here. Just leave me alone."

"I want to help..."

"Help? You've just made things worse."

"What does that mean?"

"It means you don't want to be anywhere close to me. You certainly don't want to be known as Curtis Cash's sister right now. The more distance you can put between us, the better for you."

Sam stepped up, narrowing his gaze on Curtis. "Your sister has a right to worry. You've just turned an opponent into a dangerous enemy, Curtis. When you chose to play in the big league, you had to know you'd be expected to honor your debts. You can't just walk away from a player like Dex Cantrel."

"I knew what I was doing." Curtis's eyes were bleak, his hands fisted at his sides. "I didn't have any choice."

"Everybody has choices." Sam's tone was deadly calm.

"Curtis, please..."

Before Penny could say more, Sam wrapped an arm around her shoulders. Seeing the fury in Curtis's eyes, he steered her away before this erupted into an ugly family feud where both of them would say things they would later regret.

Before Sam and Penny had taken a few steps, Curtis's friends and fellow wranglers surrounded him, all of them eager to give advice.

"That guy's bad news, Curtis."

"You almost had him, buddy. But now that you've lost, you'd better make yourself scarce."

Despite his show of bravado, Curtis's voice betrayed the nerves he could no longer hide. "I've still got an ace in the hole. I'll talk to Everett tomorrow and ask him for an advance. Then, if I have to, I'll promise to work for half wages for a year."

"Everett doesn't hold with drinking and gambling."

"Slade's right. Your best bet is to get out of town tonight. Before you have to face Dex tomorrow."

Hearing them, Penny paused at the door. "Listen to them, Sam. None of them are offering a bit of help."

"How can they? Most of them are barely getting by. They live from paycheck to paycheck. Come on." He urged her out the door and down the street.

Once in the truck, he drove through the darkened town, watching Penny twist her hands together. He knew if she could, she would jump out of the truck and run back to the Hitching Post, even though her brother had made it clear he wanted nothing to do with her.

There was no changing her nature. She was the big sister. The mother substitute. The nurturer. And right now, though she was bitterly disappointed in her little brother, she couldn't help turning the problem over and over in her mind, trying desperately to find a happy ending for Curtis.

Sam had seen a lot of winners and losers. But there was something different about her brother. Before that final game, he'd already won more money than he could hope to earn in a month of backbreaking, bone-jarring wrangling at the Lazy K. That should have been enough to satisfy his ego. But something had compelled Curtis to keep playing.

Maybe, as Penny feared, her brother had become addicted to the game, or to the lure of easy money. Or, Sam thought, maybe he'd run up a string of debts and had seen this high-stakes game as a way to get even. Whatever the reason, Curtis had stayed too long at the dance.

Dex was a longtime hustler. He'd made his reputation on winning and on being paid. The challenge he'd issued to Curtis was no idle threat. If Curtis didn't come up with the money tomorrow, he'd find himself up against a man who knew how to use his fists to get what he wanted.

Damned fool kid was in for the fight of his life.

Hearing Sam swear under his breath, Penny turned to him. "What are you thinking, Sam?"

"I'm not sure what to think." He looked over, and seeing the glint of unshed tears, he reached out and held Penny's cold hand in his, determined to give her whatever comfort he could offer.

"I'll wait until morning and drive over the Lazy K and have a talk with Curtis."

"What about tonight...?"

Sam shook his head, cutting off her protest. "Tomorrow. When he's sober. If he's learned his lesson and agrees to give up pool hustling for good, I'll take him to the bank and withdraw enough to pay off his debt to Dex."

"You can't do that, Sam. This isn't your fight."

"It isn't yours, either. But since it involves your brother, I'm making it my business now."

"But..." Penny tried to think of an alternative. Coming up with nothing, she turned. "Oh, Sam. You'd do that for him?"

He squeezed her hand. "No. I'd do it for you."

She managed a shaky smile. "Thank you. But what if he doesn't agree to your terms?"

His tone roughened. "Your little brother will be limping around with a mile-wide patch torn off his miserable hide."

He was rewarded with a muffled laugh that managed to lighten his mood considerably.

CHAPTER TWENTY-TWO

Though it was barely dawn, Sam stepped in from the barn to find Penny in the kitchen, tending to her morning chores.

She turned to him with a smile.

"I see you're feeling better than you did last night."

She nodded. "I just know Curtis is going to be so grateful for your help, Sam."

"He'd better be." He stepped closer, still feeling the heat of the kisses they'd shared last night, when he'd walked her to her room.

He'd intended merely to offer comfort, but when she'd flung her arms around his neck and clung to him, he'd been unable to leave her alone. He'd spent the night offering comfort in the only way he knew how.

Now he bent to her, hoping to take up where they'd left off. But when he heard Mac descending the stairs, Sam managed a quick kiss on her cheek before stepping away.

"Hey, you two." Mac was subdued as he poured himself a mug of coffee. "You were out late."

"Yeah." Seeing the high color on Penny's cheeks, Sam decided to deflect attention from her. "And up early this morning. I've already finished the barn chores."

"Thanks, son. Otis, Roscoe, and I will be heading into town after breakfast, once we see Mary Pat off."

"She's leaving?"

Mac nodded. "Want to come along with us to town?"

Sam shook his head and helped himself to a glass of orange juice. "I've got an errand to run…"

"Good morning, Samuel. Mackenzie. Penny." Zachariah smiled at Penny as he walked out of his room and into the kitchen. "Something smells amazing."

"Cinnamon rolls to go with your ham and eggs."

"You're spoiling us, Penny."

"And that makes me happy."

Zachariah accepted a cup of steaming coffee and took a moment to breathe in the fragrance before drinking.

Otis and Roscoe stepped in from the bunkhouse and Mary Pat came downstairs while Finn ambled into the kitchen, dressed for a day in his office in Haller Creek.

Sam elbowed him. "Don't you ever take a day off?"

Finn shrugged. "After a trial like the one we just finished, an ordinary day at work will seem like a vacation."

"It's not exactly the same as a margarita on a sandy beach."

"Highly overrated, bro. All that sand between your toes. And sunburn."

The two shared a grin.

While the family ate, Penny moved her food around her plate and let the jokes and conversation flow around her. When at last they all pushed away from the table, with Mac fussing about Mary Pat's safety on the road, Sam waited until the others left before crossing to Penny at the sink.

He slid his arms around her waist and drew her back against him, nibbling the sensitive skin of her neck. "Sure you don't want to come with me?"

She shook her head. "I've had time to think about what you said last night. It's better if you go alone. That way, you and Curtis can talk man to man and feel free to speak your minds. I'd just be in the way."

"Money, you're never in the way." He turned her into his arms and covered her mouth with his.

When they came up for air, he smiled. "Maybe I can finish this business with your brother sooner than expected, and once we go to the bank and then meet Dex to pay off his debt, I can come back here before the others get home and we'll...talk."

That put a smile on her lips and a glint of laughter in her eyes. "Uh-huh. We'll...talk?"

He shrugged. "If we're lucky, we may even find time for something more."

She pulled his face close and kissed him. "I like the way you think, cowboy."

He framed her face before slowly kissing her. "Hold that thought, Money."

As he walked from the room, she ran to the window and watched as he climbed into one of the ranch trucks and drove away.

Turning back to the sink, she was humming a little tune and thinking of the relief Curtis would feel when Sam offered to clear his debt.

Sam followed the gravel driveway leading to the Lazy K ranch that seemed to go on for half a mile or more. He'd expected to find Curtis standing outside the property line, waiting to meet with Dex. Instead, finding no sign of either Dex or Curtis, Sam pulled up alongside the first of several barns and stepped out of his truck.

Inside, he caught sight of one of the wranglers who had been with Curtis at the Hitching Post the previous night.

"'Morning." Sam strolled over. "Know where I can find your buddy Curtis?"

The bearded cowboy leaned on his pitchfork and gave him a long, steady stare. "Who wants to know?"

"My name's Sam Monroe."

"I saw you last night at the Hitching Post in Haller Creek."

Sam nodded. "I was there with Curtis's sister, Penny."

A grin creased the cowboy's face. "She was one spittin' mad female. Reminded me of a cat tossed in a rain barrel."

Sam chuckled. "Yeah. That about sums up Penny when she realized what a mess Curtis was in. I told her I'd help out her brother."

The wrangler's eyes widened. "That's decent of you. But you're too late."

"Too late?"

"Curtis is gone."

"To meet Dex?"

The cowboy gave a short laugh. "Not if he can help it."

"What does that mean?"

The wrangler turned away and hung his pitchfork on a hook along the wall. "On the ride home last night we tried telling Curtis that our boss doesn't hold with drinking and gambling. But as usual, he just had to find out the hard way. That about sums up his life so far. When Curtis told Everett Noble, the ranch foreman here at the Lazy K, about the trouble he was in and made an offer to work for the next year at half the pay if he could get an advance to cover his debts, he was fired."

Sam's heart plummeted. Curtis was learning some hard lessons. He glanced around. "Will I find him in the bunkhouse?"

The cowboy shook his head. "He's long gone."

"Gone where?"

The wrangler shrugged. "I didn't ask. He didn't say. He just packed up his duffel and left. And if he's smart, he'll hightail it out of the entire state of Montana before he slows down. If Dex Cantrel catches up with him, poor Curtis won't be able to walk. Hell, from what I've heard about Cantrel, Curtis will be lucky if he can still breathe."

With gritted teeth Sam walked back to his truck and climbed inside. On the long drive back to the ranch, he fumed over this latest twist.

Penny would be worried sick about her brother and the lack of information Sam was able to glean. And from what he'd seen so far, Curtis wasn't the kind of man who would call his sister to let her know where he landed just to ease her mind.

Curtis might be lucky enough to outrun Dex for the moment. But unless he put a thousand miles between them and gave up pool hustling forever, the two were bound to meet up again one day.

With Dex's reputation on the line, he would move heaven and earth to collect the ten-thousand-dollar debt, knowing unless he did, the next kid who came along in some seedy bar would try to pull the same stunt.

Sam didn't like Curtis's odds. He could run, but he couldn't hide. Sooner or later he'd be caught. And when he was, playing pool would be the least of his worries. He'd be lucky to get out of this mess alive.

Penny put the first loaves of cheese bread in the oven to bake. Two more were on the counter, rising under linen towels. They would be perfect with the lasagna she was planning for supper. She'd already browned the beef, and it now simmered in the big pot of sauce on the stove.

The house was redolent of Italian spices and the yeasty fragrance of bread baking.

Instead of the usual hustle and bustle of the place, it felt oddly peaceful. Mary Pat had left right after breakfast. Mac, Roscoe, and Otis were in town. Zachariah was holed up in his room, catching up on his beloved legal reviews. The ebb and flow of a familiar Mozart concerto drifted through the closed door.

She picked up a bucket of rags and cleaners and climbed the stairs, determined to stay as busy as possible, in order to keep her mind off Sam and Curtis.

She knew her brother. Even though he would be relieved to have Sam's offer of money, it would gall him to have to accept help. Being the youngest in the family, Curtis had always had this driving need to prove he could keep up with the others. When twelve-year-old Danny had managed to climb to the top of the ancient oak tree on their property, seven-year-old Curtis had crawled up to the roof of their house and fallen to the ground. Instead of learning his lesson, within a week of the cast being removed from his broken leg, he'd walked like a high-wire acrobat across the narrow railing of the bridge over a nearby creek. He'd tumbled into the foaming water spilling over the rocks below and had been knocked unconscious. If not for Danny and Cooper, he'd have drowned.

He'd always been wild and reckless. And though she'd done everything from punishing him to begging him to change, there was just something in him that made him test every boundary.

And though his brothers had always played by the rules,

and she loved them for it, Penny knew in her heart that she loved this rulebreaker just as much. It was true she worried over him, and probably always would. It was also true that she despaired of ever seeing him settle down like other adults. But she loved her wild, unconventional, daredevil brother so much it hurt. And right now, all she wanted for him was to be safe.

At least this time he would be. Thanks to Sam.

She paused in her work.

And hadn't Sam told her that Curtis was a lot like him?

A little laugh issued from her throat as the thought blossomed inside her. Of course. And that's another reason why she loved Sam. That wild, reckless side of him was so at odds with her determination to play by the rules. But despite their differences, he'd proven himself to be a man of honor. Honest, straight-talking, and willing to give Curtis a hand while he figured out how to be a man.

She was smiling as she descended the stairs carrying a bucket of rags and cleaners.

When the back door opened, sending a gust of wind to rattle the cabinet door, she turned, arms laden with rags. "I didn't expect any of you back so..."

The rest of the words she'd been about to say died in her throat.

It wasn't Mac, or Roscoe, or Otis.

The stranger in the doorway was tall, dressed in a rumpled suit that had seen better days. His dark hair was long and stringy beneath a black knit cap. His eyes were dark and narrowed on her with a feral look that had her heart leaping to her throat.

In his hand was a pistol.

A pistol aimed directly at her heart.

CHAPTER TWENTY-THREE

Reacting on instinct, Penny began to turn away, hoping to scream and alert Zachariah. A big hand closed over her mouth while an arm encircled her waist. She was lifted off her feet and hauled, kicking furiously, out the door, where a truck stood idling beside the back porch.

She was thrust into the passenger side and restrained with plastic zip ties on her wrists and ankles. She screamed in terror. Though the plastic bit into her tender flesh, she lifted her feet and bucked, hoping to kick out a window.

Swearing a blue streak, the man withdrew a hypodermic needle from his pocket and stabbed it into her upper arm.

"Let's see you fight now." It was a voice she'd never heard before.

Her vision blurred, and she could feel her movements begin to slow. She could no longer kick her legs. She moved her mouth but made no sound. Within seconds she was unable to sit up. She could feel her body sliding bonelessly to the floor of the front seat.

An engine roared, and the truck was moving.

Penny struggled to focus. Somewhere in the far recesses of her brain, she sensed that it was imperative that she get away. Nobody would ever know where she'd gone. But it was a fleeting thought as her mind began to shut down.

She whimpered once, before falling down a long tunnel of darkness.

The long drive back from the Lazy K gave Sam plenty of time to work through the wave of self-disgust at the way things had turned out. He'd been so sure of arriving in plenty of time to catch Curtis and get him to the bank and back, he hadn't even given a thought to what he'd do if Curtis wasn't there. Hell, where could he be?

Sam's attempts to phone Penny had gone unanswered. He'd left her several messages, but he still hadn't heard from her.

It had never occurred to Sam to ask Penny for her brother's cell phone number before leaving home. So far, he'd been unable to locate Curtis, and he hadn't been able to call him.

By the time he arrived home, he was seething with frustration.

As he pulled up to the back porch, Mac, Otis, and Roscoe were just stepping out of their truck, laughing and chatting after their visit to town.

Mac walked up to Sam. "Where're you coming from, son?"

Sam shrugged. "I'll tell you later. Right now I need to see Penny."

He took the porch steps two at a time and slammed into the mudroom. Seeing the pile of dirty rags, he paused for just a moment before storming into the kitchen.

Before he could call out, he stared in horror at the smoke pouring from the oven. He pulled open the oven door just as the others stepped into the room.

"What the hell...?"

Seeing smoke billowing, Otis raced across the room to open the window.

Hearing the ruckus, Zachariah opened his door and peered out. "What's all the commotion out here? And what's that godawful smell?"

"Smoke." Using a towel, Sam hauled out the burned loaves of bread and tossed them out the window before setting the pot of burned meat sauce in the sink and turning on the taps. It sent a cloud of steam rising above the sink.

"Where's Penny?"

Zachariah scratched his head. "How would I know? If she isn't in the kitchen, she's probably cleaning upstairs."

Sam stormed up the stairs and returned minutes later. "She isn't there. Not that I thought she would be. It isn't like Penny to neglect her chores. First those dirty rags and now the food. Something's wrong here."

Mac's head came up sharply. "What are you getting at, son?"

Sam shook his head. "I don't know. None of this makes any sense. First her brother and now..."

Mac held up a hand, interrupting him. "Penny's brother?"

"I drove to the Lazy K this morning, hoping to get Curtis out of a jam."

Mac's eyes narrowed. "What sort of jam?"

As quickly as possible Sam explained about the pool game and the amount of money Curtis had lost.

Mac listened before asking, "And how were you planning on helping him?"

"I thought I'd take him to the bank and lend him the money to pay Dex Cantrel. But Curtis got fired from his job and left town."

"Did Penny know?"

Sam shook his head. "She and her brother had a falling out. I doubt Curtis would have admitted to her that he'd lost his job over this and was leaving town. She was already mad at him for gambling and drinking."

"If she isn't with her brother, where could she have gone?"

Sam looked around. "The better question is, how could she have left?" He started toward the door. "I'll check in the barn to see if her ancient car or any of the trucks are gone."

Otis put a hand on his arm to stop him. "I'll go. You stay here."

While he was gone, Sam walked to the mudroom and studied the pile of rags.

Minutes later Otis returned to say, "The car and trucks are there. Nothing looks out of place."

"But this does." Sam pointed.

At the blank look on their faces he said, "What's the one thing we've all noticed about Penny?"

Mac nodded in understanding. "She's neat as a pin."

"Exactly." Sam started pacing. "I can't think of any reason she would drop a pile of rags here. Or allow those loaves of bread and spaghetti sauce to burn. Unless..."

"Something or someone forced her to," Mac finished for him.

Sam was already dialing his brother.

"Ben." He put his phone on speaker, and the others stood by while he explained what they'd found at the ranch. "I'm thinking Dex Cantrel couldn't collect from Curtis, so he decided to kidnap Penny to flush her brother out of hiding."

In the blink of an eye Ben's voice switched from concerned brother to that of an efficient lawman. "I'll pull up photos and descriptions of Dex Cantrel and Curtis Cash, and alert the state police and the local law enforcement in the area that both men are persons of interest."

"Let them know that Penny is missing, and I believe she's been kidnapped."

"Bro, I can't accuse a man of kidnapping without some sort of proof."

"I don't have any proof, except this feeling in my gut that Penny didn't leave here of her own free will."

"Did anybody there see her being taken?"

His question was greeted with silence.

Suddenly Otis spoke up. "What about that dirty truck we saw pulling onto the interstate ahead of us?"

Roscoe and Mac nodded as Mac explained. "It appeared to be coming from this direction, and at the time we figured he'd made a wrong turn somewhere, since none of us recognized it."

"Did you see a woman in the truck?"

All three men shook their heads.

Ben's voice came over the speaker. "Can any of you describe the driver?"

Otis shrugged. "I just caught a glimpse of his head. He was wearing one of those black knit caps. Underneath it, his hair was long. But I didn't see anybody else in the truck. Just him."

Ben's voice revealed a trace of disappointment. "That's not much to go on. A lone man driving a dirty truck that may or may not have come from our ranch, or may have just been lost and made a wrong turn. I can't ask the state boys for help with that one."

Sam was quick to say, "I know it's a longshot, but at least mention it to them, Ben."

Ben's voice switched yet again, from lawman to concerned brother. "Sam, stay close to the ranch, in case Penny returns or tries to reach you by phone."

"Like hell I will." Sam studied the strained faces of the men standing around him. "The others can stay here. But I have to do something."

"The best thing you can do is trust that we'll do the job we're trained to do."

"Ben, I—"

The line went dead.

Sam stared at the phone, then turned away and began pacing from the kitchen to the mudroom and back.

The others stood helplessly by, his frustration, pain, and outrage palpable.

Two hours later, when Sam's phone rang, he snatched it up. Seeing the sheriff's office on his caller ID, he said, "Yeah, Ben."

"I paid a call on the Lazy K to learn whatever I could from the ranch foreman. Everett Noble told me Curtis was a good employee, but there had been rumors about his gambling, and when Everett learned the amount of his debt, he had to let him go. The state police have issued an APB on both Curtis and Dex. I expect to hear something positive within the next forty-eight hours."

"Forty-eight…" Sam couldn't hide his disgust. "We're talking about Penny's safety. Maybe her life. We need to find her now, Ben."

"I know. And believe me, Sam, I know what you're going through. But these things take time. Just trust us to find her."

While a hundred curses played through his mind, Sam resumed his pacing.

Trust. It had never been his strong point. In his experience, the ones in authority were often the least worthy of trust.

He knew Ben meant well. If he had to trust the law, it didn't get any better than his brother Ben. Still...

He stalked off to the barn, needing to fill his time with something, anything that would keep him from going mad.

CHAPTER TWENTY-FOUR

Sam's sweaty shirt was plastered to his chest as he deposited another wagonload of wet straw and dung in a field behind the barn. He'd been pushing himself for an hour, unwilling to stop. He knew if he didn't keep going, he'd be tortured with images of sweet Penny, hurt, helpless. Was she traveling against her will with Dex, or had she tried to bargain with him? Worse, had he left her hidden away somewhere while he arranged a meeting with Curtis? Was she shivering in some cold, deserted barn or shack? Had he hogtied her in the back of that truck? The thought of it taunted him, ripping out his heart.

When Sam heard the crunch of wheels on gravel, he set aside the wagon and rushed to the door of the barn in time to see Ben stepping out of his police vehicle.

Climbing out of the passenger side was Penny's brother Curtis.

Sam was beside them in an instant.

Before they could climb the steps, the family came spilling out the back door and gathered around them on the porch.

Sam's hand shot out, clutching the front of Curtis's shirt, dragging him close. "Where is your sister?"

Ben put a hand on his brother's arm. "Back off, Sam. I'm responsible for his safety."

"His safety? What about Penny's?"

Ben's hand closed around Sam's. "I said back off."

Sam's teeth were clenched like a vise as he reluctantly released Curtis.

He and the others studied the young man's ashen face.

"I wish I could help." Curtis looked around at the cluster of men staring daggers at him. "I didn't even know she'd gone missing until the sheriff told me."

Sam wasn't about to let him off the hook. "Oh yeah? Just where did the law finally catch up with you?"

"I was trying to get out of town. I was on the interstate when the state police picked me up and delivered me to Sheriff Monroe. That's when I learned about Penny." Curtis hung his head. "I never meant for this to happen."

"You knew, by running, you were asking for trouble. Dex made it plain that nobody stiffs him."

"I wasn't thinking. And certainly not thinking about my sister. All I wanted to do was get as far away from here as possible."

"Are you saying you haven't heard from Dex?"

Curtis shook his head. "Not a word. But if he's taken Penny..."

"Your sister never would have left here on her own, especially now, when she was waiting to hear news of you. She had to be taken against her will." Sam looked from Curtis to Ben. "Have you checked her cell phone records?"

Ben nodded. "The state boys are on it. If she has it with her, they'll locate her."

"And if it's been tossed?"

Ben gave a slow shake of his head. "Don't get ahead of yourself, Sam. The state police have ways of tracking victims."

Victim.

The very word had Sam's heart dropping like a stone.

Victims were abducted and later found in shallow graves. Victims were nameless, faceless headlines in the news.

He couldn't wrap his mind around Penny being called a victim.

Not the woman he loved.

His hands tightened into hopeless fists of rage, and he turned away from the others, unwilling to let them see the deep-seated anguish he was fighting.

The woman he loved was out there somewhere, alone and afraid. And here he was, listening to the ramblings of her shiftless brother.

He desperately needed to do something.

He turned to Ben. "What are the authorities doing about Dex Cantrel?"

"They're on it. His photo has been sent to every law agency in the state. It's only a matter of time before he's spotted."

"Time?" Sam could feel his head exploding. "Ben, we don't have the luxury of time. Penny is out there somewhere with a guy bent on vengeance. We need to find her now."

Ben put a hand on his brother's shoulder. "I know how worried you are. We all are. But trust me, Sam. With all the police looking for this guy, he'll be found before this day ends."

Sam turned away, knowing the entire family could read his fear. It was so strong, he could taste it.

This was a new kind of fear, one he'd never before encountered.

Despite the hellish violence he'd endured in his younger days, he'd always had a sense that he could fight back. This was different. The threat was against Penny, and he was being told to do nothing but wait and hope. It went against everything he believed in. He hated this feeling of helplessness. He wanted to get in his truck and drive until he found the bastard who had taken her. He was itching to lash out against anyone who would harm his sweet Penny.

Ben's phone rang, and he snatched it up. "Sheriff Ben Monroe here."

He listened, then gave the family a thumbs-up.

At once they crowded around him, waiting until he'd ended his conversation with the invisible entity on the other end of the line.

He disconnected and said, "They've got Dex Cantrel. Picked him up on the interstate."

"And Penny?" Sam couldn't seem to breathe.

Ben shook his head. "Dex was alone. He claims he doesn't know a thing about her."

Sam's heart plummeted. "Give me five minutes alone with that lying bastard and I'll get the truth out of him. Where are they taking him?"

Ben tucked the cell phone into his pocket. "My office in town."

As Sam started toward the door, Ben laid a hand on his shoulder. "I want you to stay here."

Sam slapped away his hand. "Like hell I will."

Ben wrapped a beefy hand around his brother's arm, holding him when he tried to pull away. "I know you'd like to beat Dex senseless..."

"You got that right."

"But the law is my territory, and I'm not going to let you mess this up. I intend to interrogate Dex and get to the bottom of all this, but if you go to town, you have to promise to keep your distance from a man who is innocent until proven guilty."

"Innocent my ..."

Mac walked over to put a hand on both sons' arms. "We'll all go into town, except Zachariah. He'll remain here in case there's a phone call. I promise we'll stand back and let you handle things, Ben. You're the expert."

"Thanks, Dad."

Mac turned to Sam. "Agreed?"

Though his jaw was clenched so tightly his teeth ached, Sam gave a reluctant nod.

Ben instructed Curtis to ride with him in the squad car.

The rest of the family piled into several ranch trucks. As they headed toward town, a pall of silence hung over all of them.

Ben's small office felt even smaller when his entire family crowded inside.

Dex Cantrel glared at Curtis as he took the seat indicated by Ben. The two men eyed one another in sullen silence.

Finn, who had been in his office in town, had been apprised of the situation and joined the rest of his family.

Mac, Otis, and Roscoe dragged chairs from a back room and took their seats as far away from Ben as the small space would allow.

"Now." Ben sat straight and tall in the leather chair behind his desk, knowing it gave him the advantage over his two unwilling prisoners. "Let's begin at the beginning. As I understand it, you two put on quite a show at the Hitching Post. Word around town is you"—he turned the full fire of his gaze on Dex Cantrel—"won ten thousand dollars. And you"—he swiveled his head to shoot a look of disdain at Curtis—"were a willing party to this."

Curtis nodded.

Ben's voice deepened with authority. "You went into this game with full knowledge of the risks?"

Curtis swallowed before saying, "That's right."

"If you had won, you'd have demanded payment in full." Ben fixed Curtis with a frigid look. "Is that about right?"

"Yes."

"But when you lost, you were forced to admit you didn't have enough to pay your debt." Ben didn't wait for a reply before adding, "What kind of fool continues gambling when he knows in advance that he can't pay off his possible losses?"

Curtis's voice was hardly more than a whisper. "A desperate one."

"What made you desperate?"

Curtis clamped his mouth shut, refusing to answer.

Before anyone could react, Sam grabbed the front of Curtis's shirt and pulled him to his feet.

Getting into his face, he snarled, "You can answer the easy way, or you can answer to me."

Before he could land his fist in the younger man's face, Curtis held up his hands in a sign of surrender. "All right." He sucked in a quick breath before saying, "Before I came to Haller Creek, I was working at a ranch in Wyoming and got in with a rough crowd. I got sucked into some big-time gambling. Horses. Sports. Even when I couldn't always pay, my bookie carried me and allowed me to keep on betting."

"Why would he do that?" Ben demanded.

"I agreed to bring him more customers."

"You were a shill for a bookie?"

Curtis shrugged and stared hard at the floor.

"Okay." Ben's harsh tone had the young man looking up quickly. "So, what changed? You stopped bringing him customers?"

Curtis shook his head. "I kept gambling, hoping to win enough to get him off my back. But I...kept losing." He swallowed. "Finally, I owed so much, he threatened to go to my boss, so I quit my job and moved on to Montana, hoping to start over."

Sam's eyes were hard as ice. "Surprise. You didn't really get away from your past. Your bookie found you."

Curtis nodded. "I'd been ignoring his calls whenever I recognized his number. When I went in the men's room of the Hitching Post, my phone rang. When I answered and realized who it was, he claimed he was calling from a new phone and was there, watching the pool game between Dex and me. He said if I went all the way, and won the ten thousand, he'd collect it and call us even."

Ben motioned for Sam to back off.

He turned to Curtis. "Okay. We get the picture. You lost, and the scumbag threatened you."

"I thought I could get an advance from my boss. I was desperate. I figured I'd give half to Dex and the other half to my bookie, with a promise of more to come."

"And now you know he won't give up until he collects. And you know how he intends to do that." Ben looked around at the others. "But how would he know about your sister?"

Curtis hung his head. "She made an ugly scene last night at the Hitching Post. Maybe he figured she'd be good for the money I owe."

Ben looked at Sam for confirmation.

Eyes narrowed in thought, Sam nodded. "It's true. I took her back when she asked, and we saw the final game. When

Curtis lost, and Dex threatened him, Penny was like a wounded mama bear."

Ben leaned forward, fixing Curtis with an icy determination. "Give me your bookie's name, and I'll alert the state police."

With a look of defeat, Curtis was shaking his head. "We never used real names. I had a cell phone number when I wanted to place a bet. I was number thirteen. He called himself Dog."

"Dog." Ben's eyes narrowed on the young man. "Give me the number."

"I told you. He must have changed cell phones. The number he used at the Hitching Post was a new one. If I'd recognized it as his, I never would have answered him."

"Give me the latest number."

Curtis retrieved his phone from his pocket and read aloud the numbers.

Just as quickly, Ben was relaying them on a secure line to the state police.

When he was finished, he looked over. "They'll track him. It's only a matter of time."

"Time." Sam was on his feet, pacing and mentally shouting every rich, ripe swear word he'd ever learned.

"And now this guy has Penny, and who knows what he'll do to her." He turned the full effect of his fury on Curtis. "And you wasted half a day before telling us any of this."

"I didn't know." Curtis shot a pleading look at the sheriff. "I swear, it never occurred to me that this dude would focus on Penny. I was so upset about losing my best shot at paying off my gambling debts, I never even gave Penny a thought." He dropped his head down, fighting a rising sense of fear and revulsion as the truth dawned. "I never meant to put my sister in danger. She doesn't deserve any of this."

Sam's voice betrayed his barely controlled emotions. "That's the first honest thing you've said."

Mac stepped forward and put a hand on his son's shoulder. "Some lessons are harder than others. Right now, we all need to work together to get Penny safely home."

Sam looked across the desk at his brother, who was busy fielding a phone call from a state police coordinator.

When their gazes met and held, Ben gave a barely perceptible nod of his head. "They want me to keep Curtis here so they can monitor his calls. Sooner or later this guy will contact Curtis and tell him what he wants in return for his sister."

"No matter what he asks for, we have no guarantee he'll keep his word and deliver her safely."

Ben was shaking his head. "He has no reason to hurt her."

"No reason?" Sam struggled to rein in his growing fear. "She's seen this guy. She can identify him. She could mean the difference between his going free or spending the rest of his life in prison for kidnapping. What reason does he have for keeping her safe?"

In the silence that followed, Sam turned away, calling over his shoulder, "Keep me in the loop. In the meantime, I'm heading out to the interstate to look for a dirty truck driven by a guy in a black knit cap over long hair."

"That's not much to go on," Ben called.

"It's better than sitting here twiddling my thumbs while the state police try to get a name and wait for a call that may never come."

"He'll call." Ben's tone was equally fierce. "He's gone to all this trouble. He wants his money."

With clenched teeth Sam muttered, "And all I want is Penny safe."

CHAPTER TWENTY-FIVE

Penny began the slow, painful ascent from a drug-induced fog. Her eyes, when she opened them, felt hot and gritty, as though she'd survived a fire. Or maybe it was the fire raging inside her. When she lifted a hand to rub her eyes, both hands moved upward, and she stared at them in surprise. They were bound together with plastic. The loud throbbing that assaulted her ears was an engine. A truck's engine, although they didn't seem to be moving. She was lying on the floor in a heap, like someone's discarded laundry.

When she tried to sit up, her vision swam and she had to swallow back an overpowering feeling of nausea.

"Coming out of it?" The threatening voice she'd heard before losing consciousness had her jerking her head upward.

The driver gave a cruel laugh as she struggled her way from the floor to the seat, all the while wondering why her body was slow to cooperate.

Finally, heart pounding from the effort, she managed to slump into the passenger side, feeling drained beyond belief. As though she'd been climbing a perilous mountain while dragging an anchor. They appeared to be parked in a shed behind an abandoned building.

She turned toward the man at the wheel. "Who are you?"

"My name's not your business. You're my business."

"But why? Why would I possibly matter to you?"

He gave a snarl of laughter. "That's a good one. You don't matter at all. You're just a means to an end."

"Then what..."

His hand shot out. Her words were cut off by a blow to her temple from his pistol.

"I don't answer to you. And if you don't shut that mouth, I'll stick you again with that needle just so I can have some peace. You understand?"

Blood streamed from the blow to her temple, and trickled in a line down the side of her face, staining her shirt. She took no notice. For several long, painful moments, stars flashed in her brain and she thought she might lose consciousness again. Tears burned behind her lids, but she refused to give in to them, blinking furiously. She reminded herself to remain as quiet as possible so she could figure out who this monster was and what he wanted from her.

There was so much she didn't understand. But this much she knew. It had been no random abduction. He'd come armed with zip ties and a drug powerful enough to silence her and render her incapable of escape. If she were to try to fight him, she had no doubt he wouldn't hesitate to use it again.

For now, she would do as he told her. She would keep her questions to herself. She would do all in her power to tamp down the terror that had her by the throat.

Though she was desperate for answers, she could only have them if she kept her wits about her.

But while she struggled to stay alert, she prayed she could keep her poor heart from pounding clear through her chest. In her life, she'd never known so great a fear. And right now, that fear was throbbing through every vein in her body, threatening to turn her into a bubbling mass of hysteria.

Sam drove along the interstate, scanning every vehicle he passed, though he had little to go on except a dirty truck and a long-haired driver. That would fit the description of half the traffic in the state. But right now, he had nothing else to guide him.

While he drove, he was thrust back once more into his painful childhood. All those memories he'd kept locked away, hoping he would never have to confront them again, were now filling his thoughts, stealing his sense of security.

He could see himself being driven, often in the dark of night, to a new house to live with strangers. He'd been ignored by some, made to feel small and insignificant by others, and in a few instances that were branded into his mind, beaten or punished in some other way. Not that he hadn't deserved some of it. From his earliest memory, he'd been a rulebreaker. Over the years he'd morphed from a feeling of helplessness to a desperate need to take control by the only means he could—with his fists. Of necessity, he'd become adept at fighting his opponents and inflicting pain, all the while knowing that in the end he would pay a price for such defiance. The price could be as simple as being locked in a shed or cold garage, or as complicated as being sent to juvenile detention, where, as one of the youngest, he would find himself once again forced to fight for his life.

If only it were that simple now.

This time, there was nobody to fight. All he could do was race along a highway, a feeling of utter hopelessness making him want to strike out at anyone or anything keeping him from finding Penny.

Penny.

His sweet, beautiful Penny. What would she have to endure at the hands of a stranger whose only concern was collecting his pound of flesh?

Sam forced himself to concentrate on the fact that she was no pampered princess. Growing up under difficult circumstances, she'd had to fight her own demons. But was she tough enough to fight a man bent on using her in a dangerous game?

Feeling a growing sense of rage and frustration, Sam floored the accelerator, all the while studying every vehicle he passed.

Mac and the others watched and listened as Ben, pacing the length of his office and back, spoke tersely into his cell phone with a state police detective. They could tell by the tight, pinched look on his face that he wasn't getting the information he was hoping for.

When he hung up, he composed his features before turning to them. "They have a name. Actually several names. He's Emory Pittman. A known criminal. Home invasion. Assault with a deadly weapon. Home base is Canada, but he's been branching out into the States. They suspect him of being connected in some way to the Russian mob. Bookmaking is the least of his criminal activities. Apparently he only engages in that for pocket money. If you call thousands of dollars chump change." Ben rubbed at his temple, a certain sign he was getting a headache. "He calls himself Dog. Horse. The Pit Bull. Probably half a dozen other aliases they don't know yet. He assigns a number to each bettor. That way, if the authorities confiscate his records, all they have is a list of numbers, but no names. He's been able to avoid arrest by routinely changing phones and numbers. The state boys are still working on tracking the number Curtis gave them. Once they have it, they should be able to get an exact location. Unless," he added with a frown, "he's already tossed it and is using another new one."

"How long do they think it will take?"

Ben hissed out a breath. The tone of his voice revealed his frustration. "As long as it takes. In the meantime, the state boys are sending their experts here to monitor all calls. They expect this guy to contact Curtis with his plan, using yet another new phone."

"Plan?" Mac looked hopeful.

"It stands to reason he'll reach out to Curtis. Curtis owes him money. Pittman wants to be paid. By now he's hatched a plan to get what he wants."

Mac looked thoughtful. "Sam had intended to loan Curtis the money to pay off his debt. Since Sam isn't here, I'll phone the bank and make arrangements to make available whatever funds Curtis needs."

"We're talking a lot of money, Dad."

Mac gave a quick shake of his head. "We're talking about Penny's safety, son."

He dialed the owner and president of the little Haller Creek bank and instructed him to prepare the proper documents. "I'll stop by now and sign whatever you need signed."

Finn exchanged a look with his father before turning toward the door. "I've got my truck here. I'll check with Sam and try a different direction."

"Hold on." Ben's voice stopped him. "What the hell good

is it to just drive around without knowing a vehicle description?"

Finn shook his head. "Like Sam, I'll keep an eye out for a long-haired dude in a dirty truck. It beats sitting here waiting for this guy to play us like fish on his line."

Zachariah lumbered to his feet. "I believe I'll go along with Finnian."

As they left, Mac also stepped out of the sheriff's office and walked along Main Street to the bank.

When he returned, it was obvious that he'd come to a decision. He turned to Otis and Roscoe. "I can't disagree with Finn's logic. I can't stand this waiting either. I'd rather do anything than sit here feeling helpless. Are you in?"

The two men were on their feet and starting toward the door.

"I know you understand, son." Mac lay a hand on Ben's shoulder.

Ben nodded. "If I didn't have to follow the letter of the law, I'd do the same. As soon as Curtis hears from Pittman, I'll let all of you know. And, Dad..." He managed a grim smile. "Thanks for coming through with the funds for this."

The two men shared a look before Mac strode from the sheriff's office, trailed by Otis and Roscoe.

A quick phone call to Finn informed them which direction he and Zachariah had taken, and where Sam was. Turning the truck around, the three men headed in the opposite direction at a fast clip.

While Mac drove, Otis and Roscoe were silent as they kept their eyes on the road.

Mac was grateful for their quiet presence. His thoughts were on Sam, alone in his misery.

Mac had seen the bleak look in Sam's eyes when he'd

learned that Penny wasn't with Dex Cantrel, but rather with a dangerous stranger. Dex was nothing more than a gambler. A pool hustler. The stranger was an unknown quantity, who might use Penny until he got what he wanted, and then...

And then discard her.

Mac pulled himself back from such dark thoughts. All his life, the darkest moments had always been swept away by an unexpected burst of sunlight. He would cling to the hope that this situation would prove to be the same.

It had to be, he thought fervently. He'd seen the amazing change in Sam since Penny came into his life. Before, Sam had always been the wild card in their family. The hard-working, hard-playing man who regularly unwound after weeks of backbreaking work on the ranch by challenging the customers at the Hitching Post to endless games of pool, sometimes lasting all night. His had been a careless, casual existence. Since Penny's arrival, he'd been content to spend his evenings at home. And why not? It's what happened to a man in love.

A man in love.

Mac felt his heart pound.

He'd know a thing or two about love. And about losing the love of his life. It had sent him into a spiral of despair that had almost ended in tragedy.

He didn't want that for any of his sons.

Dear heaven, he thought. They had to find Penny before this madman did something that would change all their lives forever.

Sam had found love, peace, and contentment. And in one terrible moment, it could all be taken from him.

CHAPTER TWENTY-SIX

The sky over the tiny town of Haller Creek buzzed with light aircraft and helicopters.

The sheriff's office was crawling with men and women in various uniforms. The Montana State Police had sent their team of experts to set up a base of operations. The Royal Canadian Mounted Police International Crime Unit had sent their own team, since they had been investigating Emory Pittman and his link to Russia for over a year.

Ben's desk was littered with an assortment of high-tech devices ready not only to accept a call from Pittman and stream it to all interested parties, but also to collect and identify any background sounds that could be missed by regular communications. More equipment was set up around the room to pinpoint the location of his call within minutes.

Curtis was seated at the desk, looking pale and visibly trembling as he listened intently to instructions on how to speak and what to ask when the expected call finally came through.

Ben stood back, allowing the experts to do their jobs. He found these men and women to be respectful and efficient as they worked with very little interaction. They had been highly trained to keep distractions to a minimum while preparing a novice like Curtis Cash to follow their orders.

When the phone rang, everyone stopped in their tracks. Though they'd been expecting the call, the shrill ringing in the sudden silence was a shock to the system.

A detective put his hand on Curtis's arm, cautioning him to wait. As explained, this was done to rattle Pittman, who expected his victim to pounce the second he called.

At the third ring, Curtis was prompted to answer. When he did, dozens of devices were listening and operating at full speed.

At Ben's request, the call was also being forwarded to Sam, Finn, Mac, and the others.

He tried to imagine them, pulling over along the interstate, listening with rapt attention to every word spoken. As instructed, Curtis kept his words and reactions to a minimum. "Hello?"

"Thirteen?"

Curtis swallowed and nodded before the detective motioned for him to speak. "Yes. This is Thirteen."

"Dog here. You didn't keep your end of our bargain. So, to make it interesting, I've got something you want."

"Penny? You've got my sister? Penny, can you hear me?"

The detective cut off his words with a hand over his mouth. He had already told Curtis to let Pittman do the talking in order to incriminate himself.

Curtis swallowed and nodded.

Pittman's voice came back on. "Surprise. It came to me in a moment of brilliance last night. Somebody jumped in, eager to fight your battle. I thought I'd see if you'd be willing to do the same if the shoe was on the other foot. So here's the plan. You're going to bring me twenty thousand big ones..."

"Twenty? But I only owe you ten..."

Again his words were cut off by a spitting mad detective who made a throat-slitting motion to be silent.

Curtis looked properly ashamed and shut his mouth.

"The extra ten is to pay me for the inconvenience you've caused. I'll call again in an hour with the location to make the drop. I'll have an associate pick it up. He knows nothing about my plans and can't be of any help to the authorities, if they decide to stick their noses in this. But if I don't hear from him that he and the money are safe, somebody will pay. When I hear that you've followed the rules and haven't tried to be cute, I'll call again and tell you where to find your lost treasure."

"Find her? Won't you exchange her for the money?"

"Her? I don't know what you're talking about, sucker."

Around the room, the detectives winced. Pittman wasn't about to incriminate himself over the phone.

Pittman's voice was slow and deliberate. A man with nothing to fear. "Now listen, kid. This isn't my first rodeo. I'm not about to give you something you want and risk you trying to stiff me with a bag of shredded paper. First you'll pay. Then, if I'm satisfied that you've kept your end of the bargain, you'll hear from me."

"You swear you won't hurt my sister?"

The line went dead.

When her abductor ended his phone call, Penny sat, trying to make sense of all she'd heard.

This man wasn't the pool hustler from last night, but her brother knew him. There had been no names exchanged, and yet, from the tone of their voices, they both knew what was happening. He'd called Curtis Thirteen. Why? She had no idea. And the man had called himself Dog. It suited him. He reminded her of a mad dog. Angry. Snarling. Practically foaming at the mouth.

Curtis was being asked to pay him twenty thousand big ones.

Oh, Curtis, she thought with a wave of terrible sadness. *What have you done?*

And then another thought struck. This man hadn't agreed to return her in exchange for the money. He'd said only that he would tell Curtis where to find her. And when Curtis had asked him to promise not to hurt her, this madman had hung up the phone.

She shot a sideways glance at his grim profile. At that moment he turned and met her stare.

Something flickered in his eyes. Something so dark, so evil, she had to suck in a quick breath to keep from crying out. She turned away to keep him from seeing her fear. But it was there, simmering inside her, and threatening to boil over and destroy her last ounce of hope.

He didn't intend to release her. Especially since she could identify him.

That could only mean one thing.

Sam sat staring at his cell phone without really seeing it. The moment he realized that Pittman had refused to admit having Penny, his heart had taken a painful jolt.

Whatever tiny flicker of hope he'd harbored that her abductor would release her unharmed had just been extinguished.

Penny was smart enough to know there was no guarantee that she'd be exchanged for the debt.

Sam put his head in his hands as a wave of absolute despair swept over him.

The man would never allow a witness to his crime to survive. That's why he would have someone else collect the money. He would be far away before the authorities realized he had no intention of releasing Penny alive.

He looked up at the sound of his father's voice coming over his phone.

"You heard, son?"

"Thanks to Ben, I guess we all heard."

"I believe Penny is now in grave danger."

Sam's voice was barely a whisper. But the pain was evident. "I believe that, too. Dad, I have to find her before..."

"Hold on to hope, Sam. We're all here for her. Finn and Zachariah are driving south. Otis and Roscoe and I are heading north on the interstate. The police will do all in their power to get her away from this madman. We'll coordinate our efforts and we'll find her. We have to."

"I know, Dad. I know."

Sam tucked his cell phone in his pocket and struggled to pull himself together. He needed to think like a criminal. If he wanted to get away with murder, where would he go?

The thought came to him at once. With winter coming, and most of the ranchers' herds already brought to the lower ranges, the hills became a vast wilderness.

He turned his truck in the opposite direction and headed toward the distant high country, covered in mounds of snow.

Penny listened as her abductor spoke in staccato tones to someone on the other end.

"You did what I told you?"

A nameless, faceless voice answered. "Yeah. Took me hours. Damned earth is nearly frozen. If it hadn't been for that shelter, I'd have needed a backhoe."

"Just so you got it done."

"It's done."

"Now you listen. There's a fairground just outside the town of Haller Creek. It's vacant this time of year. There's a little toll booth at the entrance. That's where I told him to meet you. Don't open the bag of money there. And don't show your face. Before you arrive, pull on your ski mask. I don't trust this dumb cowboy to go it alone. By now he's probably run to the cops crying like a baby. They won't have much time to prepare, but you know cops. They're probably already racing to the scene to get a few hidden cameras planted."

The voice said something that had him swearing. "I told you. They're not going to grab you. They know I've got what they want. Just keep the ski mask on until you've driven away."

There were more words from the other end of the line, loud enough for Penny to overhear. "They'll have my license number and the make and model of my car."

"That's why you need to watch for a chance to ditch the car and grab another one. Some old lady picking up groceries. Or a teenager driving daddy's truck. Someone who won't fight back or give you any trouble. Use that to make the pickup, and then do it again afterward, in case you're being caught on camera. By the time the cops trace both vehicles, you'll be long gone. Call me when you get to the motel and let me know it's all there. Then I'll make the final call to our fish." He laughed, and the sound of it scraped over Penny's already taut nerves. "Oh yeah. I'll tell him where he can find his hidden treasure."

Penny couldn't control the tremors that had her entire

body shaking. Her thin cotton shirt and canvas sneakers offered little protection from the cold. She was grateful when her abductor cranked up the heat, but the shivering didn't stop. Nerves, she knew. They had her by the throat, threatening to break her. She was absolutely terrified.

Her abductor put the truck in gear, left the shelter of the abandoned shed, and drove a short way on a highway before he entered a narrow, rutted lane that snaked into the hills. He had tossed her cell phone out the window hours ago.

Now they were climbing steadily, and the temperature had dropped considerably.

She hadn't seen a ranch or a herd since leaving the highway. She couldn't deny the sense of doom that enveloped her. If this stranger decided to kill her in these hills, nobody would find her until spring.

As the truck came up a rise, the trail disappeared, covered with a layer of fresh snow.

They drove through a wooded area toward a windswept hill. Up ahead Penny saw a wooden shed, the roof sagging, the door swinging open and shut in a strong breeze.

The truck came to a shuddering stop, and the driver stepped out and circled the hood before opening the passenger door. He took hold of her elbow and dragged her from the seat. She stumbled and fell to her knees.

With an oath he lifted her to her feet and with a knife sliced through the zip ties around her ankles before forcing her to walk with him to the shed.

It was little more than four walls and a dirt floor. In the gloom, as Penny's eyes adjusted, she saw a big wooden box standing beside a freshly dug hole in the ground.

Her heart sank to her toes when she realized what she was looking at.

Her grave.

CHAPTER TWENTY-SEVEN

Ben stood beside his desk, watching as the money, freshly retrieved from his father's bank account, was stacked in five-thousand-dollar bundles by one of the state police officers.

Curtis was huddled in a chair across the room, looking lost and afraid, while the others bustled about, checking phone lines and tracking equipment.

When the phone rang and the caller was identified, the room went deadly silent.

Out on the interstate, the Monroe ranch trucks once again pulled off to the side of the road to listen in silence. On cue Curtis answered, and Emory Pittman's voice set out the rules.

"Twenty thousand in a canvas bank bag and deposited in the toll booth at the old fairgrounds outside of town. You drive alone. No cops. No guns. No cameras. When my associate assures me my demands were met, I'll phone you with the location of that treasure you want. Anything changes, anything goes wrong, you'll never hear from me again. And you know what that means. You got all that?"

Curtis swallowed hard. "Yes."

The line went dead.

The police led Curtis to an unmarked truck parked at the curb. After going over their instructions one last time, the authorities stepped back. Curtis set the bank bag on the seat beside him and drove away.

On his brief drive to the fairgrounds Curtis knew that every person he passed, from the driver of the mail truck to the couple racing their snowmobiles along the deserted race track at the edge of the fairgrounds, was an undercover officer trained as a sharpshooter. It gave him no comfort. He felt, as he had so often since falling into the never-ending lure of high-stakes gambling, as though he'd lost control of his own life. The man calling all the shots was a pit bull. He'd been given the nickname for a very good reason. Like a dog with a bone, Pittman wouldn't stop until he had what he wanted. At any price. Even the life of an innocent like Penny. His sister, who had never harmed anyone in her life, meant nothing more to Emory Pittman than the means of collecting a debt.

How could a man like Pittman understand just how special Penny was? When he'd been that scared little boy grieving the loss of his father, it had been his teenaged sister who had held him in her arms and promised him that she would never let anything bad happen to him. And she'd kept her promise. Though she'd had almost no life of her own, she'd seen to it that he and his brothers had everything they needed.

And how had he thanked her for all her sacrifices? By falling into the lure of easy money by gambling and drinking with the wrong crowd. The shame of it had kept him from having any contact with Penny.

And now, because of his carelessness, she was in grave danger. And like that little boy he'd once been, he was terrified and grieving the fact that he felt helpless to do anything about it.

Curtis pulled up to the little toll booth and stepped out of the car. Though he was tempted to look around, he'd been given strict orders to set the bank bag inside the little building and drive away.

He was trembling by the time he stepped back into the truck. Trembling and sweating.

A short time later he returned to the sheriff's office, looking pale and haggard.

A state police detective patted his arm. "Good job. Now we wait."

Curtis headed to the back room and stepped into the small bathroom. Dropping to his knees, he hung his head over the bowl and gave in to the sickness gagging him.

After hearing Pittman's demands, Sam put his truck in gear and continued his drive into the hills.

When his cell phone rang, he snatched it up. Seeing the caller identification, he said, "Yeah, Dad. I heard."

"I have Finn and Ben on the line, too. Where are you, Sam?"

"On the old cattle trail that leads to the hills."

"Have you seen anything?"

He sighed tiredly. "Nothing. But I have a feeling. Where else can this guy go without being seen? Half the state troopers are looking for him. He has to be someplace out of the way."

Mac shared a look with Otis and Roscoe, who both nodded.

"It sounds logical. Okay, son. We're heading that way."

Finn's voice came on. "Sounds about right to me, too. I'm going to turn around."

Ben, who'd been pacing the length of his office and back, wishing he could be with his father and brothers, listened to their conversation before saying, "I think your instincts are good, Sam."

"All right. Let your buddies know what I'm doing."

"I will."

Ben looked around his office at the beehive of activity and wished with all his heart that he could be with his family instead of here, watching and waiting.

His gut feeling was that Sam was right. Pittman would avoid civilization and head to the hills.

He touched a hand to the badge pinned to his shirt before calling for attention. A dozen heads came up, and he cleared his throat before filling them in.

When he'd finished, Curtis stepped out of the back room. "I agree with you, Sheriff. But if you're planning on heading up there, I'd like to go along."

Ben was already shaking his head when Curtis added, "My sister's life is on the line because of me. I have to be there. Don't you understand?"

Ben looked at the state police detective who was heading this task force.

The detective was frowning. "I'm not about to send an entire force on a wild goose chase. Give us a few more minutes and we may be able to pinpoint the exact location of the two cell phones we're tracking."

Ben cleared his throat. "I agree we shouldn't send an entire team without better information. But if you don't mind, I'd like to go."

Curtis crossed the room. "Take me along. Please."

Ben looked at the detective, who gave a slight nod of his head.

"Grab a parka. It'll be cold in the hills."

Ben realized he was talking to air. Curtis was already pulling on a jacket and walking to the door.

When Sam tucked his cell phone into his shirt pocket, he paused a moment, pressing his forehead to the steering wheel. What if he was all wrong? What if Pittman was already halfway across the state? What if Penny was already lying somewhere...?

He couldn't go there. He pressed a fist to his chest. Wouldn't he know in his heart if she'd been harmed, or worse, dead? Wouldn't his own heart stop beating if hers did?

He was going crazy thinking of all the possible outcomes.

He put the truck in gear and began moving along a trail that snaked high into the hills. He had to find her. *Had to.* If he didn't, his own life would be meaningless.

He couldn't imagine living in a world without his sweet Penny.

Supremely pleased with himself, Pittman tucked his cell phone away and lifted the lid on the box before turning to Penny, who sat slumped in the dirt in the corner where he'd deposited her.

"Get up, woman."

When she remained where she was, he walked over and pistol-whipped her before yanking her to her feet by her bound wrists, causing her to wince in pain.

That had him smiling. He enjoyed her pain.

He nodded toward the box. "Get in."

She dug in her heels. "I won't."

"Suit yourself. You can climb in and have plenty of time to think about how stupid your brother is, or I'll shoot you right here and dump your lifeless body in there." He gave a chilling laugh. "Your choice, big sis. A quick death? Or a long, slow one?"

Penny stared into the box. Not a box, she mentally corrected. A coffin. Hadn't he admitted as much? He had no intention of letting her live. He was about to seal her in her own coffin. The truth had her shivering violently.

He slammed his pistol against her temple hard enough to have her crying out as she staggered toward the box.

"Just a little reminder. I call the shots around here. And you have nothing to say about it. Now climb in."

On shaky legs she walked closer and paused beside the box.

"Get in."

"I can't. Not with my hands bound. I'll fall on my face."

"As if I care." His knife sliced neatly through the plastic and he gave her a shove, sending her toppling over the edge. "You're going to die anyway."

As she fell headlong into the box, he added, "If that loser brother of yours tries to rat me out to the authorities, I'll tell them I never even heard of you, and they have to believe me. Without a body, it's his word against mine. And they're never going to find your body out here."

While she struggled to untangle herself, he gave a chilling laugh before lifting the wooden lid and slamming it over the top.

Instantly Penny was engulfed in darkness.

She could hear him grunting as he slowly pushed the box to the edge of the hole. Moments later the box was sliding, and then, as it landed, she could hear the scrape of a shovel, and the sound of dirt cascading over the top of the box.

Dear heaven. He was burying her alive. By the time he was finished, there would be no trace of the grave, or of her.

She would disappear from the face of the earth, and nobody would ever know what had really happened up here.

This time she couldn't stop the tears. They fell harder and faster as she raged against her small, dark, hellish prison.

She lay in pitch blackness, alone and terrified, feeling completely helpless and abandoned by the world. She wept bitter tears until there were none left.

CHAPTER TWENTY-EIGHT

Maybe it was the horror of dirt falling on the lid of the box. Maybe it was the realization that she was about to be left all alone yet again. Whatever the reason, Penny's tears stopped, and she felt a rising sense of outrage. An overwhelming anger gripped her.

Being left alone was nothing new to her. She'd been a scared little kid the first time she faced the heart-wrenching loss of her mother. And then again as a teenager when her father died of a broken heart.

She'd gone through a range of emotions in those early years. A feeling of betrayal, as though she and her brothers weren't enough to keep her father fighting to live. And then, when she'd come to terms with the fact that he'd had no choice, she had to deal with other emotions. There had been the fear that their family would be broken up, her brothers taken from her and placed in foster care. Then there had been her own feelings of inadequacy. But despite her misgivings, she'd stepped up to care for an aging great-aunt and three small brothers.

And she'd survived, hadn't she?

As the sound of the dirt continued, she fought an overwhelming desire to curl up in a ball and give in to the rising hysteria bubbling up. But anger inside her was already taking over all her other emotions.

How dare this stranger use her as a pawn in his deadly, ugly game? How dare he think a gambling debt was worth more than her life? Did he have any idea how hard she'd fought to pick herself up from all the tough things life had thrown at her? Did he think he had the right to decide if she would live or die?

She'd won over incredible odds before. She wasn't about to give up without a fight this time.

And then she thought about Sam. He'd once told her about a particularly terrible punishment, and she'd wondered at the time how one little boy could have survived such cruelty. He'd been locked away in a cold, dark shed and forced to spend the night surrounded by rats.

He said he'd felt around in the darkness until he'd located a pitchfork, and he'd used it to scare away the vermin that had crept up in the darkness. Just having that one tool in his hand gave him courage. He knew he wasn't helpless.

How could she do less than that scared little boy?

She lifted her hands to her face to wipe away the trace of tears and realized she'd already won a tiny victory. Her hands and ankles were unbound. Maybe it was only a baby step, but even baby steps could win the race.

When the stranger finished covering up her grave, he intended to simply drive away and leave behind no trace of his vile deed. Unless she survived, he would win.

Not this time, she thought, gritting her teeth. There had to be something she could do to save herself.

As she twisted this way and that, she felt the scrape of something in her back pocket. Her father's old Swiss army knife.

There was barely enough room to maneuver from one side to the other, but she managed to dig her fingers into her back pocket and retrieve it. Though it was pitch black in this place, she knew this little tool by touch alone. How many times through the years had she blessed the clever minds that had designed such a thing?

She tugged on the various sides of the tool until she uncovered the knife blade. Lifting it above her head she began chipping away at the wooden lid of her coffin.

Baby steps, she reminded herself as fear began to creep back into her thoughts.

Baby steps.

Sam's truck ate up the miles on the upward, circuitous route. Seeing no sign of life, he was cursing himself for his lack of judgment while rounding a bend. As he came to the first line of snow, he was debating the wisdom of turning around. He'd wasted precious time trying to think like a criminal. He should have waited for the police to pinpoint exactly where Pittman's phone call had been made.

He decided he would turn around as soon as he found a level space.

Just then he spotted a line of tire tracks.

Fresh tire tracks in the snow.

Heart pounding, he dialed his dad's number.

When Mac answered, Sam's voice was suddenly alive with energy. "I'm almost at Devil's Pass. Fresh snow up here. And fresh tire tracks. I'm heading up."

Mac reached Finn on the first ring and passed along Sam's news.

Finn's voice went from weary to excited. "I'm on my way."

Ben plucked his cell phone and listened, then turned around and headed his SUV toward the hills.

Curtis looked over. "Have you heard something?"

"Maybe. Maybe not. But it's the first hopeful sign, and I'm not about to ignore it. Hold on. I'm about to set a new speed record."

Sam drove through a stand of evergreens heavy with snow. As he did, he caught a flash of light reflecting up ahead. Could it be sunlight on a windshield?

He sped up and nearly collided with a dirty truck heading in the opposite direction, right toward him. Seeing him, the driver swerved and floored the vehicle, avoiding a collision.

Sam caught only a glimpse of the driver, but it was enough to convince him it had to be Emory Pittman. The driver was wearing a black knit cap over long, stringy hair.

He turned the wheel sharply and tailed the truck until he got close enough to ram the bumper. Caught by surprise, the truck went into a tailspin and spun around until it ended up in a snowbank. The driver's door opened, and Sam saw the man crouch low using his truck as a shield as he fired off several shots.

Hearing the bullets hitting his truck, Sam snagged his rifle before crawling out the passenger side.

He took a moment to study his surroundings. The wall of evergreens offered the perfect cover to attempt to get closer and, hopefully, surprise the gunman. Moving quickly, he darted from tree to tree until he had circled the area and was behind Pittman. While he watched, the gunman got to his feet and took careful aim at Sam's gas tank.

"Drop the gun."

At Sam's terse command, the man turned. Seeing Sam's rifle aimed at his chest, he did as he was told, letting his pistol drop into the snow.

"Where is Penny?"

"Penny?" The man gave a chilling smirk. "Sorry. I don't know anyone named Penny."

Sam walked closer, keeping his rifle aimed at the man. "The woman you kidnapped. Where is she?"

Pittman gave a negligent shrug. "Kidnapped? You're talking about a federal offense. I'm too smart for something like that. But I did spot a hitchhiker. A pretty little thing. I passed her back in some hick town. You might know of it. Haller Creek. Maybe that's your missing woman."

"You lyin' sonofa..." Sam lunged toward him.

Anticipating him this time, Pittman gave a quick karate chop, dislodging Sam's rifle from his hands. As it flew into the snow, Sam grabbed him by the throat.

Pittman brought up his booted foot and kicked Sam in the groin hard enough to have him doubling up in pain. That was all the distraction Pittman needed to drop to one knee in the snow and retrieve his pistol.

In a rage Sam reared up and heard the gunfire before he realized he'd been shot. A bullet grazed his head, slamming him backward. Shaking his head to clear his vision, he kept on coming, and Pittman fired again. This time the bullet hit Sam's leg with such force it tore through his flesh and exited the other side, causing a river of blood. Sam felt himself dropping to the ground. In an instant Pittman was on him, eager to take advantage of his weakness.

Fists flying, curses muttered through clenched teeth, the two men fought savagely. They barely looked up at the sound of vehicles approaching.

As Sam's family raced toward the two men, they could see that Sam was wounded. His parka was smeared with his blood, with more blood spilling from the gaping wound to his leg.

Finn leapt into the fight, pulling Pittman off his brother and landing a punishing blow to his chin before yanking the pistol from his hand and taking aim.

Pittman went down to his knees, shaking his head in an effort to clear it.

Mac hurried over to help Sam to his feet. "You've been hit, son."

"I'm fine." Sam pulled away and raised a fist to Pittman's face. "Now you're going to tell me the truth. Where is Penny?"

Penny had managed to chip away at the lid, carving a splintered chunk barely big enough to force her hand through. A hand that was torn and bloody from the effort.

Dirt spilled down through the chink in the lid, stinging her eyes, and she blinked furiously and wriggled around until she could almost kneel. The effort had her struggling for breath, but she continued pressing her head, arms, and shoulders against the wooden lid, determined to lift it far enough to dislodge the dense layer of earth that acted as a seal.

With supreme effort she felt the lid's slight movement. It was infinitesimal, but she experienced a moment of triumph before she was forced to fall back down and gather her strength for the next attempt. When she'd caught her breath, she knelt up and began the almost superhuman effort again and again.

Though it was slow and painful, Penny could feel a measure of success. Each push now seemed to dislodge more and more of the dirt, and the lid seemed to inch a bit higher with each shove, though she knew she had a long way to go.

She sat back on her heels and thought about her father's favorite phrase. "Difficult is easy. The impossible might take a while."

She felt tears welling up in her eyes and blinked furiously. She wouldn't cry. Not when she was so close.

Taking a deep breath, she pressed her head, her arms, her shoulders once more against the heavily weighted lid and shoved with all her might.

Ben's SUV pulled up behind the other trucks, and he and Curtis were out in a flash. As they cleared the vehicles, they saw Sam holding Pittman by the front of his parka, about to land a fist in his face.

"All right now." Ben stepped up, gun in hand, his badge winking in the sunlight. "Step away, Sam."

"Not until he tells me where Penny is."

Ben looked around in confusion. "She isn't here?"

Sam shook his head. "This scumbag is going to tell us where she is, or I'll beat it out of him."

Ben turned to the scowling man. "I'm Sheriff Ben Monroe. Emory Pittman, you're under arrest for kidnapping and extortion."

The man showed no emotion. Not surprise, nor remorse. "Just who is it I'm supposed to have kidnapped?"

Sam swore and reached out, but Ben was quicker and stepped between them. "You took Penny Cash from the Monroe ranch and demanded twenty thousand dollars from her brother, Curtis. Or as you know him, Thirteen."

The man gave a half smile. "Thirteen? Sounds like a lucky number."

Ben looked over at Curtis. "Do you recognize the voice?" Curtis nodded.

"And I recognize the face from the pictures produced by the Canadian authorities." Ben snagged Pittman's hands behind his back before cuffing him.

When Ben started marching him toward the SUV, Sam grabbed Ben's arm. "Wait a minute. You're not going to leave."

"I need to get this man secured until the rest of the team arrives. They're on their way. Thanks to you, I've already alerted the state and Canadian authorities where we are. On the way up here, they were able to locate the signal from his cell phone. His last call came from this direction."

Sam was in a state of fury as he reached out and grabbed Pittman's arm. "I don't care about any of that. I need to find out where he stashed Penny."

"Penny?" Pittman glanced over his shoulder and gave a chilling laugh. "I don't know anybody by that name. Looks like you got the wrong guy, Monroe."

Before Sam could land a fist, Ben was again between them, steering the handcuffed prisoner toward his vehicle.

Over his shoulder he called, "I know how you feel, Sam. But I have a duty to deliver my prisoner to the state police. When they finish interrogating him, if he knows anything at all about Penny, they'll have the truth." He turned to his brother, seeing blood seeping from the wound to his leg. "You need to get to the town's clinic. You're losing way too much blood." Ben turned to the rest of his family. "I'll need all your statements back at my office."

"No." Sam's voice lowered to a dangerous level. "You can leave." He looked around at the others. "You can all leave. But I know in my heart Penny isn't dead. If she was, I'd feel it here." He touched a hand to his heart. "Whatever that bastard did to her, she's hurting. She could be lying somewhere right now, wounded and in pain. I'm not going anywhere until I find her."

CHAPTER TWENTY-NINE

Before Sam could say more, a convoy of trucks snaked up the hill in a long line. Up above, several helicopters circled and began coming in for a landing, sending snow swirling about, creating a near-blizzard.

Two of the uniformed state police took Pittman from Ben and headed toward the first vehicle.

As he was marched away, Pittman loudly denied knowing anything about a woman named Penny, except to say he'd spotted a hitchhiker back in town, who was probably their missing woman.

"You're not pinning a kidnapping charge on me," he shouted.

One of the officers ordered a team of medics to tend to Sam's wounds until they could fly him to the nearest clinic. One medic began wrapping his leg to stem the flow of blood. Two men carrying a gurney between them hurried over.

By this time Sam was in a fine temper. "I told you. I'm

not going anywhere with you until I find Penny." He pointed to the snow-covered hillside. "Pittman was coming from that direction. I'm heading up there."

One of the officers from a helicopter stepped closer. "I spotted tire tracks up there as we were circling for a landing."

"Thanks, Officer." That was all Sam needed to hear.

The family watched helplessly as Sam limped toward his truck, leaving a faint trail of blood with every step.

Before Ben could say a word, Mac put a hand on his arm. "Your brother's right, son. We need to find Penny now. There's no time to waste."

"But Sam's wound...?"

"You know Sam. He'll never give in until he's satisfied that he's done all he can." Mac started toward his truck, with Zachariah, Otis, and Roscoe following.

Finn raced over and caught the door of Sam's truck before he could put it in gear.

The rest of the family piled into a second truck to follow.

With a muttered oath Ben did the same. When he jumped into his SUV, Curtis raced to catch up with him, settling himself into the passenger side.

Sam followed the tire tracks in the snow until they ended near a run-down shack in the hills.

Heart pounding, he was out the door and racing toward the building, leaving more bloody tracks.

His family raced after him.

As they walked inside the shed, Sam was standing in the gloom, peering around with a look of heartbreaking sadness and despair.

He glanced at his father. "I really thought I'd find her tied and gagged in here."

Mac moved to drop an arm around his shoulders. "I know how it feels to absolutely refuse to believe anything bad can happen to the ones we love."

Sam was shaking his head. "I know you've been through it, Dad. But this isn't like that. Don't you think I'd know in my heart if Penny was gone?"

Again he touched a hand to his chest, and his father's sorrow deepened at the sight of all that pain.

Ben started toward Sam. "I'm really sorry. But if you're satisfied she isn't here, you need to come with me now. I'm really worried about you. You're still losing too much blood, bro."

Sam was shaking his head as his father and brother began to lead him toward the door, standing open and swinging in the bitter wind.

As they moved forward, Sam stopped. "Did you hear that?"

"What?" The others paused to look at him.

"That." He turned around. "Like...scratching."

Mac squeezed his shoulder. "It's the door creaking."

Ben's big hand closed around his brother's arm. "I'm worried about your mental..."

"There." Sam wrenched free and hurried over to stand in the middle of the dirt floor. "I'm not crazy. I hear...something."

Just then he saw, out of the corner of his eye, some of the dirt shift.

"There!" He pointed, and the others turned to stare.

Instantly he was racing to the spot and shouting. "Penny! Are you there? Can you hear me?"

The dirt shifted again, and this time everyone saw it.

All of them were on their knees, using their hands to scrabble frantically, clawing at the ground.

Curtis was working more frantically than any of them. With each scoop of dirt he was calling out to his sister. "Penny. Please be all right. Please, Penny."

To their amazement they faintly heard Penny's screams and saw, beneath the layer of dirt, a wooden lid. And when they'd finally managed to remove the earth from the wooden lid, it began to lift.

Otis dropped to his knees and folded his hands as though in prayer. "Oh, sweet heaven bless us. Miss Penny."

With everyone grabbing at the heavy lid and lifting it free, she stood up and was engulfed in Sam's strong arms as he pulled her from the coffin and gathered her close for a fierce embrace.

"I knew you weren't dead," he whispered against her temple. "I just knew it. I was sure you were here, but I couldn't…"

Penny stopped him with a finger to his mouth. "Shhh. I knew you'd never give up searching for me. I wanted to give in to my fear, but all I could think about was you, and the frightened little boy you once were, who had to fight for his freedom. How could I do less?"

"Oh, Money." Seeing her torn, bloody hands, he pressed a kiss to each palm. "I'm so sorry you had to go through all this…"

"But I'm safe now." She pushed a little away and realized for the first time that he'd been wounded. "Oh, Sam. You're bleeding." She looked around. "What happened to him?"

"Your abductor shot him," Ben said.

"Sam! You've been shot…?"

"It doesn't matter." He dragged her against him and pressed his face to her hair. "All that matters is that you're safe."

She stood a moment, allowing herself to savor his

warmth, his strength. Then, as she heard his hiss of pain, she pushed a little away and turned to the crowd of officials standing nearby. "He needs a medic."

"And she needs a parka," Sam said.

At once the medical team stepped forward with a blanket for Penny and a gurney for Sam.

Two men lifted him and secured him with straps before starting toward the door of the shed.

Now Penny was all business. "He's losing blood. He needs something for the pain right now..."

Sam caught her hand and gave her one of his heart-stopping grins. "I love it when you get all bossy, Money."

She gripped his hand tightly in hers and felt the first tears brimming up and spilling over.

She sniffed. "Now you've made me cry."

"I'm sorry." He pulled her close and brushed a kiss over her mouth.

"It's okay. These are happy tears."

"Good. Now let's get out of this creepy place."

Penny gave a last look at the coffin, and at the men and women sweeping the dirt and bagging and tagging evidence.

She'd thought this deserted shack on a windswept hill would be her tomb.

Now she knew it to be a place not of evil but of magic. She'd been lost and was found. She'd been in the depths of despair and was now feeling light as air.

And all because of this amazing man who could lift her higher than any mountain with just a wink and a smile even in the depths of his own pain.

"Penny." As Penny and Sam were boarding the helicopter, Curtis rushed over to wrap his arms around her neck and bury his face in her hair. A face stained with dirty tears from digging in the dirt. "I'm so sorry, Penny. I never thought any of this could touch you. I never meant for any of this to happen. Can you ever forgive me?"

She gave him a tired smile. "The question should be, can you forgive yourself?"

He shook his head and looked so remorseful, she couldn't help but draw him close. "There are lessons to be learned from this."

"Lessons?" He shook his head in wonder. "Even now, with all you've been through, you just can't help being a teacher."

"I guess you're right." She sighed. "Curtis, the lessons today were painful for all of us, but always remember that it could have ended in a much different way. I don't know how we got so lucky this time. But I do know this. You'll need to think about the path you've taken and see if you can't find a better one in the future. I can't help but think you were given a second chance for a reason." She gave him a long, steady look. "But never forget, Curtis, you're my little brother. I love you more than my own life. There's nothing you could do that would ever make me turn away from you."

"Oh, Penny." With a sob he hugged her fiercely, and she returned the hug before stepping back.

With Ben's hand on his arm, Curtis watched as she climbed aboard the helicopter. Then he was led away to join her family, waving along with them as the helicopter lifted, scattering snow as it ascended high into the sky and headed toward Haller Creek.

Penny settled herself beside Sam, who was already drifting in and out of consciousness.

She studied his rugged, handsome face.

There had been moments when she'd feared she would

never see him again. And now, with the nightmare behind her, she couldn't get enough of watching him, of breathing him in.

She linked her fingers with his and lowered her head to his chest, content to simply feel the warmth of him envelop her as she listened to the steady beating of his heart.

CHAPTER THIRTY

In the little town of Haller Creek, folks at Dolly's Diner peered out the windows as they watched a state police helicopter land in the parking lot of the Haller Creek clinic. It wasn't something they saw every day. Or the line of police vehicles pulling up to the sheriff's office, where a handcuffed prisoner was taken inside, followed by a cluster of uniformed officers.

At the barbershop one of the men remarked, "That looks like Mackenzie Monroe racing into the clinic. What're the odds it's one of his boys?"

A longtime resident chuckled. "They're scrappers, all right. And darned good with their fists. I just hope one of 'em didn't get himself shot."

Horton Duke ambled toward the door. "Since I've got some time to kill, I think I'll just head on over to the clinic and see what's what."

The men seated in the barber chairs hoped he wouldn't

take too long. His news, whatever it was, would make for exciting conversation tonight around the kitchen table.

"Now, Mac." Dr. Dan Clark held up a hand as the Monroe family gathered around Penny's bed in the examining room. "You're all going to have to head to the waiting room while I examine my patient."

Zachariah used his best courtroom voice. "I'll have you know, Daniel, this young woman"—he indicated Penny— "has just been through a life-and-death trauma."

Dr. Clark fixed the old man with a withering look. "This is my clinic. My rules."

"Perhaps I should mention that all of us experienced that same trauma." Zachariah glowered at the doctor.

Dr. Clark looked around. The old men stood with arms crossed over their chests, feet planted like trees. Mac and Finn stood side by side, forming an impenetrable wall. It was clear that none of them had any intention of following his orders.

With a look of exasperation, he motioned for his nurse, Jenny Turnbull, to assist.

While he worked he said to the others, "Sam is already undergoing surgery in the OR with Dr. Wilson. The doctor's preliminary examination showed that the first bullet grazed Sam's head. Sam was lucky. Another inch, he could have died. The second bullet seems to have passed clear through Sam's leg, without piercing anything vital. Except for the loss of blood and the pain he'll suffer for a while, he should have no aftereffects from the wounds."

After probing Penny's bloody temple, Dr. Clark nodded toward his nurse. "We'll stitch this wound and give her something for those raw hands."

Penny gave a sigh of resignation as the nurse swabbed the

area before administering something to ease the pain of the stitches.

A short time later, her wounds neatly stitched and the pain thankfully numbed, her raw and bloodied hands wrapped in soothing dressings, she was helped into a recliner chair and covered with a warm blanket.

As the others filed out of the room, Penny finally gave in to an overwhelming exhaustion and closed her eyes.

Though she fought to stay awake, hoping to be here for Sam when he was returned from the operating room, she was asleep within minutes, thanks to the drugs the doctor had given her.

The recovery room at the clinic was warm and silent, the lights dimmed to induce rest.

Penny awoke from a dark, disturbing dream and sat a minute, struggling to get her bearings.

Hearing the sound of slow, even breathing, she glanced to her left and saw Sam in a bed beside her chair. She sat up, shoving hair from her eyes, and drank in the sight of him.

Safe.

They were both safe.

Overcome with love and gratitude, she tossed aside the blanket and stepped up beside his bed.

"Hey, Money." He reached out to take her hand. "What's this?" He struggled to focus on the dressings on her hands.

"Just some healing ointment." She wiggled her fingers protruding through the dressings. "What's more important is that you're awake. How are you feeling?" She touched a hand to his forehead.

"Like I got hit by a train. But none of that matters. You're alive." He patted the edge of the mattress. "Lie here with me."

She slipped into bed beside him. He drew her close. "I've never been as afraid in my entire life as I was when you were in the hands of that madman."

"Not even when you were that little kid locked in the shed?"

"Those fears didn't even come close to what I was feeling when Pittman denied ever seeing you. I knew then that he'd stashed you somewhere, hoping you'd never be found."

"Oh, Sam." She wrapped her arms around him and pressed her lips to his throat to whisper, "I'm so thankful you found me. Ben and Finn said you refused to give up, even when the others wanted to. They're calling you Super Sam."

He grinned. "Yeah. That's me. Except right now I'm Not-So-Super-Sam."

"You're perfect to me. Do you need anything?"

"Baby, I have all I need right here." He buried his face in her hair and breathed her in.

They fell asleep in each other's arms, feeling the weight of the world slip away.

"Well." Dr. Dan Clark took his time examining both his patients before looking up. "It's plain you can't keep a good man, or woman, down. You're both doing fine. I'll sign your discharge papers and you'll be free to go as soon as you call your family for a ride."

Sam chuckled. "Check the waiting room, Doc. I got a text that they're already here."

The doctor grinned. "I should have known. The Monroe family is always a step ahead."

Sam and Penny sat close together in the backseat, hand in hand, watching as the ranch came into view.

"I don't think home ever looked this good to me." Sam squeezed Penny's hand. "How about you?"

She nodded, afraid to trust her voice she was so overcome with emotions. Home. When had this ranch, which had begun as a temporary source of income until she could find her dream job, become home to her?

Was it when she'd discovered just how much joy her simple homemaking added to one family's life? Or was it when she'd realized just how much she loved one particular member of that family? Whatever the reason, she felt such a feeling of joy at returning to this place, she couldn't think of any way to express herself.

Seeing tears welling up in her eyes, Sam drew a protective arm around her.

Finn glanced over his shoulder. "I hope the two of you are hungry. When we left, Mary Pat had taken over the kitchen and was cooking up a storm."

"Mary Pat's back?" Sam started grinning. "Now Dad can really get into the celebration mood."

"We all can." As the truck came to a halt alongside the back of the house, Zachariah stepped out and held the door for Penny and Sam. He bent to press a kiss to Penny's cheek and clapped a hand on Sam's arm. "Welcome home, you two. This is a day to remember."

Before he'd finished speaking, the back door opened and the family spilled out and down the steps to hug Penny and Sam and led them inside.

Penny breathed in the wonderful fragrance of bread baking and meat roasting, and felt the prick of tears behind her lids as Mary Pat turned from the stove to hug them both.

"I hear I missed a great deal of drama," Mary Pat said with a smile.

"I wish we could say the same." Sam winked at the others

before adding, "You should have seen Penny. She wasn't about to go gently. She fought like a wounded bear."

Mary Pat touched a hand to his arm. "And you're looking very proud of her."

"You bet." He caught Penny's hand, linking his fingers with hers. "Whenever I look at her I think of the words *I am woman, hear me roar.*"

That had everyone smiling.

"Well, woman who roars..." Mary Pat kissed Penny's cheek before adding, "And all you gentlemen, we'll eat as soon as Ben and Becca get here."

"That will give us time for a cold longneck." Finn reached into the refrigerator and began handing around beers.

Sam shook his head. "None for me. I'm already zoning out on all the pain medicine."

Mary Pat turned to Penny. "Are you up for some white wine?"

Penny held up a hand. "Like Sam, I'm on some pain meds."

"I'll drink one for you." Mary Pat filled a tulip glass with white wine and lifted it in a toast. "Here's to all women who roar."

That brought another round of laughter just as Ben and his wife walked into the kitchen, trailed by a tail-wagging, very happy Archie.

Mac's smile became radiant as he looked around the room.

When Ben and Becca each had a drink in their hands, the family began a round of toasts to their resident heroes.

And then, as they took their places around the table, Mary Pat began passing a celebration feast of pot roast, cooked to perfection, along with twice-baked potatoes, green beans with slivered almonds, a garden salad, and crusty rolls still warm from the oven. As they began filling their plates, Otis glanced toward the kitchen counter, where a chocolate layer cake stood on a pretty footed plate.

"A word of caution," he muttered. "You may want to forget about seconds if you intend to enjoy Mary Pat's dessert."

The others looked over and nodded in agreement.

Mac patted his middle. "I could have thirds, and I'd still find room for that."

Mary Pat merely closed a hand over his before offering a blessing.

"We give thanks for this food and this family gathered together in safety and love."

Sam winked at Penny as they bent to their celebration feast.

A log burned in the fireplace, filling the parlor with the wonderful fragrance of woodsmoke. The family gathered around, sipping hot chocolate or coffee, and talking in low tones about how they were feeling about all that had transpired.

Becca turned to Penny. "Ben couldn't stop talking about you and Sam, and how in tune you are to each other. He said Sam refused to go to the clinic, despite having been shot, until he found you, and you'd already worked your hands bloody digging yourself out of that terrifying tomb."

Penny shivered and Sam's arm was there at once, encircling her waist and drawing her close against him.

His reaction wasn't lost on the others.

"It did feel like a tomb. And I know that's what that monster intended. I'm just grateful that he didn't shoot me first before burying me, or no one would have ever found me."

Mary Pat gave a firm shake of her head. "Enough talk about what might have been. Let's savor the fact that the two of you are here where you belong, safe and sound with the ones who love you."

Penny and Sam exchanged a look, and it was clear that Mary Pat's words had affected them deeply.

Ben emptied his mug of hot chocolate and got to his feet. "I need to get back to work. If you don't mind driving into town tomorrow, I'd like all of you to stop by my office and sign some documents. While you're there, I've been advised that the authorities have been working around the clock and will bring you up to date on all the final details of this case."

Ben and Becca attached Archie to his leash and dispensed hugs and kisses before leaving.

When they were gone, Roscoe and Otis made their way to the bunkhouse. Zachariah closed himself in his room. When Penny offered to help clean up the kitchen, Mary Pat shooed her off to bed.

"You may have been released from the hospital, but you still need some time to rest and heal. Now go. Mac will help me clean up down here."

Sam and Finn followed Penny up the stairs, leaving Mac and Mary Pat alone in the kitchen.

She poured another mug of coffee and handed it to Mac before sitting down at the kitchen table.

"Now." She took a sip of coffee and patted the chair beside hers. "Why don't you tell me how you're feeling?"

A slow smile touched his lips. "You know me so well, don't you?" He settled himself beside her and stretched out his long legs. "I feel as though, finally, at long last, I can breathe again."

They sat, hands touching, enjoying a rare moment of peace as silence slowly settled over the house.

CHAPTER THIRTY-ONE

The morning clouds had disappeared, replaced by a brilliant sun. The countryside was ablaze with fiery autumn color that added to the festive feeling.

Mac promised the family a special lunch at Dolly's Diner as soon as they finished their business in town.

They drove two trucks to Haller Creek for their morning visit to Ben's office. Finn drove one truck with Zachariah in the passenger seat and Sam and Penny in the back. Mac drove a second truck with Mary Pat beside him and Otis and Roscoe in the backseat.

Sam and Penny wore matching smiles as they sat quietly, letting Finn and Zachariah carry on a conversation.

While the two up front got into a heated discussion of trial tactics, Sam leaned close to whisper to Penny, "Last night was special."

Penny blushed. "It was special for me, too. I just hope nobody saw you leaving my room this morning."

He touched a hand to her cheek. "I don't care if the whole world sees me. I intend to be with you again tonight. And every night, until you get tired of me."

"Tired of you?" She smiled up into his face. "Sam, that's never going to happen. Never."

As they neared the town of Haller Creek, they both fell silent. But their secret smiles remained.

They stepped into the sheriff's office and were met by Ben and Captain Donnelly of the State Police, as well as Inspector of International Operations McMasters of the Royal Canadian Mounted Police.

After signing documents, they were brought up to date on what had transpired since the arrest of Emory Pittman, and the charges against him.

Inspector McMasters was smiling broadly. "Miss Cash, the evidence provided by your brother Curtis, as well as your own firsthand account of what Pittman did to you, will be enough to see an international criminal put away for a very long time."

"I'm glad." She took in a breath. "And his accomplice?"

The inspector nodded. "A small-time criminal with a list of petty crimes. But the fact that he crossed the border made this an international crime, and he is due for some hard time. He was arrested at a nearby motel, and the money confiscated as evidence. He has agreed to testify against Pittman, in return for a reduced sentence."

As they were shaking hands with the family, Curtis stepped into Ben's office.

He kept his head down, face averted. "You wanted to see me, Sheriff?"

Ben nodded. "I've been informed that, because of your agreement to testify against Emory Pittman, all illegal gambling charges against you will be dropped. I hope you understand that you've been given a second chance. Now it's time to get your life in order."

"Thank you, sir." Curtis shook hands solemnly with Ben, and then with the rest of his family.

He turned to his sister. "Penny, I hope you know how sorry I am about everything."

Seeing that his apology was sincere, she nodded. "I know, Curtis. And as I told you, I'm just grateful that you understand and are willing to own your mistake."

"I do. I know now I was headed down a wrong road, hoping for easy money. I love you, Penny. And I promise I'll make you proud."

"I love you, too, Curtis." She hugged him fiercely. "Have you thought about what you want to do in the future?"

He nodded. "I've already talked to an Army officer about enlisting. They accepted me, thanks to Sheriff Monroe's offer to vouch for my character."

Penny looked over at Ben and her smile grew. "That's generous of you, Ben."

"The Army always needs good men. I think Curtis is ready for the next chapter in his life."

Curtis nodded. "More than ready. I leave this afternoon."

"So soon?" Penny wrapped her arms around her little brother and choked back tears. "We barely had a chance to reconnect. But I understand. You have the right to get on with your life. I'm so proud of you, Curtis."

He shrugged, clearly embarrassed at being the center of attention. "I'm hoping, if I'm lucky, that sometime in the future I'll get stationed with Danny or Cooper. At any rate, I'll get to see the world. And"—he turned to Sam—"I'll think about you and the way you love your ranch whenever I'm marching with a heavy pack, knowing I don't have to muck out smelly stalls anymore."

"You sound just like I did the first time Mac forced me and my brothers to muck stalls. We had to hold our noses to get through it."

That brought a round of laughter from the entire family.

Penny hugged the sound to her heart. If she had to say good-bye to her little brother so soon, at least he was leaving on a happy, hopeful note.

When they finally stepped out of Ben's office to make their way to Dolly's Diner, Penny was wrapped in a hazy glow of happiness.

She turned to Sam. "I can hardly believe it. Yesterday, I was at my lowest point ever. I really thought I might never see another day. And here I am, alive and being given the wonderful news that my little brother is turning his life around. And all because of you and your family. I don't believe my life could be any sweeter."

He dropped an arm around her shoulder and drew her close. "Nobody deserves a sweet life more than you, Money."

Mac led the way to the diner. "Come on. I phoned ahead to reserve a table. It's time we celebrated all the good things in our lives."

Roscoe was rubbing his hands together, just thinking about Dolly's meat loaf and garlic potatoes.

Once there, Dolly showed them to a large round table. While Loretta, their waitress, poured water and coffee for those who wanted it, Dolly told them her specials before leaving to tend to other duties.

Otis was beaming when Loretta brought him not only the meat loaf he'd ordered but also a bowl of collard greens. "Now how in the world did you manage to find collard greens this time of year, Miss Loretta?"

She chuckled. "The minute Dolly heard the Monroe family was coming for lunch, she sent me out to find some at the store. It took some searching, but here's the proof."

The old man dug into his treat, his smile growing with every bite.

Mary Pat was enjoying Dolly's pot roast and mashed potatoes smothered in gravy. She glanced over at Penny, who had ordered the same thing. "Well? How does this compare with yours?"

Penny smiled. "It's fine."

Mary Pat covered her grin with her hand and said in an aside, "You're not a very good liar. But at least we can enjoy the fact that somebody else did the cooking and the cleanup. I guess that adds to the good taste."

The two women shared an easy laugh.

Finn nudged Sam and kept his tone low enough that nobody else could hear. "You're looking way too happy for a guy who took two bullets."

"I'd take a hundred more just to see Penny looking so relaxed and happy."

Finn gave him a long, steady look. "I've been watching the two of you. Are you thinking of making this joined-at-the-hip thing permanent?"

Sam merely smiled. "I don't want to share what I'm thinking with you or the others until I've had a chance to share it with Penny first."

Finn's eyes went wide. "You're serious, aren't you?"

Sam punched his shoulder. "I think my days of performing at the Hitching Post have come to an end."

Finn moved a little away. "First Ben and now you. I hope what you two have isn't contagious."

The two were sharing a laugh when Chet Butler, head of the school board, stepped into their line of vision.

He paused to drop a hand on Mac's shoulder. "What a

surprise finding all of you here. I thought I'd have to make that long drive to your place later today."

Mac got to his feet to share a handshake. "Why would you drive to my ranch, Chet?"

"To offer Miss Cash a new contract." He looked across the table at Penny. "The town is talking about what happened to you. We're all relieved that it was quickly resolved. I'm sure my news will be frosting on the cake, so to speak." He was clearly pleased to be the bearer of good news. "One of the teachers in our district has requested an early retirement. Her husband has been diagnosed with an illness that will require long-term care. Since you're first on our board's list of replacements, we're prepared to offer you a contract to begin teaching immediately."

Penny's eyes were wide, her smile radiant. "There's nothing I'd like better than to teach here in Haller Creek."

Chet Butler gave a quick shake of his head. "Sorry. I should have made this clear sooner. Theresa was teaching in the town of Dryden. It's about a hundred and fifty miles from here, but still in our district. I can assure you it's a nice little town, and you'll have the support of some fine parents and students."

Penny swallowed. "I see. Thank you, Mr. Butler." She could feel everyone watching her. She shot a quick glance at Sam, then away. "I ...don't know what to say. I wasn't expecting this. I'm a little overwhelmed."

"Of course." He gave her an easy smile. "Why don't you drive into town tomorrow and stop by the office to sign the contract?"

"I..." She nodded. Swallowed. "Thank you."

He shook hands all around before walking from the diner.

When Loretta returned to take their dessert order, she was shocked that nobody seemed hungry enough to order.

While Mac lingered at the front counter to pay the bill, the others moved slowly out the door and down the street to their trucks.

On the drive home, the sun drifted behind a wall of thick, ominous clouds.

It mirrored the mood of the people who spent the entire ride in silence.

CHAPTER THIRTY-TWO

As their trucks pulled up beside the back porch, Mac helped Mary Pat from the passenger side. "I shouldn't be more than an hour or two. I want to check on the herd."

As he started toward the barn, Sam caught up with him. "You go ahead inside with the others, Dad. I'll check on the herd."

"But your injuries..."

"Are healing nicely. I can still sit a horse. Besides, you'll be doing me a favor. I need some alone time."

Mac nodded in understanding. "I know this offer of a job for Penny came out of the blue. I also know the way you two feel about each other." When Sam opened his mouth, Mac lifted a hand to silence him.

He studied Sam's face. "I know Dryden's a long way. Maybe she'll reject the board's offer and wait for something in Haller Creek."

Sam was already shaking his head in denial. "Teaching

has been Penny's dream for a lifetime. She can't afford to sit around and wait for an offer that may never come along again."

Mac put a hand on Sam's arm. "Son, if you love her, you need to let her know how you feel about her. It could influence her decision to stay or move away."

"And rob her of her dream?" With a bleak look Sam turned away. Over his shoulder he said, "I can't do that to Penny, Dad. I love her too much. She deserves this chance."

Mac stood watching as Sam made his way to the barn.

A short time later he watched as horse and rider moved across a meadow at a fast clip before disappearing below a ridge.

The day, which had begun with such joy and promise, now seemed as oppressive as the leaden sky.

Sam hunched deeper into his parka, the collar turned up, his wide-brimmed hat pulled down low over his forehead. The air had grown colder, and he could already taste the first drops of rain.

As Sam made a turn on the trail, the rain began in earnest. Though the comfort of home was tempting, he decided to take refuge in the nearby range shack.

He unsaddled his mount in the attached shed out back and filled a trough with food and water before making his way around to the front.

Inside he knelt before the fireplace and touched a match to kindling. Soon the little cabin was filled with warmth. After rummaging through the cupboards, he found a blackened coffeepot. A short time later he stretched out his long legs to the fire and sat, sipping strong, hot coffee and brooding about this latest twist in his life.

This shack offered him no comfort. He could feel Penny's presence. It was here that he and Penny had first given in to their passion. A passion that had grown into something deep and real.

Last night, while Penny slept in his arms, he'd been the happiest man in the world. He'd known, without a single doubt, that she was the only woman for him. Though he'd never expected to find this kind of love in his lifetime, he was convinced that he'd been somehow blessed with a gift from heaven.

That's what Penny was. A very special gift that had come unbidden into his life, leaving him forever changed. All the things that had once made him happy now seemed silly and superficial. Drinking with the wranglers. Shooting endless hours of nine ball with strangers, just to show off his skill on a pool table.

Curtis wasn't the only one who'd completely turned his life around because of Penny.

When Sam looked at her, he saw the goodness, the unselfish choices she'd made for the sake of others. She'd worked so hard, sacrificed so much in order to care for her brothers and aged great-aunt. And all for the chance to teach. To touch children's minds and hearts.

And now, finally, it was within her grasp.

Nobody deserved this honor more than Penny.

How could he dare stand in the way of her dream now that it was finally being offered to her on a silver platter?

Outside, the skies opened up and a torrent of rain mixed with ice pounded the roof of the cabin.

Sam topped off his coffee and sat, his mind circling every angle, wishing he could find a way to have all he wanted. But the more he mulled, the darker his mood became.

Mac had taught his sons, by his own example, that real

love meant putting the needs of those you loved above your own. Though it broke his heart to think about a future without Penny, he knew he would do anything for her.

He had to step back and give her room to fly without regrets.

Without regrets.

How ironic. He was aware of the pain he would suffer for his choice, but Penny deserved her shot at her dream.

He would step aside and do his best to put on a good face to hide his broken heart.

Penny paced her bedroom, from the window to the door and back, waiting for Sam. Hadn't he said he wanted to spend every night together the way they'd spent the previous night?

What was keeping him?

Hearing the sound of rain and sleet hitting the window, she draped an afghan around her shoulders before turning to peer into the darkness.

Had he returned from checking on the herd? She hadn't heard his voice downstairs, but then, she'd been too distracted to really pay attention. Once home, she'd sought the privacy of her room, hoping to quiet the nerves that had taken hold.

She shivered. Could Sam have misunderstood her behavior? Did he think, because she fled to her room, that she wanted to be alone?

She opened her bedroom door. The hallway was in darkness. There were no lights drifting up from below. Everyone, it seemed, had turned in for the night.

She made her way barefoot to Sam's door and knocked lightly.

Hearing no reply, she eased the door open and peered inside. The bed was untouched. The room empty.

He'd chosen to remain with the herd rather than be with her. That fact was like a slap in the face.

Feeling the sting of tears, she turned away and hurriedly returned to her room.

Crawling beneath the covers, she wiped away her tears and struggled to make sense of this.

She wanted to think that the man she loved was trying to make her decision easier. It was like him to be noble. But a tiny voice inside her head taunted her with the thought that maybe, just maybe, a wild child like Sam was sending the signal that he had already decided to move on with his life alone.

Alone.

That would certainly define her life. Despite the presence of three demanding brothers and a sweet, helpless great-aunt, she'd felt so alone. Her childhood friends had moved on with their lives. Her neighbors had lost contact once she sold the family home and started her new life in Haller Creek. And the minute she'd come here to the Monroe ranch, this family had become like her own.

But she'd been fooling herself. They were, in fact, Sam's family. And when she left to accept the teaching job in Dryden, she would once more be alone.

Alone.

The word played through her mind like a litany until at last, weary of the bleak thoughts that circled, sleep overtook her.

Penny walked into the kitchen to find Mac and Mary Pat seated at the table, heads bent close, talking in low tones.

They looked up as she entered and called out greetings.

"Good morning." Penny glanced around, feeling a painful sense of loss when she realized they were alone. "I'll start breakfast."

"Sit and drink your coffee." Mary Pat indicated the steaming coffeemaker on the counter. "The men are out in the barn, finishing up morning chores. They won't be in for a while yet. With the two of us working, we'll have plenty of food ready for our hungry family."

Our hungry family.

With a fresh ache in her heart, Penny poured a cup and sat across from them. "I didn't hear Sam come in last night."

Mac nodded. "I'm thinking that storm forced him to spend the night in the range shack. He should be back soon."

Penny took in a breath. "Roscoe said my old car needed work if I'm going to try driving it all the way to Dryden. Would you mind lending me one of the trucks after breakfast while he tinkers with my car?"

"Not at all." Mac smiled. "I'm sure you're eager to meet with Chet Butler and the board."

"Yes." She managed a weak smile before pushing away from the table.

Needing to be busy, she began breaking eggs into a bowl and slicing ham.

Sensing her nervous energy, Mary Pat glanced helplessly at Mac before joining her.

A moment later, when Penny sucked in a breath, Mary Pat looked over to see her dropping the knife and wincing in pain.

"Oh, Penny, you've cut yourself."

Penny held her finger under the tap and let the water wash some of the blood. "That was careless of me. It's just a little cut."

"Here." Mary Pat reached for a clean linen towel and wrapped Penny's finger before opening a drawer and retrieving ointment and a bandage. When the cut was bandaged, Mary Pat wrapped an arm around the young woman.

Her tenderness was the final straw, and Penny couldn't stop the tears she'd been holding in.

"Oh, honey. Does it hurt that much?"

Penny was shaking her head and trying to turn away. "No. It's nothing. I just feel..."

Mary Pat gathered her close. "I know." Over Penny's shoulder she gave a silent signal to Mac, and he promptly left the room.

When they were alone, Mary Pat ran a hand down Penny's hair. "Want to talk?"

Penny couldn't meet her steady gaze, instead staring hard at the floor. "I'm so confused right now."

Mary Pat led her to a chair and sat beside her before taking her hand. "Is it the job offer, or Sam?"

"Both." Penny swiped at her tears. "I've waited so long for this chance. And now that it's here, I'm feeling so... empty. I spent years studying to become a teacher. But this job will take me so far away from..." She sniffed and blew her nose. "Oh, Mary Pat. Tell me what to do."

"I can do a lot of things. But only you know what's in your heart." Mary Pat squeezed her hand. "But I know this. You're a smart woman, Penny. You'll figure things out and make the right decision."

"But how can you be so sure?"

Seeing her anguished face, Mary Pat touched a finger to her tear-drenched cheek. "I know you, honey. Trust your heart."

Penny's voice wavered. "Oh, Mary Pat. I'm so afraid of doing the wrong thing."

"You won't. Go with your heart."

"I hope you're right."

The two women embraced. And then, sensing the young woman needed some space, Mary Pat stepped from the kitchen and joined Mac in the parlor.

*   *   *

Penny descended the stairs and paused to retrieve the keys
to one of the trucks. After tidying the kitchen and watching
the others disperse to carry on their day's activities, she'd retreated to her room to dress for success. It wouldn't do to
meet with the school board looking less than her best.

She wore a stylish black fitted dress and a bright red
jacket with jet black buttons. On her feet were black heels.
At her throat a red and black silk scarf added a sparkle to her
eyes.

She'd fussed with her hair. Instead of her usual ponytail
or a mass of tangled curls, she'd used a straightening iron to
get the desired effect.

As she drove away from the house, she was painfully
aware of the fact that Sam still hadn't returned. Maybe he
would remain in the hills for days or weeks. However long
he stayed away, she knew it was because he was avoiding
her. That knowledge was like a knife in her heart.

She brushed aside the pain. For now, she had a meeting
to take. She wasn't about to let anything be a distraction.

CHAPTER THIRTY-THREE

Sam turned his horse into a stall in the barn and tossed the saddle over a railing. Filling troughs with food and water, he closed the stall door and walked from the barn before starting toward the house.

Overhead the midafternoon sky was threatening more rain.

Halfway there he caught up with Roscoe and Otis, engaged in a friendly discussion about Penny's old car outliving Mary Pat's ancient van. They were still arguing as to which vehicle would die first as he stepped into the mudroom and began prying off his boots. He rolled his sleeves above the elbows and began scrubbing the grime from his hands.

In the kitchen he was surprised to find Finn at home, discussing the finer points of law with Zachariah.

"You run out of clients?"

Finn chuckled. "Just the opposite. I'm going to have to

clear my decks to take on a big lawsuit. I figured I'd better take some time off now, before I get bogged down."

Sam gave his brother a fist-bump. "Good for you."

He glanced over at Ben. "Shouldn't you be in town chasing bad guys?"

"My day off. Becca and I figured we'd grab a free lunch."

"Nothing new." Sam glanced at Becca, tossing a salad, and Mary Pat, at the stove, stirring a pot of chili for their lunch.

Beneath the table, Archie's tail thumped his joy at being here with his second family.

Looking around, Sam's heart dropped to his toes at the realization that this would be his new normal. The others would be as they'd always been, happy, content. But his life would never be the same again. For the rest of his life, he would miss Penny with an unbearable ache. Still, he would have to gamely carry on, showing the family his best face. After a long night of mulling, he'd decided he would do whatever it took to keep his feelings to himself. Hadn't that always been the way he'd survived?

Mac stepped in from the parlor, where he'd been going over bills. The pen he'd used was tucked behind his ear. "I'm glad you're back, son. How bad was the storm?"

Sam shrugged. "The usual. Rain. Sleet. Some ice. It's melted now, and the herd's—"

Hearing the back door open, he turned. Whatever he'd been about to say was forgotten when he caught sight of Penny.

She quite simply took his breath away.

His first thought was to carry her off to someplace private and confess his love. But then he remembered his long night of soul-searching and his decision to do the right thing, no matter the cost.

It took a moment before he managed to compose himself. "Wow. I bet you dazzled the school board."

"That was the plan." She studied the way he looked, a rough stubble of beard darkening his lower face, his shirt and denims sweat-stained and clinging to his skin. "And you look about the same as you did the first time I met you."

"Yeah. As I recall, you called me a trail bum." He managed a half-smile as he looked down at himself. "I guess I'm no prize."

"Exactly my first thought the day we met."

"Well?" Ben asked the question on all their minds. "When do you start that dream job?"

Penny was still standing in the doorway, her gaze riveted on one sweaty cowboy. "That will depend on Sam."

His head came up sharply. "What's that supposed to mean?"

"The school board wanted a commitment. I told them that's what I wanted, too." She met Sam's questioning gaze. "But not from them. From you."

"What the hell . . . ?" He glanced at his father before saying, "Sorry." He turned back to Penny. "What's all this about? Didn't you tell Chet Butler and the board that they'd just made your dreams come true?"

"What I told them is that I'd like to be considered for a teaching job in the future, if one becomes available in Haller Creek. Right now, my plans are up in the air."

"Up in the air? Money, this is your dream job." Sam paused. "Isn't it?"

"For years it was. But now . . ." She took in a breath, glancing around at the entire family, watching and listening. It was so awkward having an audience. This wasn't the way she'd planned it, but she clung to Mary Pat's assessment that she was a smart woman.

Final exam time, she thought. *Either nail it, or face a failing grade.*

Though her face flamed, she forced herself to continue. "A very wise man told me"—she could see Otis turn to stare at her with a dawning smile—"that life has a funny way of happening while we're busy making plans. When the board offered me a job hours away, I realized that what I wanted was right here."

"Hold on. Just hold on a minute." Seeing the way everyone was hovering, Sam reached out and grabbed her arm before hauling her from the kitchen and into the parlor, where he slammed the door.

He stood facing her, his eyes narrowed on her with such ferocity, she was forced to swallow down her fears.

"Are you saying you turned down the offer to teach?"

She nodded, afraid to trust her voice.

"Because of me?"

"Because of me. Because of what I want." The words were barely a whisper, but they held conviction.

He was studying her so carefully, she felt her cheeks grow hot. "And what is it you want, Money?"

"You, Sam."

"Are you saying you'd give up your dream of being the world's greatest teacher for a beer-drinking, pool-hustling good old boy who ignores the rules of proper society?"

She tried to laugh at his joke, but her nerves were too tightly strung. Instead she lifted her chin in that haughty way he'd come to love. "That's who I thought you were when I first met you."

Sam nodded. "Yeah, baby. You weren't wrong. That's me."

"No, Sam. That *was* you. Or who you tried to be. But now I see you willing to step back to give me a chance to have my dream, even though it means letting me go." She took a step closer. "I can't think of anything more loving, more generous, than what you're trying to do for me. That can only mean you love me." She touched a hand to his arm. "Or am I misreading you?"

He flinched at her touch, determined not to weaken now and crush her to him the way he wanted. Instead, he made one more attempt to do the right thing. "Don't go making me sound like some hero, Money. I just want what's best for you."

"And don't you see? That's exactly what makes you my hero. My Super Sam. And the truth is, I'd give up everything for you, Sam."

He was looking at her with such intensity, she felt her heart hitch and had to force herself to go on. "I realize now, without you, all those big fine dreams are just... empty illusions. What I really want is to be with you. To spend my life loving you. And if I never get to teach in a school, maybe I'll be lucky enough to teach our children..."

"Children." His hand snaked out and he closed his fingers around her wrist. "Now you've done it."

"Sam..."

Her protest was cut off as he grabbed her in a fierce embrace and covered her mouth with his.

Against her lips he whispered, "Do you know how much I love you, Money? I was pleading with heaven to find a way to keep you here, even though I knew you should follow your dream. But now you're talking about love. Commitment. Children. All the things I've been afraid to want because I wasn't sure I deserved them." He shook his head. "I know one thing. I don't deserve you. But if you'll say you'll marry me, Money, I'll give you all the love, all the hard work, all the children you want, as long as you promise we can spend the rest of our lives together."

"Oh, Sam." She wrapped her arms around his neck and kissed him. Against his mouth she whispered, "That's what I want, too. I love you so much."

"And I love you more than my own life."

Before he could kiss her again the parlor door burst open and the family spilled through.

Otis and Roscoe were slapping Sam's shoulder.

Zachariah shook Sam's hand. "How does it feel to be a good woman's hero?"

"Feels good. At least I think it does. I'm in a daze." The two men shared a smile.

Ben grabbed his brother in a bear hug. "Welcome to commitment, bro. You're going to love being a team."

Finn gave a mock shudder. "Two of the mighty have fallen. I guess it's up to me to stay strong and resist whatever love virus is going around."

Laughing, Becca and Mary Pat took turns embracing Penny.

Mary Pat whispered, "I knew you could do it."

"Oh, Mary Pat." Penny touched a hand to her heart and gave a long, deep sigh. "I've never been so scared in my life."

"Hey, you survived being buried alive."

"That was nothing compared to declaring my love right out loud."

The two women shared a laugh.

Mac waited until all the others had stepped back before hugging Penny. "Welcome to the family, honey."

"Thank you, Mac. I couldn't have found a better family than this. I love all of you."

"Not nearly as much as we love you." Mac turned and put an arm around Sam's shoulders. "I'm proud of you, son."

"Just trying to do what a really smart man taught me."

The two shared a knowing smile.

Otis gathered Penny close. "You really pay attention, don't you, Miss Penny?"

"I do when a wise man has something to say."

His eyes were twinkling. "I'm convinced that you and Sam are all part of a heavenly plan. All it needed was a little help from you."

"Even though I was terrified, I kept hearing your words in my head."

He nodded. "And, Miss Penny, you kept riding that train until it brought you home."

"Just like you."

The two shared a heartfelt embrace.

Mary Pat called, "Come on. Time to celebrate with salad and really hot chili."

As the others started toward the kitchen, Sam caught Penny's hand, holding her back.

Very deliberately he closed the parlor door before turning to her. "If you'll give me time to shower, I'd prefer a private celebration."

He gave one of those sexy smiles and Penny felt her heart melting.

"Take all the time you need, cowboy. I'm not going anywhere without you."

As he sauntered away, Penny pressed a hand to her heart.

She'd lied to Sam. She'd once said she would never gamble. And yet today, she'd risked everything.

Everything.

On love.

And won the biggest jackpot of all.

EPILOGUE

Spring

Mary Pat and Zachariah were up to their elbows in white frosting as they topped off the four-layer chocolate torte and nestled several autumn leaves made of spun sugar on top.

When Penny opened the kitchen door, they stood together to block the cake from her view and ordered her to leave.

"It's just a cake," she protested. "Why can't I see it?"

"It's your wedding cake. That's why." Mary Pat pointed with her spatula. "Go upstairs and let Becca fuss over your hair."

"She's been fussing for an hour." Penny breathed deeply. "Is that prime rib on the counter?"

"Go. We want you to be surprised."

"But I could help."

"Absolutely not. The preacher will be here in less than an hour, and you have to put on your dress."

When Penny turned away, Mary Pat and Zachariah shared a laugh.

The old man shook his head. "Even on her wedding day, she just can't let go of being chief cook."

"Thank heaven. I hope she never tires of cooking for all of us." Mary Pat looked up when Ben and Finn walked in. "Is the table all set outside?"

The two men nodded. "And those little bowls of flowers are the perfect touch."

Mary Pat turned to Zachariah. "We're going to make wedding planners out of the whole bunch."

Ben was already shaking his head. "This was a one-and-done deal. Dad wants us up on the hill." He reached into the cupboard above the stove for the bottle of Irish whiskey, while Finn snagged rocks glasses. "Come on, Zachariah. Dad and the others are waiting."

While the men trooped out of the house, Mary Pat took a look around the kitchen. Satisfied, she walked up the stairs to dress for the ceremony.

On a windswept hillside, the men gathered around the familiar grave site.

Archie, wearing a fancy white bow attached to his collar, ran in circles around Ben's legs as he climbed the hill.

While Ben filled tumblers with whiskey and passed them around, Sam walked up to join the others. He was dressed in his best dark suit and string tie, his boots polished to a high shine.

When everyone was holding a drink, Mac lifted his glass and saluted the marble headstones standing guard over the graves of his wife, Rachel, and son, Robbie. "Here's to those we love who are no longer here, but with us always in spirit."

The men drank.

Ben, in his crisp sheriff's uniform, turned to his brother. "And here's to Sam, who lost his heart to the most amazing woman."

They drank again.

"Smartest thing you ever did, bro," Finn put in with a laugh.

Zachariah, in his best courtroom voice, added, "I'll second that, Samuel. You showed us just how clever and patient you can be, when you put your mind to it."

"Want to know the truth?" Sam's self-deprecating humor broke free. "I was scared to death she'd walk out that door and never look back. What did a woman like Penny need with a no-good cowboy like me?"

"She needed the same as you, son." Mac put an arm around Sam's shoulders. "Unselfish love. It's the very best kind." He lifted his glass. "To love."

They all intoned his words before drinking.

As Sam turned away, Mac called, "Where are you going?"

Sam paused and turned back. With a sly grin he handed his empty glass to his father. "I need to get away from here before I start believing all this bull…" He stopped, then composed himself and did a perfect imitation of Zachariah. "I believe I'll take a walk in the fresh air and clear my head. After all, the lady said yes. And if that doesn't show the power of my amazing personality, I can't imagine what would."

As he descended the hill, the sound of his family's derisive hoots and raucous laughter followed.

Mary Pat knocked on Penny's door and Becca hurried to open it.

"Reverend Grayson is here." As she stepped farther into the room, she caught sight of Penny in an ankle-length dress of ivory silk.

"Oh, my." Mary Pat put a hand to her heart. "Aren't you a picture."

On Penny's feet were simple ivory sandals. Instead of a veil, she'd tucked a sprig of baby's breath in her hair, worn soft and long, with just a hint of curls.

Becca's maid-of-honor dress was also ankle-length, in pale seafoam.

Penny handed Becca and Mary Pat pretty white gift bags.

"What's this?" Becca opened hers first and was thrilled to find a book of Penny's favorite recipes, all carefully compiled and labeled, from appetizers to desserts.

"Oh, Penny. I just love this. And I know Ben will be so thankful." She embraced her soon-to-be-sister-in-law. "I hope this doesn't mean you won't still cook for us."

Penny returned the hug. "I hope I can always cook for our family. I just love cooking for all of you."

"And we love everything you make." Becca cradled the cookbook to her heart. "I can't wait to try some of these recipes."

Mary Pat opened her bag to reveal a beautiful book. On the cover was a photo of her standing beside her old red van, with the towering Bitterroot Mountains in the background.

At her questioning look Penny smiled. "I asked Mac for a picture, and he said this was one of his favorites."

When Mary Pat opened the book, the pages were empty.

Before she could ask, Penny touched a hand to hers. "I believe this is the book only you can write, Mary Pat. It's the story of your life, through the many people you've known and helped and have come to love."

Tears sprang to the older woman's eyes. "Oh, Penny. How could you know? It's something I've thought of through the years but was always too busy to try."

"Someday you won't be nearly as busy." Penny kissed her cheek. "You're the reason this day is happening. You helped me find a job, and then you helped me find my courage."

Mary Pat shook her head. "Penny, you would have found it with or without my little pep talk."

As the two women embraced, Penny whispered, "Sam said you're the closest to a mother he's ever had. I feel the same. I treasure you. Thank you."

Mary Pat sniffed, then squared her shoulders. "I believe it's time you said those vows. Reverend Grayson is waiting outside."

Penny nodded and picked up the nosegay of baby's breath Sam had handed her earlier that day, before following Mary Pat and Becca down the stairs.

When they reached the parlor, Sam was there, pacing. His head came up sharply, and when he spotted Penny behind the other two, he simply stared.

Becca seemed about to pause when Mary Pat caught her hand, hauling her from the room, leaving the two alone.

"Money, you look..." He shook his head, lost for words.

"Is it that bad?"

He hauled her into his arms and pressed his mouth to the hair at her temple. "You're so beautiful, you take my breath away." He held her at arm's length. "You know, the first time I saw you, I was speechless."

"As I recall, you had a lot to say. You thought I was some poor, fragile old woman, and you tore a heavy box right out of my hands."

"And then I saw your face and heard your bossy voice, and something happened to my poor heart."

"Or your mind."

He grinned. "You did play hell with my mind, Money. I spent a lot of sleepless nights thinking about you." He drew her close, his eyes staring hungrily into hers. "I love you so much. I still can't believe you'd give up your dream for me."

"I haven't given up anything. The school board called to

say there will be an opening in the fall." She wrapped her arms around his neck. "I'm getting so much more than I ever dreamed possible, Sam."

He kissed her full on the mouth, and she felt the familiar jolt.

With a wink he caught her hand. "Come on, babe. Time to make it legal before you come to your senses."

With a laugh they walked hand in hand out the back door and toward the family, gathered around the town's minister.

Suddenly Penny stopped and gave a gasp of surprise at the sight of her three handsome brothers, all looking splendid in their military uniforms, standing together.

She let out a little cry and turned to Sam. "Did you know they were coming?"

He nodded. "I didn't want to spoil their surprise. They've been busy meeting all the family."

"Oh. How wonderful." She flew into the arms of Danny, Cooper, and Curtis with a mixture of laughter and tears. It had been so long, and she'd missed them so much.

As the family watched, she fussed over each of her brothers like a mother hen, admiring their uniforms, asking a million questions about where they'd been and how their lives were going since leaving Montana.

From the attention they lavished on her, it was obvious to all who were watching that they adored their big sister.

When at last Penny and Sam stood before the minister to speak their vows, the two families joined together into a crowd of handsome, rugged men surrounding them, with two pretty women, Becca and Mary Pat, in their midst.

Archie, sensing the importance of this gathering, began barking and circling, causing everyone to burst into gales of laughter.

While Becca and Ben tried to quiet their dog, Penny turned to Sam with a wide grin. "I can see what my life will be like in this big, noisy family."

"Getting cold feet, Money?"

"Not on your life." She touched a hand to his cheek. "I'm going to love every chaotic moment of it."

After the vows were spoken, the two families gathered around the big log table made festive with bowls of wildflowers and baby's breath, and enjoyed a wedding feast of prime rib, baked potatoes, garden vegetables, and a four-layer chocolate torte with white frosting, autumn leaves, and standing amid the colorful leaves, two wedding figures depicting a bride wearing an apron and wielding a school bell, and a groom in denims and plaid shirt.

As the sun slowly made its arc behind the mountains, Penny's brothers announced it was time for them to go.

"We're driving to Bozeman," Danny explained. "From there we'll be taking separate flights."

"I wish we could have had more time." Penny kissed each of her brothers, exclaiming on how they'd grown so tall and strong.

"But at least for today, we were all together," Curtis said against her cheek. "And for that, we have Sam and his family to thank."

At her arched brow he explained. "Mac sent air tickets for all three of us." He took her hands in his. "You're getting a good man, Penny. And joining a really good family."

"I know." She felt the beginnings of tears and blinked them away. She wanted no tears to mar this special day.

Sam and his family gathered around to see them off as Penny's brothers drove away.

Afterward, Sam and Penny changed into comfortable denims and plaid shirts.

As the others began to clear the table, Penny picked up a plate, and Mary Pat took it from her. "Not today, Penny."

"But you've done so much."

Mary Pat glanced at Sam, heading toward them. "I believe your husband has plans for the two of you. And they don't include kitchen duty."

Sam walked up behind Penny and wrapped his arms around her waist. Against her neck he said, "Time for that honeymoon I promised you, wife."

"You still haven't said where we're going. I had no idea what to pack."

"I told you. The less you pack, the less you can wear and the happier I'll be."

They were laughing as he caught her hand and led her toward a truck, where their bags were already secured.

After hugging each and every member of her new family, Penny was surprised when Otis took her hand.

His big, dark eyes were solemn. "Remember, Miss Penny. Life has a way of throwing us curves. It was no accident that you didn't get that first teaching contract. Heaven had something better in mind for you."

"I know." She nodded, feeling a lump forming in her throat.

"And heaven had something better in mind for Sam, too. Here, way off the beaten track, the two of you found what matters. Family, home, and good people who will always have your best interest at heart."

"Oh, Otis." With a cry she threw her arms around his neck and hugged him fiercely.

"Hey, now." Sam hurried over. "You just made my wife cry."

Penny wiped her eyes. "These are happy tears."

"Yeah. I get it." With a wink, Sam took Penny's hand and helped her into the truck.

Calling good-bye to the others, he drove along the curving ribbon of driveway, waving until they were out of sight. Then, turning the wheel, he started across a high meadow and into the woods before catching Penny's hand.

He pressed a kiss to her palm. "I don't think they were fooled. They know us too well. But I don't think any of them would dare to show up at the cabin."

"Is that where you're taking me?"

"I hope you don't mind. I thought we could spend a whole week alone, sleeping in the range shack and planning our very own home."

"Oh, Sam. A home on your property?"

"It's *our* property now, Money. And that's the plan. At least for part of the time." He winked. "But I hope you won't be disappointed if we spend the first couple of days just in the cabin."

At the smoldering heat in his eyes, she smiled. "I was hoping that was your plan."

He gunned the engine. "Money, if we don't get there soon, I may have to just stop in the woods and hope there are no bears looking for a place to hibernate."

As she shared his laughter, she thought about the strange twists and turns of her life. She'd come here hoping for a dream job and had faced such disappointments. And then, in the midst of despair, she'd found her reason for living.

Otis was right. This had to be part of some grand plan.

This man and this amazing family had forever changed her life. And she was, she vowed, going to grab this grand new life with both hands and live it to the fullest.

With the cowboy of her dreams.

BEEF TENDERLOIN

The Main Dish in the Wedding Supper for Sam and Penny

- 3 tablespoons butter, softened
- 1/3 cup kosher salt
- 3 cloves garlic, minced
- black pepper
- 4 to 5 pounds beef tenderloin, trimmed

Stir the butter, salt, garlic, and a sprinkle of black pepper together and rub over the entire length of the tenderloin. Let the tenderloin stand at room temperature for 20 to 30 minutes.

Preheat the oven to 425°F.

Place the tenderloin on wire rack on a baking sheet and bake until a meat thermometer inserted into the thickest portion registers 135°F (for rare) or 140°F for medium to well done.

Remove from the oven and cover loosely with aluminum foil. Let the meat rest about 15 minutes before slicing.

Serve with garden vegetables, garlic mashed potatoes, and warm dinner rolls.

Serves approximately 20 guests.

What cowboy and his lady wouldn't love this?

KEEP READING FOR A PREVIEW
OF *BORN TO BE A COWBOY*!

AVAILABLE IN FALL 2019.

CHAPTER ONE

Haller Creek, Montana
Monroe Ranch—Present Day

Finn Monroe unlocked the door to his law office and tossed his battered attaché case on the desk. Then he removed his fringed buckskin jacket and draped it on the back of his chair. Both the attaché and the jacket had been gifts from his mentor, Zachariah York, when Finn had passed the bar. They'd been the old lawyer's trademark and were now Finn's daily uniform, as was his longer-than-typical hair. He figured if Zachariah could look like an old lion in court, he could look like a young cub.

Finn had begun his practice here in the little town of Haller Creek by accepting every legal request that came his way, from an arrest for impaired driving to settling neighbors' property disputes. Recently he'd snagged the attention of the national media by winning a case against the county, for the largest monetary award ever, by a small rancher who had suspected officials of blocking his herd's access to his own water supply. There was now talk of submitting Finn's name to be the state's attorney general, even though he insisted it wasn't his dream.

Finn ignored all the background noise of politics while he continued to go about his business. Hearing the door open behind him, he glanced over his shoulder.

"Mr. Monroe?"

The feminine voice was soft, tentative.

He tried not to stare, but the woman standing there looked like a corporate executive and not at all like the women who usually came to his little office here in Haller Creek.

Instead of boots, denims, and a T-shirt, she wore heels, a sleek dress, and a matching jacket. Her blond-streaked hair fell in soft waves around a small, heart-shaped face. Except for the nerves that had her wringing her hands, she was almost too perfect to believe.

To put her at ease, Finn stepped around his desk to offer a handshake. "My friends call me Finn. Finn Monroe."

"Jessica Blair." She paused and tried to smile. It had her lips quivering. "My friends call me Jessie."

"Nice to meet you, Jessie. You're not from around here."

"I grew up in Arvid. It's a little town about a hundred miles from here."

He nodded. "I've heard of it. Great cattle country. Did you grow up on a ranch?"

"Yes. My aunt's ranch. My aunt Nola, Nolinda Blair, raised me after my parents died when I was five. She's the only family I ever had."

"It sounds as though you love her a lot."

Her eyes filled, and Finn had to resist an urge to wrap his arms around her and offer her comfort.

Instead he indicated the chair facing his desk. "Why don't you sit and tell me why you're here."

"Please give me a minute."

As she sat, he rounded his desk and took a seat facing her. To give her time he asked the first question that came to him. "Is your aunt's ranch big?"

Jessie nodded. "Nearly a thousand acres."

"I bet she and her husband needed a big family to keep it all going."

"Aunt Nola never married. There were just the two of us. And a team of loyal wranglers who'd been with her for years."

"So you worked the ranch with her?"

"I did until I left for college. And even then I came back every chance I had and every summer. I've always loved living on her ranch."

Seeing the glint of fresh tears, he gave her time to compose herself. "I know what you mean. My family has a ranch outside of town. When I'm not here, I'm more at home on a tractor or riding in the high country with the herds."

Her eyes brightened. "You're a rancher? Then you understand how important the land is."

"I do." He folded his hands, hoping to ease her into the reason for her visit. "If you grew up in Arvid, why are you here?"

"When I went on the Internet and researched the town of Haller Creek, yours was the only law office listed."

"Why Haller Creek?"

"My aunt mentioned it. She said that's where her new ranch foreman once worked."

"Does your aunt want me to look into this wrangler's background?"

She shook her head. "I'm here because..." Again that threat of tears. When her lower lip quivered, she bit down before speaking in a rush as though she needed to get everything out. "I believe my aunt has been murdered, and her estate stolen by a smooth-talking cowboy."

Finn let out a slow breath. "That's a pretty inflammatory statement. Did you identify her body?"

"There's no..." She tried again. "She's gone. Just...gone."

"So your aunt's missing?"

She nodded.

"And this ranch foreman..."

"Wayne Stone." She lifted a handkerchief to her nose as if she'd just smelled something distasteful.

"Wayne Stone is the smooth-talking cowboy you mentioned?"

Another nod while she twisted the handkerchief around and around her fingers.

"Have you gone to the police with your suspicions?"

"Yes." She lifted her head to glance at him. "They looked into it. They said the marriage was valid, and there was no sign of foul play."

"Marriage? When did your aunt marry him?"

"Two weeks ago."

"That must have been a surprise. Did she tell you about it before the wedding?"

"She called me the day they were getting married, on the way to town. She said after the wedding they were leaving for a honeymoon. And there hasn't been a word from her since."

"I'm guessing your feelings were hurt that she waited so long to let you know."

"This isn't about my hurt feelings." A big tear rolled down her cheek and she brushed it aside. "It isn't like Aunt Nola to do something like this. This is completely out of character."

"It may not be usual, but a lonely woman has the right to share her life with someone. That doesn't make it a crime."

"You don't understand. She couldn't bear to be away from the ranch for more than a few days at a time. And now she's been gone for over two weeks without a word. I just know something's wrong."

Finn steepled his hands on the desk. "Miss Blair, you don't need a lawyer. If the police won't help, and you want to pursue this further, I'd suggest a private detective."

"I hired one." She dug into her pocket and held out a business card.

Finn took it and read the name. "Matthew Carver. Retired FBI agent." He looked over at her. "Are you happy with his work?"

She nodded. "He called to say he had some news. He sounded...agitated. We were supposed to meet yesterday."

"Let me guess." Finn sat back, folding his hands atop the desk. "He never showed up, and you realize he skipped town with your money."

"No." Another tear slipped out and she brushed it aside. "He was involved in a hit-and-run accident on the interstate. He's dead, and whatever information he had for me died with him."

Finn experienced a little tingling at the base of his spine—a sure sign that he was beginning to get sucked into something he'd rather not be involved in. "A good investigator would have kept notes. Could you call his office and ask his assistant..."

"I called. Her name is Bev, and she's his wife. She was so grief-stricken she could barely speak, but she said when his belongings were returned to her, his briefcase, his computer, and all his notes were not among them."

The little tingling just got stronger.

Finn sat staring at the woman across the desk, mulling the consequences of what he was about to do. If he took this case, he'd be up to his eyebrows in work that could keep him from more pressing matters.

Still, there was that tingle.

And the fact that he was looking at just about the prettiest woman he'd ever seen.

He dismissed that out of hand. He wasn't stupid enough to let important work pile up where he pursued some lame story for the sake of a pretty face.

Was he?

Yeah, maybe he was.

And right now, though he could think of all the reasons why he should send her packing, the only thing that mattered at the moment was getting a chance to know more about the fascinating Jessica Blair and her story. And maybe, just maybe, he could help her.

"I'll need a lot more information than this." He lifted a packet of documents from his desk drawer and passed them to her. "I'd like you to fill these out. If I need more, where can I find you?"

She took in a deep breath like a woman who'd been plucked from a frigid lake and had been going down for the third time. "I checked into the Dew Drop Inn on the interstate last night so I could find you first thing today."

"Okay." He shoved back his chair. "While you answer everything on these pages, I'll head on over to Dolly's Diner and bring back coffee. How do you take it?"

"Two sugars and two creams."

He grinned. "So you like a little coffee with your cream and sugar."

That remark brought a half-smile to her lips.

As he started down the street, he was chuckling to himself. He'd figured that a woman like that would take her coffee black.

His smile suddenly dissolved when he realized it may not be the only wrong impression he'd had. As he began to put time and distance between them on the walk to Dolly's and back, he began to question his rash decision to take this on.

Jessica Blair could turn out to be a jealous, vindictive relative who'd just discovered she'd been locked out of a hefty inheritance. And though her nerves looked real enough, she could be nothing more than a really good actress playing on his sympathy.

"Two creams. Two sugars." Finn set the lidded cup on the edge of his desk before taking his chair and picking up the completed pages.

As he started to read, he looked up. "You're an accountant?"

"A certified public accountant with Ayers and Lanyer."

At the mention of one of the state's biggest firms, he lifted a brow. He would have pegged her for something in the public eye. Modeling. TV news.

"I've taken a leave of absence until this matter with my aunt is resolved. My boss isn't happy about it, but I had leave time coming, so he had no choice but to agree to my request."

Finn nodded. "Then there's no time to waste. I'll begin by running a check on Wayne Stone. If he worked on ranches in Haller Creek, he should be easy to find. From time to time I employ a detective, Basil Caldwell, also a retired FBI agent, and I trust him to be thorough and discreet. He should have something for me by the end of the day. Give me a number where I can reach you."

She spoke the numbers and he entered them in his cell phone's contacts before giving her his number, as well.

"As soon as I hear from Basil, I'll call you with the information."

For the first time her smile wasn't forced or nervous. "Thank you, Finn. You don't know how much this means to me."

"Don't bother to thank me yet. The police could prove to be right, and we'll find we don't even have a case."

She touched a hand to her heart. "I don't care what the police think. I know I'm right. And I know when your detective starts checking, he'll know it, too. I know my aunt well enough to know she would never willingly be gone from her ranch this long."

Finn watched her walk out the door before sitting down to read through the papers she'd filled out. Her handwriting was easy to read. He wished he could say the same for the woman. He wouldn't be the first guy to lose his perspective because of a pretty face. What he liked even more was that she had a good mind to go with the looks. Anyone working for Ayers and Lanyer had to be sharp. But that didn't mean she was to be trusted. He intended to reserve judgment until he found out more about Jessica and her aunt.

Because if he'd learned one thing since going into this business, it was the fact that a good mind and a pretty face could mask a greedy heart.

ABOUT THE AUTHOR

New York Times bestselling author **R. C. Ryan** has written more than one hundred novels, both contemporary and historical. Quite an accomplishment for someone who, after her fifth child started school, gave herself the gift of an hour a day to follow her dream to become a writer.

In a career spanning more than twenty years, Ms. Ryan has given dozens of radio, television, and print interviews across the country and Canada, and has been quoted in such diverse publications as the *Wall Street Journal* and *Cosmopolitan*. She has also appeared on CNN and *Good Morning America*.

You can learn more about R. C. Ryan—and her alter ego Ruth Ryan Langan—at:

RyanLangan.com
Twitter @RuthRyanLangan
Facebook.com/RuthRyanLangan

SAVED BY THE COWBOY

A. J. PINE

Olivia Belle has always believed in fairy tales...until the moment her boyfriend dropped to one knee. When Olivia speeds into Cash Hawkins's town like a modern-day Cinderella in a ball gown and glass slippers, Cash's careful existence is thrown for a loop. Olivia could be his happily ever after...if this runaway bridesmaid doesn't run off with his heart.

FOREVER
YOURS

NEW YORK   BOSTON

PRAISE FOR A. J. PINE

"A fabulous storyteller who will keep you turning pages and wishing for just one more chapter at the end."
   —**Carolyn Brown**, *New York Times* **bestselling author**

"Cross my heart, this sexy, sweet romance gives a cowboy-at-heart lawyer a second chance at first love and readers a fantastic ride."
   —**Jennifer Ryan**, *New York Times* **bestselling author,**
      on *Second Chance Cowboy*

"This is a strong read with a heartwarming message and inspiring characters."
      —*RT Book Reviews* **on** *Second Chance Cowboy*

CHAPTER ONE

Sheriff Cash Hawkins sat comfortably in his police-issue Chevy Tahoe. There was a beef brisket sandwich from BBQ on the Bluff cooling in the bag on the passenger seat. He'd just cued up a new audiobook on his phone and connected the Bluetooth. His German shepherd, Dixie, chewed on her rawhide in the back.

A pretty perfect Saturday night if he did say so himself. Well—except for the thick, calligraphied square envelope sticking out from the passenger seat visor. Still unopened.

He unrolled the top of the takeout bag and breathed in the savory aroma of homemade barbecue sauce and locally sourced beef.

"Damn, that Lily Green can cook. Can't she, Dixie girl?" he called back to his companion. But then he remembered that Lily and Tucker Green—the husband and wife duo who'd opened the restaurant together—had just split, Tucker having bought out her portion of the business.

"Still her sauce recipe, right?" he asked aloud. "Tucker wouldn't be fool enough to let the woman go without getting all her secret recipes." And yes, he knew he was talking to the dog. He and Dixie had some of their best conversations on quiet Saturday nights doing traffic patrol. It was why he always insisted on taking the shift, even though as sheriff he sure as hell didn't have to. He *liked* it. Not that he'd let any of the other officers at the station know.

First he set up the radar and positioned it in the direction of oncoming traffic, though he knew there'd be none. There never was. He pressed play on the audiobook, then started removing the foil wrapper from the sandwich, readying himself for that long anticipated first bite, when his teeth sank into the warm, toasted roll and all the good stuff in between.

Except something in the distance caught his eye—a car barreling down the opposite side of the street way too fast for comfort. He didn't need an official readout to tell him it was well over the limit. Still, he sighed, laid the sandwich on top of the bag in the passenger seat, and readied his finger on the trigger of the radar gun.

"Speeding down my street when I'm about to eat some damn good barbecue," he mumbled.

Dixie's ears perked up.

"Sorry, girl," he said. "No tasting the goods until I take care of Speed Racer out there."

He nodded toward the windshield just as a canary yellow Volkswagen Bug zipped by.

"Seventy-two miles per hour?" he said, shaking his head. Then he flipped on the lights, pulled into the all but empty street, and sped off after it.

It didn't take the car long to stop. In fact, as soon as the siren made its first wail, the driver hit the brakes, and he was pulling up behind the offender in a matter of seconds.

Dixie howled. She wasn't used to this much police action on a Saturday night. In the three years since he'd been elected sheriff of Oak Bluff, Cash could count on one hand the number of traffic violations for which he'd written actual tickets, and none of them happened on his Saturday night watch. Not much happened in the way of criminal activity, period, and he was planning on keeping it that way.

He hopped out of the truck and strode toward the yellow Bug but stopped before reaching the window. His brows drew together. Half of some sort of ball gown was hanging out the driver's side door. It was torn and tattered, like it had been dragged along at seventy-two miles per hour for the better part of the afternoon and early evening.

Cash shook his head and approached the window, which was still closed. He rapped on it with his knuckles.

It lowered.

Yep, that was a ball gown, all right. A purple one. And inside the gown was a knockout brunette with soft curls tumbling over her bare shoulders...A knockout brunette who'd just broken the law.

He lowered his aviators down the bridge of his nose.

She gasped. "Wow," she said. "I thought that just happened in the movies."

"Excuse me, ma'am?"

"That!" she said, grinning and nodding toward his glasses, her bright blue eyes glowing in the setting sun. "The whole shades-down-the-nose thing, the instant intimidation. It's so amazingly small town. I love it!"

Cash cleared his throat, trying to ignore how her smile lit up her face or how soft her pink lips looked. He wasn't having a ton of success. "Ma'am, do you have any idea how fast you were driving?"

Her smile fell. "Do I really look like a 'ma'am' to you? I

know some people think 'miss' is a little degrading, but I'm all for it. Call me 'miss' till I'm gray and old—not that I'll go gray gracefully." She laughed.

"*Ma'am*," Cash said with more force, and the laughing ceased. "You were going seventy-two in a fifty-mile-per-hour zone."

She bit her lip. "That's bad, right?"

He nodded. "It's breaking the law, so yeah. I'd say it's bad."

She sighed, then held both her hands toward him, palms up. "Book me," she said. "Lock me up and throw away the key—as long as I make it to Oak Bluff by ten. That's when the B and B closes for the night."

Cash scratched the back of his head. Then he glanced over at his car—the one that had OAK BLUFF SHERIFF painted on either side. He was a man of the law. Rules and regulations. This was all part of the job, which meant he should not let himself get distracted by her teeth grazing her full bottom lip—or the vulnerability he sensed beneath the brash exterior.

"License and insurance card, please, ma'am."

She smiled again, but something in it seemed forced. It wasn't as if he knew a thing about this strange woman, but he was trained to read people. Despite not flinching at being pulled over and possibly arrested, she radiated a nervous energy he couldn't ignore. He'd venture a guess she was not as brazen as she'd have him believe, and something about that bothered him. Cash didn't get pretense. He might have been a quiet man, but he was a man of meaning—meant what he said and meant what he did. Why couldn't everyone else just do the same?

"Right," she said. "I've got them both right..." She trailed off as she acted like she was rifling through a giant bag when all she'd done was click open what looked like a fancy as hell billfold.

She chuckled. "So... you're going to love this, Officer"—she squinted to read his name badge—"Hawkins."

"Sheriff Hawkins," he corrected her.

Her cheeks flushed, and he had to remind himself that he was here to write this woman a ticket—not find her in any way attractive.

"*Sheriff* Hawkins. So—Sheriff. I wasn't even supposed to be driving tonight. I left everything in the hotel room except for what I needed. That's why I only put my lip gloss, the room key, and my phone in the clutch."

"The what?"

"Clutch," she said, starting to lift the wallet-type contraption.

"Ma'am, please keep your hands on the steering wheel if you're not going to produce the items I'm asking for."

She dropped the clutch, or whatever it was, and placed her hands at ten and two with a self-satisfied grin. "It's a purse that you *clutch* in your hand. Only enough room for the essentials."

He crossed his arms. "Something's not adding up."

She narrowed her eyes. "Look, you can try to find me guilty of speeding—"

"Seventy-two in a fifty."

She rolled her eyes. "But I'm not a liar."

He raised a brow. "The keys?"

"What?"

"The car keys, ma'am. If you only put the essentials in your *clutch*, where'd you get the car keys?"

Her mouth opened, then closed. Finally she blew out a breath. "I keep the key in this little magnet case and hide it behind the back wheel. Just in case."

Good Lord, why did he even ask? He didn't have time for this. Okay. Fine. He had all the time in the world. But all he'd wanted to do was eat his damned sandwich and watch the sunset. He and Dixie would listen to a few hours of a new book, and then they'd go home and have an off-duty beverage or two. Well, Cash would, at least. Dixie would get a fresh bowl of water with two ice cubes—her favorite. But instead his sandwich was getting cold, and he hadn't even heard the opening remarks of the book, let alone gotten to chapter one.

"In case *what*?" he asked. Because how the hell long was it going to take to get to the end of this—this situation?

She shrugged. "In case I need to get the hell outta Dodge on a moment's notice."

He pressed a palm against the doorframe and leaned down to the window so they were eye level with each other. He could smell hints of her perfume—a light citrus that made him think of an orange grove.

"No license, no insurance, and twenty-two miles over the speed limit. Ms. . . . ?"

"Belle," she answered quickly. "Olivia Belle."

"Please step out of the car, Ms. Belle."

She scoffed. "You're not serious, are you? I can pay the ticket. I know my debit card number by heart. And I know you can punch my license plate number into your computer thingy and find me. It's my car, registered in—*shit*. Michael co-signed for the loan, and that damned bank put *his* name on the title. Stupid patriarchy," she mumbled. Then she groaned and opened the door, and the rest of the dress erupted out into the street as she exited the vehicle.

"Lemme get this straight," he said, averting his gaze from how the bodice of the dress fit her curves like it was meant for her body and hers alone. The dip and swell of her hips, the way the cut of the dress made a heart below her collarbone, and how the soft skin above her breasts rose and fell with each measured breath. "You were just driving twenty-two miles over the speed limit with no license or insurance in a car that is registered to a Michael?"

She winced but nodded.

He shook his head. He didn't want to do it like this, but if he brought her in any other way, the whole department would call him on it—tell him he was going soft on his first Saturday night offender in a long time.

Cash pulled the cuffs off his belt and quickly clasped one of them around her left wrist, then the other around her right.

He sighed. "Welcome to Oak Bluff, Ms. Belle. You're under arrest."

CHAPTER TWO

Sheriff Hawkins read Olivia her rights, then nodded toward the SUV. "You lead the way, ma'am."

Olivia groaned.

This was a first. Handcuffs. And not in a sexy way. Sure she was speeding, and *maybe* she'd left before grabbing the necessities like her wallet. And clothes to change into so she wouldn't have to spend eternity in this monster of a dress. But wasn't that the whole idea behind fleeing? You leave. Quickly. Without any thought other than self-preservation.

It only took her two steps to stumble on the hem of her dress, break the heel off her shoe, and twist her ankle.

"Damn it!" she cried, throwing her cuffed wrists into the air to catch her balance, but she was going down. There were no two ways about it. Except before she hit the pavement, a strong, muscular arm wrapped around her midsection, hauling her back up.

She was smack against Sheriff Grumpy Pants's chest now, and hell if he wasn't solid as the trunk of a redwood.

"You all right there, Cinderella?" His warm breath teased the skin on her neck.

"Pardon me?"

He bent down and picked up her broken shoe, dangling the crystal clear stiletto pump in front of her. "Ball gown. Glass slipper. I'd say you walked right out of a fairy tale if you hadn't ruined a perfectly peaceful Saturday night."

Olivia scoffed, then spun to face him, but when her full weight fell on her shoeless foot, pain shot through her like a lightning bolt—hot and fast. She yelped, and this time there was no one to catch her as she toppled backward and fell flat on her already-sore-from-driving-four-hours behind.

The sheriff's eyes widened.

"You're hurt," he said matter-of-factly.

She would have liked to have crossed her arms in defiance, affording herself the tiniest bit of dignity, but—handcuffs. So she settled for a glare.

He said nothing, but simply scooped her up and carried her to the passenger side of the Tahoe.

He held her with one arm—dress and all—and opened the door with the other. Then he moved something out of the way and deposited her onto the leather seat.

"You mean you're not tossing me in the caged-in area in the back?"

"Quiet a second, will you?" he barked, his deep voice tinged with an emotion she couldn't put her finger on. Annoyance for sure, but there was something else.

He dropped to a squat, then pushed back the taffeta and tulle—entirely too much material of any sort for a daytime wedding. But the bride had insisted, and everyone knows the bride is the boss, especially when she's your almost-fiancé's sister.

Emphasis on the *almost*.

Coarse hands gingerly cradled her foot.

"Does this hurt?" he asked.

She fisted her fettered hands in the pile of dress on her thighs, then pressed her lips together as he moved her foot slowly from side to side.

"Mmm-hmm," she squeaked.

"Swelling's not too bad. Looks like just a mild sprain. I can get you some ice at the station."

She huffed out a breath. "Maybe there wouldn't be any sprain if you hadn't arrested me."

He took off his sunglasses and stared at her with eyes so green she forgot for a second that she was even wearing handcuffs.

"And if you hadn't been driving without a license *or* insurance card at twenty-two miles over the speed limit in *my* town, I never would have arrested you."

He stood, pulled the seat belt across her torso and clicked it into place, shoved as much of her dress in the door as he could, then slammed it shut.

Something wet lapped at Olivia's shoulder, and she wasn't sure if she should hold still or scream. You were supposed to play dead with a bear, right? Were there a lot of bears in wine country?

The sheriff climbed into the driver's seat with a swift, fluid movement that told her he and this tank of an automobile were well acquainted.

"Is there a bear in your backseat?" she whispered.

"A what?"

There it was again. Something slobbery and smooth on her skin.

"A *bear*!" she whisper-shouted.

He froze, one hand white-knuckling the wheel. Then the other reached slowly toward the backseat, but Olivia was too scared to watch. He let out a heart-stopping roar.

She screamed as he yanked his hand back, cradling it to his chest as he threw his head against the back of the seat and—*laughed.*

She shifted toward the rear of the vehicle to find a German shepherd sitting behind her, tongue hanging out the side of its mouth and tail wagging.

"You're terrible," she said.

"And you're gullible as hell. You must be a long way from home if you think Oak Bluff is bear country." He scratched under the dog's chin. "Olivia Belle, meet Dixie. The reason I don't need a cage back there."

Olivia swallowed. "But she's sweet, right? That's why she was slobbering all over me?"

Pets weren't really her thing. For one, she lived in an upscale hotel, and it wasn't one of those pet-friendly ones. Then there was the issue of permanency. Committing to a pet was—well—committing. And the fact she was here instead of in San Francisco saying *yes* to a guy she'd left on one knee probably said a thing or two about her staying power.

He put the key in the ignition and the massive engine roared to life.

"She'd rip a man's arm off if I asked her to." He paused for a couple of beats. "Woman's, too." He set his sunglasses in the center console. The sun was setting now, and she guessed he wouldn't need them anymore. Then he shifted into gear and pulled off the shoulder of the road.

She swallowed and decided to sit very still. But then she saw her Bug sitting there as they began to move. "Wait!" she cried. "What about my car?"

He kept his eyes on the road so all she could see was his profile—the strong line of his stubbled jaw, a crooked nose that was somehow perfectly imperfect.

She, however, was just imperfect. At least when it came to relationships. She always found a reason to run. And today she'd run to the one place she thought she could find answers, the tiny town of Oak Bluff.

"I'll send a couple deputies—*licensed* drivers—out to get it after I bring you in."

She let out a relieved breath. At least he wasn't towing it.

She raised her cuffed hands to the visor above her. "What's this?" she asked, fingertips brushing the edge of an envelope. "Looks like a wedding invitation." Seemed like everyone was planning weddings, getting married, or proposing. And she was just flat-out running.

He wrapped a hand around one of her wrists and lowered both hands to her lap. "None of your concern is what it is," he said gruffly.

She groaned. "Are these really even necessary? It's not as if I resisted arrest. And I'm hobbled now, so I can't exactly tuck and roll and make a break for it."

The corner of his mouth twitched, but he held back the grin. It made her think the burst of laughter she'd just seen from him was something rare. Because a man who fought off a smile was a man who liked others to view him a certain way.

He tugged at a small key ring that was attached to his belt with what looked like a retractable cord. Without looking, he inserted the small key into the base of each cuff and released her.

"Thank you," she said softly.

He nodded.

She reached for her swollen ankle and rubbed it gingerly.

"Pain's pretty bad?" he asked.

She shrugged. She'd broken her arm in eighth grade. That had been the most excruciating physical pain she'd ever experienced. But worse was her parents arguing in the ER about whose fault the accident was when it was *their* arguing that had initially caused it. But by that point in her life, her parents had found any reason they could to scream at each other, and they'd long since stopped making sure she wasn't around to hear.

The divorce dragged on for years, finalized just months before she'd left for college. She hadn't lived with either parent since.

"That all depends. You gonna make me sleep in a cell tonight instead of the cozy bed-and-breakfast I booked?"

He sighed. "You got someone who can fax in a copy of your license and insurance?"

Emily was the night manager tonight—and Olivia's closest friend. She had a key to Olivia's room. It would just be a matter of avoiding Michael if he hadn't gotten his own room after her disappearing act this afternoon.

"Yes!" she said, feeling the tiniest bit triumphant. Because, come on—she needed a small win here.

He sighed. "If you can prove you're a licensed driver, that the car is registered with *your* insurance, then I guess that'll just leave the speeding. And making my dinner cold."

They pulled to a stop in front of a small two-story brick building that looked about a hundred years old. Yet it was charming as hell, as was every other shop or restaurant that lined the street.

"Sixteen Oak Bluff Way," she said, remarking on the address that was stenciled on the sign below the more prominent OAK BLUFF SHERIFF'S DEPARTMENT. "So the bed-and-breakfast is—"

"Across the street and two doors down, next to Lucinda's Antiques, which is closed on account of the owner having to go to a funeral."

"The bed-and-breakfast?" she asked.

"Huh?"

"The bed-and-breakfast is closed?"

He shook his head. "Lucinda's. Her third husband passed. He lived about an hour outside of town."

"Oh," she said softly. "How sad. Wait; did you say *third* husband?"

He ran a hand through dark brown hair. It was cropped close, but just long enough that fingers could get partially buried. Not that she was thinking of such things about a total stranger who—up until a few minutes ago—had a laundry list of items to arrest her for. It didn't matter that she'd been with Michael since their last semester of grad school and was now in her first year as event coordinator at Hotel Blue—the hotel his parents owned. She could count on one hand how many times she'd run her fingers through *his* hair in the past six months—or him through hers.

Eighteen months—her longest relationship to date. She'd thought he was going to ask her to move in. She'd privately entertained the thought of not living in the place where she worked. But then she'd be ten miles from the place where she spent ninety percent of her time.

But he hadn't asked her to move in. He'd *proposed*.

"Ms. Belle?" she heard the sheriff say, then realized by his tone it probably wasn't the first time.

"Huh?" she answered. "What?"

He shook his head. "I was explaining how Lucinda's third husband wasn't from Oak Bluff. He wanted to be buried by his parents, and Lucinda respected that. So she's there for a few days, getting his affairs in order."

"Oh," she said absently. "What happened to the other two husbands... if you don't mind me asking?"

He shrugged. "Lost the first one to lung cancer." He paused for a second, and she wasn't sure he was going to say more. But then he continued. "The guy was a stubborn smoker who just couldn't—no, *wouldn't*—quit. Second one got thrown from a horse who got spooked. And Earl? Well, he was older. Had a lot of health issues, but she loved him. And he treated her real good."

She didn't know Lucinda but was already fascinated by a woman who could commit to three different men. Even if they all ended in heartache, she kept on keeping on. Walked down that aisle three times. Buried three men she seemed to have loved.

Olivia let out a bitter laugh. If anything happened to one of her parents, the other would probably show up at the funeral just to dance on the grave.

"What's so funny?" he asked.

"Nothing," she said flatly. "Absolutely nothing about anything is funny."

He raised a brow, then threw open his door and hopped out of the truck. In seconds he was at her side of the car. The door swung open, but then he stood there, hands on hips.

"What?" she asked.

He crossed his arms now. "I'm just puzzling out how it's gonna look when I carry you in there and then throw the book at you."

She rolled her eyes, then slapped on the cuffs. "Does this help?" she asked. "Big bad sheriff worried everyone's gonna think he's a marshmallow?" She wiggled out of her good shoe. "And I can walk just fine," she lied. She swung her legs to the right, then looked down. It was a few feet drop to just hop out. And she'd already screwed herself into losing her balance with her wrists bound again.

"I could help you," he said dryly.

A rogue curl fell over her eyes, and she tried to tuck it behind her ear, but it wasn't so easy to do with the cuffs. She blew it out of the way, but it just fell back over her face. Then she groaned.

"Fine," she relented. "But I'm *walking*."

He said nothing as he grabbed her under each arm and then hoisted her out of the vehicle. He set her down carefully, and she put all of her weight on her good foot to start. Then she tested the waters on her injured one.

She hissed in a breath between her teeth, but she was able to do it.

"You are stubborn as hell, aren't you?" he asked.

She jutted out her chin and squared her shoulders even though she knew she was a sight. Tattered bridesmaid gown, no shoes, handcuffs, and her hair falling every which way.

"Oh God," she said as realization struck. "Am I going to have a mug shot?"

There it was again—the corner of his mouth threatening to tilt up.

"I guess we'll just have to see about that." He reached past her and grabbed a greasy-looking brown paper bag, then opened the back door to let Dixie out. The dog sniffed at Olivia's bare feet, then started licking her wounded ankle as if she knew she was hurt.

"Traitor," he said under his breath.

Olivia narrowed her eyes. "She's not really an attack dog, is she? You were just messing with me again."

He said nothing as he strode a couple steps in front of her to get the door, and her eyes instinctively dropped lower than they should have. His belt hung low on his hips, his gun holstered on one side, that ring of keys on the other. The whole uniform was black—not tan like she would have thought— and those pants fit like an absolute glove over a part of the sheriff she certainly shouldn't be ogling.

"After you," he said once the door was open.

Her head snapped up, and her cheeks flamed. Had she just been caught? If so, he could just add it to her rap sheet.

She limped past him and into what looked more like a small office than a police station. There were a handful of desks, most of them empty. Only two were occupied—one by a woman in uniform and one by a man who looked several years younger than the sheriff.

"Deputies," he said, nodding his head in greeting. "Looks like we've got some paperwork tonight."

CHAPTER THREE

Well, your license checks out. Your insurance checks out, and on account of the fact I don't want either of the deputies to have to spend the night making sure you're *comfortable* and well cared for in our seldom used cell, I'm going to write you your ticket and send you on your way."

She beamed at him, and damn if that smile of hers didn't wake something up inside him he'd thought would never come out of hibernation.

"Oh, I could just hug you!" she said, jumping up from the chair beside his desk. "Ow!" she yelped.

"Right," he said. "The ankle. Wait here a minute."

She sat back down and he strode off to the kitchen, grabbing a cold pack from the freezer and a clean towel from the counter. He rummaged through the cabinets until he found a bottle of ibuprofen, then filled a glass with water from the tap.

What if she would have done it—hugged him?

He shook his head and laughed softly. He'd long considered himself *off* the market. He had enough to fulfill him with the job, taking care of Dixie, and—the job. Did he say the job? Well, it was election year. That would keep him busy enough. Besides, he certainly wasn't setting his designs on a strange woman who was only passing through—and breaking a hell of a lot of laws on her way in.

Cash was a permanent staple in Oak Bluff, and he had no interest in anyone who wasn't.

He handed her the bottle and set the water down on the desk. "A few of those should help take the edge off the pain." He dragged another chair to face hers, then knelt down beside her. "May I?" he asked.

She nodded, and he lifted her foot and rested it on the seat cushion. First he laid the towel over her swollen ankle. Then the pack. He watched as she tossed four of the small red pills into her mouth and washed them down with a sip of water. And then another until she downed the whole glass of water.

"Thirsty, huh?" he asked.

She wiped her forearm across her mouth. "Yeah. It's been a day."

"How long were you driving?"

"I ran out—I mean *left*—at about two p.m. So a little over four hours?"

He checked his watch. It was after seven now. "You must be hungry, too."

She chewed on her bottom lip. "Starved, actually. I didn't even make it to the hors d'oeuvres."

He blew out a breath, then grabbed the brown paper bag from his desk. "It's not hot anymore, but it'll still be the best barbecue you ever had."

Her eyes lit up as he handed it to her. She reached inside greedily and practically tore the sandwich free. She paused, though, just before sinking her teeth into that perfectly crusty bread.

"This is your dinner," she said with realization.

He waved her off. "I know where to get more." Though he doubted that would be happening tonight. BBQ on the Bluff closed at nine, and by the time he got Olivia settled at the B and B, well, he'd most likely be heading home to a frozen pizza and a six-pack.

His brows furrowed. "You coming from some kind of party? I kind of figured with the dress."

Her mouth was full with his dinner, a drip of barbecue sauce in the corner where her lips met. Her eyes fluttered closed, and she moaned with what he knew was the sheer ecstasy of tasting the best local fare Oak Bluff had to offer.

She swallowed and licked her lips, and there it was again: the hibernating bear waking from its long sleep.

He wanted to brush his thumb across that full bottom lip of hers, which was just about the stupidest thought he'd had since asking Tara to marry him ten years ago.

"A wedding," she finally said.

He raised a brow. "Not yours, I take it. I mean, I know brides wear all sorts of dresses these days—"

"No!" she interrupted. "God, no. Me? Married? Ha! I…" But she cut herself off by taking another gargantuan bite. "This is so good," she said around the mouthful of food.

He guessed the whole marriage conversation was over, which was fine by him. They weren't here to hash out each other's romantic pasts—or lack thereof. In fact, they didn't need to be here any longer once she'd polished off the rest of his dinner. And that only took about three more minutes.

He sat on the edge of his desk and watched her dab at the corners of her mouth with her thumb. Then she brushed off her hands just as Deputies Adams and Walters walked back through the station door.

"Bug's parked behind the B and B, Cash," Adams said. "Am I clocking out now, or is our guest staying the night?" She nudged Walters with her elbow, and the two deputies glanced from Cash sitting casually on the desk to Olivia stretched out across two chairs. Both of his employees were fighting off grins, which meant they were assuming something they shouldn't be assuming. Because they'd be wrong.

He stood to his full six feet four inches and crossed his arms. "I'll be taking her to the B and B in just a couple minutes, so you can both clock out. Who's on call tonight?"

Adams cleared her throat. "You are, sir."

Shit. That was right. Scratch the six-pack. There'd just be the frozen pizza.

"Right," he said. "I'll see you two in the morning, then."

Both deputies nodded at him and then Olivia. "Night, Cash," they said in unison.

"Good night."

Olivia took the ice pack and towel off her ankle and stood. She looked steadier on her feet. Her bare feet.

"You got an overnight bag?" he asked.

She shook her head. "Do you have a Target around here?"

He groaned. "You don't even have a wallet."

"Right. Shoot. I did *not* think things through."

He pulled his cell phone from his pocket and dialed up Wade at the pharmacy. "You busy? Yeah, I got a customer who needs some of the necessities. Okay if I bring her by in a minute? Thanks, buddy. I owe you."

He looked her up and down and shook his head, the faintest hint of a smile playing at his lips.

"What *are* you doing in Oak Bluff, Olivia Belle?"

She shrugged. "I came here to find true love."

CHAPTER FOUR

With Michael's sister's wedding in the books, there were no other major events happening that week at the hotel. Olivia could pencil in a few vacation days. Emily was sending an overnight messenger service with her wallet, some of her own clothes, and toiletries. For now, though, as the sheriff walked her to the B and B, she was dressed in a very trendy Oak Bluff sweatshirt and a pair of drugstore yoga pants, because, yes—those were apparently a thing. Pharmacy owner Wade even had a small selection of flip-flops, which meant she wasn't exactly ready for the cover of *Vogue*, but she wouldn't have to spend the night in a ball gown and one glass slipper.

She laughed.

"Did I miss a joke?" he asked.

She shook her head. "Just remembering you calling my shoes glass slippers." She held up the pharmacy bag that was stuffed with her bridesmaid dress, one-and-a-half shoes, and a toothbrush and toothpaste. "I'm most definitely *not* anything out of a fairy tale."

It was dark out now, but the streetlights lit the hard lines of his face, and she could see that he was trying to puzzle something out.

"Got anything you want to ask me, Sheriff? Or can I call you Cash now that you bought me dinner and this fancy new outfit?" They stopped in front of the B and B, which was aptly called The Oak Bluff B and B. "You know? Something bigger with a little more pizazz might get your little town some more tourist traffic."

He crossed his arms. "Our little town doesn't need big names. We get plenty of traffic. In fact, someone sped right through the outskirts just this afternoon. Coulda gotten into a serious accident if law enforcement hadn't stepped in."

She rolled her eyes.

"And I take it you aren't in town long?" he added. "So we should probably just keep it at *Sheriff* and *Ms. Belle*."

She smiled her best customer service smile—one of the first things they teach you when you major in hospitality management. He was right. They should keep it formal. Formality kept things distant, and distance was exactly what Olivia needed.

Except this stranger of a man could have really arrested her. He could have let her go hungry and left her in her tattered gown until the messenger got here tomorrow. But he hadn't, and somehow those small gestures felt more intimate than Michael's proposal, which meant she was not succeeding at distance here.

"I shouldn't be here more than a few days," she said. "Just need to find what I came here for."

"Right," he said. "True love. That should only take a few days."

She closed her eyes for a moment and replayed Michael's words in her head.

It had been just after the ceremony—and just before cocktails. All she'd done was ask him why he'd been acting so weird all morning. Then everything had spun out of control.

It's the logical next step, babe. The practice wants a family man as partner. The condo co-op board won't put your name on the deed unless we're married. It just makes sense. Only then had he gotten down on one knee—after likening their relationship to a business maneuver. It wasn't the animosity of her parents' relationship, but it sure as hell wasn't love. Not with Michael and not with anyone who'd come before him. What had she been doing wrong?

Being with him had been safe—their chemistry a slow enough burn to take things at a gradual pace—but it was only now, standing in this ridiculous outfit before a man who'd put her in handcuffs in the first five minutes he'd met her, that she wondered what it would be like to throw caution to the wind.

Spontaneity had never been her thing—at least with men. Sure, she could run off and drive four-plus hours down the coast the second she got spooked *out* of a relationship, but she didn't just jump off the ledge the second a man made her heart go pitter-pat. Or maybe it was that her heart had never reacted like this before, but right now it was pittering and pattering beyond restraint.

Aw, to hell with it. Caution had gotten her nowhere so far, and it wasn't like this guy was proposing marriage. She'd already broken the law. How much more trouble could she really get herself into?

She drew in a deep breath and opened her eyes to find the sheriff unabashedly staring at her, his stoic expression revealing nothing. She dropped the pharmacy bag—and before talking herself out of it—rose up on her tiptoes and kissed the man softly on the lips.

"I'm sorry," she said, when his lips didn't move in the slightest. "I was just testing a theory, and it was the worst judgment ever, and—"

He shoved his fingers into her hair, his lips crashing against hers. The kiss was strong, insistent—and clumsy. Teeth knocked together, and his fingers got caught in her curls. But he pulled her closer, and she him—unable to get enough of someone who up until a few hours ago hadn't even existed as far as she knew.

But he existed now. *They* existed in this inexplicable moment of lips touching and tongues tangling and what the hell was she doing?

She stumbled backward, gasping for breath, and he scrubbed a hand across his jaw.

"Good night, Sheriff." She cleared her throat. "Thank you—uh—for the sandwich. And clothes. And no jail time."

He nodded once. "Good night, Ms. Belle. Try to stay on the right side of the law."

She laughed nervously and backed toward the door, reaching behind her to turn the knob and push it open.

Thank the stars the bed-and-breakfast was still open.

Seconds later the door was closed again, giving her that distance she craved.

Never mind that she could still feel the tingle of his lips on hers—or the scratch of his stubble against her chin. Never mind any of it. She was a twenty-five-year-old woman who'd just fled a marriage proposal—a twenty-five-year-old woman who had, in one way or another, fled every relationship she'd ever been in the moment she knew she wasn't in love.

Why couldn't she fall in love? Either she was defective or she just hadn't learned the secret yet. She liked to think it was the latter. At least, she hoped it was. Otherwise, caution or no, she was in big trouble.

This visit obviously wasn't about her own love story. It was about the only one she knew existed in real life. And if she could figure out how *they* made it work, then maybe, *just* maybe, she'd have a chance at one day getting it right herself.

Cash had just given Dixie the last slice of pizza when his cell phone alerted him to the alarm being tripped at Lucinda's. Not the shop, but the apartment above.

He picked up his radio from the coffee table. "We got a four-five-nine at Lucinda's. No request for backup yet but wanted to see which one of you was still awake *and* sober. Over."

"Roger, Sheriff. Available for backup," Walters said. "I do believe Adams is on a date, sir. Over."

"Damn it, Walters. Doesn't mean I'm not available for backup. Available for backup, sir. Over."

Cash shook his head. "Heading there now. Stand by. Out."

Breaking and entering? That kind of shit didn't happen in Oak Bluff. The town wasn't perfect. The Everett boys had had their share of hell when their drunk of a father had almost killed the oldest one, Jack. But that was over a decade ago, when Cash was studying criminal justice in college. By the time he'd come back home, the Everetts had been permanently removed from Jack Senior's custody. Now the man was dead and gone, and the three brothers were all running the Crossroads Ranch and soon a new vineyard.

The bottom line was, there were no major threats—

domestic or otherwise—in their sleepy little town. And hadn't he dealt with enough on what was supposed to be an uneventful Saturday night?

When he got to Lucinda's, he and Dixie climbed stealthily up the back steps to where they found the door perfectly shut.

Cash gripped the handle and gave it a soft twist to the right, and it opened with ease.

Perfect. Lucinda had set the alarm but hadn't locked the door.

He stepped quietly into the apartment's kitchen—and almost tripped over a pair of pharmacy-purchased flip-flops. In fact, he'd venture to guess these flip-flops were only a few hours old.

That's when he saw Olivia Belle through the open archway into the living room, kneeling on the wood floor with a broken floorboard in her hand.

And she was crying.

"I know," she said, her reddened eyes meeting his. "I'm under arrest."

Dixie ran straight to her and collapsed, resting her head in Olivia's lap.

She laughed through a sob. "This furry ball of love would never rip someone's arm off."

"Betrayed again," Cash mumbled. "She *is* trained to," he said louder. "Just hasn't had much occasion to do so, so she's out of practice." More like she never had the occasion to do so, but that was beside the point.

He made his way through the living room to the digital panel on the wall. He typed in the code to disable the alarm, and the silent alert finally left his cell phone alone.

"The door was unlocked," she said with a sniffle. "I was just going to look for— I didn't know there was an alarm." Her brows pulled together. "Wait. You know Lucinda's alarm code?"

He huffed out a breath. "Lucinda is my mother. And when she gets back, we're going to have a nice long talk about how the alarm doesn't mean shit if she keeps on leaving her door unlocked. Also, who takes off their shoes when making an unlawful entry?"

Olivia's eyes widened as she dropped the floorboard to the ground. "Oh God. I broke into the town sheriff's *mother's* home? And I stepped in a puddle out back. I didn't want to mess the place up—just find something that isn't here."

He sat down on the arm of the couch and pulled the radio off his hip. "False alarm. No backup needed." He waited for Adams and Walters to reply, then set the radio on the coffee table and crossed his arms. "Well, you didn't exactly *break* in. But you did enter private property that isn't yours. You wanna tell me why?"

Olivia scratched Dixie behind the ear and blew out a shuddering breath. Cash had the inexplicable impulse to go to her, to pull this force of nature of a woman into his arms and comfort her.

But Cash Hawkins didn't act on impulse. And he wasn't about to start with a woman who couldn't seem to go five minutes without breaking a law.

Her shoulders slumped. "Guess I have to tell you everything now, huh?"

He shrugged. "Either that or say good-bye to the B and B and hello to a musty cell."

"Fine," she said. "I suppose now that I've interrupted your evening again, I owe you that much."

"I suppose you do," he said. He could just march her back to the B and B and call it a night. But he told himself he wanted to hear her story for legal reasons—to make sure this woman wasn't going to be breaking and entering or committing another traffic violation any time soon. It certainly wasn't because he wanted a few more minutes in her presence. Because that would go against all his self-imposed rules when it came to women. Mainly—he didn't do the whole get-to-know-you thing. But here he was—getting to know her.

Olivia swiped under her eyes and sniffled again. Dixie whimpered, and Olivia went back to scratching behind the non–attack dog's ear. "My grandma lived in Oak Bluff until she was nineteen. She met my grandpa on a weekend trip to San Francisco. They had one magical night—his last night in town before leaving for basic training and then being shipped off to the war in Vietnam. They continued their courtship one hundred percent through letters for *three* years."

"I'm assuming things worked out for them since they are your grandparents and all?"

She nodded. "He proposed to her the day he got home, and they eloped the next weekend."

"Get outta here," Cash said. "One date and some letters, and just like that?"

"Just like that. They're coming up on their forty-eighth anniversary."

Cash blew out a long whistle. "Lemme guess," he said. "You're looking for the letters."

The tears started again. "This used to be her house. I didn't realize it because the address was different and—well—it's an antiques shop now. But I did some googling on my phone. Thank God for the B and B's Wi-Fi, by the way. And it turns out this is the place." She held up the loose floorboard. "See?" She pointed to small carvings in the wood. *J and A. 1967–1970.* "Joseph and Anna."

He scratched the back of his neck. "I don't get it. If these letters are so special, why'd your grandmother leave them here?"

"She didn't mean to at first. But their honeymoon turned into a year of travel. Can you believe that? A *year*. And when they finally made their way back here, her parents had up and sold the place. By that time Gran said she didn't need the letters because she had my grandfather, so she never came looking for them. They ended up settling in San Francisco, had my dad and my uncle. My dad married my mom. They had me. Years later they decided they hated each other, so they divorced and are still living hatefully ever after to this day."

"That was a mouthful," he said, still sort of reeling from the verbal onslaught. Most of his conversations warranted nothing more than a one- or two-word response from him, and he liked it that way.

She secured the plank of wood back into its spot, gave Dixie a pat, then stood up. She dusted her hands off on her Oak Bluff sweatshirt.

"I'm pretty sure I've overstayed my welcome. If you're not going to arrest me—again—I should get going."

"So the true love you came here to find...?"

"Theirs," she said. "I thought if I could read the letters I could figure out the secret. You know?"

He narrowed his eyes. "Secret to what?"

She threw her hands in the air. "*Love!* How do you find it? How do you make it last? What happened in those letters that got them to almost fifty years of marriage when I can barely make it past fifteen *months* of dating a perfectly nice guy with a perfectly good job and perfect co-op who would love to put me on the deed? Do you know I ran from a man while he was down on one knee? With a ring? Why do I keep running from commitment? How the hell do I fix myself so I can find what they found five decades ago?"

Her chest was heaving.

"Wait. You're getting *married*?"

"No! That's just the point. I'm *not*. And I probably shouldn't. Yet I keep hoping I'll figure it out, and maybe that's my problem."

Her arms were flailing at this point, and her eyes were wild—both signs that he should probably back away. Instead he found himself stepping closer, his hands gently gripping her shoulders in an effort to calm or steady or *something*.

"Hey," he said softly. "I don't know a whole hell of a lot about this stuff, but I'm sure of one thing."

She took a few steadying breaths, then fixed her gaze on him. "What's that?"

"There is no secret," he said plainly.

Her bottom lip trembled, but no more tears fell. "So I'm just—broken?"

He could feel the heat of her skin even beneath the sweatshirt, and it made the tips of his fingers tingle. He tried to rationalize that she was simply new and unexpected, and that was why he couldn't seem to stay away. But it wasn't like he was celibate. He spent his nights and weekends off at his favorite tavern a couple towns over. He'd found plenty of companions over the years who were good with keeping it casual.

Weren't they at one time or another new and unexpected, too?

"Aren't we all sorta broken?" he countered.

"Well, that's a cynical way of looking at things. Hey, wait." She paused. "If Lucinda's your mom, that was your stepdad who just..."

He nodded. "Went to the burial this morning. But a sheriff

can't quite take a week off the job. It's kind of a 'round the clock situation."

She sucked in a sharp breath. "And the first husband—the one who died of lung cancer—that was your dad."

His throat tightened. "I was sixteen. He was a good father, but hardheaded as all hell."

"Oh, Cash," she said, cupping his cheek in her palm. He didn't correct her. Didn't give her his damned spiel about *Sheriff Hawkins* and *Ms. Belle* because right now, in this moment, he liked the sound of his name on her lips.

"What if I could help you track down those letters?" he asked.

"You would do that for me?"

He laughed softly. "If it means you stop breaking laws in my town and let me get a night or two of peace."

Her cheeks flushed, and hell if she wasn't beautiful when she was embarrassed.

She held up her right hand. "I solemnly swear to stop breaking laws in Oak Bluff, California."

"Deal," he said.

"I'm sorry about your dad, Cash. And your stepdads. You and Lucinda have lost a lot, huh?"

"We get by just fine."

"And getting by is enough?" she asked.

"Has been." Until now, it seemed. Because this woman was making him think things he shouldn't think. And want things he shouldn't want.

She rested both her palms on his chest, and he could feel his heart hammering against his ribs. Could she feel it, too? And when the hell was the last time a woman had made his heart race?

He wasn't like Lucinda. She loved, lost, and loved again. He didn't know how she did it, and she definitely wasn't the norm. People were lucky enough to find love once in a lifetime, if at all. He'd had his once and wasn't about to go looking for it again when one of two things could happen: he could search and never find it, or he could be that tiny percentage like his mother who found it—and lost it—again. Either way, he set himself up for disappointment or worse. No, thank you.

Yet here was Olivia Belle, her fingertips searing his skin through his shirt, obliterating years of rationalization for why he lived his life the way he did.

This was the worst idea. Period.

"You're not getting married," he said plainly, but it was still a question.

"I'm not."

"Ms. Belle?"

"Sheriff?"

"I'm gonna kiss you again."

She bit her bottom lip, and he wondered if there was anything sexier. "I'm gonna let you."

"Good." He dipped his head.

"But," she interrupted, "let the record show that I am defective. I don't know how to—"

"Olivia."

"Yeah?"

"Stop talking, please."

He brushed his lips tentatively over hers, and when she didn't speak, he let the hunger win. Her lips parted, and his tongue slipped past. He tasted the salt of her tears, the coffee she must have had at the B and B, and something sweet, like cinnamon. She was both delicious and intoxicating, and even though he was still on call, he let himself get drunk on the strangeness and newness of wanting like he hadn't let himself want in a good long time.

Because wanting her was safe. She wouldn't be here long enough to burrow her way into his heart, just long enough to get whatever this was out of his system.

Because she'd already admitted she was a runner, and Cash knew a thing or two about being left on one knee.

Because despite it seeming like she somehow ran to *him*, as soon as they solved the mystery of the letters, she'd be long gone, and everything would go back to the way it had always been.

CHAPTER FIVE

Olivia met Cash in the lobby of the B and B at half past ten. She bounded out of the kitchen in her favorite jeans, a green cami and cardigan, and her Chuck Taylors. The messenger Emily sent had arrived a bit past eight, and just having her own stuff made Olivia feel like today, anything was possible. Plus, the swelling in her ankle had gone down significantly, so while it still hurt, walking was no longer an issue. Then there was the big, bad sheriff waiting for her in the small foyer. Only in jeans and a form-fitting gray T-shirt, he didn't look so big and bad. Or sheriff-y. But good Lord did he look—*good.*

"Coffee," she said in greeting, holding out one of the two to-go cups in her hand. "I wasn't sure how you took it, so I made one black and one with cream, sugar, and a dash of cinnamon. Figured I'd drink whichever one you didn't."

He gave her a single nod. "I take it black." He paused for a moment, then added, "Cinnamon, huh?"

She grinned. "Oh, thank goodness. I'd have run back to the kitchen if you said otherwise. I can't do without my cream and sugar. I love almost everything a little sweet."

She pressed the opening of her cup to her lips and hummed as her tongue caught the first taste. There was nothing like the first sip of coffee in the morning.

"I thought I tasted cinnamon when I kissed you," Cash said softly.

Olivia coughed, almost spitting the hot liquid all over the floor.

He took a long, slow sip from his own cup, then let out a satisfied-sounding sigh.

Right. He knew how she tasted—and she him. Who the hell was the Olivia who'd kissed a stranger last night— *twice*—and was now wondering when she'd get to do it again?

They hadn't spoken much after Lucinda's. He'd simply walked her next door and made sure she got back into the B and B okay. They'd decided on ten for this morning and then they'd said good night—with no further lip-locking.

But she was watching him drink his coffee now, and coffee drinking involved lips. She knew her focus today was the letters, but Sheriff Cash Hawkins had a mouth that was very distracting.

"What?" he asked.

"Huh?"

"I ate a donut on the walk over. I got chocolate on my face or something?"

"No!" she blurted. "I mean—wait, the cop-and-donut thing is for real?"

He rolled his eyes. "I like donuts. Who doesn't like donuts? The *people*-and-donut thing is for real." Still no trace of a Sunday morning smile.

She shrugged. "I like donuts."

He lifted a white paper bag she hadn't realized he was holding in his other hand. Probably because she'd been staring at his lips. "Chocolate cake, chocolate frosted. From Baker's Bluff. Best donut you'll ever taste."

She narrowed her gaze. "Here I thought I was taking care of you this morning, but you show up with a donut. I can't beat that."

He scanned the quiet foyer. "Everybody still asleep?"

She shook her head. "There are a few people in the kitchen. A few left already on a wine tour. And then there's me." She grinned, taking in the wood floors, the wainscoting on the walls. "This place is so charming. I'll have to tell Gran and Pop about it. Maybe they'll come back for their anniversary."

He scrubbed a hand across his jaw. "When do they hit forty-eight?"

She grinned because that's what thoughts of her grandparents did. They made her smile. Gave her hope when she thought her well had run dry. "A few months. Just after the new year."

"Hmm," he said, brows pulling together.

"*What*?" She waited while he sipped his coffee, as he seemed to contemplate the best course of action for his response.

"Well...It's just that they're selling." He turned toward the curtained front window and grabbed a sign leaning against the glass—a sign she hadn't noticed last night in the dark. A sign that said FOR SALE.

"Oh." The one word was all she could muster. Because after her inauspicious arrival—after coming up empty-handed at Lucinda's apartment—now there was this perfect place that would soon be no more.

Cash cleared his throat. "I didn't realize the bed-and-breakfast meant so much to you—seeing as how you've been here one night and all."

She groaned and grabbed him by the wrist, pulling him out of the foyer and into the sitting room to the right.

"Look," she said, pointing straight ahead.

"It's a fireplace," he remarked without a hint of emotion.

"And knotted pine floors, and that adorable love seat, and the rocking chair where I came up with the brilliant idea to see if I could get into Lucinda's apartment. I'll have you know that I *did* ring the bell. I don't know what possessed me to try the doorknob. No. I know. It was desperation. But the point is—" She groaned. She didn't know what the hell the point was. She just knew she hated the thought of this place going away before Gran and Pop got to see it.

"I mean, I like the DaSilvas as much as the next guy, but they've been making preparations for retirement for the past few years. Both their kids are grown and ended up in Arizona. As soon as they hand over the deed to the place, they're moving into a condo in Phoenix."

She peeked into the kitchen where the older husband and wife team, Rose and Marcus, had been cooking breakfast alongside two newlyweds. The younger couple was sitting at the breakfast bar eating, while the two owners slow-danced to a country song that was playing from a Bluetooth speaker.

Rose waved. "Olivia! Stay out of trouble today, huh?" Then the woman winked. "Mornin', Sheriff."

Cash smiled in Rose's direction, his eyes crinkling so that Olivia knew the gesture was genuine. She wondered how long a person had to know the man before they elicited the same response. Sure, he'd laughed in the police truck yesterday, but it had been at her expense. That didn't count.

"Mornin', Rose. Marcus." He gave the two a friendly nod. "Any bites on the place yet?"

Rose beamed. "We just got an offer on Friday. Waiting to see if the buyer's loan gets approved."

Olivia swallowed. "We should go," she said, tugging at Cash's wrist again. But this time he didn't budge so easily.

She waved good-bye to the kitchen congregation and sped back toward the foyer and then out the bed-and-breakfast's front door.

She paced the sidewalk, stopping when the breeze sent such a chill through her the only remedy was another sip of coffee.

Cash finally appeared several seconds later.

"You want to explain what that disappearing act was all about, or should we just head to the Everett ranch?"

She thought about answering him. There was no logical spin to put on the idea, but then again, she doubted he saw her as anything close to logical after the way she blew into town, knocking laws over left and right when she'd never so much as gotten a detention in high school, let alone ended up handcuffed inside a police vehicle.

"I just feel like it's all a bunch of signs pointing toward me being too late."

"Too late for what?"

She shrugged. "For finding what I'm looking for. It's like Gran and Pop's story disappeared, you know? Her house isn't her house anymore. The letters are probably gone. And now this amazing bed-and-breakfast that totally captures the charm of Oak Bluff—where they could have celebrated the best love story ever—won't even be a bed-and-breakfast anymore. I just think it was probably a mistake—running here."

She wrapped both hands around her coffee cup and

brought it to her lips—both to keep herself from fidgeting and to stop herself from unloading any more of her baggage on a man who gave up a quiet Sunday to help her find what she came looking for.

"Here's the thing, Olivia Belle. I don't believe in signs, only intent. And you *did* run here. The question is, do you intend to go home with those letters?"

She nodded slowly, lips still pressed to the small opening on the to-go lid.

"Then don't you give up before you've even started."

Her eyes widened and she lowered her cup, studying him. "You sound just like her."

Cash drained the rest of his coffee, dropped the cup into a street recycling receptacle, and crossed his arms. "I sound like a *her*? Can't say I've ever been told that before."

"No," she said, shaking her head with a small laugh. "You sound like Gran. After my first couple of failed relationships in college, she started giving me the third degree whenever I began dating someone new. Those were her words when she met Michael."

"The fiancé."

"The *not* fiancé. Look, he's a good guy with a good job, and he was good to me."

He cleared his throat. "That's a hell of a lot of *good*."

She waved him off. "But he's not the right guy. And I'm not even the right woman. It's just that you might be right. I could truly be unfixable."

He brushed a rogue curl out of her eye, his fingertips skimming the length of her face. "I mighta said something about being a little broken, but I sure as hell never told you that you needed fixing, and anyone who ever gave you that idea is a damned fool."

Her breath caught in her throat, and for the first time

since they'd met—albeit less than twenty-four hours ago—she was at a loss for words.

"Now, let's go find us some letters," he said, holding out his hand.

She placed her palm in his, and he gave it a reassuring squeeze. And in that instant, Olivia Belle's heart did something it had never done before.

It skipped a whole beat. Either this strange man was getting to her in ways no one had before, or she was in need of medical attention. She wasn't quite sure which scared her more.

CHAPTER SIX

Cash knocked on the screen door, but the main door was open. So when no one answered, he took it upon himself to enter. It wasn't like he was an unexpected guest. He'd texted Jack Everett late last night after he'd caught Olivia breaking and entering, and Jack had been more than happy to help.

"You can just do that, huh?" Olivia asked. "Walk into other people's homes when the door's unlocked and not call it breaking and entering. Is that a sheriff thing?"

He held the screen door for her. "No. It's a friend thing. Last time I checked, you and Lucinda weren't friends."

She huffed out a breath. "I didn't realize someone with as pleasant a demeanor as you *had* friends. And I bet if Lucinda met me and got to know me, we'd be BFFs in no time."

His brows furrowed, and she groaned.

"Best friends forever?"

He stared at her absently.

She jutted her chin out as she stepped through the door, and he had to bite back a grin. Of course he knew what the letters stood for, not that he'd ever uttered them in his life. It sure was fun to mess with her, though. And she was right about Lucinda. She and Olivia would be fast friends if they ever had the chance to meet. Lucinda had a soft spot for things that were strange or different yet still beautiful in their unique way.

That was Olivia Belle. Strange. Different. And absolutely beautiful. He was on dangerous ground, even though it was the same earth he'd traversed for the better part of his life.

"Jack?" he called out as they headed down the short hallway toward the kitchen. "I think I'm a few minutes early, but—"

They both stopped short in front of a kitchen table lined with slices of cake—and a half-dressed Luke Everett—the middle brother—blindfolded, his arm in a sling while he was being fed a forkful by Lily Green.

Cash cleared his throat.

Lily yelped while Luke simply chewed the food that was in his mouth, removed the tie covering his eyes, then gave Cash and Olivia a sly grin.

"Mornin', Sheriff. Who's your friend?" He raised a brow.

"Sheriff!" Lily said, with a little more enthusiasm than he was used to seeing from her. "I was just—I mean, Luke was helping me pick a cake for the wedding."

Cash narrowed his eyes. "You two are getting married?"

"Hell no!" Luke said.

Cash wasn't judging, but Lily and Tucker Green had just finalized their divorce.

Lily narrowed her eyes at Luke, then laughed nervously. "*No*. Luke and I are *not* getting married. But my ex-husband is. To Sara Sugar. From that Food Network show, *Sugar and Spice*? Right. You don't watch television. Anyway, Tucker's getting married, and I'm happy for him, and I'm sort of catering the wedding."

"What?" Olivia blurted. "I'm sorry. I don't know you, and that was rude of me, but—*what*? You're catering your ex-husband's wedding?"

Lily bit her lip and nodded. "I know it sounds crazy, but I need the job."

"And she agreed to it before she knew whose wedding it was. Not that I didn't try to stop her." Luke put his coffee mug down on the counter and swiped the fork out of Lily's hand. "If you all are going to keep on talking about Lily's excellent decision-making skills, I'm just going to take care of the cake." He dug the fork into the hunk of cake and stuffed it into his mouth.

"You're an asshole sometimes. You know that?" Cash said.

Luke just raised his fork in a gesture of cheers and kept on eating.

"Jack in his office?" Cash asked Lily.

She shook her head. "Is he supposed to be? Ava just went to meet him and Owen for lunch."

Cash pulled his phone out of his pocket to double-check his texts, then cursed under his breath.

"What is it?" Olivia asked, and he could hear the doubt seeping into her voice.

"Nothing," he said. "Just missed a text from Jack. He took his son Owen to the park for some pitching practice this morning, and now it looks like they're meeting Owen's mom, Ava, for lunch. He was going to dig up some deed history on your grandma's house since I can't find the record of sale from before Lucinda purchased it. Jack's a contract attorney, and he's got a buddy in real estate who might be able to track it down. He says he's sorry if he put us out and that he'll email me what he finds this afternoon."

Olivia's shoulders sagged.

"Hey," he said gently. "It's not a sign."

He glanced back to Luke and Lily, who both looked like they were guilty of something, but of what he wasn't sure.

"Heard about the rodeo last night," Cash said to Luke. "Bull threw you pretty hard."

Luke's devil-may-care grin faded. "I got—distracted," was all he said, and Cash could tell not to press the issue.

"You got any horses need working out since I take it you're out of commission for a bit?"

Luke's jaw tightened. After his brothers, Cash knew riding was the most important thing to Luke Everett. Being benched wouldn't be easy for him.

"Yeah," Luke said. "Cleo and Bella are always good for a workout."

Cash nodded toward Lily. "You make sure he stays put."

"Oh, I'm not here to—I mean, I was supposed to do the cake tasting with Ava." Her face brightened. "Do you two want some cake? I'm sure Luke would love the company."

Luke mumbled something Cash couldn't quite make out. And as good as some of Lily Green's homemade cake sounded right about now, he somehow felt like he and Olivia were intruding.

"We'll take a rain check," Cash said.

"I'm Olivia, by the way," she said.

"Lily," the other woman said. "And this ray of sunshine is Luke. You new in town?"

Olivia shook her head. "I mean, yes. I am new, but not staying. Just visiting—and trying to stay on the right side of the law. It was nice to meet you both."

"I'll hold you to that rain check, Sheriff!" Lily said as they turned toward the door.

"That's what I'm hoping," he called over his shoulder, and they were out the door a few seconds later.

Cash led her toward the stable. He was going to make sure this morning wasn't a loss as far as Olivia giving up hope. "I know what you're thinking," Cash said when they were a good distance from the ranch.

Olivia's cheeks were pink, and she was smiling. "You mean that there was some *major* sexual tension happening during that *cake tasting*?" She put finger quotes around *cake tasting*.

"You are aware that there was actually cake. And Luke did seem to be tasting it."

She raised her brows. "So you didn't notice it."

"No."

She took a step closer to him, and he could swear the crisp October morning grew warmer with her approach.

"You didn't feel the heat? Or you like to pretend that kind of thing doesn't exist?"

He cleared his throat. He knew that kind of thing existed. He knew damned well. But yeah, he was pretending right now. Real hard. Not with Luke and Lily, though. Whatever was going on there was none of his business. The problem was that whatever heat Olivia had noticed back in that kitchen, it had followed them to the stable. And now it was just him and her.

"We're not here to talk about heat," he said. "And apparently we're not here to talk about the deed to your grandma's house. At least not yet."

She moved in closer, that heat he didn't want to acknowledge melting the space between them, and he knew she felt it, too. "What *are* we here for, Sheriff?"

He could tell she was trying to be coy, but there was a

slight tremor in her voice that mirrored the erratic rhythm of his pulse.

He was here to clear his head. That much was true. "We're here so I can show you Oak Bluff the way it's meant to be seen—on the back of a horse."

On the back of a horse? "Whoa there, Sheriff. Slow your roll. I don't ride horses. I'm from San Francisco. I ride trolley cars. Sometimes I even ride Ubers—"

"And sometimes you ride a canary yellow Bug way too fast in a town that moves at a much slower pace."

She narrowed her eyes at him. "Horses don't move at a slow pace."

The corner of his mouth twitched, and she gasped dramatically.

"What now?" he asked.

She stepped closer and was even so bold as to touch that spot where his bottom and top lips joined, inspecting it, eyeing it with scrutiny.

He wrapped his hand around her wrist, but the touch was gentle—not full of the force she knew a man of his stature was capable of.

"I was just seeing if this thing worked," she said. "I mean, other than when you're laughing at my expense."

He rolled his eyes. "I smile."

"Mmm—no. You don't. You're that strong, silent type, so stoic, burying your feelings. I mean, if you have them."

He sighed and lowered her hand, but he didn't let go. "I'm having a feeling right now," he said dryly.

She laughed. "I bug you, don't I?"

"Yes. Because you're stalling. Come on."

He tugged her toward the stable door, and only because he'd now laced his fingers with hers did she not resist.

"Oh!" she said when he opened a stall door to reveal a gorgeous caramel-colored horse. Gorgeous and *huge*. How did anyone even get into the saddle without a ladder?

"Olivia Belle, meet Cleo. Cleo..." He stroked a hand down her mane. "Meet Olivia. You two are going to get to know each other rather well today."

"Cash," she said nervously now. Because this was getting a little too real. "I'm not sure this is a good idea. Maybe I could just watch you ride? I'm quite good at spectating. My dad's a huge Giants fan, and we go to tons of games. I can—"

"Shhh," Cash said, covering Cleo's ears. "Cleo here is Jack Everett's horse, and he's just about the biggest Dodger fan there is. You don't want to spook her with talk of another team, do you?"

She forced a smile but backed away from the stall.

"Hey," he said, his tone shifting from playful to concerned. "What's wrong?"

She fidgeted with the button on the bottom of her cardigan. "So...My parents actually took me riding once when I was in middle school. They were concerned I didn't have a thing, you know?"

"A thing?"

"I wasn't into sports or ballet or playing a musical instrument—by the way, the cello thanked me for quitting. I just hadn't found what made me tick."

He raised a brow. "Fast driving."

She sighed. "*No.* Event planning." He opened his mouth to say something, but she cut him off. "Before you make fun, I'll have you know that I am an excellent party planner, and it all started with my best friend's thirteenth birthday party. It was Harry Potter themed, and all the kids in school were talking about how amazing it was afterward. But that's not my point." She paused, waiting for him to interrupt, but he just stared at her with those gorgeous green eyes all patient and *slower paced.* "My parents took me to this farm that gives you a half-hour lesson and then lets you set off on this trail. So there we were, the three of us on horses, and my parents get into an argument."

His brows furrowed. "About what?"

"You name it. Whether we should walk or trot, go right or left at the fork in the trail even though both routes led back to where we started. Then I think it escalated into whether or not my dad's horse was brown or chestnut. At one point my mom yelled at him so loud that my horse got spooked."

"Shit," he hissed quietly.

Olivia nodded. "Threw me right off. I broke my arm in two different places and had to listen to my parents continue arguing in the ER about whose fault it was. So—yeah. Horses did not end up being my thing."

He followed her out of Cleo's stall and closed the door.

"You don't have to get back on the horse, Olivia."

She laughed at the pun even as the mere thought of the incident made her heart race with the familiar fight-or-flight response that always accompanied one of her parents' shouting matches.

"But," he continued, "if you'll let me, I'll change your memory of horses to one that's far less painful." He pulled her hands from the hem of her sweater where she'd all but torn the bottom button off.

"Are you a cowboy or a sheriff?" she asked, trying to stall her answer.

He shrugged. "Maybe I'm a little bit of both. After my—after Lucinda's first husband passed, that's when she sold our farm—and with it the few horses we owned. She bought the antiques shop, and we moved into the apartment above it, and the rest is history. The Everetts let me ride every now and then—whenever I get to missing it."

"Are you missing it right now?" she asked, already knowing the answer.

"I am." The wistful look in his eyes softened the hard lines of his face.

She sighed. "Why does hearing you talk about horseback riding like that make me want to kiss you?"

And then something wholly unexpected happened. Cash Hawkins grinned.

Her mouth fell open.

He shook his head and chuckled. "You know, I'm not stopping you."

He let go of her hands, and she used her freedom to run the tips of her fingers over his stubbled jaw. "It's sexy lawmen cowboys like you that make it awfully hard to concentrate on my unparalleled equine fear."

He raised a brow. "You talk like we're a dime a dozen."

She snaked her hands around his neck, clasping them there as if she'd never let go.

"No," she said. "I get the feeling they broke the mold when they made you, Sheriff."

"You gonna keep talking?" he asked.

She skimmed her teeth over her bottom lip. It was dangerous how much and how often she wanted to kiss this man after only just meeting him. Yet there was also a safety in Oak Bluff—in this seemingly far-off place where what she was running from couldn't catch her.

He dipped his head, and she rose on her toes to meet him the rest of the way. Their mouths met with a soft brush, then a gentle flick of her tongue. His lips parted, and she tasted the bitterness of his black coffee mixed with the sugar of hers.

She let out a hum of pleasure and felt him smile against her.

"Now you're just showing off," she teased.

"I told you I smile," he said, his voice low and sexy. "Just not for everyone."

He kissed her again, his lips firm yet gentle, and his touch—the sheer nearness of him—made her forget how scared she really was.

"Do you promise you'll keep me safe if I ride?" she asked.

He straightened to look at her, his green eyes so damn sure.

"You have my word."

She slid her hands from his neck but left them splayed against his chest.

"Then show me your town, Cash Hawkins. The way it was meant to be seen."

CHAPTER SEVEN

Riding was easy when it was on Jack Everett's mare, Cleo. But Cash could still see the tension in Olivia's shoulders, which meant the horse could sense it, too.

"It might help if you breathe," he said. "She's not gonna throw you, but if you want her to trust you, you have to do the same with her."

They were moving at a snail's pace across the pasture and toward the new Everett vineyard, but at least they'd made it past doing guided laps in the small arena.

"How am I supposed to trust someone I just met?" she asked calmly. He guessed she was keeping her voice even so as not to spook the mare. But Cleo didn't spook. She was older and set in her ways, and spooking wasn't one of them.

"That's a good question," he said. Because Cash was wary about most people other than Lucinda and his deputies. It went with his line of work. And—he guessed—his personal life, too. "But you trust me, right?"

She studied his face for a moment and then nodded. "Even though we just met, too. Is it weird that I feel like I've known you longer than a day?"

He shrugged. "Multiple arrests will do that, you know. Bring a cop and a criminal together."

She snorted. "Your job must be really boring if I'm your definition of criminal."

He watched her shoulders relax as she laughed, and Cleo began to move with less trepidation.

"See?" he said, giving Bella a slight nudge with his heels to pick up the pace. "It's all about trust."

They crested a small hill, and Cash pulled on the reins. "Whoa, girl," he said softly, and Olivia did the same. Then she sucked in a sharp breath.

"Not bad, eh?" he asked.

She shook her head, mouth still hanging open.

The Everetts' vineyard sprawled before them at the bottom of the hill, but to the west they could see the main part of town, and thanks to the clear sky, the ocean beyond.

She swiped under her eye.

"Hell," he said. "What's wrong? Tell me I didn't just make you remember something else you'd rather forget."

She laughed, then sniffled. "No. It's not that. It's just—I mean I've seen the ocean before. I grew up in San Francisco. But—"

"It looks different here," he said.

She nodded, and he understood.

"Small-town living isn't for everyone," he said. "But this is one of the many reasons I never really left."

"I don't blame you." She took a deep breath of the crisp air. "But you have been outside the town limits, right?"

He nodded once. "Four years at City University of New York."

Even behind her sunglasses he could see her eyes widen. "Eighteen years in Oak Bluff to New York City?"

He cleared his throat, then turned his gaze just past her and toward the horizon. "They had a good criminal justice program."

"Uh-huh."

He could feel her stare burning a hole straight through him. No one asked him about CUNY anymore, and he didn't exactly bring it up voluntarily. So what the hell was he doing mentioning it now?

"For someone who doesn't seem to like much change in the status quo—who has already expressed that there are many reasons why he stayed in his small town—I find it very interesting you went so far away for school." She gasped. "You followed a girl!"

He squeezed his eyes shut for a moment, grateful they were hidden behind his aviators.

"Oh, come on," she said. "I told you my story. It's only fair I get to hear yours."

He grinned and enjoyed watching her brows rise once more. "Only if you can keep up." He tapped his heels against Bella's flanks, not hard enough to make her gallop but just enough to get her moving a bit faster than before.

"Hey!" she called after him as he started descending the hill. "Not funny, Cash!"

He knew she was safe, though, whether she followed or stayed at the top of that hill until he came back up. But he could hear Cleo's hooves in the grass behind him, so he kept going, just a few paces ahead of her, until he reached the fence that denoted the end of the pasture and the beginning of the vineyard.

He hopped down and tied Bella's reins to a post. By the time he finished, Olivia was pulling Cleo to a stop beside him.

Her jaw was set, and she was *not* smiling.

He moved to give her a hand dismounting the horse.

"No, thank you," she said, chin raised. "If you're going to leave me to fend for myself, then I'm going to fend for myself."

He stepped back and crossed his arms. Damn, this woman was stubborn. But he already knew that—and kinda liked it. She was strong and not afraid to challenge him. It had been a good long while since someone had.

She swung one leg over Cleo's side so she was balancing in just the one stirrup. She yelped and he rushed to her before she fell flat on her back, catching her in his arms.

"Your ankle," he said. "Shit. I forgot."

She nodded, her face so close to his—lips near enough to kiss. Again. "I guess I forgot, too. It wasn't really bothering me until I put all my weight on it. And here you are again, sheriff in shining armor, catching me before I fall. Maybe one of these days I can swoop in on a horse and rescue *you*."

He chuckled. "What makes you think I need rescuing?" he asked.

She blew out a breath. "Oh no you don't. You don't get to change the subject. You said you'd answer my question if I could keep up. Well, I kept up." She shimmied out of his arms, biting back a wince when she landed, but she stayed standing. "Now you have to tell me about the girl you chased across the country."

He showed her how to tie off the reins, then helped her over the fence and into the vineyard. They walked slowly down a row of vines.

"All this land belongs to the Everetts?" she asked, running the tips of her fingers along the budding vines. "I thought the sign on the property said *Crossroads Ranch*."

"Mmm-hmm," he said. "And soon they'll add *and Vine-*

yard to that. It's a long story, but their father passed away recently and left them a failing vineyard in the will. For three guys who grew up knowing nothing but ranching, they've really turned this place around."

She was a few paces ahead of him when she spoke again. "You know, you don't have to tell me about her if you don't want to. I get wanting to leave the past in the past."

He sighed. Because that was exactly where he wanted the past. And he thought he'd left it there until the Saturday morning mail arrived. Now here it was, still lurking in his present.

"Her name was Tara. *Is* Tara. Shit, it's not as if she died." He mumbled that last bit to himself.

Olivia stopped walking, then turned to face him. "High school sweetheart?"

"Yep. But I didn't follow her to New York. Small-town living can get to you when you're younger and don't appreciate it, and I needed to get away to make sure staying was what I wanted. So I researched criminal justice programs on the East Coast. Lucinda had money set aside from the sale of the farm, so when I got in..."

"She followed *you*," Olivia said with realization. Then she pushed her glasses to the top of her head so he could see what he knew was coming. The pity. "You came back, but she didn't." She gasped and covered her mouth. "It was her wedding invitation in your truck!"

He let out a bitter laugh. "I'm that damned obvious, huh?" She opened her mouth, but he cut her off. "I swear, Olivia Belle, if you say *Oh, Cash,* or tilt your head to the side and give me that look..."

She crossed her arms. "What look?"

He raised his glasses, tilted his head to the side, and drew his brows together, mimicking the look of pity everyone gave him when they found out about the post-graduation proposal that got turned down. The look that everyone gave when he rolled back into town on four wheels, an empty tank of gas, and an even emptier heart. The same look Henrietta, the mail carrier, gave him when she walked up the stairs to his apartment and handed him that damned invitation just as he was leaving to take Dixie for her morning walk.

Olivia giggled, and he raised a brow.

"Oh God," she said, laughing harder now. "That *is* a terrible look. I promise not to ever give you that look."

He chuckled, realizing that up until that moment *he'd* been the one pitying himself. But now he was with this woman. *Laughing*. Maybe he balked at Olivia calling him on it, but it was something he rarely did these days.

"Much appreciated," he said. His phone buzzed and he pulled it from his pocket.

"Something wrong?" Olivia asked as his jaw tightened.

He put the phone away and met her gaze. "That was Jack Everett. Wanted to let me know that he tracked down the builder who transformed your grandmother's house into a retail space and apartment. Says anything they found as far as personal effects got dropped at a local Goodwill."

Olivia's expression fell. "They must have thrown the letters out, right? I mean, why would they keep them? To a builder they would have been trash."

A sheen grew over her eyes. Damn it; he didn't want to see her cry again.

"Maybe..." he said, and he knew he was grasping here. "But maybe not."

She sniffed back the threat of tears. "What are you saying?"

"I'm saying that Lucinda sometimes shops the farmer's market for little odds and ends for the store." She gave him a look, and he waved her off. "Not food. There's this woman who sells handmade crafts and stuff like that. But she also deals in found items, and I know Lucinda has picked up some stuff for the store from her before. We can ask her if she's heard anything about the letters."

Olivia sucked in a breath and grinned. "Well, let's go! What are we waiting for?"

He cleared his throat. "That's the thing. The farmer's market is only open on the weekends and only until noon on Sundays. It's a quarter past twelve now. *And* there's also the chance that even if we go to the market, she's not there."

He expected her shoulders to sag, but instead she pursed her lips and narrowed her eyes. "So I'd have to stay here the week," she said. "And then run the risk of still coming up empty-handed."

He nodded.

"I have the vacation time," she said. "But what would I do here all week?"

A surprise gust of wind blew her soft curls over her face. He chuckled and pushed them out of the way and behind her ears. And it must have been the brush of his skin against hers—this crackle of whatever was brewing between them— that made him lose all sense of self-preservation.

"I'm on duty the next forty-eight hours," he said. "Off Wednesday. Then back on Thursday and Friday. If you can keep yourself out of trouble for a couple days, I'd like to take you to dinner Wednesday night."

Olivia cleared her throat. "Are you—are you asking me on a date?"

He shrugged. "Figure if we keep kissing like we're doing I could at least buy you a meal. Even though you stole my dinner last night."

"You *offered*!" she scoffed. "And…then you brought me

a donut." She scratched the back of her neck. "I kinda feel like I should maybe buy *you* dinner."

He laughed. "My town, my rules. Means I get to not only buy you a meal but also continue to give you hell for stealing my last one."

She groaned, but he could tell there was a smile hiding behind her annoyance.

"So...you'll stay the week?" he asked, a little surprised by how much he wanted her to say yes.

She bit her bottom lip and nodded. "Are you gonna kiss me again, Sheriff?"

He dipped his head, his lips a breath away from hers. "Every chance I get, *Ms. Belle.*"

And then he did.

When his lips touched hers, he tried not to think about how much he enjoyed it, or how a sudden warmth spread through him, slow but deliberate. He tried not to admit to himself that Tara's wedding was starting to bother him less and less. And he tried to ignore that their date was just a date—that Olivia Belle in Oak Bluff was only temporary.

Because if he didn't try all of these things, he might realize that she was melting his long-frozen heart, which meant he was in danger of the one thing he'd protected himself from for so many years.

Falling in love and getting left again.

CHAPTER EIGHT

Cash's forty-eight hours on the job had been busier than he'd expected.

Monday he'd had to fetch Mrs. Middleton's fifteen-pound cat from her oak tree. Twice. And he had the scratches on his neck to prove it. He'd made a note to himself to start forwarding Mrs. Middleton's number to one of his deputy's phones, even if it was their day off.

Just a couple hours ago he'd received a call from The Night Owl, Oak Bluff's one and only tavern, that Walker Everett was drunk and disorderly again. Hell, Cash knew the Everett brothers had a messy past to contend with, but Walker—the youngest of the three—had been *contending* worse and worse these days. Nora, owner of The Night Owl, tried her best to deal with Walker on her own, but sometimes things got out of hand. It had just been one of those nights.

Actually, it had been a day—or two—to say the least. Now, at mere minutes past midnight and the end of his shift, all he wanted to do was collapse into bed, Dixie at his feet. But something felt off.

He'd already let the dog out, so that wasn't it. He'd tossed his uniform into the washer and locked his gun in the safe. Everything was as it should be.

He scratched the back of his head and stared down at his phone charging on the nightstand. The screen lit up with an incoming text. The sender? Cinderella, the name he'd programmed into his contact list for Olivia Belle.

Cinderella: Hope the residents of Oak Bluff obeyed the law better than I did. ;)

Cash laughed out loud. Then, even though he stood on the cold floor in nothing but his boxer briefs, that inexplicable warmth spread through him.

He sat on the side of the bed, picked up the phone, and unlocked the screen.

Cash: Isn't it past your bedtime?

Cinderella: Nah. I like to wait till everyone's sleeping before I try breaking and entering.

He chuckled.

Cash: But I'm the sheriff, and I'm still up. Might be a flaw in your logic.

Cinderella: Wasn't counting on you being awake. Figured you'd crash as soon as your shift ended, but I'm glad you didn't.

He leaned back against the headboard, and Dixie gave him a knowing look. That was when he realized he was wearing a dopey grin on his face, and he rolled his eyes at himself. He was damn glad Olivia Belle was still awake, too.

Cash: Been thinking about me, huh?

Because he understood, now, the reason something felt off. Missing. As busy as he'd been, thoughts of Olivia had lingered in the back of his mind these past two days. While he'd been saving a cat, what had she been doing? When Walker Everett needed a police escort home—and Cash to be a friend and sneak him into the house without waking Jack, Ava, or their son Owen—where had Olivia been?

Cinderella: A lot, sorta. Is that bad?

Cash: Not at all. Been thinking about you too. You enjoying our little town?

Cinderella: YES! I love that even though you let me have my car back, I can walk anywhere I want to go. Been to the bakery, to that little craft shop where some of Ava Ellis's paintings are. She's really good, btw. And tonight I cooked dinner at the B and B with the other guests. It was so fun! And we made sangria. I had a glass. Or maybe two. Delish!

Cash laughed at her rambling. She texted like she spoke, but he liked it. He liked hearing about her day at the end of his.

"Huh," he said aloud. That was a first—wanting to talk to someone other than Dixie before he went to bed.

Cinderella: Also I ignored texts from my mom, dad,
grandmother, and Michael. Basically everyone in my
real life. So that was fun. Also I might be buzzed.

Cash's small bubble of whatever he was feeling deflated
just a little at the sound of that name. *Michael*. The guy who
wanted to marry her.

Cash: Don't you think you should maybe deal with all
that?

He regretted hitting send as soon as he did. He was nothing more than a pit stop on her way to who knows where.
Who was he to tell her when she should deal with her life?

He watched those three dots hovering where Olivia's next
text would appear, his chest tightening as he did.

Cinderella: They all think they know what's best for
me. But right now real life isn't best. I want to live in
the fairy tale a little longer … with my fairy tale straight
and narrow lawman. Is that okay? ;)

He blew out a breath. Yeah, he'd say that was pretty okay.
After all, wasn't he living in a fantasy, too? In a few days,
they'd be strangers again—she back to her life and he back
to his.

Cash: It's okay.

He thought the response maybe merited some sort of
emoji to let her know he wasn't going to pry into her life any
further, but Cash Hawkins had never used an emoji in his
life. He sure as hell wasn't about to start now.

Cinderella: Good. I'm kinda sleepy.

Cash: Sangria? Or because it's past midnight.

Cinderella: Both, I think. But I just wanted to say hi. So...hi.

Cash: Hi.

Cinderella: Now I should probs say good night. Good night, Sheriff.

Cash: Good night, Cinderella. I'll see you tomorrow.

Cinderella: You think you might kiss me again?

He chuckled.

Cash: I think I just might.

He waited a few minutes, but there was no response. She'd probably fallen asleep. As tired as he was—make that exhausted—he lay in bed, eyes wide open, for a while after that. She'd thought about him...and he her. Correction. He was *still* thinking about her right now.

Dixie let out a long sigh, then nudged his foot with her nose.

"I know, girl. I think we're in trouble, too."

CHAPTER NINE

Olivia stood in front of the mirror and twisted back and forth. She loved the rich blue color of the dress, the off-the-shoulder style and bell sleeves. But what really topped off the look were the black suede ankle boots.

"You look fantastic."

Olivia startled, then spun to find a familiar-looking blond woman standing just inside the door of the small clothing boutique.

"Lily," she said. "Lily Green? We met at the Everett ranch. I was feeding cake to Luke Everett." She winced as she said Luke's name.

"Oh!" Olivia said. "The brother who got thrown off the bull. And you're catering..."

"My ex-husband's wedding. Yep. That's me."

Yeah. Olivia remembered. She also remembered the tension in that kitchen between Luke and Lily that seemed to have nothing to do with her ex's wedding. "Right." She let out a nervous laugh and then glanced down at the dress. "It's not too much?" she asked.

Lily shook her head. "Why would it be too much?"

Olivia's cheeks flushed. "I don't look like I'm trying to look all cowgirl to impress a sometimes cowboy?"

Lily shrugged. "You look like a woman who's going to blow Sheriff Hawkins's mind when he picks you up tonight." She gasped and threw a hand over her mouth. "Was I not supposed to know about the date?"

Olivia laughed. "How many people live in this town?"

Lily was laughing now, too. "Yeah, okay. The whole town knows about the date. Cash hasn't gone on one—at least not around here—in a long time. We're all kinda rooting for him."

Olivia's heart sped up, but then she remembered waking this morning to a text from Michael asking if she'd reconsidered his proposal and a text from her mother asking if she was crazy passing up a guy who could give her so much more than her dad ever gave to *her*. This afternoon her dad had actually called, and she'd let it go to voice mail just so she wouldn't have to listen to him asking when she was going to grow up and come home to face her problems.

Reality.

"I'm just here for the week," she insisted. "So whatever this is with me and Cash, it's temporary."

Lily nodded with a knowing grin. "Mmm-hmm. That's why you're buying a new dress for a first date with a guy you don't plan on seeing again."

Olivia's mouth fell open, but she had no comeback.

"He's a good guy," Lily said. "If you can get past that gruff exterior, there's a real sweetheart underneath."

Olivia blew out a breath. She'd seen that sweetheart already, not that Cash would admit it. "What about you and the cake-eating rodeo star?" she asked Lily, trying to get the attention off her and Cash.

Lily shook her head. "Luke Everett hasn't been able to stand me ever since Tucker and I started dating. Now that we're divorced, seems I get under his skin even more."

"You know what they say about love and hate," Olivia said. "It's a very thin line."

Lily's cheeks grew pink, and Olivia wondered if they'd already crossed that thin line.

"Do all the Everett brothers look like that?" she asked.

Lily rolled her eyes but nodded. "It's really not fair. Blond-haired, blue-eyed, all that cowboy-rancher swagger with a sun-kissed California vibe. They're like a pack of horseback-riding Hemsworths. Though I'm guessing you prefer the dark-haired brooding type."

Olivia laughed. What she preferred was not worrying about the future because the *What comes next?* was the part that terrified her. All she knew was that kissing Cash Hawkins was as easy as breathing because he had no expectations of her beyond the present. She didn't know how to be anything other than who she was—a runner. That was why she'd run here, to the town where Gran and Pop fell in love through the words written on the page. But for these next few days with Cash, she could just be herself. With him. Until their time ran out.

"Something like that," was all she said.

"Well, I should go." Lily started backing toward the door. "I was just walking by and saw you. I hope it's okay I stopped in to say hello."

"I'm glad you did. I was a little on the fence about the dress, but now my mind's made up." Olivia yanked the tag that was hanging from her sleeve and walked it over to the small checkout counter where the owner was helping another customer. "I'll take it all," she whispered.

"Good choice," Lily said and then waved. "I have a good feeling about you, Olivia."

And then she was out the door.

After a hefty but worthwhile dent on her debit card, Olivia soon was, too.

She checked her phone once she got back to the bed-and-breakfast. She had exactly thirty minutes before Cash was supposed to pick her up, so she decided to head down to the common room and see who was around.

Everyone was around because Wednesday nights were apparently game night, and just about all the guests plus the owners, Rose and Marcus, were seated around the long wooden table setting up Trivial Pursuit.

Olivia bounced on her suede-booted toes and clapped. "I love this game!"

"Come join us!" Marcus said. "We're just getting started."

She worried her bottom lip between her teeth but then grinned. "Okay, maybe just a couple rounds. I—I sort of have plans."

Rose raised a brow. "You mean with the sheriff."

Enthusiastic mumbling broke out among the guests, and Olivia groaned.

"How does *everyone* know?" she asked.

"I saw him at the market this morning in the produce section," Marcus told her. "Cash never shops for fresh produce. I knew he had to be doing something special for *someone* special."

"And I bumped into Carol from the boutique at the bank who said something about Lily Green and a new customer talking about the sheriff," Rose said. Then she looked Olivia up and down. "New outfit?"

Olivia blushed so hard she thought her face would actually catch fire. "I guess there's no point in my *answering* any of your questions since you seem to know everything already. So there's only one thing left to do."

"What's that?" Marcus asked.

"Kick all your butts in Trivial Pursuit." She sat down at an empty spot on the bench seat, her chin held high. Then she glanced at her opponents, who all seemed to be sitting in pairs. *Couples*, to be exact. "That's okay," she said in response to her own thoughts and most likely what everyone else was thinking. "I can hold my own against teams."

A throat cleared in the open archway of the common room.

A *man's* throat. And hell if Olivia couldn't recognize said man just by that sound. Still, she spun slowly to find Cash Hawkins standing behind her.

"I've played on a team or two," he said.

Rose waved him off. "High school football doesn't count," she teased.

Cash slid into the empty seat beside Olivia, barely giving her time to take in his plaid shirt, the sleeves rolled to reveal his muscular forearms. His dark jeans hugged his hips and—well, speaking of *butts*. Cash Hawkins was a sight to behold. And she was enjoying a long moment of beholding.

Olivia swallowed. "I was running early."

He leaned in close—even with the whole table watching—and whispered in her ear, "So was I."

His breath tickled her skin, and he smelled—*mmm*—she had to fight to keep from sighing.

"Rosemary," she said out loud. "And mint."

"Should we get started?" Rose asked, reminding Olivia that she and Cash were not alone, and oh how she wished they were now.

"Do we still have time?" Olivia asked Cash, hoping he'd tell her they were in some rush to make a reservation. Then her brows drew together as her eyes dipped from his to three small but fresh cuts on his neck. "What happened to you?"

He sighed and shook his head. "Mrs. Middleton's cat. Twice."

Her concern morphed into a giggle. "Please tell me you actually saved a cat from a tree. Twice. That really happens?"

Cash nodded and she noticed a slight tinge of pink spreading over his cheeks. Somehow him blushing made her blush, and she was sure everyone could see. Her heart raced even though she was sitting still, and as much as she'd been looking forward to tonight, something as simple as a first date suddenly felt—dangerous. She'd thought her time in Oak Bluff would be a welcome diversion from the mess that waited for her in San Francisco. But physiological reactions like this were not in her repertoire. Cash Hawkins did more than divert her attention. He captivated it.

The sheriff pulled out his phone and fired off a quick text. To whom she had no idea.

Then Rose handed him the dice, and he rolled. "You're in Oak Bluff now, Ms. Belle," he said. "We've got all the time in the world around here."

A whole ninety minutes later Cash held the door and Olivia exited the bed-and-breakfast out onto the pavement.

"I can't *believe* you knew that Denmark had the oldest flag design," she said, walking backward so they could continue their conversation.

He raised his brows. "Hey. You got us the sports and leisure piece by being able to name what teams all those NFL coaches coached. Impressive," he said.

She shrugged. "Why? Because I'm a woman?"

He laughed. "No, because they're not current. You'd have had to be a young kid when they were all in their prime."

Her smile faded. "My dad's a huge football fan. Sunday afternoons and Monday nights used to be our thing—until he and my mom started arguing louder than the flat screen with surround sound. Kinda lost my love of football after that." They got to the corner, and she finally turned to face the street they were about to cross. "You were good?" she asked. "In high school?"

He shoved his hands in the front pockets of his jeans as they continued to the other side of the street. "Mighta been able to play in college. But I blew out my knee the week Dad went into hospice."

Her throat tightened. She pulled one of his hands free and laced her fingers through his, giving him a gentle squeeze.

"I'm pretty much the worst, aren't I?" she said.

He tugged her across the street perpendicular to the one they'd just crossed, only answering her when they were on the sidewalk again. "How do you mean?"

"I've been complaining about my parents and their messy divorce pretty much since you met me. And as much as they both drive me to drink—heavily—I can still say that word. *Both.* Because they're both still here, and you've lost—"

"Hey," he said, pulling her close. Then he glanced up and down the street, from shop window to window.

"You worried about who's watching us?" she asked, knowing that just about the whole town probably was.

"I'm not worried about a damned thing," he said. "Especially you thinking your pain is anything less compared to mine. It's not a competition. We all have our baggage—our pasts that shape us. It's what we do with all that shaping that matters."

She narrowed her eyes. "You're talking about me, aren't you? How I run from my baggage?"

He chuckled. "Or how I keep mine sealed up in a really fancy envelope."

She looked over her shoulder, only then realizing where they were standing.

"Sheriff?"

"Ms. Belle?"

"Am I under arrest?"

"You break any laws today?" he asked.

She pretended she was counting her fictional offenses on her fingers. "Nope," she finally said. "Unless you count the liquor store I robbed before breakfast."

He shook his head and chuckled again. "Well, I guess I'm harboring a known criminal. We better get you inside before the rest of the town is on to us."

He grabbed her hand and pulled her toward the department's front door. But once inside, instead of continuing straight into the office, he veered left, to a staircase she hadn't noticed the last time she was here. When she *was* under arrest.

She followed him up the stairs and to a sparse hallway that had one door at the far end.

He opened that one door and ushered her inside. There she found a small apartment, modestly decorated and furnished, with a German shepherd curled on a doggie bed on the floor next to a bookcase. Dixie.

But it wasn't the sweet, non–attack dog who didn't even stir when they entered that caught Olivia's attention. It was the round wooden table set for two, a bottle of red waiting to be uncorked, and the smell of something absolutely delicious.

"You—cooked for me?"

He pushed the door closed behind them. "I figured if we went to eat anywhere in town we'd be dealing more with the stares and whispers than anything else. Thought if I took you somewhere outside of town you'd think I didn't want anyone to know I was taking you out. Decided that if I had the whole day off, I might as well make use of it. So yeah, I cooked for you."

This made her smile. "So you *do* want people to know you're with me tonight?"

"I want my damned privacy," he said. "And to show you a good time. The rest doesn't matter as long as it's you and me tonight."

Dixie barked and looked up from where she was tearing apart a piece of rawhide.

"And your ferocious beast," Olivia said, laughing.

She dropped down to a squat and gave the dog a scratch behind the ears. Dixie responded by rolling onto her back, exposing her belly for additional scratches. The dog wriggled back and forth, and Olivia lost her balance. She yelped with laughter as she collapsed right onto her butt.

"You okay?" Cash said, extending a hand.

She let him help her up, and she brushed off the skirt of her dress. "Yes, but I do seem to have trouble staying on my own two feet when I'm around you, Sheriff."

"Any idea why that is?" he asked.

She looked deep into those green eyes of his, hoping for some sort of logical answer as to how, just a few days ago, she'd run so far and fast from that forever she'd ended up in handcuffs, yet now she was already wondering how in the heck she'd be able to walk away from this man and never look back.

"Guess you just make me weak in the knees," she said, voice shaky.

He wrapped an arm around her waist. "I don't think there's one weak bone in your body, Olivia Belle, but far be it for me to argue with a beautiful woman who knows her obscure trivia."

She wrapped her arms around his neck. "And far be it for *me* to go one more second without kissing a man who cooked me dinner."

CHAPTER TEN

And just like that, her mouth claimed his.

Cash felt Olivia smile against him as she parted her lips, and somehow that made the kiss even sexier—knowing how much she was enjoying it.

His hands slid up her sides, and she sucked in a breath as his thumb grazed the side of her breast. That was all it took to unleash something in him he hadn't known still existed.

It was more than hunger. More than want. Cash Hawkins *needed* this woman, and he wasn't sure how to wrap his brain around that. He'd let himself believe for so long that he didn't need any*one* or any*thing*. Because needing someone and then losing them? That was something Cash had experienced too often to write off as coincidence.

He'd loved and lost, in more ways than one. And until Olivia Belle blew into town, he'd whittled down that circumference of love to the only two females he'd let past his barriers: Lucinda and Dixie.

Cash's tongue tangled with hers, but he needed to come up for air. So he kissed down the length of her neck, breathing in her sweet citrus scent. He paid equal attention to each of her bare shoulders, lips brushing across skin pebbled with gooseflesh.

But he still couldn't quite catch his breath. He couldn't let go of one, singular thought.

In the span of four days he'd gone from wanting to get Olivia Belle and her disregard for rules and regulations out of his hair to needing her in his bed tonight—and all the nights to come.

The oven timer went off, and he silently thanked the buzzer for a moment of reprieve.

"We should eat," he said, backing away, his voice hoarse.

She straightened out nonexistent wrinkles in her dress and stared at him. "How the heck did you cook me dinner while we were playing Trivial Pursuit at the B and B?"

This, at least, got him to grin. "Walters and Adams have a key to the place. I texted them when to come on up and preheat the oven. I prepared everything and left it all marinating in the fridge. Just had to be thrown in to bake while I was—detained."

She breathed in deep, then closed her eyes and sighed. "Mmm. I'm starving, and whatever you made smells unbelievable." She strode toward the table. "Can I pour you a glass of wine while you're getting everything out of the oven?"

"Sounds perfect."

A bottle of pinot noir later, he watched as Olivia swirled her last bite of steak in the marinade. "Seriously?" she said after she swallowed. "I thought single men subsisted solely on canned beer and frozen pizza."

He coughed on his last sip of wine. He wouldn't confirm how close to the truth she was. It wasn't that he *couldn't* cook. Her empty plate was evidence enough of that. It was that he didn't see the point of putting in so much effort just to eat alone.

"Guess I'm not your typical single man," Cash said.

She polished off the rest of her wine. "I guess you're not," she said. She reached down and rubbed her ankle under the table.

"Still bugging you?" he asked.

She winced slightly. "It wasn't," she said. "But I think walking around in heels mighta made it a little angry."

He stood and offered her his hand. "Come here."

She didn't question him, just placed her palm in his and let him lead her to the couch.

"Sit," he said, and when she gave him a pointed look, he added, "*please.*"

She sat, as did he, a little farther apart than he might have liked. But he had work to do before—well, before anything went further than the couch. *If* it, in fact, did.

He unzipped her boots and pulled off her ankle socks. Then he swung her legs so her feet were in his lap, cherry-red painted toes and all.

"What are you—*oooh*," she said as he started massaging her foot. She sank into the arm of the couch and hummed. "God, that feels good."

He worked his way up her calf, kneading her tight muscles.

She sighed with what he hoped was pleasure.

"Ever since the knee injury, I see this athletic masseuse every now and then. When the muscles get too tight. The trick is that you gotta take care of the muscles around the injury because when they seize up, it makes it hurt more."

"*Mmm*," she said, eyes falling closed. "Was something hurting me? I can't seem to remember." Then she flexed and pointed her uninjured foot. "I know this one isn't hurt, but I might walk funny if the muscles in this leg are all tight when the other one is soooo relaxed."

He laughed softly and happily turned his attention to the other foot. "We wouldn't want that to happen, now, would we?"

She opened her eyes and shook her head. "I could injure myself so badly I might not be able to drive home in time to get back to work on Monday."

His eyes met hers. "Would that be so bad?"

"Being too injured to drive?"

He shook his head. "Staying longer."

She was silent for a long moment, and he knew he should take the words back—words that were full of pressure to commit, to plant her feet in one place for the long haul. Something she'd made clear she didn't do—and something he had convinced himself he no longer wanted.

"You know what?" he finally said. "Don't answer that."

Her mouth fell open. "What if I want to answer?"

"If you wanted to, you would have. But you don't because you didn't. So let's just take the question off the table."

She yanked her feet from his lap and straightened. "Do you think you know what's best for me?"

"Whoa," he said, hands raised in surrender. "I wasn't—"

"You were deciding what I needed, just like everyone back in my real life who thinks I need to deal with reality."

His jaw tightened. "And you don't see me as reality."

Her hands balled into fists. "I didn't say—"

"But you did."

Now she groaned through gritted teeth. "Cash Hawkins, you are infuriating."

Infuriating? She was going to call *him* infuriating? "Well, you, Olivia Belle, are one-hundred-and-fifty percent *maddening*. Guess we're quite the pair if we're not talking about the real world."

She crossed her arms. "You met me *four* days ago, and you think you know me well enough to want me for longer?"

He straightened as well because two could play at this game. "What I know is that you make my blood damn near boil."

"With anger," she interrupted, but her voice had softened.

He nodded. "And downright irritation."

She scoffed.

"But what I also know," he added, "is that in four days you've made me realize the daily routine that's worked so damn well for me might not be enough."

She sucked in a deep breath, most likely to continue tearing him a new one, but then her shoulders relaxed as she blew it out.

"I make you want more out of your life?" she asked, the momentary anger in her voice fizzling to nothing.

"Yes," he admitted.

"I also make you smile sometimes."

"Yeah," he said, the corner of his mouth turning up. "You do that, too." He slid closer to her, then scooped her into his lap. He figured her wrapping her arms around his neck was a good sign. "I know it's only been a few days, but here's the thing: San Francisco and Oak Bluff—it's not as if the two are on opposite sides of the planet."

"True," she said. "But you already know I'm no good at this. It's not just Michael. I dated three guys when I was an undergrad. Ended it each time one asked me to go home for the weekend to meet his parents or even mentioned the idea of looking at engagement rings. If I can't make it stick with someone I see every day, what makes you think I'd be any better with you?"

He pressed his hand above her heart and felt it race against his palm.

"Can I ask you something?" he said.

She nodded.

"Any of those other guys make your heart do this?"

She shook her head slowly.

He raised a brow. "I have a theory, Ms. Belle. I think you've been so damned scared you'll end up like your parents that you've made sure you never get that far. We're a lot alike, you know. I've kept everyone at arm's length to protect myself from loss while you've surrounded yourself with people you know will keep your heart safe."

"And how do these *people* keep my heart safe?" she asked, though he was pretty sure she knew the answer.

"Because." He shrugged. "You never truly give it to anyone. That way it never gets broken."

She blew out a breath. "*You* could break it."

"And you could destroy mine. I have no doubt about it."

She pulled him closer, resting her forehead on his. "I don't want to destroy your heart, Sheriff."

He laughed softly. "And I sure as hell don't want to break yours."

"So what do we do?" she asked.

He kissed her once, soft and slow, and she hummed a sweet moan against his lips.

"We take these next few days to figure it out."

She nodded.

"Stay with me tonight," he said, deciding to go for broke.

She squeezed him tight, then kissed the line of his jaw all the way to his ear, her breath against his skin driving him completely mad.

"Okay, Sheriff," she said. "You got yourself a deal."

He stood with her in his arms and strode to the bedroom in ten easy steps, kicking the door shut behind them before lowering her to her feet.

Wordlessly she unzipped the back of her dress and let it pool around her ankles so she stood before him in nothing but a pair of black lace panties.

For a second it was as if all the breath had been sucked from his lungs, and he could barely breathe, let alone speak. Even though Cash was a man of few words, he felt like now would be a good time to say something. To say the *right* thing. But he wasn't quite sure what that was.

"I didn't realize it until now," he said, finally recovering his voice.

"What's that?" she asked.

"Maybe it can happen more than once."

Her brows drew together.

"All these years I've told myself I had my chance and blew it," Cash continued. "I convinced myself that Lucinda finding happiness again and again—even after losing it— was an exception to the rule, but I'm not so sure anymore. Maybe I didn't put my life on hold all these years just to play it safe. Maybe I did it—because I was waiting for you."

"That's a lot of maybes," she said, and he noted the slight tremble in her voice.

"Sure is."

She stepped toward him then and unbuttoned his shirt, pulling it down his arms and letting it fall to the floor. She unbuckled his belt, helped him out of his jeans. Gone went the boxer briefs, too.

"Wow," she said softly.

He raised a brow, then hooked a finger inside the seam of her panties.

"May I?" he asked.

She nodded, and he lowered himself to one knee, carefully sliding the undergarment over her soft skin, the tips of his fingers exploring her as they trailed the length of her perfect legs.

Perfect because the legs belonged to *her*.

"I'm on the pill," she blurted with a slight wince. "In case you were wondering."

He grinned. "I was prepared if things were otherwise."

He pulled her to him, her soft breasts against his torso, and she let out a sweet sigh.

"I forget to breathe around you sometimes." She kissed his neck.

"I guess that makes two of us. Because you take my damned breath away."

He backed her toward the bed, which he'd actually made to impress her. He realized now there wouldn't be much *looking* at it, though. And he was perfectly okay with that.

He laid her down on her back and just stared at her for a long moment. Then he dipped his head, kissing her soft lips, then her neck and her collarbone until he came to the swell of her breast. Her stomach contracted, and he could tell she was holding her breath. He grinned as he flicked his tongue out, tasting her hardened peak.

She gasped and dug her fingers into his hair, which was all the encouragement he needed to continue kissing, licking, nipping.

"More," she pleaded.

God, he loved that sound in her breathless voice, a sound that echoed everything he couldn't quite put into words.

Need.

Hell yes, he craved her touch, hungered for the taste of

her skin on his tongue. But something more than physical was happening here, wasn't it? Did she feel it, too?

"Cash," she said, and he heard it again. That something more. "Please."

"Whatever you want, Ms. Belle." He crawled over her, kissed her, then entered her as her legs fell open, inviting him in.

Every dip and swell of her curves was brand-new, unexplored territory. Yet at the same time it was as if he'd known her all his life. They moved to a rhythm that was solely their own. When she kissed him, he didn't taste the bottle of wine they'd polished off with dinner. He tasted *home*. Because hell, that was what this woman was for him.

He brushed his lips against hers, teased them with his tongue, and she gripped him tighter, pulled him closer. Deeper.

"Cash," she said, a breathless plea, and he knew she was close.

"It would be worth it," he said, slowly sliding out and then entering her again.

She gasped and opened her eyes. "What would?"

He rolled to his side, pulling her with him, hooking her leg over his hip.

"You—destroying my heart. It'd be worth it."

Her breathing hitched, and he wasn't sure if it was because he'd just snuck his hand between the place where they joined or if she felt it, too—the falling.

Because it wasn't that he *could* fall for this woman.

He *was* falling. Had possibly already hit the ground with deadly, destructive force. But he didn't care. All that mattered was this moment, showing her how well they actually fit.

Like Cinderella's glass slipper.

He chuckled, but she was too close to the edge to notice, and soon he would be, too.

He fell onto his back, pulling her on top of him and letting her take the wheel for the final moments.

"God, you're gorgeous," he said, staring up at her, her wild curls spilling over her shoulders and a look in her eyes that made it feel like all she could see was him.

She leaned down—he *thought* to kiss him—but instead nipped at his ear.

"And you," she whispered, her breath warm against his already heated skin, "are the most beautiful, wonderful, genuine man I've ever met. If I knew how to give someone my heart, Cash Hawkins, it'd be yours."

And before he could speak the words that were on the tip of his tongue, she kissed him and took them both the rest of the way home.

Hours later, when she was still naked and asleep in the crook of his arm, he realized all the work he'd done protecting himself—*convincing* himself he'd already had his one shot at love—was complete and utter horseshit.

It didn't matter if she was unable to give her heart away. She had his now, and with it the power to crush it into a million irreparable pieces.

What the hell had he gone and done?

CHAPTER ELEVEN

It had been two nights since Olivia had slept in Cash's arms and two whole days since she'd seen him. She'd shopped, hiked, and cuddled in the B and B sitting room with a romance novel she'd found on the bookshelf. Her days had been both pure bliss and pure agony as she ached to see him again, which made no sense. Olivia Belle had never ached for anyone before. Except now she did.

She hoped Cash slept during those forty-eight hours on duty. Maybe that was why he lived above the station. What a solitary existence that seemed to be—just him and Dixie behind a desk or in that small apartment.

Where he'd cooked her dinner and made love to her.

She checked her texts as she swung her feet beneath the sidewalk bench where she waited for Cash's Tahoe to pull up. First she reread the one he'd sent her late last night.

Cash: Wish your head was tucked against my shoulder right now.

It was the only text he'd sent during their separation. She hadn't seen it until she woke up this morning, which had both relieved and confused her. She'd left the ball in his court after her texts during their last time apart, and it had been radio silence. She knew he was the strong and silent type, but the other night had been—*Wow.* But where in the world did they go from here? Where *could* they go? So she decided not to respond, especially since Adams or Walters could be around. She knew Cash would hit the office even though he had the day off because that was just what Sheriff Cash Hawkins did. He took care of things even when he didn't have to.

Michael: The co-op would like an answer. Have you reconsidered?

She groaned. She was more than a name to add to a deed.

Mom: Where the hell are you? Your father thinks it's my fault you ran away. Says you're just like your mother.

Dad: I blame your mother.

Gran: Am I doing this right? I've never texted on this new pHone. Oh darn. How do I get rid of that capital h? Sweetheart, are you where I think you are?

Mom: Your grandmother thinks she knows where you are. Can you just answer one of us? Actually, no. Answer me before your father.

She answered none of them. But then she felt bad about Gran. Gran was the reason she was here. She at least owed her the truth.

Me: Yeah, Gran. I'm here. I'm gonna find the letters.
Just don't tell Mom and Dad. Please? Luv u.

And because he had impeccable timing, that was exactly when Cash pulled up, effectively rescuing her from the life she still wasn't ready to return to.

He hopped out of the truck and she stood, holding up the cup carrier with two coffees from Baker's Bluff.

"Hey," she said, not sure how she was supposed to greet him after two days.

"Hey yourself," he said, then dipped his head to kiss her—like, *really* kiss her—and yeah, that was exactly how they should greet each other after two days.

"What's with the uniform, Sheriff? Thought you were off until traffic duty tonight."

She looked him up and down, from what she assumed were steel-toed boots all the way to his sheriff's badge and crisp collar.

"Scratch that," she said. "The uniform is hot as hell. You can wear it whenever you want."

He smiled, but his eyes didn't crinkle like they did when he laughed, and she could feel there was something he was holding back. But he'd kissed her like he meant it and, boy, had she meant her part in it, too, so she wouldn't pester him about a smile.

"Wasn't sure if I'd make it back home before it was time for official business, so I figured I'd look—official for the whole day. But it seems to me that you don't mind it much."

She shook her head. "I don't mind it at all. Is Dixie not

riding along later tonight? If you need someone to keep you company..."

Ugh. What was she doing? He was being nice and taking her to the farmers market, but he didn't need her with him at work. He'd already told her he'd stop by the B and B when his shift was up so they could spend whatever was left of the night together. Because she'd be heading back to San Francisco tomorrow. She had to. There was a job, and a life to deal with even if she wished she could avoid it for one more day. Or week. Or maybe even the rest of her life.

"Dixie's in the back. She'd never forgive me if I went to the market without her. There's this vendor—Felix— makes the best damned dog treats from scratch. She goes nuts for them."

Olivia laughed. "And you can't just bring some home for her? Man, does she have you wrapped around her paw."

This, at least, elicited a genuine chuckle.

"Yeah," Cash said. "She sure as hell does. You're welcome to join us, though. Tonight, I mean. Traffic duty's *usually* pretty quiet on a Saturday night."

She raised her chin. "I was in a hurry," she said haughtily.

He took the drink carrier from her and opened the passenger side door. "You ready to go find what sent you to Oak Bluff in such a hurry? The answers to true love?" he asked.

"I guess." She wasn't sure what made her more nervous, not finding the letters or finding them and realizing that what her grandparents had was something impossible to replicate. She used to think that if she could just see *how* they fell in love, she'd understand what was missing from her own romantic DNA and would be able to fix it.

But what if Cash was right? What if she kept choosing guys she knew wouldn't be *forever* guys because that was what kept her safe from having to commit and get hurt?

Despite how amazing the other night was—how being with him was unlike being with any other man she'd been with before—wasn't she still doing the same thing by choosing a man she couldn't commit to because he lived over two hundred miles away?

She climbed into the truck, her heart suddenly heavy. Here she thought she was finally doing something different, but despite how she felt about Cash—and *oh*, there were feelings—his life was here, and hers was not.

As soon as she settled in her seat, Dixie gave her a wet kiss on the back of her palm. Olivia laughed hard, and with it some of that weight on her chest dissipated.

"She give you a proper welcome?" Cash asked when he settled into the driver's seat.

Olivia nodded. "I've been properly welcomed by both of you this morning, so thank you very much."

He leaned over and kissed her again. "I plan on welcoming you a few more times today, if that's okay with you."

"*Mmm-hmm*," she said, sneaking one more sweet kiss. "It's very okay with me."

The ride to the farmers market was long enough to warrant turning on the radio, which made Olivia thankful she didn't have to fill the silence with all her talking. For once, she just wanted to be. So she let country music take up the space between them as they got closer and closer to finding the letters.

"You wanna grab lunch first?" he asked.

"Yes!" she answered with a little too much vigor. The truth was, now that they were here, she was terrified of finding what she'd come for—and terrified of the letters being lost for good. Lunch was the perfect distraction.

"Good," he said. "I know just the place."

The three of them—Olivia, Cash, *and* Dixie, strolled through the rows of market stalls. Finally Cash pointed up ahead.

"There it is," he said, and she followed his gaze to what was no more than a food cart. A *one*-type-of-food cart.

"Corn dogs?" she asked. Not that she had anything against the popular carnival delicacy. But they were at a farmers market. It seemed—wrong.

"Corn dogs," he confirmed. "The best you ever had, made with cornmeal sourced from a local farm and most likely some sort of illegal secret ingredient that keeps patrons coming back week after week."

She eyed him in his sexy uniform, then narrowed her gaze. "Does a woman work the corn dog cart?" she asked.

He cleared his throat. "I'm not sure. Haven't been in a while. Might be."

Olivia placed her hands on her hips. "Sheriff Cash Hawkins, does the pretty girl at the corn dog cart give you free food because you're a tall, dark, and devastatingly gorgeous officer of the law?"

Dixie barked, and Olivia nodded emphatically.

"See? Even your longtime friend agrees that flirting for food is very unbecoming of a sheriff."

A vendor walked by with a basket of Calla lilies. "Flower for the pretty lady, Sheriff?" he asked Cash.

Olivia blushed and smiled at the young man, who couldn't have been much older than eighteen.

"Sure," Cash said. "How much?"

Olivia waved her hand. "Oh, it's okay. I don't need—"

"For such a beautiful woman," the guy said, "it's on the house. Just—uh—don't tell my employer over there at the florist stand, okay?" He nodded back toward the way they'd come, then pulled a lily from his basket and handed it to Olivia with a wink.

"Thank you," she said as he backed away.

Cash cleared his throat and then smugly raised a brow.

"*What?*" she asked.

Dixie barked.

"Looks like my longtime friend is calling bullshit on you, Olivia Belle."

She groaned. "It's not like I come here weekly to score a free lunch or anything." She squinted toward the corn dog cart. "Wait, speaking of lilies...isn't that Lily Green and Luke Everett?"

Cash turned his head back toward the corn dog cart, and as soon as he did Lily seemed to glance in their direction.

"Hide!" Olivia said, grabbing Cash by the wrist and pulling him behind the side of a tent where a couple was selling soaps and lotions.

Dixie barked again.

"Shh!" Olivia said. "Come here, girl!"

She was more than a little surprised when the dog obeyed, and she grinned with satisfaction.

"What in the hell are we doing?" Cash asked. "Why wouldn't we just go and say hello?"

Olivia shushed him, too, and he raised a brow.

"Oh, stop, Sheriff. I'm not afraid of you." It was only a half-truth. She wasn't scared of being ticketed, arrested, or possibly thrown in jail. But there was the whole issue of how her heart hadn't quite returned to its regularly scheduled rhythm since Wednesday night. *That* was more frightening than anything she'd experienced to date. Including being thrown from that horse in middle school.

"Remember what I said about the sexual tension between those two?" she asked.

His brows pulled together. "Lily and Luke? I told you. He's her ex-husband's friend. There are certain rules when it comes to that stuff. Plus, they can't stand each other. I've seen 'em go at it—bickering and arguing about who knows what."

She rolled her eyes. "*Yes*, Lily and Luke. I'm telling you there is something going on between those two, and saying hello is not going to do them any favors."

"So we're just going to hide out back here until..."

Olivia tiptoed to the back of the tent where she could sneak a peek at the food cart in order to check her theory.

She gasped.

"What's the matter?" Cash asked, rounding the corner.

"Nothing," she said. "But I rest my case."

She turned Cash's attention to where Luke and Lily were still standing in front of the food cart—doing something that looked an awful lot like kissing.

"Aw, hell," he said. "Nothing good is going to come of that."

Olivia licked her lips, thinking of the last time she'd experienced a kiss as steamy and romantic as the one Luke and Lily were basically broadcasting for all to see. At least it looked steamy and romantic from several yards away. Based on whatever she saw simmering between them in the Everett kitchen, she didn't doubt being right. As far as the last time she'd had a kiss to rival theirs? It had been with Cash.

He wrapped his hand around *her* wrist now, gently tugging her with one hand and Dixie's leash with the other, until they'd made it at least a hundred feet in the other direction.

"What in the hell are we doing now?" she asked, parroting his words.

"That's none of our business," he said. "Whatever's going on between them is none of our damned business—and now

I have to find us somewhere else to eat because who knows how long they'll be there doing—what they're doing."

Olivia *was* still hungry. But it was no longer for food. "Do you wish *we* were doing what they're doing?" she asked, giving her lily an innocent sniff.

"Jesus, Olivia," he said.

"What?"

"I thought we came here to find your letters."

She took a step closer. "We did, but I thought you said you'd planned on giving me plenty of proper welcomes today."

He shook his head and chuckled. "I did say that. Didn't I?" Then he slid his fingers under her hair, cradling her neck.

Goose bumps peppered her skin. Her breath quickened, and her heart felt like it was beating double time. What was it with this man? A week ago she hadn't even known him, and she'd been doing just fine without his presence in her life—if you didn't count fleeing a wedding where you were a bridesmaid and the bride's brother had just proposed to you.

Other than *that,* Olivia Belle was just fine without Cash Hawkins in her life. But what if *just fine* wasn't enough anymore?

The second his mouth touched hers, it was as if her whole being woke up from a long sleep. She pressed her palms to his chest and swore his heart was doing the same thing as hers. When her tongue slipped past his lips, she grabbed on to his shirt, fingers grappling at his collar as the kiss grew from sweet to something so much more.

Then as quickly as the kiss began, Cash let her go and backed away.

"I'm sorry," he said. "I just—"

"You're in uniform," she interrupted. "And we're in public. It's not professional. I'm the one who should apologize."

Dixie tugged at her leash.

"She can see the dog treat stand," he said with a soft laugh. But Olivia could tell it was forced. Something was up, and it was more than just professionalism.

"Everything okay, Sheriff?" she asked.

He nodded, then pulled his sunglasses out of his shirt pocket and threw them on, effectively hiding from her any trace of emotion.

"Let's get Dixie a treat," he said. "Then we'll find what we came here for."

He was quiet while Dixie enjoyed her grain-free pumpkin biscuits and while she gnawed on her sweet potato slices. Conversation was like pulling teeth when they finally settled on roasted corn on the cob as their so-called lunch, since neither was too keen on checking out the corn dog stand again.

Dixie lay on the ground beside their picnic table while she and Cash avoided eye contact as they ate.

Well, *she* kept trying to gain his visual attention, but he seemed plenty taken by his corn.

"What in the world is going on?" she finally asked.

He stood, dropped his plate and napkin into the trash and the stripped cob into the compost bin.

She rose and did the same, then crossed her arms waiting for him to answer.

"Cash Hawkins," she said. "Is kissing me so terrible that you can't even stand to talk to me anymore?" Because the way she'd seen it, that very first kiss the day he'd arrested her had been the start of something in her she couldn't quite name, so how in the hell could it have been the *end* of something for him?

"It's not terrible at all," he said flatly. "I just think we might be losing sight of the agenda. You came to Oak Bluff to find something, and it wasn't there. So here we are, chasing down your answers, and I think we should stick to the plan, is all." He picked up Dixie's leash from the grass. "Come on, girl."

The dog looked up from where she was still enjoying what was left of her sweet potato treat and whimpered.

"*Dixie...*" he said with a little more force.

She rose slowly, the treat hanging from between her teeth.

"Sure," he said. "Bring it with you."

Her ears perked up.

Olivia grabbed the rest of Dixie's goodies and followed Cash as he started walking.

"Her stall is usually in the second row," he said.

"Cash."

"Just keep in mind it's been a lot of years since the house was remodeled into a retail space and apartment. She might not have any clue what in the hell we're talking about."

"*Cash*," she said again.

"What I'm saying is that you should prepare yourself— for whatever we may or may not find."

She was having trouble matching his gait, so she was now a few paces behind. "Damn it, Cash Hawkins, will you shut the hell up about the letters and just *talk* to me?"

He stopped suddenly, turning to face her, and she plowed right into his solid wall of chest.

She groaned. "What the hell has gotten into you?"

"I'm in love with you, Olivia!" he snapped.

Her eyes widened to saucers, and her jaw fell open. Passersby slowed at his very vocal declaration, and Olivia shooed them away.

She pulled his aviators from his face so she could see his eyes. His gaze, always so steady, was now a raging sea of emotions she didn't recognize on him.

"You're...*what*?" was all she could seem to muster.

"I'm in *love* with you, damn it. And I don't need a pile of letters to tell me if what I feel is real or if I'm doing it right. Because there is no right. There's just me fooling myself into thinking I could avoid getting my heart stomped on again and *you,* blowing into town, messing up the status quo, and then leaving."

She swallowed, her throat suddenly dry. "Cash, I—"

"There," he said, pointing. "Cora's Collectibles. That's our spot."

He strode in the direction of the stall, Dixie at his side.

"So you're just going to drop a bomb like that and walk away?" she asked, scrambling to catch up. "Don't you even want to hear what I have to say?"

He stopped and blew out a long breath. He looked so— tired.

"What happened to us getting through this week and figuring it out?" she asked. "Wasn't it you who said that San Francisco and Oak Bluff aren't opposite ends of the earth?"

He scrubbed a hand over his jaw. "You *are* leaving tomorrow, right?"

"Well...yeah. I have to work on Monday."

"And when do you think you'll be headed back this way?"

Her brows furrowed as she flipped through her mental calendar. "Well, I have the Goldman bar mitzvah on Saturday and a baby shower brunch on Sunday...The next weekend there is that small dental convention..."

"That's what I thought," he said.

"Hey," she said. "That's not fair. It's my job." A job she wondered if she'd still have on Monday. After all, she did run out on the hotel owners' son, which—though having nothing to do with her professional qualifications—could possibly cause some friction at work.

"You're right," he said. "I'm sorry. I was out of line. I just—I wasn't counting on you, Olivia. And now I'm not sure how to make heads or tails of all this."

"Cash Hawkins? It *is* you! Get on over here and say hello!"

They both glanced over Cash's shoulder to find an older woman—presumably Cora of Cora's Collectibles—calling him as she stood in front of her stall.

So that was that. The end of their conversation for now, and she still hadn't addressed the elephant in the farmers market.

He *loved* her.

"Mrs. Abbott!" he said with a wave and what she recognized as his "for the public" smile.

Cora scoffed as they walked over. "You're not in high school anymore. I think you can call me Cora." She looked over the frames of her glasses. "And it looks like I need to start calling you Sheriff. Has it really been that long since you came here with Lucinda?"

She reached up to hug him, her short white hair and petite frame reminding Olivia of Gran and of why she'd come to Oak Bluff in the first place. Because she'd been starting to lose focus.

"Been a little more than ten years," he said. "But you still see Lucinda from time to time, don't you?"

"I sure do. About once a month." She frowned. "So sorry to hear about your stepdaddy."

"Thank you," Cash said; then he checked his watch. "I was wondering if I could ask you a business-related question. It's kind of why we're here."

Cora's blue eyes brightened. "You mean you're actually here to see me? Well, that is a treat. What can I do for you two?"

Cash put his hand on the small of Olivia's back, and she sucked in a breath.

"This is Olivia Belle. Olivia—Cora Abbott of Cora's Collectibles."

Olivia extended her hand to shake, but Cora just pulled her into a hug, too.

"Oh!" Olivia said, then laughed. "It's—nice to meet you."

She cupped Olivia's cheeks in her palms. "Aren't you a pretty one. And where do I know that name—Belle?"

"My grandfather," Olivia said, her voice suddenly a bit shaky. She wasn't sure why, but she felt like she was on the verge of something. "He wasn't from around here. My gran was, though. Oak Bluff, actually."

Cora slapped her knee. "Anna Moretti!" she exclaimed. "Married that boy who went off to war. His name was Belle."

"Holy hell," Cash said.

"Oh my God," Olivia added. "I didn't expect you to *know* them. I just thought you might have their letters."

Cora laughed. "*Know* them, sweetie? Your gran and I were in school together. Lost touch after she and your grandpa ran off and got married, though. And letters? What letters?"

Olivia's heart had just begun soaring to new heights when four words—*four* words—sent her heart and her hope on a collision course with the ground.

Her throat tightened, and her eyes started to burn.

"Damn it," Cash said under his breath. "I'm sorry, Olivia."

Cora put her hand on Olivia's arm. "What letters, dear?"

Olivia drew in a shaky breath. "Their whole courtship was letters," she explained. "They had this one magical night together before he left for the war. But he courted her for years via his letters, and she gave him something to come home to with hers. When he got home, he gave her back the letters she'd written that he'd been able to save, and she kept them safe beneath a floorboard in her bedroom when they eloped."

Cora's eyes widened. "And then she never went back for them?"

"Said she didn't need to once she had *him*." Olivia shook her head and swiped at a tear. "I know it's silly to react like this over something that was never mine to begin with, but…"

Cora gave her a reassuring squeeze. "I bet it would be a great love story for you to read. But if I'd have come across that sort of treasure, I never would have sold it. Though I'm not sure I'd have read them, either."

"Why not?" Olivia asked with a sniffle.

Cora opened her mouth to respond, but Cash cut her off.

"Because it's *their* story," he said. "It's theirs and no one else's, which means whatever worked for them in their time and place could have only ever worked for them."

His voice was gentle, but Olivia's sense of loss was slowly morphing into anger. Because who was Cash Hawkins to tell *her* there were no answers in those letters?

"Thank you, Cora," she said, taking the woman's hand. "It was really nice to meet you, but I think we should probably get going."

Cora patted the top of her palm. "I hope you find what you're looking for, honey."

Olivia forced a smile and then started for the car. She only slowed her gait when she realized it was Cash's car toward which she was heading. She supposed she wouldn't get very far without him.

"You're mad," Cash said from behind her, and she spun to face him.

"*Yes,* I'm mad," she admitted. "You just discounted my whole reason for coming here. Do you have any idea how that made me feel?"

His jaw tightened. "Do you have any idea how it feels to tell a woman you love her and have her unable to respond without having the definitive answer of what love is from a relationship that originated decades ago?" He ran a hand over his close-cropped hair. "Damn it, Olivia. I know you told me you're a runner, but hell if there isn't something real right here in front of you, and you're still running."

She placed her hands on her hips and huffed out a breath. "I am *not* running," she said. "I'm standing *right* here telling you that you made me feel like shit back there. Has this whole week just been you silently judging me for why I came here? *Oh that silly Olivia, thinking she'll find the answers in some stupid letters.*"

"That's not what I said."

"But it's what you implied." Her shoulders slumped. Because even if that wasn't what Cash had been thinking, had *she*?

Olivia had come here on a whim, but up until today she'd all but forgotten why. Now that the letters—or lack thereof—were staring her in the face, what had really been the point?

"Can you just—take me back to the B and B?" she asked, her heart sinking as she thought about saying good-bye to Rose and Marcus. Would she get a chance to see Lily Green again before she left? Olivia guessed she had her hands full with planning her ex's wedding and figuring things out with Luke.

She hadn't found her grandparents' letters in Oak Bluff. But she'd found—*something.*

"Olivia..." he said softly.

Dixie, ever the intuitive dog, whimpered.

Olivia squatted in front of her and gave the German shepherd a scratch behind her ears.

"I'll miss you, too," she said. Then she straightened, meeting Cash's gaze. "Please," was all she said.

"Yeah. Okay."

They rode in silence until they hit the outskirts of Oak Bluff. This was it—the street where they'd met.

Olivia laughed mirthlessly. How had she gotten herself into such a mess in the span of only seven days?

"Aw, hell," Cash said, looking in his rearview mirror.

In a flash he pulled onto the shoulder of the road, grabbed his radar gun, and pointed it at the window.

Seconds later a black sedan flew by—a sedan she recognized all too well.

Cash clocked the car at eighty miles per hour. Then he threw on his lights and put the Tahoe in drive.

"Aw, hell," Olivia mumbled, parroting his words.

The car pulled over as quickly as it had passed, and Cash slowed to a stop.

"So," she said. "When is it a good time to tell you that's my father?"

Cash let his head thud against his seatback. "Of course it is."

CHAPTER TWELVE

Olivia's father would have been enough, but when Cash approached the driver's side window, he could hear the crescendo of voices with the glass still up.

He knocked, but the driver's back was to him as he engaged in a heated argument with the woman next to him.

"Oh my God," Olivia said, coming up next to him.

"This is official police business," he said. "It's safer if you stay in the car with Dixie."

She let out a bitter laugh. "Yeah? Well, that's *both* my parents in there." She pressed her nose to the glass. "And Gran, too! Good Lord, they sent the cavalry after me!"

Cash pounded on the window with a little more force, and this seemed to get the occupants' attention.

The glass lowered, and the car fell silent—until Olivia poked her head over his shoulder.

"Livvy!" her mom yelled from the passenger seat. "Oh, sweetie, I was so worried. I told your stubborn father to slow down, but does he listen? Even his own mother told him he was driving too fast, and—"

"Elizabeth!" Olivia's father yelled. "There's a damn sheriff at the window!"

"I can *see* the sheriff, George. He's standing right next to our daughter, the reason we're *here*." She rolled her eyes.

Jesus. This was what Olivia had grown up with?

Olivia's grandmother met her gaze and Cash watched her mouth, *I'm sorry.*

"Just remember that I *let* you ride with us," her father continued. "Even with a GPS you still would have ended up halfway to Vegas before you'd realized you made a wrong turn."

"Oh, yes," the woman responded. "Thank the heavens I came with you so you could endanger us all with your daredevil driving and then get arrested." She turned her attention to Cash. People usually did this a lot sooner in the whole pulled-over-for-speeding scenario. "You are going to arrest him, aren't you?"

"Enough!" Olivia yelled.

Cash crossed his arms and took a step back.

"What are you even doing here? All of you?" she asked. "I didn't ask you to come. I'm a *grown* woman. I should be allowed to take some time for myself."

Her father threw up his hands. "You didn't answer any of our texts. Is that something a grown woman does? We were worried!"

Olivia shook her head, then pointed an accusing finger toward the backseat. "You promised, Gran. I trusted you."

The old woman's eyes narrowed, but instead of responding from where she sat, she opened the door and got out, standing to face her granddaughter.

The two women were the same height and even had the

same slender build. But where Olivia's wild brown curls whipped around her face in the breeze, her grandmother's white hair was short and straight. But they both had the same fire in their brown eyes, and for a second Cash's mind flashed forward fifty years. He imagined himself in his early eighties, Olivia looking much like her grandmother did now, and the thought knocked the wind clear out of his lungs.

"Anna," the older Belle woman said, holding out her hand to Cash but still staring straight at her granddaughter.

"Cash," he said, giving her a firm shake. "It's nice to meet you, Anna. I've heard a lot about you."

This got her attention, and she looked up at him. "Let me guess," she said. "The letters?"

"The letters."

"Can't say I had any clue about *your* existence," she added. "Unless, of course, you've only just met my granddaughter because you've arrested her for whatever reason."

He chuckled. "No, ma'am. That was last Saturday."

Anna shook her head and laughed, too.

Olivia waved a hand between them.

"Um . . . *hello*? Remember me—the person you're talking about as if she's not even here?"

"Sheriff, may I have a word alone with my granddaughter?"

"Am I getting a ticket?" Olivia's father said, still sitting in the car.

"Yes!" Cash, Anna, and Olivia's mother said in unison.

Cash pressed his hand to the top of the car and leaned down to the window. "And if I hear any more arguing between you two, I'll write you both up for disturbing the peace."

This effectively shut them both up.

He nodded to Anna and Olivia, a silent *I'll take it from*

here, and the two women set off a bit down the road where they found a slice of privacy in a bus depot.

It wasn't his business what they were talking about, but that didn't mean he wasn't curious, so he kept himself busy by heading back to his truck and writing a ticket to the second San Francisco Belle he'd met this week.

"Mr. Belle," he said, handing the man the citation. "You were close to thirty miles over the speed limit. I'm letting you off easy by giving you a ticket that says only half as much. This way you don't have to go to traffic court in Oak Bluff."

The man let out a relieved breath. "Thank you, Sheriff."

Cash shook his head. "That's not the end of our bargain. I'm gonna need your word on something—both of you—and I hope there's honor to that word, sir. Ma'am."

Olivia's parents both nodded.

"I've known your daughter for a week, which isn't long. And I don't pretend to have learned the entirety of her family history in that time, so I know what I'm about to say may be overstepping, but I'm going to say it anyway.

"I don't reckon the end of a marriage is easy, and it gets even more complicated when children are involved. But I think Olivia's been hurting for a lot of years, and maybe it's time you two put your differences aside long enough to ask her why."

Elizabeth Belle's jaw tightened, and she narrowed her eyes. "You got a lot of nerve, Sheriff. You don't know anything about our family, about Olivia."

"You're right," he said. "I have a hell of a lot of nerve, but it's only because I'm in love with your daughter and want to see her happy—even if it's over two hundred miles from here." He handed Mr. Belle his ticket. "I do apologize for any disrespect, but I hope we have an understanding here."

He straightened just in time to see Olivia and her grand-mother approaching, hand in hand. Both women's eyes were damp. Anna let Olivia's hand go when they got to the car.

"It was a pleasure meeting you, Sheriff," the older woman said. Then she shook his hand and got back in the car. "Close the window and turn on some music, George. Let's let these two have a moment."

George Belle seemed none too happy to give Cash a moment alone with his daughter, but thankfully, it looked like Anna's word was gold.

Olivia worried her bottom lip between her teeth.

"You're going home," he said. It wasn't a question.

She nodded. "I can't keep hiding," she said. "I have to go back, face the mess I made, and try to clean it up."

He'd known this was his last day with her, but somehow it hadn't fully registered until now.

"Time to turn back into a pumpkin, huh?" he asked, forc-ing a smile.

She laughed, and a tear leaked out the corner of one eye. "It always was. Maybe I should have answered their texts so you didn't have to deal with all this."

He shrugged. "It's all part of the job."

"See?" she said. "I'm not a fairy-tale princess. Just a woman who needs to stop pretending. Though I did enjoy playing make-believe with you."

His chest felt like it was caving in, but he wouldn't put that weight on her. She *had* to go. Even if he somehow con-vinced her to stay in Oak Bluff, how would that be fair to her and figuring out what she really wanted?

"I'm sorry for diminishing your reason for coming here," he said. "I was frustrated, and it was a shit thing to do."

"Is that really what you believe? That I ran here for some silly letters that don't mean anything?"

He shook his head. "I think you ran here hoping the letters were the answer, and I get that. I really do. I just hope, now that you know they're gone, you can still find what you're looking for."

"What about you?" she asked. "You gonna go to your ex's wedding?"

He raised a brow. "I was sort of hoping you forgot about that."

She nudged his shoulder with hers. "Hey. If I have to face my future, don't you think it's about time you faced your past?"

He laughed. "We're quite a pair, aren't we?"

She smiled, and he realized how much he'd miss seeing her do that for him.

"The sheriff and the reckless driver?"

He shook his head. "I think we're a little more than that."

He waited a beat, letting this moment—their parting—be her call.

She stepped toward him—thank the stars—and splayed her hands on his chest. "We're *so* much more than that." Then she rose on her toes and pressed her lips to his.

He didn't care that they had an audience or that said audience was almost her entire family. Cash Hawkins kissed Olivia Belle with everything he had. He didn't hold back. He didn't worry about self-preservation. He just kissed her like it was the last time he ever would.

Because it probably was.

She melted into him, and for this one tiny pocket of time, he let himself forget there was anything other than her, right now, in his arms.

Only when they both needed air did they part, though oxygen couldn't compare to how much he realized he needed *her.*

"I have something for you," he said, letting his forehead rest against hers.

"What?"

He led her to the back of the Tahoe, where he opened the door and removed a shoe box. "I'm not good with gifts or good-byes, so just do me a favor and open it when I'm not around, okay?"

"Okay," she said. "But—I feel like this is too quick. I need to tell you—"

"No," he said. "You don't. I think this will be easier if we leave—certain *things*—unsaid from here on out."

She narrowed her eyes at him. "Easier for whom?"

Him. Which he knew was selfish. But she already knew how he felt. Knowing her feelings either way wouldn't change the fact that this was good-bye.

"It's okay," she said. "How about you don't answer my question and I don't say anything else. Not even good—"

He kissed her again.

She was right. They shouldn't say good-bye. Because the truth was, he couldn't.

Cash waited until Olivia's father pulled back onto the road, and then he watched the car fade into the distance as they headed into town. When he climbed into the driver's seat, he pulled the fancy cardstock envelope from the passenger visor and fished out the response card. Then he grabbed the pen from his shirt pocket, clicked it open, and checked off the box next to where it said *Will attend.* He even added a little note.

Tara—
So happy for you and Tim. Congratulations.
All my best,
Cash

He stuck the card in the envelope and sealed it shut, closing the door on past heartache just in time to open a new one for Olivia Belle.

CHAPTER THIRTEEN

It didn't take long to pack up her stuff. When you were used to living with one foot out the door, packing became second nature. But when Olivia opened the small closet in her room at the bed-and-breakfast, her breath caught in her throat when she stared head-on at that giant, poofy dress.

"Nope," she said aloud. "No one wears a bridesmaid dress twice. Plus, first step in facing my life is facing the fact that I'm not a part of Michael's family anymore." Which meant leaving the dress behind and telling him—in person—why she ran.

She didn't love him, not the way she was supposed to. But he didn't love her either, and they'd both ignored the truth for far too long.

She slid the closet door shut but then threw it open again, checking the floor. Then she looked under the bed, *around* the bed, in her small bathroom, to no avail. Nowhere in the room were the shoes—those gorgeous, clear, four-inch heeled pumps. It didn't matter that she'd almost broken her ankle in them *and* had broken the shoe. They could be repaired, and it wasn't as if she planned on getting arrested in them again. If worn and used properly, those shoes were spectacular. And they were gone.

Then something caught her attention out of the corner of her eye. On the striped upholstered chair in the corner of the room sat the still-unopened box from Cash. A *shoe* box.

She sucked in a breath as she approached it, then picked it up and hugged it to her chest. The shoes were in there. She knew they were, but she couldn't bring herself to open the lid, not while she was still here. Because if she confirmed her suspicions, she might never leave Oak Bluff.

She let out something between a laugh and a sob. Because didn't that just take the cake—Olivia Belle having wild and crazy thoughts of staying put.

Instead she tucked the box under her arm and threw her weekender bag over her shoulder. Rose and Marcus were waiting at the foot of the stairs to help her to her car.

"Thanks," she said, a little teary. "But this is all I have."

Rose took the bag and the box from her anyway, then set it on the floor. "But how am I supposed to hug you with all of that in your arms?"

Olivia laughed as the woman drew her into a warm embrace while Marcus quietly picked up her things and brought them out to her car.

"When do you close on the offer?" she asked.

Rose sighed. "The buyer has had some trouble getting a loan, but we're hoping to finalize everything soon."

"What if the new owners don't want to leave it a B and B?" Olivia asked. "Can you make it part of the sales agreement that this has to be a place for tourists to have a home away from home? Or that Trivial Pursuit on Wednesdays is a must or no deal? What about group dinner prep—or using fresh blueberries in the waffles?"

Rose laughed. "Those are all very important stipulations, but I'm not sure we can make the sale contingent on those requests."

Olivia sighed. "Okay," she said reluctantly. "But maybe just say you'll think about it so I can sleep better tonight."

Rose grabbed her hand and gave it a soft squeeze. "I'll think about it."

It was well past dark when she hit the outskirts of San Francisco. And though the first thing on tomorrow's agenda was to face Michael, his family, and whatever came after that, tonight she just needed quiet—which was how she ended up in Gran and Pop's spare room.

Olivia sat in bed, a cup of tea on the nightstand, and the box from Cash beside her, staring at her, *waiting* for her to finally make a move.

A knock sounded on the door.

"Come in."

She'd expected Gran, but it was Pop. He sat down on the edge of her bed. He was a contradiction of a man just to look at him—in his worn jeans and flannel shirt hanging open over an old T-shirt, he looked more like a teen than a man of seventy-four. But then there was his tan but weathered skin and the thick salt-and-pepper hair that always seemed to need a trim.

"Sounds like I missed one hell of a trip to your grandma's hometown. Sorry I had to work this weekend, but you know...if the garage closes, people take their business elsewhere."

She laughed. "I know. And you're the best mechanic, Pop, but when's it gonna be time to retire?"

He grinned. "When I stop loving what I do or when your grandmother tells me I have to. Whichever comes first. Now, let's get back to this little trip of yours. I've heard a lot about it from Gran, but I think I'd like to hear your take on it."

He patted her feet, which were snuggled under the duvet.

She shrugged. "Michael proposed, and I panicked."

"He proposed to you at his sister's wedding?"

She nodded. "I know. But he'd just heard from the co-op board that he could add a fiancée to the deed, and he was really excited." She winced. It didn't matter how many times she said it out loud or what kind of spin she tried to put on it, the proposal never got any better. But the truth of it was that she hadn't wanted it to be better. She hadn't wanted it to happen at all, and she wasn't too sure Michael had either. "A little tacky, right? I mean, if I had said yes, that would have totally stolen the bride's thunder."

Pop laughed. "I think your little disappearing act might have done that anyway."

She sipped her tea, then hugged a pillow to her chest. "I wanted to find the letters. Yours and Gran's. I thought if I read them I could learn your secret."

This time Pop's laugh was loud, straight from the belly. "Oh, darlin', why in the hell would you want to see those? I was an idiot teenager who had no *idea* how to talk to girls. Hand me a wrench and pop the hood of any vehicle in existence, and I could talk for days. But I'm lucky your gran even answered my first letter let alone married me when I got back."

Olivia rolled her eyes. "I think you're downplaying a great romance, Pop. But it doesn't matter. The letters are gone."

"Look, I get that you've grown up with what looks like two extremes—your gran and me"—he groaned—"and then your dad and mom. Sometimes relationships work, and sometimes they implode so damned badly that you wonder how two people ever could have loved each other in the first place."

Her throat tightened. "Did Dad love Mom when he married her?"

"Oh, sweetheart." Pop's face lit up. "I never saw your daddy so head over heels for a girl before your mom *or* after. And she with him. But they expected it to always be easy."

"But it was easy for you and Gran." Olivia had never seen her grandparents fight. Not once. When it came to her parents, she couldn't remember them *not* fighting.

Pop shook his head. Then he leaned over and kissed her on the cheek. "Do you want to know the real secret that you'll never find in some lovesick teenage boy's letters home from the war?"

Olivia nodded, tears in her eyes. "God, yes. I really do."

"Falling in love is easy. Staying in love is work, *hard* work. When you find the man who makes you fall, then makes you want to do everything in your power to keep on falling, that's how you'll know." He raised a brow, grinned, and then left the room.

She thought about the past week—Cash catching her when she tripped in those ridiculous but sexy-as-hell shoes only so she could fall ass over elbow in the middle of the street seconds later. He caught her again when her ankle gave out on their horseback riding adventure. Then she collapsed right onto her behind while petting Dixie the night Cash had made her dinner.

In one week's time, Olivia had *fallen* for Cash Hawkins not once, not twice, but *three* times.

Her heart sped up as she tore the top from the shoe box to find what she'd known was there all along—her glass pumps, the broken heel repaired.

But it wasn't the shoes that stole her breath. It was the envelope on the bottom of the box.

Cash had written her a letter.

Dear Olivia,

Well, now you know why I didn't want you opening the box while I was around. It's bad enough that words aren't really my thing, but having to watch you read those words? Well, it would have been torture—almost as much torture as letting you go.

I let myself believe that not getting my heart stomped on again was better than risking it, so I closed myself off to even the possibility of love a long time ago. I wasn't counting on some wild-haired beauty to speed through my quiet little corner of the earth and turn it way the hell upside down. But damn it if you didn't do just that. Now I can't seem to put everything back just like it was. Funny thing is, though, that I don't think I want to.

I wasn't lying when I said you destroying my heart would be worth it. But the real truth is, you didn't destroy a thing.

I watched Lucinda love and lose in the worst possible way three times. And I kept wondering how she did it—how she could take risks like that again and again. But I think I get it now.

You saved me, Olivia. Falling in love with you might hurt like hell right now, but you know what would be worse? Never having let myself do it.

I'm going to give you your space to get things back on

track, but I'll be here if you ever speed into town again.

So, here are your glass slippers, Cinderella. Good as new. I hope you enjoyed the ball.

I love you.

~Cash

CHAPTER FOURTEEN

Two Months Later

Cash still didn't know how to fill his nights off, now that heading to crosstown taverns and pubs didn't have the same appeal. Tonight was warm for early December, so he'd decided to take Dixie for a walk up and down Oak Bluff Way.

Things were uneventful until he happened by the bed-and-breakfast and saw something peculiar—a missing FOR SALE sign.

He pushed right through the front door without a second thought.

It was Wednesday, so he found everyone in the common room playing Trivial Pursuit.

"Sheriff!" Rose said. "We were wondering when you'd join us for another game!"

He'd loved playing the one time he did, but he hadn't been able to bring himself to do it since Olivia left. Half the fun had been watching how much she'd enjoyed it. The other half had been—well—*her.*

"The sign," he said. "The *For Sale* sign. Where is it?"

Marcus grinned. "We got a new offer, just last week! The buyer was approved for the mortgage today." He held up a glass of red wine. "We're celebrating if you want to join us."

Before he could answer, his phone sounded with an alert—one he'd heard at least two other times this month.

He radioed the station.

"Walters, it's Hawkins. I'm off duty, but there's a B and E at Lucinda's. I'm next door, so I'll take care of it. She probably just forgot she armed it again. This weekend I'm installing one with an earsplitting siren. Maybe that'll help."

"Roger that," Walters said with a chuckle. "Here if you need backup, boss."

He groaned. What he needed was for Lucinda to remember when she armed the alarm.

"Come on, girl," he said to Dixie. Then he turned his attention back to Marcus and Rose. "I think I'll take you up on that glass of wine in a few. Let me just check next door."

Rose bit back a grin. "See you soon, Sheriff."

He and Dixie were up Lucinda's back steps and at the apartment door in less than ninety seconds. The main door was ajar, the screen door shut. When he entered, he nearly stumbled over a pair of women's hiking boots.

"Damn it, Lucinda, how many times do I have to remind you to *disarm* the alarm when you walk in the door? And since when do you wear hiking boots?"

His mother appeared in the archway between the kitchen and living room, her long gray hair pulled into a braid that hung over one shoulder.

"I think I need an alarm that makes noise," she said, echoing his thoughts. "And the boots aren't mine."

His brows furrowed.

"Cash, did I ever tell you about the letters I found beneath the floorboard in the living room?"

His stomach dropped.

He hadn't told her about the letters. *Or* Olivia. The truth was, despite what he'd said to Olivia in his letter, the hurt was still too fresh, and Lucinda had been dealing with a far greater loss. He wanted to be strong for her when she needed him most. When she was through the worst of it, he'd planned to tell her what she'd missed the week she'd been gone.

"No," he said. He cleared his throat.

"It was right when we moved in. I was cleaning before the furniture came, and one of the boards sorta jiggled when I was vacuuming. I pulled it out to inspect. It was the edge of a yellow ribbon that caught my eye. The letters must have shifted from just beneath the board during a quake or something, but the light caught the ribbon, so I stuck my hand in there to grab it, and there they were. A stack of letters with postage marks that were older than you."

His hand gripped Dixie's leash so hard he thought the leather might slice straight through his palm.

"What did you do with the letters?" he asked, trying to keep his voice calm.

That was when his mother stepped out of the archway to reveal the woman standing behind her.

"She gave them to me," Olivia said, voice shaking.

Dixie barked, and her tail started wagging.

"Oh, come here, you," Lucinda said. "Let's go take a walk and give these two a few minutes to themselves."

She grabbed the leash from Cash, then whispered, "I really like her, son. Don't mess this up."

He let out a nervous laugh as his mother and Dixie headed back down the steps.

Olivia fidgeted with the stack of envelopes in her hands. "I drove down to deliver some paperwork, and I realized I never got to peek inside Lucinda's shop. We got to talking, and I told her about the letters, how you tried to help me find them, how I realized I didn't want to live and work in a hotel where I was really good at my job but not in love with it, how I fell in love with Oak Bluff *and* her son and decided to use all the money I'd put away not paying rent to put a down payment on the bed-and-breakfast, and—"

"W-w-*wait*," Cash said. "Back the hell up, Speed Racer, and say that again."

She bit her lip. "I used my savings to put a down payment on the B and B."

He shook his head. "Back up further."

"I...fell in love with Oak Bluff?"

He narrowed his eyes. "O*livia*..."

"I fell in love with *you*, Cash Hawkins. And you let me leave here without ever telling you."

"Wasn't the right time," he said. "You needed to figure out you, and I wasn't about to mess with that."

But she'd just said she'd fallen in love with him, right? And she was buying the bed-and-breakfast. Did that mean she was still in love with him?

He braced a palm on the kitchen counter. "I think I need to sit down."

"What's wrong?" she asked, concern lacing her words.

He shook his head. "Not sure. This has never happened before. My knees..."

She threw a hand over her mouth, then dropped the letters on the kitchen table. She approached him slowly.

"Sheriff? Is that your old football injury, or do I make you—weak in the knees?"

He straightened and blew out a shaky breath. "Hell yes, you do, Ms. Belle. You gonna catch me if I fall?"

She threw her arms around his neck, that beautiful smile knocking the air from his lungs like only her smile could.

"You're way too heavy," she said. "I'd fall right with you."

He raised a brow. "Some knight in shining armor you are."

She laughed. "Cash Hawkins, I want to fall for you and with you as many times as you'll let me. And when things get hard and messy, I want to work at it so we get right back to this place."

"And what place is that?"

She rose on her toes, her lips a breath away from his. "The place where I tell you I know there is no secret to getting it right. The place where I admit that I'll always be afraid we'll end up like my parents. The place where I remind you every time it gets too hard that I love you, and that's why I'm not running anymore."

"I love you, too, Olivia Belle." Then he asked, "Are you gonna read those letters?"

She shook her head. "I'm gonna give them to Gran and Pop for their anniversary. I already read the only letter I need."

His letter.

He dipped his head to kiss her, but she backed away.

"Wait!" she cried.

"What?"

She grabbed one of her hiking boots from in front of the door and handed it to him. "Try it on me!" she insisted.

"What the hell are you talking about?"

She groaned. "Put the boot on my foot and see if it fits."

His brows pinched together. "It's *your* boot. Of course it fits."

"It's a *metaphor*!" She shoved the boot into his hand. "Cinderella?"

He rolled his eyes but laughed; then he knelt down on one knee, boot in hand.

She lifted one foot in the air, balancing on the other. As soon as he tried to slide the boot on, she fell backward onto her rear end.

Cash barked out a laugh, and Olivia swept her foot beneath his, sending him off balance and onto his own ass as well.

He crawled to her side and leaned over her.

"Is this what you meant by falling for me and with me?"

She winced. "Maybe not quite so literally, but then, I never could stay on my own two feet around you, Sheriff."

He shrugged. "Works for me."

And then her arms were around his neck again as she pulled him to her, their mouths colliding to seal the deal.

"You're gonna have to start driving slower," he said. He kissed her again—lips touching lips, then along the line of her jaw, down her neck...

"How else am I supposed to get the attention of the town's sexy sheriff?" she asked.

He rose to his knees and scooped her into his arms. "You got a room at that B and B?"

She grinned. "I sure do."

"Well then, Ms. Belle, consider yourself in police custody for the rest of the night."

She pressed her forehead to his. "You mean yours, right? Would now be a bad time to tell you about the speeding ticket I got on my way into town tonight?"

He stood, set her down on her feet, then held out his palm.

She reached into her pocket and pulled out her car keys, handing them over without protest.

"You're not headed anywhere this weekend. At the rate you're going, your license will be suspended by the new year."

She shrugged. "Keep 'em. No reason to run off in a hurry anymore. I'm right where I belong." They kissed once more, her knees buckling against his, ready to fall and save each other again and again.

LOOK FOR MORE IN THE CROSSROADS RANCH SERIES:

ABOUT THE AUTHOR

A librarian for teens by day and a romance writer by night, **A. J. Pine** can't seem to escape the world of fiction, and she wouldn't have it any other way. When she finds that twenty-fifth hour in the day, she might indulge in a tiny bit of TV when she nourishes her undying love of vampires, super-heroes, and a certain high-functioning sociopath detective. She hails from the far-off galaxy of the Chicago suburbs.

You can learn more at:

AJPine.com
Twitter @AJ_Pine
Facebook.com/AJPineAuthor

Looking for more cowboys?
Forever brings the heat with these sexy studs.

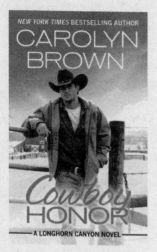

COWBOY HONOR
By Carolyn Brown

After her SUV runs off the road in the middle of a Texas blizzard, Claire Mason is stuck in a remote cabin with her four-year-old niece. Lucky for her, help comes in the form of a true Texas cowboy...

TOUGH LUCK COWBOY
By A. J. Pine

Rugged and reckless, Luke Everett has always lived life on the dangerous side—until a rodeo accident leaves his career in shambles. But life for Luke isn't as bad as it seems when he gets the chance to spend time with the woman he's always wanted but could never have.

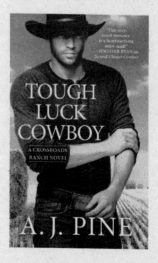

BIG BAD COWBOY
By Carly Bloom

When Travis Blake gets the call that his young nephew needs him, he knows he has to return home to Big Verde, Texas. His plan is to sell the family ranch and head back to Austin, but there's a small problem: The one person who stands in his way is the one woman he can't resist.

THE CAJUN COWBOY
By Sandra Hill

With the moon shining over the bayou, this Cajun cowboy must sweet-talk his way into his wife's arms again...before she unties the knot for good!

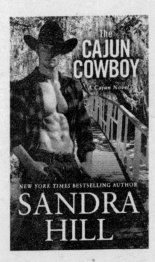

Find more great reads on Instagram with
@ForeverRomanceBooks.

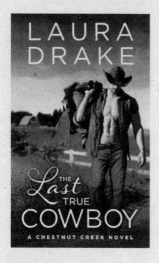

THE LAST TRUE COWBOY
By Laura Drake

Rodeo rider Austin Davis will do anything to win back the love of his life. But Carly's definitely hiding a secret—one that will test the depth of their love and open a new world of possibilities.

LONG, TALL TEXAN
By Lori Wilde

Texas socialite Delany Cartwright is a runaway bride who hopes a little magic will unveil the true destiny of her heart. But be careful what you wish for...

(previously published as *There Goes the Bride*)

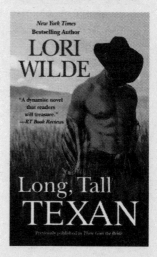

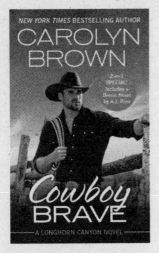
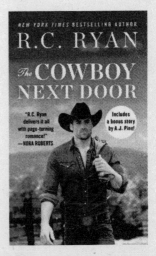